SHADOWLESS

B. JOYCE

For my mom.

MOON BEETLES SERIES

Book One: *Moon Beetles*
Book Two: *Soul Tether*
Book Three: *Mind Fracture*

Moon Beetles Companion Novel

Shadowless

Note: Shadowless can be read at any time. This novel takes place during the same time period as Moon Beetles. It is a stand-alone novel that provides more exploration of Illyson and the beloved characters within the Moon Beetles series.

CONTENT WARNING

In this book, Adrianne experiences intense anxiety. For her, the symptoms of anxiety are very physical and cause her to feel nauseous and sometimes vomit. She will often not eat breakfast or eat too much during the day because of nerves. I want to point out that this is disordered behaviour. It may be triggering for people who also have such intense anxiety or for those who have experience with eating disorders.

There are also instances where people make comments on Adrianne's eating patterns, weight, and suicide attempt. Please note that I believe this behaviour is deplorable. I explore these topics to illustrate how our society's unhealthy relationship with food, body image, and mental health has long lasting and heavy impact on individuals. Adrianne's story is here to explore real feelings, real struggle, and real self-discovery in the midst of hardship. I hope in the end it is encouraging to the reader to accept yourself.

This book contains instances of suicidal ideation, account of a previous suicide attempt, anxiety, depression, fat phobic comments and concerns about body weight, vomiting, blood, violence, death, and near-death experiences. Please only read on if you are safe to do so.

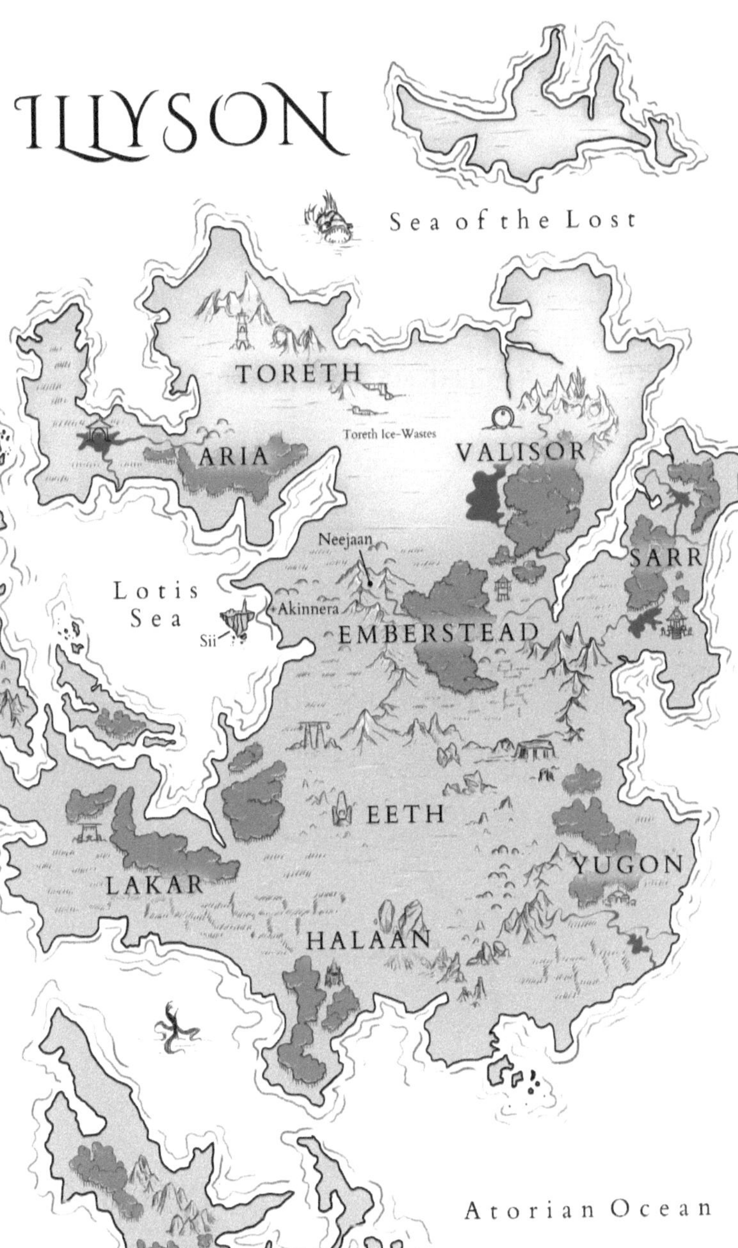

ILLYSON
Sea of the Lost
TORETH
Toreth Ice-Wastes
ARIA
VALISOR
Neejaan
SARR
Lotis Sea
Akinnera
Sii
EMBERSTEAD
EETH
YUGON
LAKAR
HALAAN
Atorian Ocean

THE LESSER WORLDS

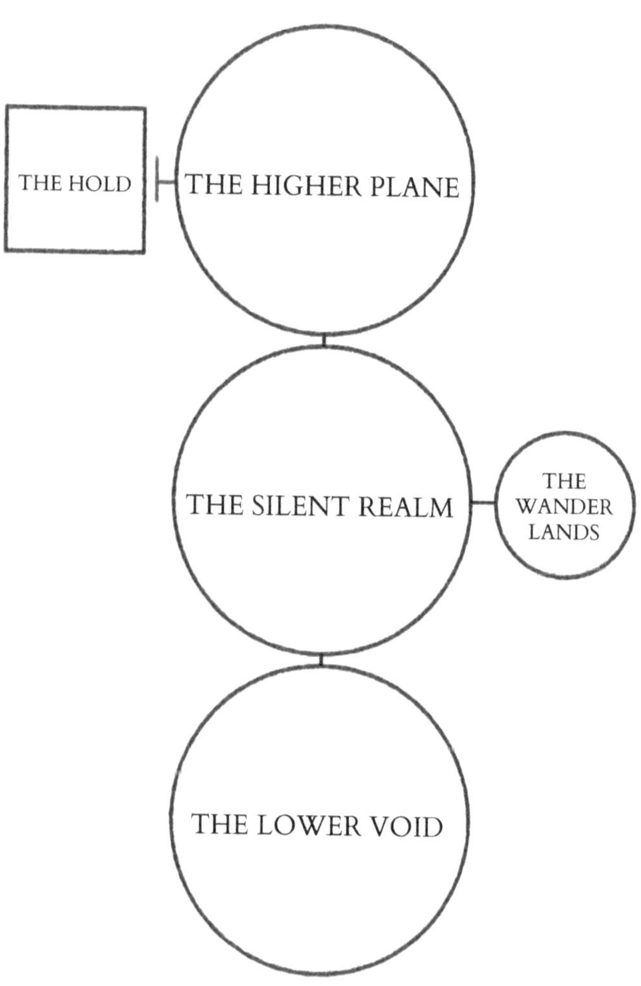

ENERGY ALIGNMENT

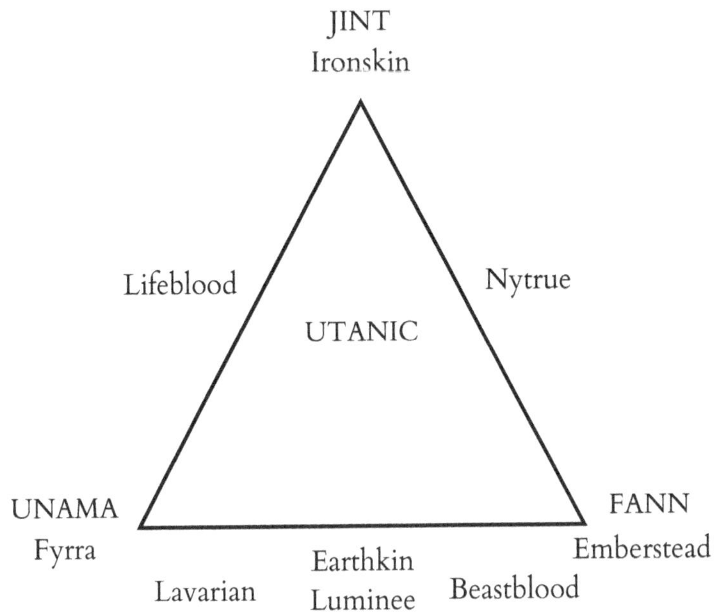

CHAPTER 1

NO MATTER HOW MUCH I PREPARE, the stress always comes at me like a hit to the tits.

The bathtub ledge presses cold through my thin shorts, numbing my butt as I brace my arms on my knees. My bags are packed. I've printed my schedule. I've picked out my clothes for tomorrow. There is nothing I've forgotten, and I've made it through all my years at the Akinnera Academy for Guardian Training alive—barely. Every fucking year my body resists leaving home. I can do it one more time. I can, even if I'm stuck here in this moment, in the same bathroom I was potty trained in, drenched in a cold sweat.

A stab of pain in my gut sends my breakfast lurching to the back of my throat. Resting my head in my hands, I still myself with my breath. One deep breath in quells the gurgle in my esophagus. Letting the air go, my mind grabs hold of the last time this happened. A scene just like this a year ago with early morning stomach spasms pounds its fist into my ego. I'm never getting over this.

Heat blisters over my neck. My stomach seizes. I keel forward and vomit my toast into the toilet. My hair spills around my head to caress the toilet seat. Acid coats my teeth. A shudder creeps through my nerves.

Holy Dien, you son of a tit-punching asshole, you're the one who cursed me with this, aren't you?

All I want today is to rest before stepping back into the world of Guardians. But it is customary for Beastbloods to receive blessings from their elders before their year of training. All the blessings dinner really does is eat up time I could use to calm my mind. My grandparents' blessings are more of a pinch than a balm anyway. They have the highest expectations, and yet I've lowered them significantly since I left home for the first time. If I can bite my tongue long enough, the sting from their visit will be quick.

There's a tap at the door.

"Adrianne?"

I groan and the door opens. My scraggly orange kitten slips in first. She rings around my feet, and I dangle a hand to stroke her fur.

"Hi, Eeny girl," I mumble.

I stare at the floor and blink in an attempt to bring the cool morning light into my foggy brain. My matta's skirt rustles into view and her red toenails poke out from under the blue fabric. Kneeling on the multicoloured rug we made together years ago, she gathers my hair away from the porcelain pot.

"Aw, sweets." She puts a cool hand to my cheek, and I put mine over it, pressing the cold into my skin. "I know you're nervous."

"I'm so stupid, Matta," I whisper.

She shakes her head, her wavy, sand-brown hair shifting around her shoulders. "We don't talk like that." Taking my chin, she tilts my head up to look at me. Her earthy eyes twinkle, and her soft brown skin is creased in laugh lines. She pulls a smile to her face, making her fluffy cat ears on the top of her head twitch. "This is the way you are, and it doesn't have to drag you down."

I've heard these words so many times. One day, maybe they'll be true.

"No shame, sweets."

I match her smile with quivering lips, an acidic worm still wiggling around in my stomach and tension in my spine.

"Tell me what's in your head," Matta says, settling on the floor beside me. Her hand rubs my knee, and her words take the weight from the air so I can breathe.

Tears leak from my eyes, taking a tumble down my cheek, neck, and minimal cleavage. "I can't imagine any other academy student barfing their guts out the day before heading out for training." I squeeze my eyes shut, sending a rush of tears down the same trail. "I hate that I'm older than everyone in my class. I hate having to tell people why."

Guardians are the Protectors and Warriors of Illyson. Warriors fight military conflicts, Protectors keep citizens safe in cities, enforcing the laws, calming conflicts. Guardians are brave and honourable. Just the thought of leaving home fucks me over every time. And I signed up to be a Medic of all things.

Matta takes a wad of toilet paper and dabs the wet from my face. "It's hard to tell the story of your pain. But please don't worry, you know you always get through."

She takes my darkest parts and polishes them like gold. Gold they may be, she loves the lustrous shimmer, but it's dense and heavy inside me. She asks me to tell her my demons, and every time I do, it's a short conversation—she is quick to shine the gold. There are stacks of heavy metal inside me.

"Up now."

She helps me up and positions me in front of the mirror. Taking a brush, she runs it through my hair. With every loving attack on the knots, my scalp prickles. Once the strands are smooth, she weaves it into a clean, strawberry-blond braid like a tail reaching down to my knees. I can't raise my chin to meet my eyes in the mirror because the length of my hair wasn't my choice—it was a Vow I didn't choose for myself.

"Get dressed, then come help me with the beading on a dress for a little while."

I let her tug me to my room by the hand with Eeny at my heels. She deposits me with a kiss to the cheek and a pat to the butt.

My body shakes as I open my window, letting the mountain air ice out the nausea kicking around in my gut. The breeze dances with my long red curtains. Not a colour I would choose, but Matta insisted my room needed more energy. I disagreed. She said the colour would honour Zenta. I said she might be right. Marking Zenta's sign above my head, I close my eyes and ask my ancestor for a little extra fire in my heart today.

I throw on an oversized sweatshirt and sit on the edge of the bed to put on a pair of my dad's socks. My feet swim in them, but he's closer now, even if he's in prison across the province. I scoop Eeny off the floor and settle her in a ray of sun. She licks my finger in thanks as I take a moment to settle, eyes locked on the rays of sun and shadow making an artistic rendering of calm across my mint-green walls.

With only a dull shake inside me, I straighten my bedspread and the one frame on my wall. In it is an embroidered heart with every vessel and valve stitched to perfection by Matta. I love that she put our initials into the vena cava. I told her it's the vessel that brings blood back to the heart, so she said she would put them there because the best day of the year is when I come back to her.

I meet Matta in the living room. Compared to the simple decoration of my space, this room is like an extension of her inner vibrance—her spirit flowing over so everyone can touch it. Every time I walk in, it's like I'm seeing it for the first time. Today, the pillows embroidered in all colours, bells, and mirrors are stuffed neatly across the green velvet couch. Most days, the pillows hang out on the floor, spreading glimmering dots of light throughout the room.

Blue vision tech stand. Pink lace curtains. Plants fill every available surface and hang from the ceiling in front of the windows, basking in sunlight. Family pictures adorn the room, just me, Matta, and Dad. Vibrant yellow walls surround our possessions in a constant glow. Last year, Nima McCarthy, my dad's mom, said it looks messy. My Nana reminded her that colour is good energy. It's definitely energy, and there's a lot of it, and the yellow walls are starting to look a little too much like bile. I rub my stomach and blink a few times.

"Feeling better?" Matta asks, sitting in the middle of the room on the soft red carpet. A client's dress is splayed over her lap, and she beads an intricate pattern on the base of the skirt.

I get down on the ground with her, taking the other end of the skirt. "A bit."

The dress has a silk slip and a black chiffon overlay. Matta has sketched out a flame pattern using red, orange, and clear crystal. It's probably for an Emberstead woman's wedding, or a funeral. Emberstead wear black for all occasions.

I take a needle, some thread, sort out enough beads, and get to work.

"Just one more year. I know it's long and hard. But you will feel so accomplished," Matta says. Her voice is low, confident in her words.

"I know," I mutter.

"You are so strong, my sweets. You'll make it through."

With busy fingers and Matta's words combatting any berating phrases my mind can throw at me, the ache in my stomach subsides a bit.

"Now tell me what you're looking forward to."

I coax my lungs to take even breaths, my eyes transfixed on my work. "I'm looking forward to working with the advanced team."

The silk sifts over Matta's legs. I can almost hear her jaw drop. "What's this?"

A chuckle tickles my throat. "Headmaster Evelyn wants me to teach an advanced first-year team defensive combat. I didn't tell you because I didn't know if I was going to do it." Good grades don't always cut it, so working with the advanced team could ensure that I get a good recommendation for Medic placement from Evelyn. "It'll mean my time will be split between work study hours at the Guardian clinic and advanced team training at the academy."

"What's your schedule then?" Matta asks.

"An eight-hour shift on the first day of the week. Then for two days I'll work with the team in the morning and do clinical in the afternoon. The last three days I'll have advanced team training in the morning, and a full afternoon of Medic classes."

It'll be hard, but a good recommendation will be worth it. The sooner I can get a good Medic placement, the sooner I'll be able to help Matta with our expenses.

My stomach prickles with fire, but Matta's eyes glaze over with tears, a smile she wears so well warming her face.

"You'll do well teaching them," she says. "You have so much to offer."

My cheeks burn and my beads tumble off my needle. They roll through the pleats of the dress. As I gather them, I say, "This dress is gorgeous. Who's it for?"

Matta hums a song she used to sing to me when I couldn't sleep. She gets lost in her work sometimes, so I ask again. "Who's it for?"

"Someone very special." She snips a thread with the scissors we've spent hours looking for over the years. No matter how many times they disappear, they're never replaced. "Someone who knows the depths of hédin pain, the joys of family, the importance of hard work."

My eyes prickle and the beaded fire pattern blurs. It's also a little clearer.

"She carries the essence of the Beastblood and the Emberstead lineages in her body. The woman this dress is for has overflowing compassion for all hédin and animal life. I've even seen her tear up when she hears beast slaying reports on the vision tech."

I wrap my sweaty fingers into the soft chiffon. "Matta, this is for me?"

She nods. "For your graduation, my sweets."

These intricate flames are for me. Matta knows me like she knows her sewing kit. The kit is a disaster of tangled threads, needles, thimbles, and stray snacks. I am just like that sewing kit—a fucking mess—but she orders everything back into their compartments when things get out of line.

"Thank you," I say, bowing my head.

The open door to the garden creaks. Mar isn't nearly warm enough to keep the door open, but Matta insists we let fresh air through the house ten minutes a day. I shiver, struggling to keep my grip on my needle while Matta's strong fingers weave her needle in and out of the fabric like they don't feel the cold.

Leaves and petals trail from the door to the dining table covered in freshly picked winter flowers. I set my needle down and rub my hands together, sending my essence coursing through my fingers in easy pulses.

Matta smiles at her work and says, "Why don't you take care of the flowers, sweets?"

I nod.

She knows how to keep me calm. She knows I like to be prepared with time to spare and activities to busy myself. Yesterday, I fixed syrup-glazed fruit and fresh bread for today's traditional Beastblood blessings dinner. Ever the first to jump in a mess and save the day, my Beastblood ancestors were at the forefront of establishing the Guardian system. To this day, Beastbloods take great pride in sending their youth to the Academies. And yet here I am, my spirit quaking at the thought of going back. But Matta takes that Beastblood saviour mentality and softens it in a knowing direction. I'm not sure I know how to direct myself yet.

"What time did you tell Nipan and Nima McCarthy to be here?"

"I told them to come around five," Matta says.

"Great, so that means they'll be here at four thirty." I run a clammy hand over my face. "Why does the Emberstead Lineage insist on being early?"

"Your father always said it ensures the best seats. But we know they won't stay long. My parents will barge in right on time, dinner will be quick and snappy, they'll all leave, and we can watch something on the vision tech when they're gone."

I chuckle and set aside the lovely beading. It's safer in Matta's hands anyway. Mine are jittering again, and a flower arrangement is more forgiving than fine stitching.

Matta picked an assortment of pale-green jaden lilies, energy suckles, and a few white prickle buds. I cup a golden energy suckle in my palm. It glows over my tan skin and the warmth soothes the shake in my hand. I reach for the vase in the cupboard. A small packet of rillia bush seeds leans against the vase. The warmth from the energy suckles vanishes. Seeds trickle through the packages as I take them from the shelf. I wanted to plant them with the rest of my flowers. Rillia bushes have beautiful dusty-blue blossoms, but they're associated with death, only used for funerals. No Beastblood would associate themselves with death unless through the guidance of a Helpful mystic beast. And that is just one of the reasons I lost my grandparents' favour; I associated myself with death too many times.

Even with tasks to distract myself, my stomach is angry. I pocket the seeds and push down the nausea with a long breath.

This year, I'll show them they can expect more from me.

After hours of preparation for tonight's meal, Matta paints my feline *Vishal* on my forehead as spices float to me from the sweet tomato zolza simmering in the kitchen. I feast on its heavenly scent instead of my Emberstead Nima's musty perfume from the other room. I run my hands down the creamy silk of my wide-legged pants. My fingers have finally calmed enough to grasp the tiny buttons of my orange blouse, so I pinch my collar closed and hide the tail ends of the long pale scars that span my forearms under the cuffs. Matta makes me wear long sleeves to hide my tattoo. My Beastblood dano would have a heart attack if he saw any marks on my body that weren't a *Vishal*. I wear them to hide my scars. None of my grandparents like to see them.

"All right, I'm done. It's a miracle I didn't mess it up with all your fidgeting, but it's done." Matta smiles down at me with a matching feline *Vishal*. She taps her finger to her forehead and then taps it to mine. "Out you go."

Standing, I sigh. "Why'd they have to come so damn early?"

"Just go talk to them."

With a buzzing heart and churning stomach, I leave the bathroom. I collect Eeny from the hallway floor and tuck her in the crook of my arm. She licks my finger with her rough tongue, giving my heart a little warmth with the simple touch.

Nima and Nipan McCarthy sit on the couch, pushed to the very edge by the sparkly pillows. Nima wears a black velvet pantsuit. Her silver hair is in a sleek bun, her mouth a straight red line. Nipan wears black slacks and a black dress shirt. His hair, still auburn, is combed neatly to the side.

They stand in unison, touching two fingers to their heads, then their hearts. "Strength of the ancestors, Adrianne."

"Strength of the ancestors," I say, returning the touch.

Sitting across from them on a footstool, I nestle Eeny on my lap.

"How is your fire manipulation coming along?" Nipan asks.

I clear my throat. "Good. I've started on protection barriers to make safety zones when treating injured comrades."

"Just started, you say? Most Embersteads with essence level three perform that technique upon essence maturity. Your younger cousins have just mastered it."

My hand pauses on Eeny's head. "Yes . . . but I'm also Beastblood. I have a few natural fau essence markers that can't be manipulated for fire techniques like fann can. It's taken a while to get a hang of it."

The energy molecules in essence channels are different for each lineage; a particular combination of jint, unama, or fann energy. Beastbloods have some unama molecules and a large amount of fann. Emberstead have pure fann, Ironskins have pure jint, Fyrra have pure unama, and they all take great pride in this purity.

"Ah, I see." Nipan nods. "Well, work hard at the technique. I'm sure it will be very useful to you." His tone has a little too much air to it. He wrings his hands. "And your beast transformation, still no luck?"

Fucking hells, he sounds so much like Dad right now. He would always ask me the same thing. My family believed my Beastblood ability was shapeshifting rather than summoning because at a young age I could transform my eyes. Doctors studied the anatomy of the transformation and matched it with a tiger's eyes. They thought a tiger must be my beast form. I was never able to transform, even after seventeen, when my essence was fully mature, only my eyes. But I lost even that ability.

"Nope," I say.

"Mm. And what is the word the Beastblood use for . . . for your condition?"

I clear my throat. "Shadowless," I say—blunt and unforgiving, just like the word itself.

They all want to see my beast form. If I have mixed affinities, then I could at least be powerful. They would love that.

Pulling my eyes away from the frown on my nipan's narrow face, I glance at Nima. The scent of her perfume is the only thing about her that moves. I pet Eeny in rapid swipes that can't be relaxing, yet the kitten snuggles deeper into the folds of my pants.

"I see you've kept the weight off," Nima says in her deep rasp that travels through me like gravel in my veins.

I give myself permission to snort. "Daily training will do that to ya." I stand, letting the kitten slide off my lap.

I move to the dining table and grab plates with whispers behind me. My hands snatch a spoon, and I scoop artichoke dip onto two plates without asking if either of them wants any. After stacking a few carrot crackers on each, I shove the plates in my grandparents' faces for them to fill their traps before Nima can ask about my mental clarity and Nipan insists on testing my Firtōn vocabulary. He would be disappointed again.

The plates leave my hands, and the hairs on the back of my neck stand straight as the energy surrounding the house shifts. The front door opens. My heart leaps to my throat. A clatter of boots, voices, and the clang of the bells to ward off Wander Wraiths jumbles through my brain. Even though I'm desperate to stuff my face with crackers and dip, I leave my munching McCarthy's and shuffle to the door to greet my Atherie grandparents.

Nana Atherie marches up to me with a deep scowl on her leather-brown face. She is a tiny woman, dripping in yellow silk and orange beads. If she were to hug me, her head would just graze my under-boob. I offer her my hand and put my left fist to my heart in a Beastblood formal greeting, the only embrace she would ever accept. She gives my hand a jerk and slinks further into the house on light feet.

Dano Atherie fills the doorway with wide-set shoulders and a paunch fit for an ale-guzzling king. The pale skin of his forehead is marked with a summoner sage *Vishal*. He wears his green Warrior uniform with his rank and metals on his chest. Straightening the lapels, he steps to me.

"Strength beyond strength, my girl. The ancestors salute you today. You may be Shadowless, but all the more, their strength is granted to you." Dano's voice booms through the entryway, and he turns me around with massive hands. "Lead me to your table and we shall eat."

There is no time to respond. A spark lights in my belly, fuelling the sickness. My face twists with the effort to stay calm as I usher us into the dining room. I sit at the head of the table, Matta to my right with Dano and Nana Atherie, Nima and Nipan McCarthy to my left with a seat empty for Dad beside me.

"We will start the blessings for Adrianne with silence as Bowen is not present to lead us," Dano Atherie says.

My first time going off to the academy was the only year Dad was able to bless me. That day, he'd stood, straightened his suit jacket, and dished out bowls of zolza. *"Ancestors,"* he had said, passing the first bowl to Nipan McCarthy, *"for Adrianne, I ask that you bless her with an open mind, an open heart, and swift hands to aid her comrades."* He didn't know I was going to choose the route of a Medic, but somehow his blessing guided me.

Nipan McCarthy serves us the zolza today. His face hangs long and ashen in the silence for his incarcerated son. Once each of us has a bowl of zolza, I cover my face with both hands to receive Dad's blessing that has never changed and forever stays in my heart. I place my hands back in my lap.

"Zenta, light your fire in Adrianne so she has strength to protect the province of Emberstead." Nipan McCarthy sets aside the zolza and takes a pitcher of water. His hands are careful as he shuffles around the table to fill the glasses.

Zenta and Fōsten's essence fight inside me at his prayer, pulsing blood to my cheeks. I shield my eyes from my family for a moment to receive the prayer for only half my being.

Nima McCarthy stands. "Ancestors, may she not be ruled by appetite but by regard for healthy eating." She breaks pieces of yellow-fenn bread to pass to each of us.

After accepting the bread, with hands wet from sweat, I hide my face once again, then set my hands back in my lap.

"May Dien damn her desire for death." My hands curl into fists under the table as Dano Atherie grinds pepper into a dish for us to season the zolza. He takes his seat, and my fists unfurl swollen red fingers to hide the heat in my cheeks.

Tiny Nana rises. "Fōsten, let her beast soul be fierce and terrify her cowardice that it may never return."

My hands rest in my lap. Nana Atherie passes fried whisper weed stems around the silent table. The stems won't be half as bitter as her bite.

Is this it? Is this me? I've always taken their advice. Ever since I was little, they all taught me what they knew of fire manipulation and beast transformation. My inability to perform as well as they'd like must make me seem dense, like I don't listen. So their blessings become harsher and harsher warnings. The sick in my stomach moves up, and my body braces against it, but instead of a lurch of acid, a pressure fills my chest. It pulses. It keeps my hands in place. They want me to take their judgement, but what if I don't want to stack it up with the gold bricks? I don't want to be a girl who hides anymore.

"Receive, Adrianne," Dano Atherie says in a low rumble.

All that escapes my lips is a trickle of breath with a curt chuckle. Nana Atherie's back straightens, growing her presence tenfold. I grab my bread and take a bite. "This is beastshit." I roll the bread into the pouch of my cheek. "Beastshit," I say, eyes still turned downward.

Dano Atherie stands again, shaking the table with his hulking thighs. "Insolence."

"These aren't blessings." I get up from my seat, pressing my shoulders back and raising my eyebrows at Dano. "These are fucking insults."

"Anipa, have you taught your daughter no respect?" He leans on the table to look down the way at his daughter. But Matta only brings her gaze to meet mine. Her eyes are bright, her ears twitch toward me.

"Every year you say back-handed blessings, insulting my past instead of bringing in hope for my future like Dad." I chuck my bread down. It plops in my soup, splattering my blouse with angry red spots.

"Girl, when you try to cross the Voids, there is no fight in you. We must ask for all the strength we can," Nana Atherie says. "Even halfies of your essence power should be able to transform into their beast form, and yet here you are, Shadowless, and unable to even make your own Vow."

I grab hold of a long chunk of my hair. Though I stand still, my blood rushes, my knees threaten to collapse, pressure builds behind my eyes as deep, growling thoughts in my head want to agree with them and damn myself to be fractured in the Lesser Worlds.

"Your halfie blood has gone cold, child." Nima McCarthy's gravelly words send a wave of itchy heat over me.

"Yes, yes," Matta says. "Mixed affinities trouble the soul. One tail is better than two. Fangs of fire are neither one nor the other. We've heard this all before." She waves her hand to ward off repetition. "Now, let's finish the blessings and eat. We'll all feel better once we have something in our stomachs."

"We just want Adrianne to find a path that will honour her family names," Nipan says and crosses his arms over his thin frame. "Perhaps her suicide attempt was a warning that she is not fit for Guardian work."

I grind my teeth; my breath is trapped by a lump in my throat. It was three years ago, four years in the fall.

"I've been working so hard, can't you see that?" There's a squeak in my voice, a residual adolescence, mirroring the defiance that stuck my hands to my lap a moment ago.

"Adrianne." Dano stares at me, eyebrows lowered. "Your actions when you are home for the break don't speak to your claim."

His stature and standards are mountainous. I open my mouth to speak. My body trembles, sending a fat tear down one side of my face.

"Guardian work is sacred, it is to keep the peace between the provinces of Illyson," Dano says. "You may work hard at school, but when you are home, without the structure, what do you do? Sleep all day. The times of freedom from command are where a true Guardian is made."

"It's my choice to be a Medic." My voice shudders out of me.

Dano scoffs. "Leave the Medic work to someone who has essence abilities suitable for healing. The Lifebloods, the Fyrra. What can you do for a dying comrade with only a flame?"

Stinging pulses of blood race through my body. "It's my choice, and I'm going to stand by it. No Beastblood or Emberstead in this family has ever been a Medic, but this Shadowless halfie will be. I'll show all of you I can make it."

My tongue has cast a spell over the dining room that quells any retort. I turn on my heel and leave with tears streaming from my eyes. I knew the hit was coming. I was ready for it. I even prepared myself for it. It hurts all the same, maybe more.

CHAPTER 2

I SLAM THE DOOR. Dano's voice carries above the rattle of the shutters and the bells. My essence churns within its channels, hot and wandering aimlessly from head to toe as I round the side of the house. One sentiment rings louder than the rest. "That school changed her, Anipa. I do not condone her finishing," Dano says.

The words cut so deep in a wound that has been gouged and ripped and torn too many times to count. The wound doesn't bleed red blood but a dark, sludgy grey, smothering and slow. I escape behind the house to find a place to bleed in peace.

"We went through all the trouble of the Monitor checkups that first year, and what does she have to show for it?" Dano says.

"She's still alive, isn't she?" Matta says. The tension she rarely shows me is tied around her words.

The replies are murmured, and I'm not sure if I want to know what the rest of them think of that statement. I use the force from those words to hoist myself up the vines crawling the wall to the roof. It's the place I've gone to be alone with my thoughts since I was little.

I was assigned a Monitor when I got my scars. A Monitor is a Guardian Medic trained to help hédin who have had essence bursts that ended up killing someone and those who are a danger to people around them. They also help Guardians through the traumas they face in their work. It's a new branch of Medic. Beastblood Guardians like my dano think it's irrelevant. If you can't hack Guardian hardships, then you shouldn't be a Guardian, and we already have Psychological Health Professionals.

In my case, I was assigned a Monitor because I was a danger to myself. If I wanted to continue my Guardian training, I had to have someone keep tabs on me. The only reason I'm alive today is because my body transformed where I inflicted the damage. My arms became a bloody mess of corded muscle and fur. The strength in that form kept me from bleeding out. But because of that, my scars remain since they weren't healed on my hédin body and my beast body. How could they? I couldn't transform at will. For weeks after the incident, my essence surged randomly. My Monitor, Officer Pellen, would sit beside me holding my hand and rubbing my shoulder where one of my transform points kept spasming. In a calm voice, my Monitor told me that my essence might never be the same, that when our vital energies touch the Void between this world and the Lesser Worlds, they can change. He lowered his head, found my eyes, and told me I might never transform into my beast form, that I'd be Shadowless.

Any hédin who touches the Voids is bound to have some essence dysregulation. But for Beastbloods it's far worse. The Shadow refers to how, when Beastbloods summon and transform, they are closest to being their true, integrated selves. Some people call it a second soul. Without a Shadow, the only way to fully integrate your spirit, mind, and essence is to find that little piece of essence and spirit that got stuck in the Lesser Worlds beyond the Voids. Integration can only be achieved after death.

My grandparents use the term Shadowless as a consequence. My Monitor spoke of it as a tragedy. Without him, I doubt I would have made it this far. I should attribute my life to my mother, since she gave it to me, and she encourages me daily. Or my father, with his outlandish dreams for me, the freedom he gave me to express myself and experience things maybe I shouldn't have been experiencing just yet, from taking me to Dawnranfet matches and letting me sip his ale at age twelve to restricted vision reels. My grandparents saw my suicide attempt as a disgrace, my mother was caring but didn't know what to do, and my father saw it as something to be fixed. But my Monitor made my rehabilitation feel like it was truly part of my life. Life implies death. Life is full of tragedies like becoming Shadowless. My Monitor made me feel hédin. To me, that made him heroic.

I've never been sure of anything in my life. The world would go on without me. The Karess spins. The moon and sun switch places. Pain stays, wounds get deeper. Sometimes it seems like there's not much point healing Guardians who keep causing more pain. But that kind of thinking was how my first year at the academy went down hill so fast. I do want to be a Medic. I can't explain away that gut feeling and try something else.

"I just think there is too much of Bowen in her and not

enough of you, Anipa," Nana says. "He was a passionate man. We all saw that. But he was everywhere and nowhere."

Chairs scrape the floor. Lowering my self to sit on the ridge of the roof, I drop my head to my knees, as Nipan says, in his slow, measured tone, "I believe that's our cue to leave."

My heart breaks. I left my matta to take the brunt of their accusation even though I'm the one they're disappointed with. Matta has to deal with so much. Dano's wrath should be piled on me, not Matta. I hate myself for it. Who's going to direct my hands, so they don't idle in a trembling stupor on my lap? How could I use such language against my grandparents? I am insolent. Wasted essence.

Which is why I have to make them see that I'm fit to be a Guardian, to stand on my own two feet and take the burden off Matta.

I inhale the sweet notes of spring in the evening air and gaze over Neejaan. The town is nestled in a valley between one craggy, pointed mountain and one with a steady slope and a single prominent peak. Sunlight toys with their snowy crests as it fades. Everyone is home at their dinner tables. The empty streets are lit in amber from lightstone poles, undisturbed by the rumble of cruisers. Neejaan is ignorant of the whistle of wind through the thatched rooftops and the angry voices from within my home.

The bells ring as my grandparents leave, muttering to each other and splitting ways so they don't have to spend another second in each other's company. Their cruiser doors slam. Engines sputter to life, and they roll away, right over my trampled heart.

Without their presence to cut into me, my shoulders drop. For a moment, my body is heavy with no sense of bone or muscle, just heavy and aching.

I don't want to continue to be the girl who hides. I want my wound to heal.

Taking a breath, I lift my head back up to the divide between the mountains.

The sun winks on the horizon, leaving the green starlight to flood the sky. There's a thud and a scrape behind me. I turn to find Matta in her lynx form, climbing up the roof to sit next to me. She lingers a while in her beast form, letting the wind brush her whiskers, lifting her chin high, eyes closed. A flash of white light brings her gifting smile and warm skin back to me.

"A mess as usual," she says, nose still in the air.

Her ears twitch in the wind. Beastbloods who become deeply connected to their beast form or their beast familiar often have a part of their body that remains transformed. Sometimes patches of scales, long sharp fingernails, or tails. It stings to see how connected Matta is to her beast form when mine has vanished.

My essence has stilled, leaving me stiff and cold. I rub my arms. The scars are firm ridges under the smooth silk.

"Sorry," I whisper.

"Don't be." She nudges me with her elbow. "I liked what you had to say."

"I'm sorry I cause you so much trouble."

"Ah, sweets." Her voice lowers again to a register that soothes me. Her truth voice. "I chose trouble a long time ago when I chose your dad. I'm quite fond of trouble." She winks at me. "Your dad and I don't love all our choices in life, we don't love the ones that landed him in prison, but we love the ones that let us choose each other and choose you."

If going to the academy causes me so much stress, why do I continue? Someone without anxiety-induced vomiting would probably be a better body working in a Guardian clinic.

The wind sends shivers over my skin. "I guess the academy is my trouble."

"You still want to go?"

My chest is tight as I hold back tears. I pull my knees in close.

"Yes," I say. "As much as you appreciate my help with the beading, I fucking hate it."

Matta chuckles.

"And I love to learn as much as Dad does, but it kills me inside to think of going on to advanced ed." I scan Neejaan in the green starlight. "I feel okay once I'm there, training to be a Medic. Okay is the best I've felt in years."

Matta soaks in the chill with her smile glued to her face.

"This realm is only the Beginning," Matta says. She is radiant in her colourful skirt pooling around her and starlight caressing her face.

She always says that. It's to remind me of what she's told me ever since I was little, that there is experience after death. In this life, our spiritual, mental, and physical energies learn to be one. In death, if these vital energies aren't joined, we stay split through the Lesser Worlds. But our energies can find each other again. She reminds me to stay in the present, that there's life to be lived in the Beginning. It's true, but it churns my blood. She, like every other Beastblood, thinks I'm linked to the Lesser Worlds, the world of the dead. My Shadow is waiting for me there, but I have to gain whatever experience I can before reuniting. And, well, that's not easy.

I crumple into myself. "Don't, Matta."

She takes a long breath, looking down at her hands. "The ancients wrote about Helpful mystic beasts. Helpful beasts were the ones the ancients could summon. They weren't feral and could aid their summoners in both the Beginning and the Lesser Worlds. One beast in particular walks through the Lesser Worlds, guiding dispersed energy back to unity. She senses their vibration, their desires, and helps them pass into the Beyond, if that's what they want." Matta turns her smile to me.

My brow furrows. "Why are you telling me this?"

Cupping my face with soft hands, Matta says, "I'm saying that beast has an intuitive spirit, just like you. Trust your intuition, even if it means looking paranoid or doing something uncomfortable. You instinctively know the way that is right for you, the path that'll keep you whole."

Letting go of me, she reaches into her pocket to reveal a glittering gold chain with a small triangle pendant. "When we look at all sides, we stay whole," she says as she drapes the delicate gold necklace around my neck.

The metal is cold as I run a finger along each edge, but this gold isn't so heavy. I smile at Matta and nod. She taps her forehead and then mine as if she could imbue her knowledge with a simple touch. I press my fingers to the spot as we climb down the roof. I won't disappoint her.

CHAPTER 3

T HE STRIP OF LIGHT FROM UNDER THE DOOR faded an hour ago when Matta went to bed. As the minutes pass, the subtle vibration in the house stills as sleep takes her in, leaving me to lie here, alone, with tension gripping my shoulders.

Starlight washes my room in a pale-green glow, and shadows from tree branches etch dark paths along my walls. My breaths are shallow, quick. I fluff my blankets and smooth them around me for the tenth time tonight, only for my skin to crawl and my heart to squirm. A sigh breaks through my lips. I press my eyes closed as if the dark can push away the nagging urgency at the back of my mind.

Is this lingering pressure from the day? Is my body unsettled from my fucking grandparents? Matta quieted that ache for me a little, so I don't think it's that. I know I'm nervous about tomorrow. But those nerves make me sick, they make my eyes blurry, and my breaths acidic. There's a pressure in my chest now, like a hook stuck in my sternum, tugging upward.

Hands pressed to my face, I sit upright, following the pull. Breathing through my fingers, I shake my head. My hands fall to my lap and my head hangs back, my spine bowed. With a grunt, I throw off the blankets. "What the fuck am I doing?" I mutter, swinging my legs over the edge of my bed.

I can't lie here because sleep is not interested in me tonight— the most aggravating thing that can happen right now. I need my sleep. Something drives me to put my socks back on. Something stuffs my body into my sweater and a jacket and a hat.

I ease my door open. Even with the slight motion, the air shifts through the house. Matta's door is closed, but as I step into the hall, the stagnant quiet of the night lights with energy as she wakes. It's been like this as long as I remember. I know when she is awake and when she's resting. I would feel her presence when she would pick me up from school, even if she was in the parking lot and I was in the back play yard. The house is dull without her in it. She can sense my movements, but not as intensely. I think it has to do with our feline essence alignment. Nana's beast form is feline and so is Dano's familiar, and I can sense their essence when they get close. So, I make my footsteps quick, crossing the house to the back door with my shoes in hand. She'll want me to stay inside, want to comfort me, but I can't stay inside.

I slip through the sliding doors and jerk my hands a few times to set my essence in motion to warm me as I put on my shoes. I hurry with my laces, as if the motions of my body will aggravate my mother's senses more. Laces tied, I lunge off the steps and through the yard, soggy grass squelching beneath me. I cross to the front of the house with my arms wrapped around my body and eyes on the ground. Matta is at her window; her eyes are on my back. My essence shudders, as if blushing, and my eyes prickle as I continue to follow the pull in my chest up the hill and along the city wall. This escapade into the night is unfounded; I don't know where I'm going. I'm like a child following my imagination on a quest that I'll make up as I go. A small quest, and just as for a child, it's so important. I don't want the adults to interfere.

A tear drips from my eye now that I'm out of her sight and the houses are clearing. I hike up the hill with my arms still hugging my chest. The cobblestones break into bits of gravel and then into soft dirt, still drying from the winter snow. Energy suckles glimmer along the stone city wall. The wall is tall and blocks half the sky, leaving me in deep shadow. It's here, the climax of my quest. My essence pulses in gentle waves in my central essence node, right below my sternum.

Taking a long breath, I trap the pleasant, honey scent of the energy suckles and wet earth, and I hold it in my chest for five seconds. My eyes are drawn to the ground. A squeak pricks my ears. Metal clatters, and a low warble rolls through the dark.

My feet carry me over a lingering pile of snow and through the bushes. The energy suckles tap warmth into my numb legs as I brush past them. The metallic clatter continues. Crouching low, I find the source. Tucked between two pinichu berry bushes is a metal cage with a small Rover trapped inside.

My heart drops and my essence is a dense curl in my chest. The Rover scrambles back, pressing into the corner of the cage. Its mouth opens, revealing small pointy teeth, and a hiss escapes it.

"Mm," I say. "Are you the little monster keeping me up tonight?"

Its warbles stop short at my voice. A sliver of starlight touches its charcoal-brown skin and his narrow head tilts to the side.

"Poor baby," I say, taking a step closer. "I bet there were some tasty snacks in there for ya, huh? Yeah, it would fool me too."

I'm just a foot away from the metal bars. Snowmelt seeps out of the ground, cooling the soles of my feet. The Rover watches me with gleaming yellow eyes. Its breaths come in quick bursts, rumbling through its little body and creating ripples through its chest—the way my essence ripples. My throat constricts.

"You know, I'm supposed to report little buddies like you who get into the city."

The beast's breaths stay steady and urgent, but it flicks its tail, twanging the metal bars.

I'm not going to do that, am I?

The LPs will kill it if I report it. If I leave it, the patrol will come by and kill it later. My stomach lurches. I shake my head and drop my face to my hands, still crouched in a snowbank in the middle of the night when I should be resting for my final leg of Guardian training. I stay still, curled into myself, breathing and unable to stir. The Rover's breaths rush in my ears. Minutes pass and the breaths slow. Its claws scrape the metal bottom of the cage. Prying my face from my hands, I find the gleaming eyes trained on me. A ruby-red tongue snakes between its teeth and back in. I can't shake its stare.

"Fuck it." I tip forward onto my knees and get to work unlatching the cage. Slowly, I stick my hands inside, the air warm around its small body. The Rover shuffles back, but it doesn't make a sound. Reaching a little more, I wrap my hands around its bony frame. "Just don't be a little shit and bite me."

The Rover squirms and I clamp his hind legs in one hand and its front legs with the other, lifting it out of the cage. I cradle it to my chest. Its breaths revert to the ragged rhythm, but it doesn't fight me, and I run a hand over the skin of its back. Its fine hair gives a suede-like texture, soft one way and course the other.

We tromp through the brush, green starlight sprinkling us through the canopy above as we search for a break in the wall—because, of course, Guardians would rather cage a beast rather than fix a hole. The Rover watches too, its little lizard head bobbing around in my arms. I scratch my nails in the folds of its skin, and it nips at me.

"Hey, I thought we had a deal, bitch." I chuckle and a shudder of breath vibrates through its body.

After a few minutes, the Rover's yellow eyes blink rapidly, and it kicks at my breasts. I keep my arms tight as it squirms, searching the dark for what excites the Rover. My foot sinks, wrenching my ankle, and I tumble to the ground. The Rover slips out of my arms, an excited sniffle escaping it, its claws ripping my sock as it propels itself down the hole.

With my ass soaking on the damp ground and my ankle tingling, essence prickles in me like the cadence of the little Rover's excited breaths once it saw its escape. The pull on my chest recoils like it's following after the small creature. I suck in a clean breath. It comes out, and my body relaxes from my head to my stinging ankle. The breaths are clean, and I am clean and full and calm, even with numb butt cheeks, muddy pants, and the stench of Rover shit on me.

I stand, my knees shaking with adrenaline. Saving this Rover is good. It is true. The day I made my choice to be a Medic, I had beast slaying training and then after that I saw a slaying report on the vision tech. Everything about that day felt wrong, except the choice to be a Medic.

Up this path is the shrine of my revered Beastblood ancestor, Fōsten, where I should have made my Vow almost four years ago. If there's a truth in me, then there's a Vow. I can make that Vow tonight. Being Shadowless, I don't really fit anywhere, and I can't be who my family wants me to be. But if I say a Vow out loud, and cling to this bit of Beastblood culture, maybe I'll finally have a guide for my life.

The night is crisp and thrumming with the hope of spring. The energy pales in comparison to the new drive in me to make my Vow, so I follow it to the shrine. The crunch of gravel spooks a fox snuffling down the way, and it scampers off. A deer stares at me with ghostly eyes before bounding off after it. As I enter the shrine grounds through a low arch, a gentle thrill passes over me. Birds rustle in the branches overhead, and on the steps to the open door sits a scrappy black cat. I reach a hand to the cat and stroke its head. It mews and winds through my legs.

The shrine is no more than a small hut. Moss grows around the planks and energy suckles sprout in the corners, sprinkling the peeling paint with light. The paint is still bright—orange for the vibrance and tenacity of the Beastblood Lineage, the white line three-quarters of the way down the walls represents the light that flashes during summoning and transformation, and the purple strip signifies the link to the Lesser Worlds through Helpful mystic beasts. Despite the age of the structure, the sturdy floorboards are swept clean and there is no sign of leaks in the roof or snowbanks piled too close that would make a mess as they melt. This place is continually tended to maintain cleanliness but not to keep the forest out.

I sit on my knees in front of the painting of Fōsten. He could summon a mystic beast named Annat'an, a great stag with essence alignment the same as all Beastblood energy. Mystic beasts are said to have bodies of coursing essence not captured in flesh. They appear ethereal but have a physicality just like the essence within me. Over the centuries, the lineage became adept at summoning animals and then transforming into animals because of its lower energy cost. And here I sit, in front of a man who could summon from another plane of existence, and I can't even transform into my beast form.

Fōsten's eyes are kind though. A warmth settles on me as we stare at each other. He's not so petty that he would compare us. I know I'm always welcome here with him.

I light the incense provided and bow my head. All Beastbloods make Vows at eighteen years old, a year after essence maturity. Vows to protect hédin, Vows of valour, Vows to protect animals, to never eat meat, and so on. Most importantly, Vows show your commitment to a well-lived life.

I didn't make a Vow—another disgrace to rub in my grandparent's wounded pride. What could I feel so strongly about when all I wanted was to die? Instead, the elders gave me a Vow to never cut my hair until I could make a Vow for myself.

My true Vow is inside me though. It was evident with that little Rover, and it will help me become a better Medic if I speak it out loud.

I lick my lips and my breath makes white curls between me

and Fōsten.

"I Vow . . . " My throat tightens, pressure builds behind my eyes, and I swallow hard. Vows are supposed to have a poetic quality. I was given a list of potential Vows to study before my ceremony. Their flowery language had swarmed my mind, twisted, and lodged in my throat as I sat right here. I'd serenaded my audience, Matta, my dad, my dano and Nana, with graceless silence.

"I Vow to protect all life, to never kill any animal, hédin, or beast. I will not eat of the meat an animal can provide. My hands will not touch a living being's blood unless it is to"—I gasp, tears heating my cheeks—"unless it is to heal or save a life." I swipe my hand over my wet chin.

The visage of Fōsten is blurry in front of me. I made my Vow. Something no Beastblood has ever Vowed before. Most justify killing beasts to protect hédin, but I left the scripts behind.

I blink away the cloud of tears and take in the space around me. There is a shadow where my grandparents should stand, a hollow that should be filled with my parents. My skin is cooling with the calm in my essence. I might as well be naked without the tension in my chest. Without a friend at my side, I almost wish the anxiety would return to provide some company.

Hands steady on my knees, my head bows, and my hair falls around me in tangles. I'll keep it. Just until I know I can make good on my new Vow. Maybe both Vows will strengthen me this year.

The breath of every bird in the trees, the scraggly cat, the deer, rushes in my ears. I clutch my chest, my heart picking up pace with a surge of fire hot essence through my body. They see me; they heard my Vow. I tremble, and my stomach sinks as darkness claws at my vision. Heat fills my arms with a pulsing pressure at my nail beds. Taking a breath, I sink my awareness into my essence, urging it to calm with a palm over my heart. It flares hotter. The transform point between my eyes pulses and my vision clears for a moment. The skin around my eyes stretches and fur fans across my brow.

This can't be happening. Am I actually transforming? The sensation of my cells becoming other is a comfort from my childhood, but my heart is angry at the change as a sharp pain strikes through my jaw muscles.

"Shit." My lips fumble over the curse, spit trickling out the corner of my mouth.

I barely remember how to control the transformation. I focus my eyes on the ground as the clarity of my feline sight is swallowed by darkness. Flares of light sparkle all through the dark. They multiply as my pounding heart comes to a stop. I scramble in the dark, breathing but not breathing, writhing, but still. What the fuck is happening to me? This isn't right.

My body is unresponsive to my distress. Something presses on me. An energy, a presence just paces away. It is hot and yet my skin has evaporated from existence. It is heavy even without pressure on my joints. A light crawls out of the blackness, golden, not like the white lights littering the expanding darkness. A pair of eyes flash before me. Though I want to scream, my voice is stuck; I have no connection to my mouth.

Those eyes, they look just like mine. Am I . . . Is this . . . Am I seeing the Lesser Worlds? Those eyes can't be my Shadow, can they? Because if they are, that might mean she's calling me, asking me to join her—finish what we started. It's such a gentle call, whispering around me.

No. I still have things to finish, goals to accomplish. My grandparents would tell Matta they were right, that I can't handle this life, and she doesn't deserve to be shamed like that.

She's still alive, isn't she?

All I can do is think of Matta's words, about my body, where I was just sitting in the cool of the shrine, the dark, the smell of the moss and soil surrounding me.

My voice bursts into the dark void. "I'm not going. I'm not dying today."

The air presses on me from behind, hot and wet like breath. Still blinded and without a pulse, I jerk a hand to the nape of my neck and wrench my body around. One arm outstretched, I shuffle back. My back slams into Fōsten. A flash of light bursts in front of me, just where I was sitting. Searing pain stabs through my shoulders on both sides as my essence pulses in my transform points. I shriek as the light blinks out, leaving a phantom image burned onto my eyelids—the pair of eyes blinking back at me, an otherwise shapeless presence. This other entity heard my Vow. And I'm not sure I wanted it to.

My essence cools. The darkness swathing my eyes peels away, leaving a blurry image of those eyes glowing in my mind as I collapse. I lie motionless, breaths shallow but sweet on my tongue.

A shiver shakes my body as it rests on the mossy slats. With a few blinks, the orange and purple walls come into focus beyond specks of dust curling in the starlight. Pressing away from the ground, my hair trails around me, collecting the dust. I pat my cold hands over my body. There are no pulses in my transform points, no spasms, just a subtle pressure like something gripping my shoulders.

My hands slide down my chest to rest on my breasts. My heartbeat shakes me with strong, even beats. *Still alive.* "Thank Carnity."

And that's the way it's going to stay. Whatever just happened here, I have to fight it. Because if my Vow is my truth, then I have to stay in the Beginning to live it out. And this experience, this transformation, will stay with me, because I don't know how to explain it to anyone, nor can I explain my Vow.

CHAPTER 4

T HE NEXT MORNING, I roll out of bed and snatch my glass ancestral beads. Dropping to my knees, I run my fingers over each of the cool spheres and start my essence in an easy wave through my body, head to toe.

I start with prayers to Zenta and Fōsten. Over the years, I've collected a charm for each ancestor of the nine lineages and even ones for our great ancestors, Carnity and Dien. Matta taught me we all have a bit of them in us through our eternal essence—the essence passed from mother to child—so I give them acknowledgement too. Eternal essence can call to them, bringing them close to give us strength. I'll need all the help I can get to maintain this Vow and get through this year. And maybe only they know what's wrong with me, how to get my pieces to fit in this world, even with something missing. I never believed in gods, only people with good will, even people long gone to the Beyond.

Once I've made it through eleven ancestors, I tidy up my space, making sure everything is just the way I like it. I change into the clothes I set out for the day and head out with my bags. My arms are stiff from the strange essence movement in my transform points last night. I set my bags by the door and search the house for Eeny. Even though she's fast asleep on a high shelf, I pull her down. Cradling her in my arms, I stuff my face in her fur and breathe in the sweet scent of fluff. Matta's eyes are on me all the while. I can't meet them. Something shifted in me last night that I have no words for. So I spend the rest of the morning in silence, force feeding my sore stomach a bowl of oats until it's time to leave.

Matta waits by the door with her cruiser keys and her purse, with wavering, questioning eyes, and yet she's quiet. There are tears waiting to be spilled if she speaks.

I kiss her cheek and push past her to load my bags into the trunk.

We are quiet on our drive to the train station. I clench my hands in my lap. My nails scrape my knuckle and I flinch. Matta's eyes are quick, taking in my hands and my face in one swipe. I smile and then snap my eyes shut as I lean my head back.

The cruiser comes to a stop and my hands are unravelled by Matta's. As she squeezes my fingers, I focus my attention on the day. A quick train ride and then orientation. I just need to focus on each of the tasks this year will bring me.

Matta sends me off fast with a hug strong enough to be one from her and one from Dad. She kisses me, says, "You are strong,

Sweets," and sticks a Muncho bar in my hand. She ends the send-off with a butt-swat on my way up the steps into the train.

I plop down in the first seat I come to and breathe. Five seconds in, five seconds out. My Monitor taught me another way of using breath to calm myself a while back. Something about four seconds in, hold five, and breathe out for six. Or was it longer than that? I always forget the counts, and it's too far from normal breathing to be helpful when I need to keep moving. Five counts became my go-to last year. It's deep enough to cleanse and fast enough to be used any time, even in the middle of combat.

The train lurches. I lean to the window and wave to Matta, who's hiding her tears behind a smile. From Neejaan to Akinnera it's only an hour trip. I stare at the Muncho bar. Part of me wants to rip it open and devour it, the other part is startled by the thought. My stomach pinches in response. Nima would roll her eyes if I ate it. This presses against the squirm inside me and I tear open the package. Kicking off my shoes, I sink my teeth in.

As I chew, last night's events rush through my mind. I made a bold Vow. It gave me a sense of calm, but that calm turned into a rush. My hand meets my chest, where I lost the beat of my heart. Those eyes, the ones that flashed through the dark that took my sight, come back to me now with a challenge. Is it even possible to maintain a Vow like that as a Medic Guardian?

As I try to manage a wad of Muncho that is probably an unsafe amount to be eating in a moving vehicle, the person in the four-seat compartment next to me stirs. I stare at her with chipmunk cheeks. Her eyes are pressed shut, and she shifts again in a fitful sleep. Her face is all sharp angles and pale skin, creating shadows under her cheekbones. She has bags under her eyes and her eyelids twitch, trying so hard to keep the images of her mind at bay. She clings to an old canvas backpack that used to be standard issue for Protectors before the uniform redesign.

The ticket inspector comes through the automatic doors that separate the train cars.

"Ticket," he says.

I hand it to him, swallow, and ask, "You know where she's headed? I'd like to wake her if her stop comes up soon."

"I believe she had a ticket to Akinnera. A student discount, too, so my guess she's on her way to the Guardian Academy." He punches my ticket.

"Thanks." I smile and take another bite of my Muncho bar.

The doors close behind him with a hiss.

I am drawn to the girl across the aisle again. Her clothes are plain—jeans and a light-blue striped shirt. Even if the lineages have diversified their wardrobes in the recent past, people will often wear something that marks their lineage if they don't have physical features to make a distinction. Most Luminee have purple hair, many Nytrue have blue hair, and Lavarians are unmistakable with large wings sprouting out their backs. She doesn't wear any distinguishable articles of clothing that identify her lineage. No Lifeblood healing rings in her ears, no colours, no Vishal. An Emberstead would have red hair for sure. She could be Beastblood, her skin tone is just a little lighter than Dano Atherie's, but a Beastblood would never wear such dull colours.

I shove the last chunk of Muncho in my mouth.

Under all this little girl's ambiguity, she has a light. It speaks to a part of me, a part I don't know yet. That something squirms inside me, chafing against who I've been and who I am now. Tapping my fingers to the triangle pendant Matta gave me last night, her words whisper to me. *You have to look at all sides to stay whole.* I don't know why I felt like I was breaking last night when helping the Rover and taking my Vow made me feel whole for one brief moment.

I have my shoes tied and a hankering for another Muncho bar just as the train pulls into the Akinnera station. I gather my bags and I cross the aisle to give the sleeping girl a shake.

"Hey, you getting off?" I say.

Her head twitches and her eyes flutter open. Grey irises like the glint of a steel blade pierce me straight through. She turns to the window, giving me a moment to recover from her shocking gaze.

"You're going to the Guardian Academy, right?" I ask.

"Yeah. How did you know?" Her voice has a rasp to it, an edge like the bones carving out the structure of her face.

"I asked the ticket inspector if he knew where you were headed so I could wake you. I'm going to the academy too," I say, stepping back into the aisle so she has room to take her suitcase off the overhead rack.

"Thanks. You really saved me there."

My stomach sinks just thinking about the possibility of missing a stop on the way to the academy. I wouldn't wish that on anyone. I step off the train and turn around to wait for the girl, hot air from the firestones powering the train, mingling with the Akinnera sun on my skin. Maybe she doesn't want to walk together, but her eyes gravitate back to me. My parents were with me the first time, and I was grateful to have someone help me navigate.

The crowded station steals her gaze from me. Her lips part with a spacey glaze invading her eyes as she takes in the crowd. I wait a moment for her to follow as the sun takes the chill out of my hands—always a welcome touch.

"My name's Adrianne, by the way," I say over the voice on the ampliphone announcing the train's departure. The girl follows close behind me as I push my way to the exit. Out of the station building, I take in a five-second breath of the sea salt air. It's thick in my lungs without the mountain chill. The sky is big and open and filled with airships. It's bigger than the Neejaan sky, no mountains to steal away the open space.

The sky takes the girl too. She cranes her neck as a hulking powerstone supply ship roars overhead. I suppress a chuckle. I must have looked just as stupid my first time here.

Her head whips back to me. "Oh, uh, Rinnaya. My name is Rinnaya, but I prefer Rin."

Her name rolls around my head like one of the old songs my dad loves to share with me. Rinnaya. Up and down, singsong, but the shortened version is perfect for her—a stab to the heart, open and bleeding. I smile at her.

"Rin it is then. Nice to meet you. We have to walk about ten minutes to get to the academy. This way."

My feet lead us up the cobblestone street I dread each year. Today, my steps are easier, if not a little jittery. My stride is long but slow to allow Rin to keep pace with me. The cadence of my breaths is steady and only picks up when I acknowledge the strangeness of the anticipation inside me. I slip a pack of gum out of my pocket and pop a stick in my mouth for something to focus on.

"Want a piece?" I ask Rin. "It's cinnospice."

I didn't wear sleeves today. The light scar on my right forearm points straight to the gum. I keep my arm strong and smile.

She takes a piece with small, quick hands. "Thanks."

Tension grips Rin's shoulders, pulling them close to her neck, her fingers fiddling with the stick of gum. Silence is a friend in situations like these, when there's something to look forward to but there's so much new, all you can do is take it in. I grant silence to her and myself. I don't want my mind to wander—I just want to be here.

Something in the Akinnera air always makes me stuffy. Somehow, I always forget about it. My eyes water and my nose itches. It's probably the sorrow-blossom trees. I rub my nose but catch sight of Rin staring at me. She lets her eyes linger. Quiet, not shy.

"What year will this be for you?" she asks.

"I'm a fourth-year." Glancing over the half-lie, I ask, "You excited for your first?"

"Yeah, I guess so."

"Don't really know what to expect, huh?"

"Kind of." Her voice is soft and her eyes flit from person to person as we head up the hill. "Everyone looks so excited."

As much as my feet are content to go up the hill this year, I wouldn't say I'm excited. That acidic worm in my gut yesterday would never allow me to say that. I know the process this place puts each student through. Being the nation's heroes is no small title. It tests you time and time again until you leave, or you figure out why you're here. I'm still figuring it out, and I've been here longer than most.

"Yeah," I say as two new faces chase each other up the hill.

"It's fucking annoying. You've always got the excited ones, then there are the ones who are scared out of their minds. Then some that just don't give a shit."

But none of those attitudes make a good Guardian.

My back itches as we near the bend in the road that will bring the academy into sight. For Fōsten's fucking sake, am I breaking out in hives? It's happened before. I was sitting at my desk studying for an exam and I just got super itchy, ended up with welts all over my body and to this day, I don't know why. Anxiety, maybe. What a bitch.

I scratch under my bra strap, my hand lingers on my skin checking for any hot raised patches and say, "I'm not gonna lie, for the first week or so it's kind of a mess. But you'll get into a rhythm and things get better."

"Good to know."

And here is a good place to stop talking, let the silence do its work. I've never talked this much to a stranger right away. I don't often say what I think. Telling off my grandparents was a strain and a release.

This girl makes me feel like I have something to say. So I open my mouth again. "Mind if I ask your lineage?"

"Ironskin."

"Really?" I say. "I had you down as a Beastblood. Hard to tell lineages these days, hey? I've never met an Ironskin before."

Rin's expression is impassive as she locks her eyes forward.

Shit. I don't think I should've said that. The province of Emberstead's history with the Ironskin Lineage is everything from messy to tragic, and personal views on Ironskins are just as wide in range. Their affinities, the life and death spirit affinities, spark fear in most. I'm under the impression we don't know as much as we should about them.

I give her a little nudge. "I'm a halfie," I say, my nervous chuckle gracing the air.

"Do you—"

"Yup, got both essence affinities. Beastblood and Emberstead."

Blood rushes to my face. Beastbloods are extremely proud of their beast form. I'm trying to be. My beast form did save me, and that's why I got the tattoo in the first place, to honour her sacrifice. But the pride is a suffocating mask. It's my lineage's pride, not fully mine. But since Rin isn't a seventy-year-old Beastblood sage stuck in the old ways, she might appreciate my ink. I slap my hand on my arm and yank up the sleeve of my t-shirt. The stark black lines of my tiger tattoo stand out in the sunlight. As Rin takes in my Beastblood form, the first sign of emotion cuts across her pale face in a small smile.

It fades before it can reach her eyes though.

The academy looms before us with its pompous buttresses, stained glass windows, and airy courtyards. It is a gaudy, white building that makes everything look unnecessarily small. To the right is the arena, a dome building with metal braces and reflective panelling. It's where I'll be working with the advanced team, in one of the training rooms on the outer edge of the building. To the right is the sea, and hovering over the bay is the great floating boulder home to the city of Sii.

Rin lags behind me, biting her lip with a furrowed brow.

"New students have to go sign in over there at that table." I point to a mob of first-year students. "They'll tell you what to do. It was nice to meet you, Rin."

The sun doesn't seem to touch her skin. But she brings the

ghost of a smile to her face, warming her cold exterior. Maybe there's some hope inside her. It's what she needs to get her to where I am. I almost lost my hope.

"Thank you," she says.

"No problem. See ya around." I wave and my heart thrums in my chest, hoping she'll be all right.

The second my feet hit the red carpet in the entryway, I steel myself, urging my brain to function as best it can. The grand lobby lies before me with marble floors, lavish seating, and a gallery of past graduates and renowned Guardians. It's museum quality, displays of the past encased with reverence and polish. I run my hand over the worn leather of a wingback chair with a stream of sunlight warming it. Midsemester first year, I waited here while Matta discussed my dropout with Evelyn. That year, this lobby didn't feel so old. It clamped down on me like a gaping mouth—the windows were glistening teeth, the crystal chandelier a dangling uvula.

I slip my hand off the sun-warmed leather.

Headmaster Evelyn marches down the hall from the central courtyard with clicking heels and an echo pressed to her ear. Her brown curls bounce, and her clean-cut burgundy pantsuit accentuates her slender figure.

"Adrianne, good." She shuts off her echo. "My office, now."

I nod, hefting the strap of my bag further on my shoulder so it doesn't slip off as I pick up my pace to follow Evelyn, immersed in a cloud of jaden lily perfume and cigarette smoke.

Evelyn pushes the door to her office open, and I'm greeted by more faces than I'm prepared for, but hells, I'm not slowing my pace, and I sure as shit am not going to throw up. Professor Hans Griven stands by one of the windows, backlit, a glowing, grey-haired, sourpuss angel. He's taught me history and Guardian Pathfinder the year I took it. He was the first to witness my choice to be a Medic. I nod to him, and a shadow of a smile marks his face. Next to him is a woman dressed in a ceremonial green Warrior's uniform. Her blond hair is tied in a tidy bun under her hat and her light-brown skin is speckled with a few freckles under one eye.

One head is turned away from me. I know that head. I know the exact shape of where his hair line ends, and the collar of his shirt begins. He holds himself strong but inflexible, like he has a stick up his ass. I used to stare at this head every day in first-year Guardian Basics, until I didn't, and I came back to Guardian Basics again the next year, but he had moved on like everyone else. As he turns to me, his scruffy jawline stops my airflow.

"Marcus," I say before I can stop the enamoured surprise from shooting out of my mouth. I drop my bag by the door, turning my face away from him to give my cheeks a chance to cool before looking back.

Futile. Blood rushes to my face as I bend to set my backpack down. In the time it takes to turn myself into a tomato, he doesn't respond. Letting my eyes be drawn back to his, he tilts his head to the side.

"Adrianne," he says, his mouth unsmiling. A rim of gold glints around his brown eyes. His rusty red curls are cut short to his head, and his deep-brown skin is warmed with red undertones. He wears a green, ribbed sweater over a white shirt, leaving me the only one in a t-shirt and jeans—an orange t-shirt at that.

Marcus points to my shoulder. "Is that new?" he asks.

My face couldn't get any hotter. I roll my sleeve back down, the edge only covering half the tattoo so the bared tiger teeth are still visible. "A congratulatory gift to myself for finishing third year."

"I see." There's a waver in his gaze. His eyebrows pull together with a hesitant flicker. It's my lack of sleeves again, revealing so much of the past, too much even. Dipping his head, he hides his hands in his pockets, and I run mine over my forearms.

His was the first face I saw when I came to after my suicide attempt. I don't remember how it felt to fall into the dark, only waking up to the glow of morning light on his eyelids as he slept in the chair by my hospital bed. Over the last few years, I saw little of him since we didn't have class together. He's Emberstead and Earthkin, a halfie like me, and exceptionally skilled. Lots of people were vying for his attention: students, teachers, Guardian scouts looking for their next prodigy.

Time and distance can take the sting out of memories so they fade to black. I'm not sure if I want him to remember our shared moments from first year. I don't want to remember the girl I was back then, but I'll never forget her. She's always with me.

"Thank you, everyone, for gathering unprompted like this," Evelyn says, settling herself in a leather chair behind her desk. Silver fish in the tank beside her send flickers of light across her dark-brown skin. "I have something to attend to at our original scheduled meeting time."

I brave a step closer to Marcus and Hans. The Warrior woman straightens to attention as Evelyn flicks open a lighter.

The room fills with the warm ash scent of her cigarette.

"I have selected each of you to teach our advanced team this year," Evelyn says. "You all have skills I admire and will fuel their advanced learning. Most of you know each other, but you may not be familiar with Commander Brand Highcaller."

The Warrior woman nods to me.

Evelyn leans back in her chair, crossing her legs and setting her hands on the armrests. "Commander Highcaller will be heading up most of the instruction, focusing on expanding the students' knowledge in the different combat styles. Hans will help the students hone proper technique, Marcus will focus on essence control, and Adrianne will teach defensive combat."

A twitch in Marcus' jaw catches my eye. With just that slight shift in his collected presence, I can imagine his heart sinking to the pit of his stomach. I could always tell he was more determined than most to be a Protector. Even as he moved on to second year and I was held back, I would catch him studying late in the library or training through the meal hours. But during his first real mission after graduation, he was injured. It was covered in the news, and I quietly followed his recovery on social networks, but I guess he kept one thing to himself—he didn't fully recover or else he wouldn't be teaching.

"Tomorrow, I will have Marcus assess which of the students will make the advanced team cut. Commander Highcaller has reviewed their entrance exams and indicated six that have exceptional skill. Jeff-Ray Warden, Niko Carper, Ace Dalaan, Eliote Nohar, Johanna Kingsman, and Rinnaya Burgheim."

The sing song name swishes through me.

"Since Marcus is the only one whose schedule is open tomorrow, he will decide if there will be any other students joining those six.”

“What about weapons training?” I ask.

“Right. There is no one better with a blade than Master Lotera, so I have left it to her to be their weapons instructor. Now, there is a rather sensitive element to the construction of this team. Brand, would you elaborate?”

Commander Highcaller faces us, her silver eyes shadowed under the brim of her cap. “Since the Fourth Great War when all Ironskins with the life and death affinity were eliminated from the living world, an Ironskin with both spirit affinities has not been known.” The Commander’s voice fills the room. Its powerful clarity warps away all other thought. “However, the Death Ritual that accomplished this horrific event was imperfect. The spirit affinities still exist in the small Ironskin Lineage. In the essence registration tests last year, it was revealed that Rinnaya Burgheim possesses both affinities. These affinities give people who possess them enormous strength, speed, enhanced eyesight, and unique essence projection abilities. We don’t know how much experience Rin has with them since, by law, she would have needed an adult present with the same affinities for her to learn.”

Marcus shifts. “But she doesn’t have that here either, unless—”

“You’re right, Marcus.” Brand paces between the line of us instructors and Evelyn’s desk. “There is no one at this establishment who has the same essence alignment and affinities to teach her. Which is why having a set of designated instructors with unique skill sets to promote the safety of both Rin and her peers is essential. On top of this, there are those who would use Rin’s power for ill. Training Rin mastery over her own power is a top priority.”

I roll my gum through my mouth and my stomach rolls with it. Blowing a bubble, it pops with a snap through the quiet. "Does Rin know?" I ask. "Does she know this is why you're creating the advanced team?"

The Commander's gaze locks on the ground. "Rin, just as the others, will know that she has been chosen because of her partial mastery over combat skills. In her entrance exam, she demonstrated knowledge of Telando, Dawntimdato, and a mixed martial arts form."

Pressing my lips, I hold back a chuckle. The only well-known mixed martial arts form is Dawnranfet. It's developed a foul reputation for its brutality and use in illegal fighting rings with zero rules.

"It's unclear how she became proficient in these forms," Brand says. "The others, such as Niko and Jeff-Ray, were part of the Akinnera junior Guardian training program, and Johanna, it seems, comes from a long line of Guardians. Ace stood out for his excellent essence control, and for the opposite reason, Eliote Nohar is adept in weapons handling as she appears to have a null essence strength reading."

Evelyn slides a stack of folders across her desk and motions for us to take one. I open mine and flip through the list of candidates for the team. It's a mixed bag of strengths, but it sounds like the six standing out the most have skills that balance out each other's weaknesses.

As the Commander removes her cap and braces it under her arm, her uniform pulls around the defined muscles. "I expect that all of you will give equal attention to the students. Keep the information of the basis for this team at the back of your mind and carry out your lessons with caution and consideration." She nods and steps back to her position facing Evelyn.

"Are there any other questions?" Evelyn looks us over, her cigarette poised by her lips. "No? Then I would like a written copy of each of your lesson plans by tomorrow morning. You may leave."

I let Hans, Brand, and Marcus file out of the office before me so I can handle my large bag without bumping into them. As I pull the door closed behind me, Evelyn says, "I'm looking forward to seeing what you will teach my students, Adrianne."

I turn to her, and she smiles an elegant but skeptical smile.

Outside, Marcus is still standing near the door, looking at his echo. I duck my head and step around him, my stomach twisting. But I don't want to be the girl who hides any more. Besides Eila Nor in my Medic classes, Marcus has been the one person to really catch my eye at this school. For years, I couldn't get up the guts to make my presence known.

I rest my hand on my stomach as it grumbles and turn to Marcus.

"I heard about the accident," I say. The words leave me breathless, and my heart thumps its way into my throat.

He lifts his head to me, but his eyes don't meet mine. Taking an audible breath, he pockets the echo. "Yeah, it was unexpected."

"This may sound creepy, but I follow you on socials. Ruptured essence channels in your left leg?"

Marcus shifts from foot to foot. Landing back with his weight evenly distributed, he crosses his arms over his chest. "Right. I still have to be checked for essence accumulation in my muscle tissue, and it can be pretty painful."

My awareness is pulled to my own leg—a tightening in my thigh, a discomfort in my calf. "I'm sorry. It's good that Evelyn asked you to teach though."

"Yeah." Shadows fill his eyes as he drops his gaze to the floor. "It's not fieldwork though."

I twist my grip around the strap of my backpack. "This will be amazing work experience."

With a shrug, Marcus starts to walk away. "It's just not where I want to be, you know?"

"I know." My voice echoes through the lobby as a wave of new students clears out. Marcus stops. My heart pounds hard and my hand rests on my leg, the same one as Marcus' injury. "But things can change."

Marcus looks back over his shoulder, and I pull my hand away from my leg.

"Is that really how you feel?" His eyes meet mine for the first time in years. Their brown is soft under his furrowed brow, I lose them way too fast. He presses his lips together and limps away.

He remembers enough. If he didn't remember, he wouldn't question me. That positivity I just forced on him isn't mine. Those were Matta's words. I'm not sure what I really want to say to him, but it's not that. And there really hasn't been much change in me between that first year and now. It's like I couldn't make my presence known to someone like Marcus, to anyone, because my presence has always felt wrong—swallowed. Starting with my first clinical tomorrow, I'll make myself known, at least to myself. Besides, my decision to become a Medic was the only one that has ever felt right.

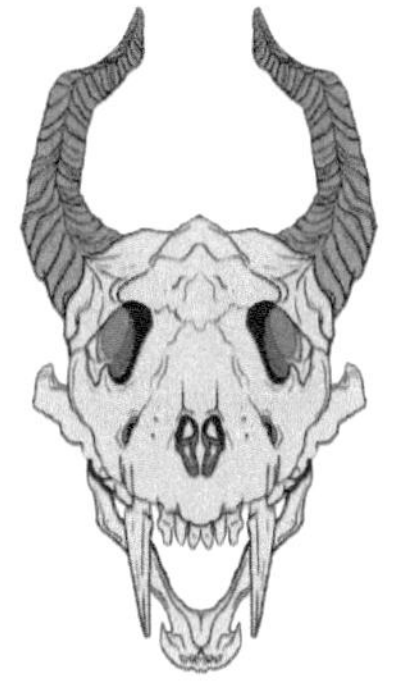

CHAPTER 5

I've been assigned to carry out my clinical and fieldwork through the central Guardian station in the heart of Akinnera. It has the largest Protector precinct and clinic of all the stations in the city. It's quarter to nine in the morning, and the workings of the clinic hover just outside of my awareness with a distant beeping and a weak scent of astringent cleaning products. My Medic uniform waits in my hands. I sit on a bench in the locker room urging myself to move, change, get out there. My head buzzes. Where is the file of Medic stuff I've stashed in my brain? Medic stuff. Stuff. It's just stuff. I can't even name it. Gibberish beastshit. What the fuck am I going to do with that?

I take a breath of five counts, dropping my shoulders, letting my eyelids fall closed. *Come on brain, now it's your turn to relax.*

The buzzing persists with a ringing in my ears. Breath slips from my lips for five counts.

If I had to choose to be a field Medic or clinical Medic right now, I think I would choose field. I'm more suited to it. Being able to use fire manipulation in barriers or quick combative manoeuvres gives me an edge over Fyrra and Lifebloods. Lifebloods have hédin cellular healing and air affinities. It's extremely hard for a Lifeblood to create solid barriers, though, and I wouldn't think it would be easy to aid a bleeding comrade in the middle of a protective cyclone. Fyrra have non-self cellular healing and vegetation affinities, and they don't particularly like to harm their plants to protect themselves. I can use heat to ease pain and speed healing and then curestones for major wounds. But in this clinical, the head Medic will assess my capabilities and knowledge. In part, it's what will clear me for my fieldwork assignment in the second semester. This clinical means everything right now.

I toe off my shoes and change into the loose-fitting teal pants, doing up the drawstring with shaking fingers. The shirt to match cinches in at the waist a little, keeping the otherwise baggy material away from my arms. I clip my Medic trainee badge on the shirt, smooth the edges of my braid, and tuck my triangle pendant under the collar of my shirt. Washing my hands, I revel in the water sending warmth to my bones and roll out the stiffness in my ankle.

The buzz and the ring in my head have finally stopped, or maybe I've just drowned it out with simple tasks. I think today will require a lot of ignoring—not ignoring what's around me but what's inside me. Focus will be my best friend here.

I leave the locker room and report to the head Medic.

There are a few other Medics from my class on rotation today. We gather together. The stench of nervous sweat is a comfort because, thankfully, it's not just me sweating like a rabid Rover.

A Lifeblood doctor with brown skin, grey hair, and fourth-level healing rings in his ear marches up to our group with a clipboard.

"All right, I'm Dr. Valencie, and you will be under my watch for the extent of your clinical study. I should have a Dentin, Nor, McCarthy, and DiHan." Peering over his thin spectacles, he scans our badges.

Dentin and DiHan are Lifebloods. Eila Nor is Fyrra; she gave me a ride in today. Of anyone here, she understands my Vow, even if she doesn't know it. Fyrra are pacifists and maintain a strict moral code to withhold violence, even lowering their eyes when angry to avoid a cutting glance. Selhet, the Fyrra's hand-to-hand combat form, is less combat and more dance that turns their opponents' brutish force and momentum into their downfall. Eila apologized profusely, bowing her head to the floor at my feet when she landed me on my ass in combat class last year. She apologized to me again this morning.

Valencie turns to converse with another doctor joining us. Taking my hand, Eila smiles at me, her purple skin flushing at the cheeks. Her inky eyes search me carefully. She smells like sugar blossoms. Closing her eyes, she whispers a prayer over me in Halaanese. Face flushed, and pits sweating, I squeeze her hand in thanks. Her girlfriend is a very lucky woman.

Out of the entire clinic staff and trainees, I am the only Beastblood and the only Emberstead.

"In your clinicals, you'll get a sense of the general flow of the clinic environment. Whether you're on the path to be a Warrior

Medic or a Protector Medic, clinic spaces are something you'll all need to be familiar with. I'll be watching closely to make sure you use good practices so when you do your Medic fieldwork, you'll be prepared. How many of you are headed down the Protector path?"

Eila and I raise our hands.

"You'll most likely be sent on a fieldwork mission only requiring one Medic. This means there's minimal risk, therefore minimal tasks for you to carry out. This also means you don't have someone to fall back on. This isn't to say that Warriors aren't going to work alone. It's just a heads-up for your fieldwork. I expect to see exceptional teamwork and competency in my clinic."

"Nor and McCarthy, you're going to be aiding returns. The rest of you are doing physical checks for departing Guardians. Those of you in departing, follow Dr. Levis. You two, you're with me." Dr. Valencie points to me and Eila and starts walking the opposite direction of Dr. Levis and her trainees.

The hall to the return ward is long, with white walls, squeaky blue flooring, and bright fluorescent lights. Valencie takes a long stride, turning right around the corner. Ensuring I'm one hundred percent awake, the scent of sour sweat, vomit, and ash twist through my nose in one whiff. My stomach flip-flops, and I squeeze my thumb to quell a gag reflex. A groan hits my ears, triggering my eyes to find the source. Rows of Protectors and Warriors wait for treatments and assessments. Their faces are darkened by lack of sleep, blood, and grime.

"In our section, we have three, four-man Protector squads in at the moment and nine Warriors," Valencie says, and stops us at a workstation separated from the next by a white curtain.

A row of Protectors sits just outside the curtain. "This squad just came back from a beast hunt where there was a core-energy pocket burst that did most of the slaying for them. They didn't have a Medic, so we have a lot of cleanup to do. What's our plan of action? What are we assessing these Protectors for?" Brown eyes and a stone face stare at me and Eila, inviting an immediate answer.

"If there was an explosion, we want to check for concussions. Neurological tests, Cognitive assessments," I say.

Valencie's brow furrows, and he waves his hand as if to fan away the stench of beastshit. "Sure, but you've got to give me a plan of action, McCarthy. Before that."

I take a step into the station. The first Protector grips a poorly wrapped wound on his right arm. He bares his teeth and grunts.

In a sweet, elegantly accented tone, Eila says, "We treat wounds, checking for breaks in essence channels. Essence dysregulation will aggravate a concussion, yes, and we can monitor for symptoms of a concussion as we work. Concussed or not, we can't waste time checking for it until we close breaks in the skin. Our biggest concern is regulating essence pressure through the brain."

"Good. Who are we treating first?" Valencie asks. He looks straight at me, patience draining out of his eyes with each second, and he taps his foot.

Of course. He asked for our process and assessment. I didn't listen to what he was asking, only caught on to bits. So I jumped. But I can fix this, I can wipe that disgusted look off Valencie's face and show Eila I'm not a dimwit.

The man with the bleeding arm bends over, his face pinched, and a pendant with Thesta's crest dangles from his neck. He must be Earthkin. "The Protector with the brachial laceration," I say, losing too much breath in one go. "His unamafann intermediate essence alignment wouldn't have taken well to the . . . the jint energy pulse." A flash of red hair catches my eye. "And the Emberstead Protector next. Emberstead always have high essence pressure." My voice wavers through each word as they rush out, but I know they're correct.

"You two tag-team treatment. Nor, be selective about your healing techniques—I don't need you passed out on my floor. Get to work." Valencie steps out of the way with a nod.

Eila smiles at me. Hand to my back, she nudges me into the centre of the stall. "How would you like to split up the work today, Adrianne?" Her tongue rolls through my name, giving it extra energy.

"I'll start cleaning up his wound. Can you calibrate an essence pressure cuff? Once I've cleaned the wound, you can heal it and take the pressure reading while I start on the next Protector."

Eila nods and locates a cuff in a stand filled with medical supplies.

"Come forward," I say to the Earthkin man.

The acrid remains of core energy permeate the air inside the workstation. I motion for him to sit on the bed, and I straddle a stool beside him. In the stand next to the bed, I find gloves and a face mask. I put them both on with shaking hands and prep my station with a wound kit and saline to flush the laceration.

Taking a pair of scissors, I hack off the crude bandages. The wound is still spilling blood and without the pressure of the bandage, his essence escapes into the air in wispy, silver spirals. The mask blocks most of the essence from my airways, but I still get a metallic pinch at the back of my mouth.

"McCarthy!"

Ice flies through my veins. I jerk away from the bleeding arm and bash into Eila behind me. The essence cuff leaps from her hands and smashes to the ground with an ear pricking crack of the glass monitor face. Eila yelps.

"Clean that shit up. This is not a fucking slaughterhouse. I never want to see blood on this floor again." Valencie's nostrils flare.

My mouth twitches with a croak as a drop of blood splatters the floor. Valencie tilts his head, eyes bulging.

"I'll fix it," I say with a disorienting swell of static through my skin.

My hands are possessed by the spirit that stole all the "Medic stuff" I couldn't access earlier. I fumble for a towel and wipe the floor, and then another to catch the blood from the man's arm. I get back to work on the wound, stopping the bleeding, cleaning, and disinfecting.

Throughout the shift, my breaths are short, my chest is tight, and my hands fumble along, performing unfamiliar tasks with my minimal knowledge to guide them. Voices hit my ears, overlapping each other, creating nonsense words like shit-syringe-beasty-mother at the back of my head as I narrow my focus to five-second breaths and exhausted Protectors.

I break three syringes, bust four veins, and drop a clipboard on the head of a Warrior with a concussion. Eila is quiet and focused the entire shift, while I swear everyone in the clinic can hear me breathing. Valencie swears at me seven more times.

At the end of the eight-hour shift, my scrubs have taken on the smell of every rank substance a Guardian or beast could spill.

Valencie gathers the rest of the interns as I sniff the aroma caught in my hair.

"All right, that wraps up our first shift together. Be prepared to swap positions tomorrow. Those of you in returns will be doing physicals and vice versa. You're dismissed. McCarthy, stay back a minute."

I drop my hair from my nose. Blood rushes in my head and my feet ache. Eila takes a few steps back but waits for me with her hands folded in front of her and her eyes cast away.

"Don't wait for me, Eila, I'll take transit home," I say.

"Don't be silly, Adrianne. I'll wait for you," she says, bridging the gap to brush a hand to my shoulder.

"Well, if I'm not back by the time you're changed, come find me in case I pass out on the way to the locker room."

The sheen of gloss on her lips shimmers as she smiles, and her thick, pink curls bounce with a nod.

"How old are you, McCarthy?" Valencie swipes his eyes over me.

How old am I? Fuck, that's the kind of question that gets me into conversations I don't want to have. But he's my superior, so I resituate my face into an unbothered smile that strains the muscles in my cheeks too much.

"Twenty-two," I say.

Valencie squints at me, tucking his ever-present clipboard under his armpit. "Older than the rest. You start late or get held back?"

"Uh, I left halfway through my first year and re-did it the next."

"Wipe that fake smile off your face, McCarthy. This is serious. Nothing much to impress me today. You need to tighten up," he says.

Heat flares in my cheeks, and the nausea sitting at the bottom of my stomach swishes inside me. Nothing. I've come all this way, claiming the path of a Medic, for a nothing?

"What does this have to do with my age?" *Mother fucker.* My smile cracks and fizzles down my spine, pooling in my aching feet.

"Medic training is intense. For some, taking extra time helps them solidify their choice. For others, well, they're burned out by the time they graduate."

My mind takes in his response, but it slows down while processing. His words are even, neutralized by his commitment to their weight, but my eyes block off half the light in the clinic. My nose has stopped identifying smells, and I'm stuck with an ever-present rank odour stuffed in my nostrils.

"Great, thanks for the input," I say.

With no feeling in my feet, I turn away, just in time to hide the tears rushing hot down my face. I regulate my feet into an easy pace until I turn the corner and stop completely. I lean into the wall, my knees buckle, and I slide to the ground, breaths shuddering in and out.

Head rested and a moment without responsibility, my body sinks into the supportive structure of the building. The hall is empty, like my mind. Moments tick by, and the rush of my breath fades from my ears; my heart stills. My eyes sting as they close.

The wash of black behind my eyelids sparkles. A swirling motion fills the essence in my face. The motion touches my ears, and a murmur works into my mind, like the speech of an elder. Rounding my head with a soft hush, it sinks into me. Words I don't know, stars I've never seen before, shift around me with a pulse in my forehead. An image accompanies the whisper. Like a dream unfolding too fast, too early in sleep, an environment lies before me that I've never seen. A vast mountain range of inky-black stone. In front of the range are those glowing eyes. Their vessel takes a shadowy shape, but I can't make it out. The darkness lengthens and shortens the shape of the body too fast.

"Adrianne!"

Someone shakes me hard.

I open my eyes, but the darkness sticks to them. With a hitch in my breath, I shake my head. The dark clears with strangling tendrils stretched across my eyes. Eila's face comes into focus in front of me.

"Eila," I say, my voice raspy.

"Holia's goodness, what have you done?" Her sugar blossom scent tangles around me, miraculously untouched by the stench of the clinic's horrors. Her eyes are shaking though, dark lips parted.

Pushing myself up from the ground, I ask, "What do you mean?"

She taps on my temples, her fingers spread out wide and her eyebrows furrowed. "Your eyes, they didn't look right."

My stomach plummets. *Another unintentional transformation.*

I take her wrist and slip away from the confines of her hands, heat crawling up my neck.

"It was like your eyes had transformed, but your eyeballs were . . ."

My nerves send a shock across my skin. "Were what?"

"Turned backward." Scooting closer on her knees, Eila lowers her voice, her eyes still watching the hall. "Adrianne, were you Void Watching?"

"I was not," I snap.

Intentionally looking beyond our world to the Lesser Worlds is frowned upon for lineages other than those with pure essence alignment. Even then, they are only able to gaze past the Voids into the realm that aligns with their essence. The Fyrra can see into the Lower Void, the Emberstead into the Silent Realm, and the Ironskins into the Higher Plane. Earthkin are only known to Void Watch through the help of ancestor energy imprints. Eila has the highest reverence for the ancestors of anyone I know, so what kind of offence to her is Void Watching without pure essence or a guide? And my dano, he told me he would set me out in the cold of Neejaan in winter if he ever caught me Void Watching.

I wipe the sweat forming on my brow. "Come on, let's just go. We're both exhausted." I start to the change room. Without the sound of a second set of feet, I turn back around, a wide gap between me and Eila. She's changed into a chunky pink cardigan and a white crop top. The strip of smooth skin sends a pulse through me, and I drop my eyes.

"Void Watching is serious, Adrianne. If you're not blessed by a priest of Carnity, then it's a serious offence to the souls of our world, past and present." Her eyes droop under full lashes. "And it's dangerous without a Shadow."

It's not something I talk about, but Eila is more sensitive to other lineages' needs and practices than most. I suppose after a few years in classes together, she pieced together why I haven't transformed in front of her. Most Beastbloods jump at the chance to be in their full beast form. It's home to them.

She scurries to catch up with me. "I'm sorry," she whispers.

The apology seeps into my skin with the pressure of her hands wrapping around my arms as we walk. The touch of the many silver and gold rings on her fingers cools my skin.

"It's fine," I say. "But I told you I wasn't . . . doing that. Look, I just want to eat and get to bed so I can teach tomorrow and put this awful day behind me."

Eila grasps the ancestral charms on her wrist, and we fall into step.

My face is still wet with tears. I swipe them away but freeze. "What do you mean it's dangerous without a Shadow?"

Stopping, Eila turns me to face her again. Hands to her heart, she whispers, "It's just, well, if you aren't fully here"—a Medic passes us, and she eyes him, staying quiet until he turns the corner—"then you run the risk that the rest of your vital energies will be pulled into the Lesser Worlds by your Shadow. Physically."

That's exactly what it felt like the first time I saw the eyes after my Vow. I let out a sigh and press my hands to my eyes. "Look, I get that being Shadowless is like an affront to all that's holy or whatever, but don't dance around it, okay?"

Sheepish and gentle, Eila nods.

"If I was Void Watching, but it was unintentional, then what does that mean?"

"Well, I suppose, since Void Watching is a spiritual act, maybe you're searching for your Shadow."

My eyelids twitch and my body is only standing straight because all my joints are stiff. What she says makes sense, and it might just be the fatigue talking, but I lean into it.

"Eila, can you Void Watch?"

Touching a hand to her curls, she bites her lip. "No, well, I mean yes. My grandmother taught me and my sisters, but I've only done it once and I . . . I—"

"Eila." I shake her out of her stammer.

"What I mean is I know how."

"Can you teach me?" I ask. Her eyes are wide, wide enough for me to understand the gravity of what I'm asking her. "If it's possible to be pulled by my Shadow into the Lesser Worlds, then couldn't I pull my Shadow out?" My heart is skittering inside me. I might be grasping at an impossibility, but at least it's something. I have to try. "Maybe I can call my Shadow back to me."

"Is it normal for Shadowless to find their Shadows again?"

"It's not normal to be Shadowless at all. But if there's a possibility to fix it, then I want to try."

"We could get in a lot of trouble," Eila says.

"From whom?" I throw my arms out to the side. Eila starts and pulls away.

"There are forces out there that we . . . "

Squeezing my eyes closed, I grab her by the arms. "Please, just help me. I need this."

Pink hairs quiver around her head as she clamps her hands together. "Well," she swallows, "I suppose it would go against Holia's code if I refused to help someone be whole again. But we have to do this the right way."

I nod and link arms with hers. "Take me to a shrine of Carnity."

CHAPTER 6

The shrine of Carnity lies at the south end of Akinnera. The drone of cruiser traffic and construction in the city is strong since the southbound motorway gate is just beside it. Eila holds her cardigan closed around her as she leads me up the steps of the shrine. The walls are pink granite, and the windows are arched, pointing to the night sky.

We stop at the top of the steps and line our shoes behind those already here. At the door, a priest of Carnity stops us with a hand stretched out. He wears long, white pants and a white cotton shirt with designs stitched in pink and green thread. Carnity's colours—her energy.

"State your purpose," the priest says.

I glance at Eila, pulling my braid across my shoulder and

rubbing my thumb over a smooth section of hair.

Eila places her palms together and bows. "We seek Carnity's blessing of protection."

That's not all we seek. But I have to trust Eila. I've never been to a shrine of Carnity, so I have no idea what the procedure is. For someone like me with a casual reverence for Carnity, my prayers aren't very specific anyway. Usually, I just ask for my ancestors' spirits to be with me. Carnity was the first woman with essence manipulation abilities. She had a healing affinity which allowed her to heal plants, animals, and hédin. Today, we call it non-discriminatory cellular healing. Carnity is revered and worshipped for her soul's ability to grant strength, healing, and protection. I guess Eila just chose one of these blessings to focus on. And it seems that the priest accepts this need for privacy.

The priest bows to both of us and turns to a small table next to the door. Two candles are lit by a smoking stick of incense. There are three pearlescent dishes filled with oil at the front of the display. A hushed chant spills from the priest's lips as he dips a thumb into one of them. Marking the oil on Eila's forehead, he chants louder, repeating his phrase. It's ancient Slyvic, so I only catch a few of the words—*Kinownolada Carnity,* ancestor Carnity, and *tuyosho.* I know *tuyo* is the word for strong and *sho* is the word to cover or skin. It must be a word for protection.

I breathe in as the priest marks my forehead. The scent of rosemary wraps around my face. The scent grounds me, but the oil is heavy on my skin, more like a brand than a blessing. Part of my being has already crossed through Carnity's Gate to the Lesser Worlds. Why couldn't she have closed the gate before that part stepped through?

The whites of the priest's eyes are a little too bright as he catches my gaze. I drop my eyes to the floor and follow Eila into the shrine.

There is a fountain trickling just inside the pink hall where flowering plants line the windows, crawl up the walls, and sit in terracotta pots filling the air with perfume.

"This way," Eila says, linking my arm again.

She hurries me down a flight of stairs just to the right of the main hall. The pink granite lines the floors and walls of every passage she takes me down. There are candles set in alcoves, incense next to each one. I can barely take a breath without smoke.

I cough into my sleeve. "Where are we going?"

"Somewhere no one can disturb us."

We come to a mural of Carnity herself with flowing hair of polished black onyx and star crystals in her eyes. There are pink and green succulents in small pots at her feet and a patch of earth filled with clovers. Eila stops in the middle of the hallway.

"Here?"

She nods, candlelight flickering across her skin. "We're at the centre of the building with an equal number of chambers to either side of this hallway. It's a liminal space, a crossroads."

The smoky air drags around us, and the only sound is the distant rumble from the motorway.

"So, what do I do?"

Eila draws me down to the pink floor. "First, the basics. Void Watching is essentially letting our consciousness penetrate into the Rithra Onta, or the Lesser Worlds as you call it. You won't be physically travelling."

"Right, but then, why is it dangerous for me?"

"There are a few reasons. I find the term Lesser Worlds

confusing. In Halaanese, we use the word *rithra* meaning separate, and the word *onta* means home or dwelling. As Void Watchers, we see past the veil of the Voids into another's dwelling. But if your Shadow has taken up residence in the Lesser Worlds, then part of you has found a dwelling there too. You and your Shadow want to be made whole, either here in the Beginning or in the Rithra Onta."

"That's just one reason, hey?" I let out a breathy laugh, running my hands along my braid.

"Yes, the second thing is that Void Watching with a transformation is, well . . . unnatural, but not unheard of. It's difficult to maintain the transformation while in this altered state of consciousness. My grandmother told me a tale of a Beastblood who Void Watched, and to this day she remains in her beast form."

"Well then, that's not a problem because I've never fully transformed." My voice hits every surface in the hall. It comes back to me in an awkward rhythm like teenage angst.

"Maybe. But that's why I will stay with you. There's no telling what will happen if you don't have much control over your transformation abilities. I can send energy through your cells urging them back to their hédin form if need be."

"Oh."

She's just going to sit here and watch me as I do this. I run my hand over my face, not sure what else to say.

"It was pretty though."

"What was?"

"Your transformation. It was like a mask across your face. All coppery and glossy." She clears her throat. "But it was good I woke you. Under Carnity's eyes, we show reverence to her sovereignty over our humble beginnings as we cross into her lover's realm."

Eila is so reverent with her language, so put together, while I sit here floundering for words in my ripped jeans and orange sweatshirt with a hole in the elbow. I'm grateful for the hole, actually. It's the one source of air getting to my underarms.

"This space is the first step," Eila continues. "You want to become aware of everything in this space and aware of yourself."

Her presence fills most of my awareness. Even with Carnity's powerful presence watching over us, the curves of Eila's figure kneeling before me bring heat to my cheeks. Her dark eyes glisten as she watches me take her in, wisps of floral incense floating through her curls. A small smile curves her lips, sending my heart into a rage. It doesn't help that she keeps using such intimate language for all this. I shut my eyes and skitter my nails over the rough floor.

"Okay, then what?" I ask, my voice cracking.

"Well, most Void Watchers engage their essence with their highest ability. For the Fyrra, we draw on the physical energy of plants, so I would turn to the clovers here. They would guide me to the Lower Void. An Emberstead uses Mind Fire to let them see into the Silent Realm, and an Ironskin would engage their spirit affinity to travel to the Higher Plane."

It's that essence purity again. The Ironskins are the oldest of the lineages, and yet, so few remain after the Fourth Great War. The Embersteads and Fyrra are the next oldest. It makes sense for Eila to have such reverence for Carnity, since she belongs close to her. Her unama essence affinity is closer in nature to the great ancestor than any other lineage. The Embersteads' fann essence is closest to Dien's heat manipulation affinity, and the Ironskins' is a mutation of the two. Is my essence just an abomination in the eyes of Carnity? Fōsten doesn't see me like that, and Zenta doesn't care. Carnity and I haven't had the best track record though.

Huffing and jaw canted, I say, "Well, my fire manipulation is pretty shit. I'm nowhere near Mind Fire level."

"Adrianne, don't swear in a shrine." Her voice lowers a little, like my nana's.

"Sorry."

"So, your eye transformation then?" Eila asks.

My stomach turns itself over. I should have eaten before doing this, but there's no turning back now. I give my back a scratch. "Fine. I'll try."

"Once you engage it, wait patiently for your consciousness to shift to the frequency of your essence. When you see your Shadow, call to her. I'll be here to bring you back if you stay too long."

Heat and smoke build over my forehead. I'm not sure what she means by the frequency of my essence, but I'll try my best. I've spent far too long like this; I'm ready to try anything. I snap my eyes shut.

"One last thing." Eila sets her hand on my knee. "I don't know which world you will see. But in the Lower Void, there's what the Fyrra call the Poison. Don't engage with it."

"How will I know—"

"It looks wrong. You'll feel wrong. The one time I was able to see past the Voids, I saw the Poison. It's why I became a Medic." A hush falls over us, accompanied only by the flutter of wind through a candle flame. "Void Watching is a responsibility. What you see there affects our Beginning. I believe I saw the

Poison for a reason. It strongly affects our world in some way. As a Medic, I can gain the skills I need to prepare for whatever that might be."

I open my eyes for a moment. Eila leans forward, still gripping my knee, eyes trained on me. I swipe my forehead, and the rosemary oil rubs off on my hand. Marked twice now, I send my essence in a wave up to my eyes.

Pressure fills my face and my eyeballs twitch. With each pulse of essence, I become accustomed to the rhythm, the frequency. I rock back-and-forth a little, and I clench my hands on my knees to keep myself grounded in my body. Once the energy in my eyes has settled, I ease them open. Darkness wraps around me, a blank slate. The mountains I saw before rise above me. My thoughts string together in a loop at the back of my mind. *Where are they, the eyes, where are they?*

Over the loop, I count the seconds as I sit in the darkness. Each one passes, and the details of the mountains fade. The eyes never come. I try to call out, but I don't know what name to shout. My own? I don't know what words to use. I don't think I know any words. I have nothing here. Even the darkness is fading. My heartbeat crashes through the nothingness with a blistering of heat through my chest.

Adrianne.

It's faint. But I know that word.

"*Adrianne*. Please, Adrianne, wake up!"

A cry crackles through the darkness. Vibration in my body, in my shoulders. My head nods back-and-forth, hairs slip over my face. Cold hits my back. Air in my lungs. Heat stings my chest between piercing heartbeats.

I blink, and Eila's face looms before me, stricken with tears, her hands braced over my chest swarming with a neon-green light. I gasp as a pain shoots from my chest to the top of my head and back down to my toes. Energy blisters over my skin.

"Oh, Adrianne, thank Carnity you're okay."

As I press away from the floor, Eila wraps her arms around me, shaking me with her sobs.

"What happened? How long was I out?" I ask.

"Everything was fine until your transformation started to move down your face and . . . and . . . Your heart stopped," Eila blubbers into my shoulder, rubbing a hand on my back. "I should have never let you do that. I'm so sorry. Carnity forgive us. All Creator forgive us. We should never have sinned against you in this way."

My hand is as cold as ice as I hold Eila close. My heart is an inferno, blazing, raging against her words. Is that what this was? A sin? Or was it a sin that led me to being Shadowless in the first place? This one prayer to her god is more violent than taking me down in combat class.

Throat dry and stinging from the smoke around me, I swallow a cry and push her away from me. "Then why did you help me?"

The skin between her brows twists and her full lips part. Shuffling away from me, she stands. Her chest rises with quick breaths as she looks down at me. "Don't you know?"

I heave myself off the ground with a hand on the wall to steady myself. My legs wobble, heavier than they should be. Eila pushes past me. She stops short with her back turned and arms wrapped around her waist.

"Can't you tell that I . . . that I have feelings for you?" Eila whispers.

The confession sinks another stake in my aching heart. I hold my hand to my chest and reach for her. "Oh, Eila, I—"

She jerks away. "It doesn't matter. I have a loving girlfriend. I shouldn't even have thought about it. This was all wrong." With a loud sniff that grates along the granite hall, she stalks away.

I can't even make the words out to tell her I had feelings too. I pushed her, unwittingly taking advantage of her feelings for me, and then she found that I am too much for her, and her accusation of sin is just too much for me.

Stuffing my hands in my sweater, I follow Eila before I lose track of her down the winding halls. I can never Void Watch again. I have to put it behind me. Maybe I can learn to transform my eyes without it, but I can't search for my Shadow. I should have never let my focus waver from my goal. I'll become a Medic. That's my calling—my purpose. This is why I made my Vow, so I wouldn't stray.

C H A P T E R 7

LAST NIGHT, I drove us home with Eila in the passenger seat, sniffling and mumbling prayers. I fell asleep at my desk and woke with my notes stuck to my face and a pinch in my chest. Thankfully, Commander Highcaller had the advanced team start with a team building drill—making their way up and down Moon Hill. Quite the challenge with beasts in the forest and a strict timeline. By the time they returned, the pain had subsided. I've checked each team member's essence pressure now, with only Rin to go.

I shouldn't have tried to use an essence pressure cuff on an Ironskin. Evelyn's skeptical smile flashes through my mind. Valencie's unimpressed report of my performance yesterday digs a spike into my heart. Eila's sobs are caught in my mind and wrench my stomach into a knot. I can't be making mistakes like yesterday. If I'm shit in the clinic, maybe teaching can be a backup for me. They always need Medics to teach.

Red dots and a blood pressure reading. The dots skitter, dancing over the black screen of the essence pressure cuff, waving it in my face that it won't work. Rin waits, her arm held out for me patiently, the cuff wrapped twice around it. There's an aroma of fresh air and her morning coffee around her. In the exercise today, this frail-looking girl released the power of her life affinity. Through the feedback monitors, the energy wrapped her vision in blue. It threw her body into motion. It was like something dead inside her came to life.

It reminds me of what Eila told me about Ironskins Void Watching in the Higher Plane, the realm where spirit energy is collected after death. But an essence burst like what she just did can disrupt the system. Is that what happened to me at the shrine of Fōsten? Did I have an essence burst yesterday, leading me to transform my eyes and to Void Watch? It didn't really feel like a burst. I don't know what to do about this, especially since when I checked my essence pressure last night, it was fine.

Glancing around the training room, my eyes catch on Marcus. He talks to Commander Highcaller with his arms crossed. There are extra shadows beneath his eyes, and he lifts one hand, giving them a quick rub. He turns. My face bursts with heat. Marcus dips his head and gives his attention to the Commander, nodding and turning his body away from me.

Clenching the monitor attached to the cuff, I say to Rin, "These monitors are shit at detecting cellular essence."

Ironskins' jint essence is housed in cell membranes instead of essence channels. This gives their lineage a number of physical enhancements and the spirit affinities. According to her physical records, Rin has impenetrable skin and enhanced strength in addition to the spirit affinities. She glances at me, like she can sense the analysis looping through my head.

More skittery red dots. This method can work sometimes. Maybe it will read if I leave it a little longer. The dots blur as I stare at them.

"I'll have to do it manually."

"Oh." The waver in Rin's voice draws me back to the goal.

I'm here to help her, all these advanced students. Yesterday I was all over the place. Today, I need to get myself together, stay calm, and show Evelyn she made the right choice with me. She made the choice; I just don't know if I believe she's right.

It's been about an hour since Rin activated her life affinity, so if her essence pressure is still high, we have a problem. More than one problem. Niko glares at us from the other end of the room with his arms crossed. The life and death affinities strike fear into most, and in the past, the other lineages waged war against the Ironskin nation to wipe them out. It doesn't bother me though—the war was evil, not their affinities. As a halfie, most people think my essence is tainted because it's not the natural balance of unama and fann energy molecules for a Beastblood, and it isn't pure fann like most Emberstead either.

I wish I didn't have to make Rin go through this process. "It's a little unpleasant," I say, crouching down to my med kit. I also wish I didn't have to do it for my own sake.

A scalpel waits for me in a pouch on the right side of the bag, right where I left the little bastard, but I move a pack of bandages and stick an expired pain tonic in the side pocket to dispose of when I get the chance. Blood chugs in my veins like the fluid has turned into those red dots dancing through my body. Unzipping the pouch, I wrap my hand around the cool metal—all my fingers clenched and turning white.

"I have to make an incision on my thumb so that when I press it to your arm, the essence in your skin will pulse through my thumb as it interacts with my blood," I say with shaking hands. I had to do it yesterday when I broke the essence cuff, and my hands shook just as bad. All I could think about was the Protector staring at my exposed scars. As I stand back up, I make a quick adjustment to the sleeves of my windbreaker.

"You have to hurt yourself to test my essence pressure?" Rin's grey eyes grow wide like two moons.

"It's fucked up. But most of the time when I don't have a cuff, people are more horrified that I have to bleed on them than me cutting my thumb to do it."

I bring the scalpel to my thumb but stop. Rin's gaze is magnetic. Her lips are parted, and she holds her hands in fists.

"My gosh, stop looking at me like that." I tap my foot to hers. "I'm not sacrificing my first-born child for you."

My eyes travel back to the knife in my hand. I Vowed not to spill blood. I didn't think about this when I made the Vow. But it is to heal, I suppose. Pressing the blade to my thumb, my nerves lean into the pain and the path the sensation takes, sparking like fire through my hand. Blood and essence spill from the cut. My head spins, so I press the cut to her arm.

Rin clears her throat. "So, after three years of being here, is this year exciting, or are you ready to get out of here?"

As I hold my thumb to her arm, the essence in her cells thrums along the line of the cut. One pulse sends a shock through my entire body, not painful, but it skates through my blood vessels, highlighting every twist and bend. My heartbeat seems to match the thrilling pulse.

"Four years actually," I say.

"I thought you said you were a fourth-year."

"I did. I just had to do first year twice." I take a sterile wipe from my bag and make sure to take away every mark of red from her skin. "But to answer your question, I'm still happy to be here. I think I took the amount of time I needed."

Happy is not a truthful word, but half truths have been the best way to skirt around conversations I don't want to have.

"You didn't mean to engage the life affinity, did you?" I ask.

Shaking her head, Rin drops her wide eyes to the floor, cracking her knuckles as I press my cut to her other arm.

"Unexpected essence bursts can interfere with the electrical conduction of the heart, so I'm going to check your heart sounds when we're done with this."

"What does it feel like?" she asks.

"Prickly," I say. "Gritty?" Maybe happy is a truer descriptor for this moment, because with her strong essence connected to mine, happiness does fit and I giggle. "Alive. Healthy. I gauge the pressure by how far I can feel it through my body. It should reach the same place for every part of your skin I test. I can feel the prickle all the way to my toes on both sides." The few times I've done this before, the prickle barely made it through my arms.

Rin's breathy laugh slips into the space between us as I wipe away my blood once more. I pick out a creamy-white curestone and glide the tip along my cut. Similar to Rin's essence sending shooting energy through me, the curestone soothes and awakens as it heals the wound.

Pressing a stethoscope to her chest, each beat is strong and full, enduring in a steady rhythm. "Okay, you're fine and healthy. Better get over to the others."

"Good. Thank you."

She crosses the training room to join the others and I watch like an old woman admiring the younger generation. I still can't place it, but when I look at Rin, it's like holding up a mirror, showing me my younger self. That's not fair though. I don't wish my younger self on anyone.

Brand Highcaller leads the advanced team through a simple drill. Each of them takes a turn striking a punching bag with a star crystal embedded in it to absorb energy and produce a reading of the strength behind their attacks. The crystals usually absorb essential energy, but this one has been manipulated with technology to absorb kinetic energy.

I come up beside Marcus to watch the drill. He wears black sweatpants and a grey t-shirt that shows every line of muscle in his arms and back, which is entirely unfair. How dare he look so damn good in gym clothes?

"You only chose the original six that Brand identified for the team," I whisper, leaning close enough for him to hear me, and way too close because with one wrong move my shoulder could touch his, and if that happens then my hands will want to slide up his sculpted arms, and then we'll have a big mess resulting in me locked in the bathroom too embarrassed to come out. Like yesterday with Eila. We got too close. I lean away from him.

"Yeah," he says and crosses his arms, further stretching the fabric to twist around his deltoids, biceps bulging.

Damn.

My body heats, starting up a nice nervous sweat, but the ice on his tongue bites through me.

I focus back on the team. Jeff-Ray is an Earthkin who rivals Marcus in size. In fact, I think Jeff is a bit taller. He has kind eyes and a great combat form. The Beastblood boy, Niko, is a tiny, scrappy dude with blond hair and a wild grin. He gives Jeff-Ray a punch on the arm as they pass each other in line. The red-headed Emberstead girl, Johanna, is striking in every way—piercing green eyes, a snarl, and an attitude. Her arms and legs are fabulously toned, her form impeccable, producing impressive kinetic energy output. Eliote is a lanky Luminee girl with long purple hair, smooth, smoky-brown skin, and a graceful technique. Ace lags behind the others in combat skill. He's Nytrue with spiky blue hair, brown skin, and kind blue eyes that seek out Rin whenever they can.

Brand gives commands and tips on their form, making careful notes, picking up things I could never see.

"Remember doing a drill like this?" I ask Marcus.

Marcus side glances at me. "Mm."

Not even a full word to reply? I shift from foot to foot, running my hand over the back of my sweaty neck.

"Ace's strikes are a bit weak," I say, as they rotate through the drill again for a power strike. Ace pushes up his glasses and focuses on the bag. Throwing a punch, all the power comes from his shoulder. He winces and shakes out his arm as he returns to the line. "I know this technique that directs essence flow to the feet just before the punch and then lets it shoot to the fist with the strike. It helps you engage your whole body with the movement."

Marcus rubs his chin. "That sounds like a risky technique

without a specific essence manipulation. We can't teach bad habits."

Crossing my arms to match him, I say, "It's not a bad habit if it's done correctly."

"What I'm saying is that it's not basic."

"He was picked for his essence manipulation abilities, wasn't he?"

A vein in his neck pops out, and his brows crinkle like two angry caterpillars getting ready to fight each other. "Yeah."

"Well, it's good to learn new combat techniques with essence techniques." The glow of the star crystal paints his face in gold for a moment after Jeff strikes the bag.

"Adrianne, I'm trying to concentrate. I'm not teaching a first-year student a technique that sounds like something that would be used in Dawnranfet rings." He drops his arms with a slight turn of his body to me, and he sighs. He caught me there. I shrink a step away from him, out of his glare and his shadow.

Fire licks my tongue. "Dawnranfet has legitimate techniques."

"It's illegal."

My heart twists in my chest, creating an ache as it presses on my lungs. Dad had held my hand the whole time we were at fights. He was there to gamble, sure, but we were also there to be together, just us. We kept it a secret from Matta. I was there to hold his hand and observe. The techniques were brutal but effective. Splatters of blood had hit my clothes. Once a tooth had hit the ground by my feet. *Did you feel that, kitten?* Dad had said. *Feel how the air got warm as he performed his double fist strike? That's because he shifted his essence with his motion to make it more powerful.*

I haven't held his hand in over three years.

"The fighting rings are illegal because they don't have rules," I say. "The techniques aren't illegal."

Marcus rolls his eyes and faces the team.

Where is this attitude coming from? It's like I stepped in shit and tracked it through his house. Somehow, I've ended up kicking that stick further up his ass.

I cross my arms and pay attention to what's going on with the team. Rin steps to the bag and performs a quick punch. The smack of her fist echoes through the room and the energy metre ticks past the other students' readings as the bag swings back-and-forth with a squeal of the metal chain. She could kick all our asses in a fight. Her ease facing the punching bag and technique is unmatched. Out in the field today, she pulled out a Dawnranfet move. I wonder if Marcus caught that. Professor Hans, however, dissects everything wrong with her form and its link to her unexpected manipulation of her life affinity.

"The key to manipulation is essence flow, then for cellular essence, mental and physical awareness of oneself is the key to engaging the spirit affinities." Hans' voice, haughty and tamed, grates my nerves.

Rin stands in the middle of the room with all eyes on her, twisting her sleeves into her fists.

In a hushed tone, Marcus says to Hans, "Maybe we should have her do some extra training every month to ensure she has good control over it."

My shoulders tense. Making a student do extra work outside of class doesn't send a great message to this team. As a halfie, Marcus should know better than to single her out based on essence abilities.

I give Marcus a quick swat on the arm to get his attention. He turns to me, jaw set and eyes stern.

"What are you doing?" I mouth to him.

A puff of breath escapes him. "I think it's for the best."

I swallow hard, pushing down the fire and bite the inside of my cheek until Brand hands the session over to me. With the tang of metal on my tongue, sweaty pits, and a buzzing head, I sort through the mass of lesson plans I've thought up. I never settled on my opening words. How do I start off?

Stepping forward, I try to keep my face neutral so no one can see my ill-prepared mind grasping for a tactic.

"Hi," I say and clasp my hands together, so they don't shake. "I . . . uh . . . I'm Adrianne. I'm a fourth-year Medic student here. I'm a Beastblood–Emberstead halfie with feline and fire affinities. I'm here to teach you how to use defensive combat at an advanced level."

"We know all this, get on with it," Johanna says. "Do you even know what you're doing?" She sighs so everyone can hear, her hip popped to the side, curly red hair pulled into a ponytail high on her head.

With my jaw canted, her sour words swim in my veins, and my head pounds from Marcus' butt-stick conking me over the head as if to say, "Stay back bitch, we don't need any of your nonsense."

Without warning, I have to pee. But with both these aggressions, one born out of impatience and the other born from a resistance to change, I know where I have to start. This is a team, and they have to act like it.

I take a step toward Johanna and punch her straight in the face. The team takes a collective gasp as Johanna's head snaps to the side. Behind Johanna, Brand smiles and nods, marking something down on her clipboard. Hans takes off his glasses and rubs his eyes.

"Damn it. What the hells?" Johanna yells, clutching her face.

Knees bent, fists ready, I say, "What are you going to do?" I look from Niko to Jeff. "What are you going to do?" I repeat, scanning the rest of the team. "Come on. Do something."

Of all the wide-eyed first years standing around me, I know it's going to be Niko. The honour of defending your comrade will push his little Beastblood heart right into gear. I shift my essence away from him without following it with my feet.

Niko lunges at me. Just as he's about to punch, I lean out of the way fast, drawn by my essence. His momentum caries him past me. I grab his face and slam him down to the ground. Niko stares at me from the flat of his back, eyes wide, gasping for air.

I smile at him. "So, Niko. What did you do wrong?"

Niko sputters, eyes fluttering, and he pushes himself up with a grunt. "I don't know."

"Jeff, what did Niko do wrong?" I ask.

Without missing a beat, Jeff says, "You were already in position, putting Niko at a disadvantage. He should have got himself and Johanna out of harm's way, or at least waited for you to attack again and counter it."

"Exactly." I help Niko up. "Unfortunately, none of you did that either, so you all failed." Johanna glares down her nose at me, her freckles blending into her red cheeks. "Lesson one. You're not the only one you need to protect. Think. Assess. Your goal is to get everyone on your team out alive. Get that through your head."

As the red-hot adrenaline cools inside me, my bones turn to

ice as Marcus shakes his head, his arms still a barricade over his chest. My heart plummets. After all these years of watching him, maybe I was right to watch. I'm too unpredictable for him, and he's too rigid for me. I swallow hard, pushing the raw feeling in my gut further down and stirring up that urge to pee.

I turn back to the group. "Everyone, partner up."

Eliote takes Rin's hand, and Niko shrugs as Ace gives him a tap on the shoulder. Still holding a hand to her face, Johanna fumes as Jeff gives her the sweetest smile to partner up. Yesterday, I made Eila do something drastic with me and it left her in tears. Now Johanna, chest heaving with breath, is moved to fury.

Shaking my head, I drag my medkit over to her and find a small curestone.

"Johanna, turn here, hun."

Jeff takes a step back to give this blazing inferno of a hédin some space. His lips are pressed as he glances at me. Clasping his hands, he turns away. I was so sure it was the right step. Everyone is uncomfortable with me now.

"See, Ace? I told you halfies were crazy," Niko says in a hushed voice behind me.

I grit my teeth.

"This proves nothing. Marcus is a halfie too."

"Yeah, but he only has a fire affinity, and he hasn't decked any of us. It's the mixed affinities, man."

"Niko, I really don't think essence has any effect on personality." Ace's voice is quiet and even.

"I don't know," Niko says in a melodic tone. "You've obviously never met any avian Beastbloods. And feline Beastbloods"—he draws out a long pause—"they're the worst."

Would it be so bad if I punched him too? I shake the thought away and tap a finger on the aggravated skin of Johanna's pale face. The skin between her eyebrows is bunched, and her eyes narrow on me, unwavering. Setting the curestone to her cheek, I am careful to not rub it too much and gently lay a hand on her arm to steady her.

"I didn't hit your nose, did I?" I say, lowering my voice for just the two of us.

"What the fuck is this?" Johanna snatches the stone from me.

"What do you mean?" I ask, keeping my voice soft.

"Playing all nice and sweet after smacking the shit out of me." Heat radiates off her as she leans in close. The chatter in the room fades for a moment. My teeth clamp together, caging my tongue. Johanna steps even closer. Lips by my ear, she says, "Two-faced bitch."

Is that how you really feel?

Wipe that fake smile off your face, McCarthy.

Two-faced bitch.

Too much, not enough, and nothing to seal them together. I have a missing side.

One of Johanna's curls grazes my neck. The lock on my limbs snaps. I shove her away from me.

Her head cocks to the side as she takes a step back. "Do you feel nice inside?"

"Just shut up. I don't want to hear from you for the rest of the day," I say under my breath.

Johanna runs her tongue over her teeth. Her chin raises and slowly lowers as if she knows something I don't, sees something I can't see, can't feel. As she turns away, a smile crests her lips.

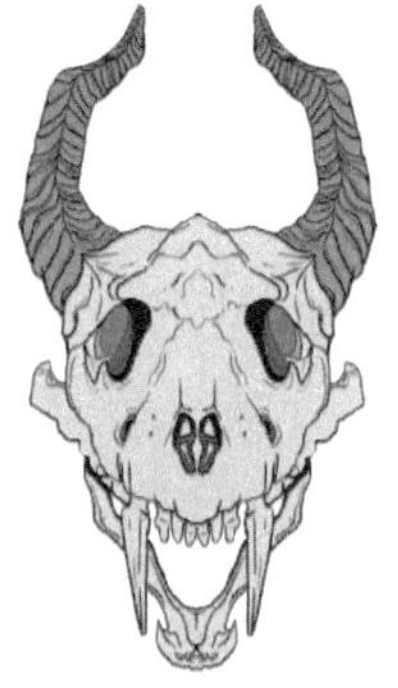

CHAPTER 8

After the morning classes, I am about to fill my plate with food in the dining hall, but Evelyn calls all the advanced team instructors to her office. I leave the hall empty-handed and empty stomached, hoping the meeting won't take too long so I can have time to eat before catching transit to the clinic. I enter Evelyn's office to a familiar scene of the other instructors waiting for me.

"Adrianne, please close the door and take a seat," Evelyn says as her eyes follow me, peering above her gold-rimmed spectacles.

As I sit, she scribbles something down in an open journal on the desk. Glass ancestral beads click together around her wrist. The air in the room is thin, either that or my throat is closing up. Evelyn removes her glasses with a sigh.

"It has come to my attention that a student was harmed during training this morning."

With my hands gripping the arms of my chair and my knees tilted to the door, I swallow hard.

"We teach combat," Evelyn says, her voice clear and low. "We do not condone violence. I hope to keep today a singular incident and that you all will keep each other accountable for your training tactics. Now"—she picks up her pen again—"Adrianne, why did you hit Johanna Kingsman?"

Digging my nails into the wood, I try to sort through the buzz in my head to figure out a reason for it. I don't think "Johanna's a bitch" will go over well. I didn't plan to hit her; she presented an opportunity for illustration. We're taught to identify the aggressor in tense situations. I identified, and I executed a counterattack to get the lesson rolling. Lowering my eyes to my lap, I say nothing.

"If I may," Brand says. "Though it shouldn't be applied in other situations, I do think the lesson had the effect it needed. Unconventional, yes. She taught them to think before they react, elevating the safety of their squad over brawn. Those students are going to remember this lesson for years."

Evelyn purses her lips as she considers this.

If only she knew that I felt threatened by Johanna, that she flipped a switch inside me and got under my skin.

I glance at Brand. There's a hint of a smile on her face as she folds her hands behind her and paces the length of the room. "To provide context for the matter, Johanna was extremely disrespectful in expressing her impatience with Adrianne's introduction to the lesson."

"All the more reason for Adrianne to model behaviours of

composure for her underclassmen. Although, frankly, I'm not sure if having a student teach other students is the best idea to begin with," Professor Griven says.

The cushion under me is like a brick, and my spine is strung tight. The clock ticks and I don't want to move or speak because the longer we stay here, the less time I have to eat, walk to the station, catch a city train, and change in time for clinical. If I say nothing, then there's nothing to discuss. Marcus is quiet, even though the other instructors have weighed in on my stupidity.

"No, Hans. Adrianne understands defensive procedures and utilizes them very well. She is an exceptional asset to the team." Evelyn pauses for me to make eye contact with her. "I chose you, Adrianne, for a reason. This kind of behaviour isn't it."

Evelyn is a vision of strength in her wingback chair, curls tied behind her head, books backing her. They testify to the vast accumulation of experience as a field Medic and as the head of medical research before her time as headmaster.

"It won't happen again," I say.

"Good. Because if it does, you will no longer be instructing. Is that clear?"

"Yes, very clear."

"Then you all may leave."

As we file out of the office, something I better get used to it seems, I officially have lost my chance to eat before leaving. The tension in my spine creeps up to my jaw and my stomach churns.

"This is ridiculous," I mutter to myself, giving the muscles in my jaw a rub.

"Is it though?" Marcus says behind me.

He's silent through all of that and now he chooses to talk? Sure, punching someone in the face is a stupid thing to do, but it's not that stupid. I turn around to face him, heat prickling the skin of my neck.

"Yes, it is," I say. "Maybe Evelyn did choose the wrong person to do this. Or maybe people just need to get punched in the face sometimes." All the fire I blocked off earlier is ready to seethe through my tongue.

Marcus scoffs and takes out his echo. "You do know how twisted that is, right?" He presses the lightstone and scrolls through his socials with a flick of his thumb.

"No, no. You don't get to do this."

"Do what?" Pausing his scroll, his sharp, brown eyes dart to me.

"This." I gesture to him with no particular focal point. "You've been talking down to me all day, and I'm not here for it. It's fucking rude."

Marcus switches off his echo. He runs his hand over his beard. The scratch of his whiskers against his skin sends a thrill through me. Pocketing his hands, he turns to face me head-on, and the heat steams from my cheeks. "If I was rude, then I was rude. I'm not apologizing for thinking your teaching strategies and tactics are terrible."

"But you think I should apologize to Johanna? Get on my hands and knees and pray for Evelyn's good graces?"

He shrugs. "No, I just think you shouldn't have hit her in the first place."

"Well, I did, and it's done." I take a few steps to bridge the gap between us. A citrusy scent wafts off him, and my head spins.

"Look," he says, "teaching like that isn't going to get them anywhere. When teaching a group, the lesson has to be neutralizing, something everyone can relate to and incorporate.

It doesn't have to be flashy."

"Great. Thank you for your unsolicited wisdom." I glare at him for a second. But his brown eyes are kinder now. The scowl he's had on his face since orientation day is softening into a neutral line.

"It's not my wisdom. Emberstead and Earthkin elders all agree that a simple lesson is the best lesson. And I'm not going to budge on that."

All the wisdom I've gotten from my elders has made me into what I am today. It's left me dangling in a weird in-between space.

"Maybe not everyone is looking for lessons," I say, running a hand over my grumbling stomach.

"You might be right on that. But in the future, I wouldn't go around being all nicey, nicey with Johanna." Marcus takes his hands out of his pockets and flairs his fingers. "It doesn't seem like she responds to . . . soft touches."

With a curt chuckle, I fish my echo out of my pocket.

"Shit." My stomach growls. I need to get going right now if I don't want to be late. My feet don't move though, my mind is swirling, and my nerves are tingly, but I just can't get myself to move. I'm not going to make it through the day if I don't eat, and if I do take the time to eat, Valencie will cuss me out, guaranteed.

"Are you all right?" Marcus asks.

My fingers fumble with my echo as I try to put it back in my pocket, and it clatters to the marble floor. "Fuck it all." I snatch my echo and shove it back in my pocket. "I have to get to my clinical, but I haven't eaten. I left my cruiser in Neejaan, and the girl I cruiser pooled with yesterday doesn't feel comfortable around me anymore. And I can't get my ass to move because . . . " I don't want to go to my clinical. It was long and tiring and it smells. And Valencie obviously doesn't think I'm cut out for it. "Never mind. I fucked up in training today. Now I'm paying for it."

I turn away from Marcus, not wanting to look into his condescending face.

"I'll drive you."

There's a clink behind me. I spin around. Marcus has his cruiser keys in his hands.

"What?"

"I said I'll—"

"I heard you. I just didn't expect you to offer."

"Well, I'm offering."

"Are you sure?"

"Yes, it's not a problem."

I grab a chunk of my hair and run my fingers over the smooth strands. "It's in the city centre."

"I know where it is."

"I have to eat."

"Then go get yourself something, and you can eat on the way. Meet me out front." He motions to the entrance, a square of blue light hitting his dark skin from the stained glass.

I start toward him, ready to throw my arms around him, maybe even give him a big kiss on the cheek, but I step back. "Thank you, I'll be right back." My face flares and I sprint to the dining hall.

Marcus drives a plain, green cruiser. It is old and rusted in places but runs smoothly like it was bought new, which it wasn't. He talked about it for weeks in first year—where to buy and a price range—before taking the plunge to buy the out-of-date model. I will not for the life of me tell him that I remember this. Eavesdropping is not an attractive quality.

The floor mats are clear of dirt, the windshield is spotless, and the only smell caught in the cab is my spicy lentil fenn wrap. Marcus drives with both hands on the steering wheel like a first-time driver, but his grip is loose. At each intersection, he comes to a complete stop and is patient with long lights. Besides the bag with a change of clothes in the back, the only sign that an actual living hédin owns this cruiser is the sticker for a band on the dash. What would play if I turned on the audio system?

Swallowing a bite of my wrap and picking up a few crumbles off my shirt, I speak for the first time during the ride. "Marcus?"

He turns his head to me for a second. "Yeah?"

I continue to retrieve crumbs that have fallen between my legs so they don't get ground into the seat. Marcus' hands shift on the wheel.

"Do you remember me?" My voice is blunt, not harsh though.

"What kind of question is that?" He rolls his shoulders back. "We've been at the same school for four years."

I take a long breath as red sorrow-blossom petals flutter past my window.

I had imaginary conversations with him all the time in first year—what I would say if we ran into each other in the hall, or if we got to chatting at the lunch table, maybe a late-night study session, but those conversations never happened. They were nonsense, just scrambled words in my head because I thought he was hot. He may know who I am, but there's not much to remember other than the one real conversation we had together. The real words he chose to speak to me were few and quiet. They dug inside me, and I felt something for him that I've never felt for anyone else—a softness, a tug, a lightness. That feeling never left. I just don't know if it meant as much to him because I was sent home too soon to find out.

"I mean, do you remember what happened?" My hands lie sweaty on my knees. "Do you remember meeting, well not meeting, we had met before, but it felt like the first time because we hadn't spoken more than two sentences—"

"I remember." The words are soft and unintrusive. They sit in the car with us, dense like a perfume. They soothe my rambling train of thought that has wondered for years about that night.

"We never talked about it." I can barely get the words to come out. They almost seem unnecessary, just him remembering might be enough, except that my heart burns to know his side of the story.

"I wanted to," he says. The ball of his throat bobs. "There was a big chunk of time between you leaving school and the next year that I didn't know how to bring it up. I didn't think you would want me to."

"I'm not sure if I wanted you to either. It was still raw when I came back and I was just happy to keep my mind on training, finish what I started." I take my last bite. My stomach calms, and my nerves are quieter than I thought they would be talking about this. I stick the paper plate in my bag and make sure I haven't crumbed up the seat too much. "I think when you're eighteen, you don't really have the words for something like that. Maybe we have them now?"

Marcus takes a long breath, the rush of air audible in the small space. He nods, his eyes ever on the road. "You were in and out of consciousness when I found you. The first thing I think of is how dumb I felt. I was angry about a critical review on my weapons exam and went to the roof to get some air. But I saw you and couldn't breathe."

The confession breaks his hold on the wheel. He puts his elbow on the windowsill and leans his head on his hand. I am too stiff to turn away. I have no thoughts to add to his story, no desire to interrupt. But my arms ache. He must be leaving so much out. So many descriptions that we're both thankful not to reexperience.

"I called for help, but no one came, so I carried you from the roof to the lobby, where Evelyn called the emergency Medics. Evelyn said she would go with you, but I insisted I go too. I didn't know if you would want me there when you woke up"—he clears his throat—"if you woke up. But I couldn't get myself to leave."

My head was foggy when I woke up. Everything was so surreal that having one familiar face around was precious. I grabbed hold of it. Marcus sat on a chair beside me, leaning to one side, his head on his hand just like now. I wanted to cry or yell or smash something or hurt myself so I would fall back into the dark, but I didn't want to wake him. I watched him until he stirred. He didn't ask questions. Until Matta arrived, he told me the information he got from the doctors while I was unconscious instead. Questions I needed answering were somehow answered through him. He told me he was glad I was awake. I couldn't admit how sweet those words were to me because I had to learn to admit I was glad I was awake too. So I'd let the years pass.

"Thank you for staying," I say.

"I'm just glad a beast was the first being I saw die and not someone I cared about."

My tongue is tied, and my mind is stuck on all these things that I'd never known about Marcus. He cares, he remembers, and even thinks about what happened from time to time. All this weighs on my chest. I hate that he was there, and I hate that I'm thankful he remembers.

"I'm sorry you went through all that," Marcus says as he returns his grip to the steering wheel.

We ride the rest of the way in silence. At the clinic, I gather my bag and open the cruiser door. With one leg out the door and one inside, I turn to him. "Um . . . talking about this helps me. Time makes impossible situations a little more bearable. Allow yourself that grace too."

This time, he doesn't question me.

I can't touch his leg—it's too far away and too intimate. Instead, I grasp his wrist for a moment. Marcus' eyes follow and a small smile lifts the corners of his mouth. "Maybe. What time is your shift over?"

"It's just a five-hour shift."

"I'll be here at six then."

"No, you don't have—"

"I'll be here at six." The smile lingers on his face even as he turns his eyes to the steering wheel again. His fingers tense around the grip and relax. With a slight flex in his jaw, his lips press together.

Drawing my leg back into the cruiser, I shut the door. "Is there something else?"

Marcus' golden-brown eyes dart to me. The gold is like a pool, shimmering and shifting—unguarded by ice. He swallows. "It's about Rin, her extra training. I thought she might prefer to work on the spirit affinities in private."

My grip on my bag loosens. "Oh," I say, eyebrows raising.

"I can't imagine working on essence manipulations so closely linked to your inner being would be easy. Peace and quiet might be good." He drops his eyes again and shrugs. "You'd better get going."

I nod. A stray hair slips from behind my ear. I tuck it back, gather my things, and exit the cruiser. My heart buzzes as Marcus drives off. So, there's an underside to his hard edge. It's something easy. I already knew it was there, he just doesn't show it much. And I'm excited to see him again, to work with him.

CHAPTER 9

"So, you sick of me yet?" I ask as Marcus pulls up to the academy and kills the engine.

My shoulder blades cinch together, waiting for his response. We have a system that seems to work even though it must break up his day to drive me to and from the clinic. I'm just worried he's starting to think I'm taking advantage of him or, well, I don't know, my friendships and other relationships have always been short.

"What's with you and asking such . . . abrupt questions out of context."

I roll my gum through my mouth and blow a bubble with a shrug. "You've been driving me for a few weeks now. Just thought I would check in. Also, I was kind of thinking we could work on coordinating our lessons a little better before you head home."

Marcus checks his watch. "I've got some time. I was thinking the same thing, actually. Maybe some lessons about protective essence barriers and projections," Marcus says.

The knot of tension in my back unravels. "Yeah, that would be good."

"But to answer your first question"—he reaches behind him to grab a tote bag from the back seat—"I'm not sick of you. A little sick of the smell though."

"Smell?" I shove my nose in my armpit and recoil, slapping my arms to my sides.

"The antiseptic, Adrianne." A smile quirks his lips as he opens his door.

I scramble to gather my backpack and slip out of the cruiser.

The sun is low and warm over the quieting campus. The waves beyond the cliffs provide a gentle hush at the back of my mind. Marcus shoulders the beige tote and grips the straps. "The weapons training room should be free. Want to work in there?" he asks.

I fall into step with him. "Ooo, we could somehow incorporate sword and shield techniques into barrier work, attaching barriers to your arm like a shield."

"That would be great because Eliote can join in using an actual shield." Marcus holds the door open for me.

"Yes, exactly. Now, should I start with some footwork drills to get into position where it's safe to use a barrier or projection? Then you teach them how to create one?"

Pushing his sunglasses to the top of his head as we walk through the lobby, he shakes his head, eyes down. "No, I think it's best if you take point on the essence technique on this one."

"Why?"

"Since my injury, I haven't been able to make barriers very well. The whole shifting your essence through your body to get enough force is a bit difficult." He pushes his hands forward and clamps his hand over his wrist like he would for a barrier, then drops them to his sides with a slap. "Plus, you can teach Niko and Rin cellular projection from your transform points, can't you?"

I consider this for a moment as we pass through the corridor between the dining hall and the central courtyard. The tiled floor is sprinkled with light filtered through the large sorrow-blossom trees beyond the glass to the courtyard. Voices echo and dishes clank from the dining hall. "Barriers aren't my strong suit, but I can do them. Projections, on the other hand, I need to practice."

"So, it's a good thing we plan this lesson sooner than later." Marcus peers through the training room window at the far end of the hall. "Hm, looks like it's occupied."

"Think we can work next to them?" I come up beside him.

In the centre of the room, Rin and a Lavarian boy spar with Illyson long swords.

"Hey, I think I know him. Yeah, that's Lance Hira," I whisper.

For a moment they stop their spar. Lance switches places so he stands next to Rin. He demonstrates a strike, and they perform it together.

"Why are you whispering?"

"I don't want them to hear us. They're so cute together." I set a hand over my heart as Lance nudges Rin's arms into correct form. Rin glances at him as if taken aback by his touch, and Lance's large black wings twitch behind him.

Marcus leans closer to the window, his neck stretched long so his shoulders don't get too close to me. "What makes them cute?"

"You can't see it?" I gesture to the window.

Marcus is quiet, still squinting at the duo. "Are they dating?"

"No. I mean, I don't know, but you can just tell that they would make a good couple."

"Well, I don't know, I've never talked to the guy." He steps back and crosses the hall to another, smaller training room.

We shuffle in and drop our bags at the door. The room has a sparring mat with a single square marked out on it. There are two small windows at the top of the far wall. Dust particles float above the mat in the stagnant heat that's built up throughout the day. The air is thick and musty.

Marcus squats down with his Personal Automated Technology device and opens a new document to make notes. He writes "protective essence manipulation lesson" at the top in crisp lettering with a stylus.

I kick off my shoes and step onto the mat, shaking my arms out and stretching them over my head to loosen up after my five-hour clinical. "You don't have to know them to know they're a good match. I can just feel it." My shirt rides up, exposing my midriff, and I peek over my shoulder to see if Marcus notices. He yawns into his fist, head bent over his PAT.

I roll my eyes at myself. *Grow up, Adrianne.*

"I don't really know what that feels like." I barely make out his muttered words behind me, and he covers them with a quick cough. "So, do you want to practice your projection first?"

Turning, I tilt my head to the side as I take him in. Mouth neutral, eyes focused, that hushed statement is lost now, and he's locked into our goal.

Sighing, I say, "I guess. Just . . . don't laugh."

Marcus balances the PAT on his knees and clasps his hands. "Of course not."

"Okay, so I think I would start the lesson with barriers, what they are, and how they're different from armour. Then move into, like, a demonstration and overview of steps. Then I'd talk about projections, no, break into groups, then projections, and—"

"Just do it. We can't teach it if you can't do it."

My stomach lurches, and I whirl away from him with my eyes shut, my braid swinging like a rope around me. I press my hands to my chest and take a long breath. My essence heats and takes a trickling path through my arms and legs. Sweat beads on my forehead as the transform points tingle at my shoulders, stomach, hips, and knees. In a quick motion, I take one step and thrust my hands out. My eyes fly open, and a globe of orange light wobbles out into the centre of the room. It shimmers and rolls to one side. Two ears pop out of the globe, then a fat tail, and two, wide-open eyes. The projection shudders, leaps, and crashes into the wall, bursting on impact.

A whimper escapes me, and I flop to the ground, heart pounding from the pathetic projection. Pieces of orange energy drift back to me and sparkle as they get absorbed into my skin.

"See that," Marcus points at the wall with his stylus, "that was cute. It was like a tiny, baby, ghost cat."

"Shit. I was going for mean and scary."

Marcus chuckles. I told him not to, but it's low and smooth, a balm for the burn of my failed, basic manipulation. "You want to try again?"

"Not yet. I need to catch my breath. Let's see your barrier."

The PAT makes a dull tap on the ground as he sets it aside. He springs up and takes a wide stance, drawing in long, controlled breaths. With eyes trained on the same spot my kitty cat projection detonated on, he thrusts one hand forward and claps his hand on his wrist. The temperature in the room rises and the air around Marcus wavers. A few seconds tick past and no light spills forth, not even a flicker of fire, just a stammering heatwave.

"Huh," I say.

Marcus drops his arms.

"Right, so I'll just do the essence demonstration myself then," I say with a wry smile.

"It doesn't make sense," Marcus says. He swishes a hand in front of him. Delicate flame threads spiral through the air, making a web around him. "I can do things like this that require so much control, but when it comes to something like a barrier, I can't do it."

"Well, the technique requires a build up of energy. Essence travelling from the tips of your toes to the tips of your fingers is where the force comes from. If you can't move essence in one leg, then that's a long stretch of energy accumulation that's inaccessible."

We both try our projections and barriers a few more times while discussing the best way to present the techniques for the team. The heat in the room is a helpful source of energy to draw on and keeps my essence flowing smoothly. By the time my projections have individual legs, even though they are barely flat stubs, I'm sweating but energized. Awake. All the times my eyes transformed on their own and I accidentally gazed past the

Voids, I was exhausted, physically and mentally. Maybe now would be a good chance to try out an ocular transformation and hold on to it.

"You know, transforming my eyes was the first essence technique I was able to do," I say.

"Yeah?" Marcus says, absently inspecting the swollen, reddened skin of his palm. He holds it above his head and wiggles his fingers to get the essence to drain.

"I haven't been able to do it for a long time, but recently it's come back to me. I think if I could master it, then maybe my other abilities would follow suit. But I need your help."

"My help, how?"

"I kind of go into a trance if I try to do it if I am too tired or if . . . " If I'm emotional or there's too much incense messing with my brain. "I just need someone to wake me up if the transformation goes beyond my eyes."

"Anywhere beyond your eyes? Don't you want to transform fully?"

"No. I think that's what causes the problem. I just want to be able to master my ocular transformation because it gives me night vision. It's a skill that could make me a better field Medic."

A soft smile spreads across Marcus' face. "You're so determined."

I sit down cross-legged on the mat. "Something like that."

I want something to show for all the years of essence practice. Something that might get my grandparents off my back, something that might show my second soul to my matta. If she saw just a bit of it, maybe she'd stop seeing me as her death girl, even if my Shadow is off chilling in the fucking Rithra Onta.

"Well, you are, too, aren't you?"

"Not in the same way, I don't think." Avoiding my eyes, he sits down, and we face each other.

I brush stray hairs out of my face and set my hands on my knees, eyes closed. They twitch a little with the sting of sweat slipping in-between the lids. With an inhale, I draw essence up to my eyes and set my awareness on the twitching muscle, the crinkle of skin between my brows, and the heat flooding my face. It pulses but the change never comes. I am rigid, keeping my breaths small to avoid any sudden chugs of essence. In the quiet, Marcus' breaths cover mine, and I start to match them.

Still nothing.

"Have you tried visualizing?" Marcus asks.

"Not really, I usually focus on the physical feeling."

"When I'm doing a difficult manipulation, I try to visualize the essence inside me, focusing on where it is, giving it a colour and a texture. You could try that."

Essence itself is silver. If I give my transform point a colour, it would give me a focal point instead of trying to track the rush of essence, the transformation, the pulse in my eyes. I bring a picture of myself to the forefront of my mind, as if I was sitting facing it instead of Marcus. My face is serene, and I mark a bright-orange X on my forehead. Streams of silver glide up my arms and neck, roll over my cheeks, swell through my eyes, connecting in the orange essence node.

My muscles relax, and another image takes hold. I am young, small, with short hair and a bright smile. My face appears in a mirror, euphoric as I gaze at the striking narrow slits of my tiger irises.

As I open my eyes now, the sun has left the sky and the training room is dark, but the lines made by the four corners of the walls are crisp. There are no odd, twinkling lights that accompany the eery darkness and the mountains, only the brightness in Marcus' eyes. He smiles at me and my heart swells.

"Looks like it was successful. Still conscious?" he asks.

"Yeah." The depth in my voice is out of place. These eyes don't know this body, the maturity of my essence. We have to get reacquainted.

I blink a few times and release the visual of the orange mark on my head. It flickers and goes out like a neon sign.

"Well, I think we give it a shot and teach this lesson tomorrow, what do you think?" Marcus asks.

"Ugh, maybe." I slap my hands over my eyes and give them a rub. Building the lessons comes so easily. I always know what I should say, but when it comes time to say it, my brain goes blank.

Marcus offers me a hand up. "I'm surprised you didn't give me a Dawnranfet technique to help me with my barriers. How do you know so much about Dawnranfet anyway?" His tone is playful, but all the ease I've felt in this room jumps out the door before I can.

"My dad took me to matches, okay?" Tension twists through my back.

Bending down to gather his tote and his PAT, he doesn't seem to notice. "Your father brought you to Dawnranfet? That's illegal, and terrible parenting, I might add."

"Yeah, well, he's in prison now, so I guess you're right."

His jaw drops as he matches my rigidity. "Oh, Adrianne, I'm sorry. I didn't know about your dad. When did it happen?"

"First year." I throw my backpack on before I freeze.

"Was it before . . . " He runs a hand over his face and turns away.

My heart kicks up into my throat. No one can ever say it, and yet my grandparents say it too much. Suicide is a cursed word. It stops up throats, steals eyes away, and infests rocks into stomachs. You can't talk about it even though talking about it is the only way to take its power.

"Yes." My braid is stuck under my strap. I yank at it, but the bag is too hefty.

The braid trails behind getting more tangled and making my nerves more aggravated. Marcus moves to help me, but I jerk back and pull the braid out, losing the tie in the process. The three strands start to unravel.

"That must have been extremely hard to deal with," Marcus says.

Within the span of two weeks, my dad and I had disappointed each other. He confronted me about my grades before we went to the shrine to make my Vow. They weren't lining up with my usual marks in academics. *"Maybe you should transfer to an essence academy instead. You can transfer as many times as you want, I don't care. But you can't just slack off."* I'd shrugged. My apathy was like a slap in the face to him. He always told me to do everything with my whole heart. I couldn't tell him my heart felt rotten. Then I fell silent when I should have made a proud Vow. Dad sighed, and said, *"Zenta, help me."* And after that, he was ripped away from me. Matta was overwhelmed and alone without him. I didn't know what I could do, what I wanted.

Why can't I tell Marcus any of this? I told him it was healing to hear his side of the story, but this? I can't.

I motion to Marcus' watch. "You still on schedule? You have somewhere to be?"

He doesn't look at the time, only at me, crinkled brow, unreadable eyes. "My cousin's having a party."

"Oh, that's nice. I hope you have fun," I say, drawing a smile to my face and a lightness to my tone. "We'll do the lesson tomorrow. I'll just get more nervous about it if we put it off." I whip the door open.

"Okay, see you tomorrow."

I leave him with a giant twisting pain in my gut. My dad is one of those things that shakes my focus. Too many memories are attached to those months surrounding his imprisonment, too many ties to the girl that lost her way, lost her enthusiastic tiger eyes, and this girl right now is just trying to keep her feet on the ground. Marcus is too gracious with me. I can only hope that working closely with him will allow some of that to rub off on me.

CHAPTER 10

THE NEXT DAY, I meet the advanced team in the arena training room. The hot air moves around me with the breeze from the open door. Sweat beads on my forehead and my lungs pinch. We're a quarter of the way through the year, and my voice still shakes every time I teach.

"All right, everyone, listen up," I say.

Conversations between the advanced team persist. Niko idly punches one of the red punching bags as he tells Jeff some story about shenanigans of last night. Johanna still has her butt in the air as she touches her toes, Rin stares off into space, and Eliote and Ace are taking a warmup lap around the training room.

I clear my throat. "It's time to start—" My air escapes too fast to be commanding.

All morning my skin has been crawling like it's rubbed raw and my insides want to burst out. I've taught so many classes already that this should be easy. Nothing about teaching is natural for me. I'm not a wealth of information or poised under pressure. I sweat and swear when things heat up. But no one wants to see that.

One more time. Stay calm. Marcus isn't here yet though; we planned this together, and I would feel better if he was here in case I mess up. He probably slept in after his cousin's party, but he won't be late. He'll be here soon. *Breathe.*

"Everyone please line up," I say as loud as I can without yelling and plant my hands on my hips to assert dominance, a guise to air out my pits.

Rin jolts out of her daze, but the rest of the team steps toward me like they're trudging through water.

Marcus comes through the doors from the arena behind them. "Let's get to it, everyone," he says, and they all step to, forming up in a straight line. I clench my teeth and dip my head as my heart beats the drum solo of an exasperated fool.

I shift from foot to foot. The floor of the training room has bounce to it that is great for athletics but shit for grounding. The little give with every movement leaves my toes eager to stay put, but the jitter in my body denies me that pleasure.

As Marcus joins me at the front, the heat in the room shifts around me with his body coming close to mine. His bright, orange-peel scent swipes past my nose. Giving me a quick nod, he turns to the team with his hands clasped behind his back.

"We're going to be working on protective essence techniques, specifically barriers." I project my voice in a steady stream like the sunlight spreading over the floor from the door open to the training grounds. But the effort is like blowing through a clogged pipe, leaving me winded and hot in the face.

"You've already been taught the use of small, repetitive hand movements to get your essence flowing steadily when trying new techniques. Creating barriers is just the opposite. You use wide motions, stabilizing hand signs, and focus."

"How much focus do you need to make a wall? Isn't that like super basic?" Niko asks. He folds his arms over his chest, eyeing me with half a smile. The kid's a Beastblood, with a bear as his beast form. He's never made any kind of essence wall before, and projection training will kick his ass if I don't do it first.

Jeff nudges Niko in the ribs. "It's harder than it looks."

"Though Niko has no idea what he's talking about, it is a good question." I step out of Marcus' bright scent so my head can stop spinning. "As an Earthkin, Jeff has made countless earth walls. It takes practice and focus, yes, but the walls he makes are breakable. He puts them up, but no matter how thick they are they can be broken because elemental walls and armour manipulations are highly energetic and volatile. Use enough force and the energy scatters. A barrier, on the other hand, stays up until the builder brings it down. Jeff will manipulate his own essence and draw on the energy emanating from the physical earth to create the barrier. It takes precision and time. Because of this, it's used as a precaution rather than a battle technique. Let me demonstrate."

I step away from the team. Facing the sunlight, I crack my neck. My feet take a wide stance, my left leg bent low like a lunge and my right foot back. Breath is ever my flighty friend. I close my eyes, centring on the rise and fall of my chest to make amends with my tortured lungs. Constricting my throat to gain control over the rush of air, my essence matches the flow. From my lunge, I lean back on my right leg, dip low to trail my hand along the ground as I push forward into my left leg. I thrust my hand forward, palm open, fingers spread wide. My essence courses to the tips of my fingers. Clasping my right hand over my left wrist, I trap the flow in my palm. I clench my fist. A flash of white light fills the room, and a shock wave punches the hot air. A five-sided fire plate bursts into being in front of me. It is translucent with peachy colouring. Shimmering and radiating, it hovers above the ground like a plate of stained glass, five feet tall.

Turning back to the team, my eyes skip around them to Marcus, who gives me a nod, a smile hidden within his scruff. My heart flies up to my throat. I swallow hard to keep it from bursting.

"So, let's break down the steps," I say. "First, I focused on a strong stance to engage my muscles, which propels the movement of essence. By rocking back-and-forth, I directed my essence to my left side. My right hand served as a vice to capture more essence into my left hand than would normally be there. Finally, when I clenched my fist, it put strain on the captured essence, resulting in a burst of energy. My hand served as the template for the barrier, giving it a clean five-sided shape."

The team shifts, each flexing their hands and trying out stances with focused brows. But Eliote stays put, her arms wrapped around her middle. She bites her lip making eye contact with me. She's Luminee, a lineage that can manipulate the light around them. But Eliote doesn't have any Luminee abilities. She can see auras though, the combination of a person's vital energy that escapes their body into the environment. It's fascinating, and my guess is that she has a little essence in her eyes. All hédin have essence that they inherit from their mothers, but it's probably not detectable. I could be wrong—it's just a guess. The poor girl had Marcus bark at her for not doing his drill in the first week of school. She barked back that she can't, and they were both red in the face for the rest of the session.

"Eliote, I'd like you to work on shield and sword techniques with Marcus. Niko, you'll be doing an essence projection from your transform points, which is a little different. Rin, a spirit affinity projection, like the well-known life affinity wings, is a projection of your cellular essence as well, so you two will be working with me. Does anyone have any questions?"

A muggy breath fills my head with heaviness, stifling my thoughts. I hope to loving Carnity they don't have any questions.

"All right then, Johanna, Ace, and Jeff help each other with elemental projections as I work with these two." I motion for Niko and Rin to follow me off to the side.

Rin follows right away, her feet making soft, pleasant taps on the bouncy floor, but Niko lags. He saunters in an uneasy step. "You know, I'd rather work with the others." His eyes bore into the back of her head. The muscles in Rin's neck tense, shoulders twitching a pinch closer to her chin.

My mind scrambles. Do I make him suck it up? Do I force Rin to work with the dipshit? I just have to make the best of the moment. I just have to hide the circles of sweat on my shirt.

"Niko, you know with your transform points and Rin's full-body cellular essence, you guys could learn a lot from each other."

"You're kidding, me and a cutch—"

"I don't condone language like that." I lock eyes with him.

Niko gives me a dark glare with his jaw canted. "Our elders

fought to keep this province free of Ironskin tyrannical rule."

"And all you're here to do is train, so you're going to do as I say."

A clang of sword and shield sounds behind me as Marcus engages Eliote in their lesson. The clatter fights for attention in my scrambling head. Rin stares at me with unwavering, silver eyes, her face a blank sheet.

Pinching the bridge of my nose, I say, "Beastblood cells have essence in their cell membranes, just like Ironskin cells. In Beastblood cells, there's not as much essence present as in an Ironskin cell but just enough to allow back-and-forth transformation between beast and hédin."

A flash of fire bursts from the other group. Johanna is shot backward by her own flames. She topples over, her fingers smoking and her curls sprawling over her face.

"You really need to clamp that hand tight, Johanna. Take your time, don't rush," I say.

"How in the hells am I supposed to know how hard you held?" she asks, pushing herself off the ground.

"Just use your head."

"Bite me." Her green eyes flash.

"It's no use telling her to use her head," Rin says. "It's empty."

Zenta, give me strength. I don't know what kind of rivalry Rin and Johanna brought from their hometown, but I do not have patience to deal with it.

"Niko, energy from transform points can be projected as an energetic visual of your beast form instead of transforming your body. You can knock back your opponents with the force of the projection. It's the same with life affinity wings. You project energy from your cells to form the wings."

Rin's face pales, and she wraps her arms around herself.

"Well, let's see you do it," Niko says to me.

My pulse pounds in my temples. I would give anything for a lick of wind to blow the itchy heat off my skin and quell my desire to smash his face in. *You do know how twisted that is, right?* I huff with Marcus' words sticking a pin in my ego.

My throat is slimy, and my pulse has switched locations to my fingertips. The course of my essence is rough, a churning river during a storm. *No baby ghost cats.*

I get into my stance, breathe again, and close my eyes. My mind travels through my body, marking imaginary orange X's on both my shoulders, my stomach, hips, knees, and feet. I circle back to my forehead and paint an invisible Vishal. I rock back-and-forth, thrust both arms out as my essence crackles along my muscles and away from the points I marked for projection.

My arms glow the same peachy-orange as my barrier. An outline of light spills from my hands, starting the projection in the shape of two feline eyes.

A clatter bursts behind me, sending a twitch through my shoulders. The light is sucked back into me. My head snaps to the side like I've been slapped in the face. Stumbling a moment, I cradle my forehead in my hand. Behind me, Niko cackles.

"Wow," he says between bouts of laughter that singes my nerves.

I turn on my heel.

"Maybe you shouldn't teach something you don't know how to do," he says.

Rin's face twists, her dark eyebrows pinching together. "Niko, she got distracted."

Niko rolls his eyes. But they make a circle right back to me.

A smile spreads his lips, slick, and mischievous. "Are you the girl that got held back?"

I clench my teeth so hard I might break a tooth. Movement in the training room slows, and pairs of eyes glance in our direction. I let my eyes wander a moment too. Marcus and Eliote have stopped their spar. Eliote rotates her shoulder a few times, and Marcus stares right at Niko with a glare as heavy as death.

"Yeah, you are. I've heard about you," Niko says.

The kid just doesn't know when to shut up.

"I know why you keep your hair so long." His beady eyes flick away from my face, trailing down my hair. "Why would I take any advice from a Beastblood halfie who can't even make their own Vow—"

"You're a little shit." The words are like a snarl from the caged beast inside me. Sparks are on my tongue, energy courses through my body, and it's not my essence. It prickles up my spine and makes my vision tilt. Heat and ice vie for my attention in my blood, appearing at my skin in places they shouldn't, making a patchwork of temperature over my body that is all wrong. "You have no right to discuss any of that."

I stare at Niko with his one eyebrow raised and arms crossed, chest puffed out. Rin takes a step back, one arm circling her middle and a hand over her chest as she plants her dagger eyes on me. If I didn't know better, I would think the temperature patches were turning my face red and blue.

"None of you get it. None of you really get what it means to be here, what it means to learn. You're all a bunch of disrespectful, snot-nosed shits with your heads up your asses—"

"Adrianne." Marcus' hand is on my shoulder. I shrug it off.

"Sprints. Everyone, now. On the line." My arm whips away

from my body, pointing them to one side of the training room. But everyone is still. Silent judgement passes through the air like the stench of garbage. *I'm garbage.* "Now!"

My voice slaps a heartbeat into their frozen bodies, and they shuffle to the line.

"They don't have to do sprints, Adrianne. Especially not all of them," Marcus says under his breath.

"If you don't listen to your teammates and instructors, you don't get anywhere. You're stuck running back-and-forth. Now run."

The team sprints to the other side of the room.

I've sweat a second skin, my shirt is soaked through, and my hands are shaking. I drop my eyes to the ground and prop my hands on my hips.

Marcus nudges me to the door. "Take a minute—"

"Pick up the pace," I yell as he gently steers me away from the team.

I break from his grasp and march myself through the automatic door to the outdoor training ground just as tears spring from my eyes.

What the hells is wrong with me? I can't keep punching and screaming my way through these training sessions. Niko's right. I'm not cut out for this.

"Niko, a word." Marcus' voice rolls past the door to meet my ears. "Never speak to Adrianne like that again. Do you hear me? Look at me. When you do this projection, remember who taught it to you. Remember that she's mastering two affinities at once."

"Yeah, whatever," Niko mutters.

"It's not whatever." There's a slight waver in Marcus' words, but no sharp threats, and each word presses into the silence with an authoritative shove. "And Rin. She is your comrade, flesh and blood just like you. You are no different."

There's a squeak of rubber soled shoes and a sigh. "Yeah." It's almost swallowed by the rush of sprinting feet. "I get it."

"Good, now run."

Sunlight beats down on me, flaring around my eyes. I slap my hands over my face, but it only makes my face hotter, stuck in a fleshy sauna. I drop my hands. My breaths come faster. I want air, clarity, relief, but all I pull into my lungs is hot.

"Adrianne, come out of the sun."

I wipe at my eyes with a sweaty hand. It stings, making me cry even more. I make my way back into the shade. Marcus meets me with a bottle of water. The thunder of sprinting feet sends an ache through my gut. I lean against the wall, pressing the skin of my arms to the cool cement.

"Drink," Marcus says, nudging the water into my hands.

The water splashes through me, soothing just a little.

"I'm so stupid," I say after another gulp.

"No, you're not stupid. He was pushing your buttons, and he shouldn't have." His eyes find mine. Sweat streaks his face. I shake my head, turning away from him.

The training field grass is greener than I've ever seen it, with a short, manicured cut. The city wall rises up behind it with a gate that opens to a path up Moon Hill. Heat waves stream away from the stone wall.

"I'm always the first to break." A fresh prickle hits my eyes.

A sigh escapes from Marcus, and he runs his hand over his sweaty face. "You've got more on your plate than most of us."

"That's not true."

"It is. You have clinical three days a week, combat training, Medic skills, the advanced team, and you still have to do your fieldwork. Midterms are coming up, and I've heard Medic exams are crazy hard."

Sliding down the wall to sit on the ground, I swallow the slimy lump in my throat. Marcus crouches down in front of me.

"You had to do just as much as I did last year," I say.

"No, I didn't. I did the minimum fieldwork hours, minimum public-aid, and my classes. You've been at this school for four years, these kids will only be here for three total. I think you deserve to be a little"—he rolls his eyes like he's looking for the right word and sighs—"pissy."

A snort bursts from me. I have never heard any remotely foul language come out of Marcus' mouth. Marcus chuckles, sitting back on the cool cement and bracing his arms on his knees.

Leaning my head back, I let my eyes fall closed for a moment. My eyelids are heavy, puffy, and still stinging. "I'm not good at this."

"Good."

My eyes fly open. "What the hells is that supposed to mean?"

"All this stress would be for nothing if you didn't learn anything about yourself."

"I guess that's a good thing." I press my palms to the ground, creating a dark grey sweat print. "Do you like it? Teaching?"

The panting and rushing of feet are louder now, bashing my ego again, but I keep my eyes on Marcus. He looks off to the side, his eyes finding more interesting things than my tomato face.

"I haven't decided. I think I still want to pretend to hate it for a while longer." He flicks his gaze to me for a moment. "It's not what I wanted, but I guess that doesn't mean I can't like it."

I nod. Feeling pinched into something and not being able to fight it, that's a terrible pain. What does it mean to hate something I wanted though? Why do I hate what I want? Clinical. Teaching. So far half of what it means to be a Medic makes me physically ill. Without this option, I don't know where I would be, and maybe that void is worse.

"All right, I get it. Can the lesson be over now?" Niko shouts from inside.

"What do you think? Ready to put them out of their misery?" Marcus asks.

"Let them suffer," I say. "I'm not cool yet."

"You have a point." Marcus lies down on the ground, his arms splayed out on either side.

A laugh bubbles through me. It lifts the gut-punch feeling from my stomach and lets some of the hot air escape.

"Marcus?"

"Mm?"

"How do you keep your cool all the time?"

His eyes flutter open. "Well, I do try to meditate each morning, which is what I would make those brats do. But . . . " The small smile on his lips vanishes. He folds his hands over his stomach, and says, "I don't think I keep my cool."

"What do you mean? Ever since first year, you've been so good at everything. Everyone wanted to know you or be you. But it never seemed to faze you."

A lick of wind brushes the side of my face. My stomach drops as Marcus swallows hard, a furrow carving between his brows.

"It did faze me," he says. "Still does. All the attention made me uncomfortable and then the judgement for how I dealt with it was ridiculous. People always think I'm rude, like I was above them or something, or apathetic. I just didn't want the attention, didn't need it."

I lean over on one hand so that my face is above his. His eyes find me.

"Sometimes I wonder if I really was being rude, or arrogant maybe," Marcus says.

"No, some people are just like that. More people than we think," I say.

"What? Rude?"

"I mean you don't get energy from people, they drain you."

Pressing his lips together, he keeps my gaze for a moment. A tingle cascades down my spine. I've always been drained by too much time with people, too, but with him, it's different. The gold in his eyes is like a shock, his stern face melting into a soft smile—it's all energy to me.

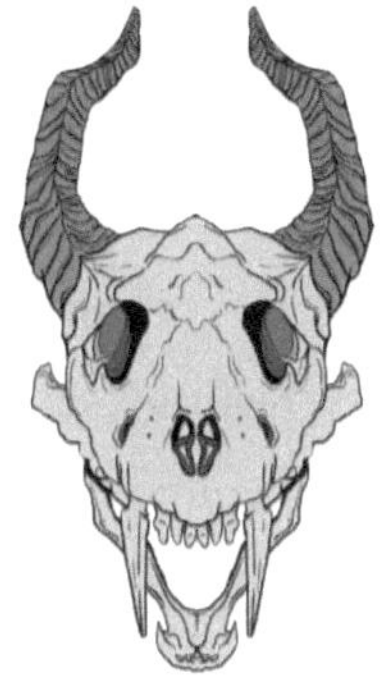

CHAPTER 11

A WEEK HAS PASSED, leaving my blowup behind, yet tension lingers like a cloud above my head with each lesson I teach. I don't know if it's a reverence or a fear from the advanced team, or maybe just disregard, but working with them each day feels stale. I instruct and they do. On top of that, classes are moving along, consuming all my free time with advanced medical first aid, mental health care, and powerstone qualities.

"Death stones are unique in that they don't affect all hédin in the same way," my professor says. He leans against his desk with his arms crossed. "Curestones can cure a break in any hédin skin. Hold a waterstone long enough, and you'll begin to feel calm. You might be wondering, why even talk about Death stones if they're so rare? Guardian work takes place in all sorts of places, exploring the new, the old, and the dangerous. We have to be prepared for everything. As a Medic, that means caring for your squad's physical and mental health under a wide range of circumstances."

I scribble mental and physical health into my notes, palms sweaty. If only waterstones weren't so damn expensive.

"Death stones amplify feelings, and as the name implies, it amplifies desires for death in hédin. That might look like fuelling a desire for the death of another person or yourself. Close proximity to a Death stone may bring up suicidal thoughts in some or desires for vengeance in others. And yet many don't feel any effect at all. Since access to Death stones is limited and illegal these days, it's unclear if beasts might be agitated by proximity of a stone or even be drawn to it from far away."

"The most important thing for you to do as a Medic is to assess your own wellbeing. Keep yourself strong and healthy with plenty of food and rest. Check in with yourself. Notice what feelings build naturally over time and which come to you abruptly. When you return to class after your Freeday, we'll dive deeper into how to provide psychological support to your comrades as well as how to identify and work through your own amplified feelings from Death stones."

The professor nods to the class, his lips pressed thin and a sombre look in his eye. He pushes away from his desk and starts handing out the study guide for our midterm exam before fieldwork assignments start up.

Dropping my pen, I press the sleeves of my sweater to my eyes. The tap of the professor's shoes comes closer, and the shift of papers rubs against my senses. I pull my hands away from my face.

Picking up the study guide, I sit like every one of my Medic classmates with the sheet in my hands, biting my lip in the process of identifying the areas that need the most study. All of it. There is no topic not accounted for, which of course is not a surprise, but there are units from my first semester training as a Medic that I barely remember learning last year. I started studying for the test earlier this week but only things from this year.

The bell rings. Chairs scrape the floor around me. Someone's bag hits my shoulder, and my fellow Medics become walls around me. The words at the top of my study guide scream at me: **You must obtain at least 75% on this exam to be cleared for fieldwork.**

It's a manageable grade. The paper crinkles as my fingers spill the tension between rational thought and my escalated heart rate. Grabbing a fistful of hair, I flip and twist it into a knot. The classroom is empty as I gather my bag, notebooks, and papers. I'll get to work right after dinner. *It'll be fine.*

"Adrianne." The sweet voice accompanied by the sugar blossom scent sends a jolt through my stomach.

"Eila," I say, scrambling to stand and keep the leverage on my belongings. "H-how are you?"

"I'm fine." She tucks a perfect pink curl behind her ear. "I was just wondering if you've got a handle on your . . . " Pressing her lips, she looks away. "Your transformation?"

"Oh." It's been months since our Void Watching excursion, months since she made eye contact with me. "Yeah, I've found a way to control it, and it's best if I transform as fast as possible." I also have to be wide awake and have an empty bladder—absolutely no distractions or altered consciousness. "See." I send a rush of essence to my eyes to the big, imaginary, orange X.

With a prickle and a pulse in my eye sockets, the room blurs, all but Eila's face.

Drawing her arms around her textbooks, she steps back. Eila's gaze is too close to what it was when I found her above me, pumping plant energy into me to wake me up.

I release the transformation and clear my throat. "Would you like to go down to dinner together?" I say, but my throat is still tight, infusing my words with insufferable sweetness.

"No, I'm meeting my girlfriend."

"Are you two okay?"

"Yes. We worked it out. I just wanted to make sure you were doing all right." Eila ducks her head and skirts gracefully around me and my mess.

Once she's out of sight, I venture out of the classroom. My jaw muscles flex, cementing my teeth together so they can't even grind. It is a stagnant energy filling my head. The hall is abuzz with activity that I want no part in. My stomach growls, but the only smells of dinner that waft up the staircase are greasy meat. My matta isn't vegetarian, we only abstained from meat when my grandparents came to visit because they both took that Vow. Meat still makes my mouth water, but I'm not breaking my Vow today. Starting down the stairs, one hand on the banister to keep my jittering body steady on the steps, a kind face appears on the landing.

"Adrianne, good. I was looking for you." Marcus waits for me to meet him on the landing. The sun comes through the stained glass, painting him in red, yellow, and blue. His beard has been trimmed, the scruffy edges along his cheek bones cleaned up. He wears a black button-up shirt with short sleeves that looks like it could be crocheted, maybe even homemade.

"Did you have a meeting?" I ask.

"Yes, with Commander Highcaller." He lets a student pass him and steps closer to me.

"Wow, I can't seem to get up the nerve to have a direct conversation with her."

"She's impressive, that's for sure. The youngest Warrior to make Commander status in the whole history of the Guardian system. But she's level-headed, open." He dips his hands into his pockets. "The day you were away for clinical this week, she made the team do a drill I think you would've liked."

I hold my books tight to my chest to hide the jitter in my hands. "Yeah, what was it?"

"Let's just say it involved the whole team carrying me to the library while they were loaded up with Guardian gear."

I stop short. The image runs through my head, knocking the tension out of me in a burst of laughter. "I can't believe I missed that. Did someone have to carry a medkit?"

"Yep. Full med supplies with max amount of curestones. Eliote took it. Everyone was mad at her for slowing them down. It was a disaster and I felt sick after."

"I bet. But they really need to learn to work together." I peer at him out of the corner of my eye to catch his face and try to hide the burning in my cheeks. "Um, you said you were looking for me."

"Right, are you going down to eat?" Marcus asks.

"Yes."

He runs his hand over his hair. "I was thinking we could eat together."

My heart leaps. "Sure. Academy food only gets better with company."

"Actually, I was thinking we could go get food somewhere else."

I stop on the last step. He's already on the ground, so I'm at eye level with him.

"Like just you and me?"

He looks at me straight on without a waver in his eyes and no curl of his lips, either down or up. He just waits. There's so much energy inside me. How is he so calm?

"That was the idea," he says.

My underarms are like a swamp, my heart pounding. "Like as a . . . " I gesture my hand in the air, trying not to bring my eyes to him to avoid butterflies in my stomach.

"A what?"

"Like a date?"

Marcus' lips part. His eyes lose mine, flashing gold at me that cuts like a knife. "No, I wasn't really thinking it would be a date."

Oh fuck.

My stomach lurches to my throat. "Right, of course not." Breath gushes out of me, leaving my head spinning and I follow the spin backward up a step. "You know, I think I'm supposed to meet with a professor now actually."

What am I, stupid? Why would he want to go out with me? I'd be way too high maintenance. He already has to wind me down when I get upset.

Marcus' hand lands on my arm. He tugs me to face him again. The weight in his eyes locks me in place. The energy in my arms is at a standstill, waiting in limbo.

"Don't do that."

"Do what?"

"Don't be embarrassed. You had every right to think it was

a date. I'm sorry that it's not, but I do want to spend time with you outside of training." The words are precise, like they're practiced, like he picked them beforehand and tried them out in front of a mirror.

I am embarrassed though. I took a shot after all these years and fell on my ass. It stings, but his hand is still on my arm, gently holding me to him, and my muscles lean into the grasp. So I nod and my jaw clicks as it loosens, letting me smile at this beautiful man in his clean shirt with his clean shave who does *not* want to go out on a date with me.

The essence in my feet churns, keenly aware of my mismatching socks and the runners I wear every day. I still have on my gym shorts and a baggy sweater. And then there's the dilemma of my knotted hair and the sticky swamp contained by the sweater.

"Should I change?" I ask.

"If you want to, I'll wait."

My hand wanders to the rat's nest behind my head as I consider the thought of climbing the stairs, searching for something to wear, and coming back down before even deciding where to eat. My stomach flips over. "I don't want to."

A smile grows on Marcus' face. I have never seen him so pleased. My heart gushes inside me, filling my face with heat, but releasing the store of unneeded tension in my muscles. Marcus lets go of my arm and shifts his hand behind me. He doesn't touch my back, but the energy I feel from him urges me on and we head out together.

We find a small booth downtown that sells multiple vegetarian options for me and just as many meaty dishes for Marcus. The booth has a wooden countertop with a cherry-red finish littered with nicks. I run my fingertips over the little indications of other hédin enjoying a meal here. The booth is warm against the cooling night. Lightstones in painted lanterns cast a soft glow about the booth.

Marcus glances at me as we sit. The light looks good on him, though it highlights the hollows under his eyes. They seem to be commonplace on his face.

"Ever been here before?" he asks.

"No, I haven't been to many places in Akinnera actually. Mostly at dinner, I grab a plate from the dining hall and escape to my room for the evening."

A note of recognition slips into the air as Marcus nods and the cook hands us menus. I select a side of bean dumplings wrapped in lassa leaves with terrin sauce, and a vegetable medley with weckler-nut paste. Marcus goes for a bowl of noodles with chicken, green onions, and fire-pepper oil.

As we wait, I unravel my hair from its knot and pull the strands back into a neat ponytail. Marcus faces forward, watching me from the corner of his eye, his arms crossed over the table. There's a crinkle between his brows as I smooth a few strays multiple times and tuck them behind my ears so I won't get food in them. I press my lips together and lose his gaze.

Marcus clears his throat. "Niko said that your hair had something to do with a Vow?"

If this were a date, would I tell him about this? Most would hold their tongue about such a blatant screwup for a Beastblood. Even if he may be rigid in his beliefs, I feel like I can tell him things, well, some things, not all, and only to a certain capacity.

Maybe the truth is I can tell him anything, but I have to allow my lips the freedom to do so. No matter what label is or isn't on our relationship, the relationship is what matters, and his desire to spend time with me. I want to honour that tonight.

"Beastbloods make a Vow to guide their lives at eighteen. I didn't make one, so the elders told me to keep my hair long until I could make a Vow of my own which . . . " The strength in my voice vanishes as a hot plate of food is set before me. "Which I have made now."

"I think I've made a Vow of sorts for myself," Marcus says.

"Yeah?" I put a steaming hot dumpling in my mouth so I don't have to continue about my own Vow.

Marcus bends his head and closes his eyes, his lips moving in quiet prayer, finishing with, "in the name of the All Creator." He moves his noodles around a bit to dig out a piece of chicken. "At the beginning of the year, you said you followed my injury and recovery?"

He pockets the chicken in his cheek. Opening his mouth as if to speak, he shakes his head and stuffs noodles in to meet the chicken.

"I did. The media said your squad was attacked by a threat-level four beast, that it was a tragedy such a promising Protector was injured so early in his career." I lower my eyes to my food, taking a wide mouth full of the nutty green medley. I chew a moment as the air absorbs the weight of my words. "But I don't get how the injury could be so bad that a curestone or Lifeblood healer couldn't fix it."

"It wasn't just a torn essence channel. My femoral essence node was completely obliterated."

My brow furrows. "But you were just outside Akinnera.

What kind of beast could do that around here?"

Marcus doesn't reply. He eyes the street behind us. Turning forward, he waits until the cook has gone to the back. Lowering his voice, he says, "Our mark was an essence syphoner."

"Wasn't that in the mission brief?" I ask through a mouthful of dumpling.

"It was misidentified as a common Noltwyn, but it was a Wraith-Wing essence syphoner, level five. The media never gave the details because Akinnera's head Commander was the one to give us the mark, kept it a secret so he wouldn't lose his job. If he had identified it correctly, I shouldn't have been assigned to the hunt." A vein pulses in his neck. Shifting in his seat, he continues to stab at his noodles, moving them around and breaking up the bits of chicken.

Still working on the wad of dumpling in my mouth, I say, "That . . . that's not right."

"Yeah, well . . . " He stabs his fork into his food and lets it clatter into the bowl.

The cook peeks at us from the back, his brow wrinkling at the clatter. I hold up my hand, reassuring him everything's okay. I resituate myself, bringing my food closer, and turn to Marcus so I can continue to eat and listen with more attention.

Marcus' chest rises. He holds onto the breath for a moment. As he releases it, both his hands fly up. "I became a Guardian because I thought it was my purpose. I have a high essence level, I'm strong, and I grew up with good family support. I'm the perfect candidate for the system." His palms slap down on the counter. "And I respected the system. It keeps people safe, it's honourable, it allows work to be done and the world to move forward without innocent people having to worry about being eaten by raging beasts. And then something like this happens."

At the slight waver of his voice, a crinkle in his brow, I sense the darkness clouding over his mind just as the street darkens behind us and the crickets sing.

"And maybe I shouldn't have been so surprised, but I was." Marcus looks right at me. The anger on his brow melts in an instant. His lips part as his eyes bore into me. "I trusted the head Commander. I trusted the system. Innocent people trust the system. I trusted . . . And then just like that, it all crumbled when I was face-to-face with a threat-level five Wraith-Wing essence syphoner drawing the essence out of my leg. That beast got past the outer wall patrol. It destroyed fields. A farmer and his family died. And I was told to lie about it just so some guy didn't lose his job."

Chills crawl across my body. My taste buds lose their love of flavour as a new type of nausea makes a home in my gut. I always knew there was a dark underbelly to the system. I don't go into this work ignorant to the fact that there will be disputes, pain, and horror. But it's different seeing it firsthand, seeing what it has done to Marcus and the family that lost their lives—simultaneously believable and atrocious.

"I thought I was meant for this work. Now I'm stuck teaching kids who don't know what they're getting into." Marcus' whole body deflates. His head sinks to his hands. "All I could do was Vow to never let something like that happen again. I won't let innocent people get hurt just to save someone's ego."

Manoeuvring around his arms, I slide my last dumpling into Marcus' bowl. The ghost hands of the cool evening breeze wrap around my bare legs. I take a long breath, looking into Marcus' eyes. Mirroring me, his chest heaves again. He picks up his fork.

"I understand, hun."

Compared to my fake smiles, the deep frown that takes hold of me is a relief, only because we share it. We breathe in the frustration of brokenness, and as we exhale, the heaviness of it thins.

There's not a direct link between what he's told me now and his meeting with Brand, but the two bits of information find each other in my mind nonetheless.

"Is that what you were talking to Commander Highcaller about?" I ask.

He glances at me, eyes squinted. "Sort of. It was more prompted by how Niko spoke to you and Rin. I hear disrespect directed at me or other halfies, Ironskins, and lineages not their own all over the academy and at the Guardian stations, even in the squad I worked with. I thought having a conversation with a Warrior Commander about the social climate of our work would . . . make a difference or something."

I finish my veggies, and Marcus works on his entire portion that has now gone cold.

"Thank you. Strength of the ancestors," we say in unison to the cook and leave the booth.

"Do you want to walk for a bit, or do you need to get back?" Marcus asks.

The exam is in a week. There are mountains of notes I need to study. Goosebumps cover my legs, but the cold is just skin deep, and my heart is so warm in Marcus' presence that ending this night too soon might shock my system. Nodding to him, I step a little closer, and we fall into a stroll.

"And do you think it will make a difference?" I ask. "Talking with Brand?"

"I don't know, but I hope so. It's important to try. Maybe it's my purpose now that I can't work in the field."

The street is lit overhead by lightstones against the green starlight. Laughter rides the chill in the air, and happy chatter chases off the bite. All around us are yellows, hearty orange hues, and rustic wooden booths. The rumble of cruisers from the motorway reminds me I'm not in a dream.

"I've never felt like I have a purpose," I say into the night. "I came to the academy to find it. I have so many people telling me what I could be or should be or shouldn't be, but I've never felt called to anything."

"What about being a Medic?" Marcus asks.

My hand brushes his. The heat of his skin is subtle but electric, and I pull away, hiding my hand in the pocket of my sweater.

"It was the first thing that felt right in the moment. I like to learn about the body and how to heal it."

The academy crests the hill behind this street with a white glow. I came my first year because I didn't know what to do. At least a Guardian academy gave me a couple years to decide what path I wanted. My dano went here, most of my cousins are Guardians, and I had a good handle of Fōsttimdato. It all made sense. But I don't make sense. I crash and burn at every obstacle.

"Now, as I actually do the work . . . I feel empty doing it. I don't like teaching, I don't like working at the clinic, and who knows if I'll be any good as a field Medic. I put so much work into it, but I've come up empty."

The lines of Marcus' face are deeper in the glowing light, sharp and severe. He moves his jaw back-and-forth as if he's chewing on my words. "Have you ever considered being a

Monitor?"

I scoff. "A Monitor? No, I can't do that. I'd lose all respect from my dano, and I already have so little."

"Hey"—he holds up his hands—"I just ask because on the first day of training with the team, I watched you with Rin. You were calm and attentive. It seemed like working one-on-one suited you."

A jolt strikes my heart. Calm in one moment. What about all my other moments? I shake my head.

"I guess it might have crossed my mind." The words are soft, as I admit them for the first time. "But I can't do it."

I drop my eyes to the ground, my mouth going dry, but a warmth sits in my chest. I admire Monitors so much. The challenges Monitors help people with are so close to my own. I feel like the things I would see as a Monitor, the emotional toll, would bring up too much for me.

"I think you could." Marcus' tone is low, hushed. He moves closer to me as we walk.

My fingers have gone cold, but Marcus wraps his hand around mine and gives them a squeeze. He lets go, and I clench my fist to hold on to the heat.

"Anyway, the most important thing right now is passing my midterm so I can actually do my fieldwork."

"You ready to head back to the academy then?"

I'd rather walk all night, listen to your voice, or just be close.

"Yeah, I think so. Thank you for dinner."

"My pleasure."

The features of his face are all relaxed. They are in a serene neutrality, like he's completely satisfied with the time we've spent together. And I am, too, I am. Except the satisfaction is only for this moment.

CHAPTER 12

I RETURN TO MY ROOM WITH STUDY TIME TO SPARE. In the light of my desk lamp, I set out a few coloured pens on my desk and line up my texts along the wall with their spines facing out so I can grab them whenever I need. With my notes spread out in front of me, the quiet presses in. I read through the exam outline and a squeeze takes my throat. It's a digging pressure, like someone pressing their finger into the soft spot right above where my clavicles meet. The warmth of Marcus' company seeps from my skin. I stare at my notes with glazed eyes.

I spin my pencil between my fingers. What Marcus told me, what really happened, sits in my mind like a virus. It collides with the gnawing fact that I've spent all my time training here, and I might not even like the work. I've put myself through all this stress just to be the same nervous wreck I was when I showed up. I can't get through exams without rock-hard shoulders, a sick gut, and a fucked-up sleep schedule. This midterm is going to bring all that back. If I don't get 75% on this, then I won't be cleared for fieldwork, and if I'm not cleared for fieldwork, I won't graduate, and if I don't graduate, I'll have to be at this damn school for another semester. With Dad in prison, Matta can't keep making house payments on her own.

A ringing sound fills my ears. Maybe the Medic stuff slips out of my brain because I don't want it bad enough? But in second year, when I was choosing a Guardian path, it's all I wanted. It doesn't make any sense, and my heart pounds like it is life or death.

And then there are the times my heart stops.

When the eyes come.

I haven't seen them in a while. Even though I've gained control over the ocular transformation since I went to the shrine with Eila, I haven't figured out why this ability would spontaneously come back to me, and why I can't transform beyond my eyes.

I get up and pace. The quiet makes my head louder. Taking a long breath, I press my hands to my chest, using the pressure to help myself focus. I got through my second year by running in times like these. Last year I was stable enough to rely on five-second breaths and coffee.

The energy in my body needs to go somewhere. Putting my shoes back on, my fingers fumble over the laces. The room is too empty and too full at the same time—a bed, a dresser, a desk, and a window—it's madness. I throw open the door and rush down the steps to the lobby. I burst through the front doors, full sprint. I disappoint my grandparents; I yell at the advanced team. I'm completely losing it. Now it's my turn to do sprints.

The night has taken up a wind that slices across my face. My feet pound the pavement. Pushing my legs faster, my mind sinks into the motion and away from the crazy. The unsteady rhythm of my lungs evens out as they get put to good use.

My sprint leads me to the transit hub. It is bathed in the hazy, nighttime glow, and empty with wide spaces between each loading station. The space grabs at me and pushes me on my jittery feet. A single airbus trundles into the spot right in front of me. It's the route I take for my early morning clinical. I don't think I'm done with the conversation I had with Marcus. The path of the Guardian Medic is always looming before me with darkness and emptiness surrounding it.

I get on the airbus, panting and sweating a cold sweat. The stale air of the bus crawls over my skin, inching back the cold. The glow of the firestones powering the vehicle as it slows and accelerates is hypnotic, and it's the only light from the outside that makes it past the harsh glare of the cab lights. My eyes fix on my face reflecting back to me until the airbus comes to the Guardian clinic.

With my blood distributed evenly through my body, I step off the bus.

I take the central walk to the front entrance with arrows on the sliding doors to the Guardian precinct and the clinic. The doors open and close as Guardians pass through to their specified destinations indicated by badges and uniforms and medals of rank. I cross my arms, staring, my hair shifting behind me in a circular motion. Something is draining from me, nothing physical, but every bone and muscle and organ is losing substance, my heart most of all. I'm left clinging to my younger, self-loathing skin.

"Adrianne."

My name is fuzzy in my ears. I blink.

Dr. Valencie appears at the doors. I'm not sure how long he's been there. "What are you doing here?"

I sniff and scratch under my bra strap. Scoffing, I motion to the drab building before us. Valencie shifts to stand next to me and takes it in. This station is practically his home. He oversees the clinic, advises field Medics, coordinates fieldwork placements for trainees.

"What's wrong?" he asks. He's not asking me what's wrong with the building, I know that. The question is digging.

I shake my head. There's a plastic bag and an empty cup laying on the ground a few paces away. I grab the cup and reach for the bag, but Valencie takes my arm.

"Leave it. Sit," he says and leads me to a bench.

The bench screeches under our weight, sending a jolt through me. A pressure crawls into my eyes, a wave of heat, and I lean over my knees.

Valencie and I don't talk. He watches and yells when I do something wrong. All that watching—maybe he's finally got a read on me. Something is wrong. It's written all over me, unhidden, dripping. A siren from a returning med-ship winds through the night. I shiver and gather myself, holding my stomach tight and drawing my knees in close.

"I don't know if it's worth it," I say to the ground.

"If what is?"

I can't bring myself to elaborate. There's not much more to it. This is the deepest I can go. This is the truest I can be because this is my block. I do all the things, I try my very best, but it all comes to this. Is it worth it to strive?

Leaning back, Valencie crosses his arms and says, "Not a lot is worth our energy."

Without context, he's still given me a direct answer, hitting the soreness around my wound. Some things are worthy of energy, and others, not so much. My energy though, the anxious, two-faced-bitch energy, is what's worthless in the eyes of the world. I don't know what to do with that, and I don't want to burden others with it.

"I should go." I stand and wipe at a tear trickling down my cheek.

"Should you?"

Eyes caught on the cement, the world is a blur of light and shadow around me. The rumble of cruisers outside the clinic fades away.

"When we question our worth," Valencie says, "it's best not to leave the question unanswered. This moment is for you."

The one tear I brushed away is the only one that escapes. The rest shower inside me, filling the hollow pit of my stomach as I slump back to the stool. Now that I'm seated, safe, I run my nails over my itching skin. All my academy years are sour vomit creeping up my throat. I hold a lot of heavy parts in my body. I contain them and mould them and stack them up. Matta shines them and keeps them organized. I think the reason I told Evelyn that I would train the team was because, for a second, I did see the weight inside me shine, and I wondered if I could give some of that light to someone who needs it. The least I can do is offer what I've learned from the little life I've lived to someone who's got a light of hope in them. Because if mine is dying, then theirs might not if I hand it over.

"I'd like to drive you back to the academy." Valencie stands, but then crouches down beside me. His eyes find mine. My face stiffens with the effort to keep the tears at bay and resist the mask of a smile. "I don't feel comfortable leaving you like this."

I nod.

He leads me to his cruiser.

Is he doing the same thing for me? He doesn't waste words to praise his interns in the clinic. He only barks when we do something wrong. And by we, I mean me. He's barely addressed the others. I must be exceptionally unimpressive, and somehow worthy of his energy.

CHAPTER 13

The next day, I pace around the advanced team as they work in pairs. One person in each pair kicks and the other lets the kick make contact, but they have to keep their leg loose, manoeuvring it away from the strike to minimize impact. To keep my instruction neutral and simple, I've focused on repetition—gruelling repetition. It's how I learned Fōsttimdato with Dano. It's how Medics train. In every aggravated exhale, the team's resentment washes over me. They might hate it, but I see the improvement in their form. I want to help them improve on a different level though.

"That's about it for today," I say. "Remember, the more times you get hit in practice, you'll learn how to avoid the real hits."

Niko glances at me, wiping the sweat from his forehead. His beady eyes are cold, squinting a little as he takes me in. With a quick nod, his mouth pulls tight. "My inner thigh is going to be red for the rest of the day. Thanks a lot."

It might have been a joke. If it was with anyone else, he might have delivered the line with a smile. But with me, it's forced. With me it's flat. "Put some ice on it."

Niko rolls his eyes.

As I turn the class over to Marcus for essence control, the team's attention snaps to him the moment he takes my place. Their eyes get brighter, their movements quicker.

"Toes on the line, backs straight," Marcus says, taking the same stance on a line parallel to the team.

I pull up next to Brand, who's been in to observe today. My own back pulls straight as I square myself to watch the team with my hands behind my back. Brand's eyes follow me without a twitch of her head. Deep inside me, I know I have something that this team needs. Just sitting next to Valencie, I realized how drawn I am to this opportunity. I don't want to waste it.

"Who remembers how Adrianne taught you to shift your essence?" Marcus says.

Niko's hand flies up.

"How many times have I told you, you don't have to raise your hand?"

"Just a sign of respect, boss," Niko says with a grin. Chin raising, his grin melts in an instant, and he says, "Broad body movements to shift the essence to where you want it to go."

"Very good. And what if you can't move, not even your fingers? How can you move your essence then?"

"Can you move it with your breath?" Eliote asks.

"Absolutely. The muscle contraction of the diaphragm pushes essence toward the central essence node in the chest. Quick breaths create quick chugs of essence. A long, sustained breath is like opening floodgates for your essence to build up energy."

Marcus takes the team through breathing exercises, and I use my breath to build the courage to open my mouth in front of Brand.

"Spit it out, Adrianne." The Commander turns to me. She wears a pair of round glasses but glares at me overtop of them. The severity in her stare is lessened by the quirk of her lips.

I clear my throat. "I like that Eliote still engages in essence training. She learns everything she can."

Nodding, Brand points a finger at Marcus. He lights a flame in the palm of his hand. As he draws in a deep belly breath, free hand on his stomach, the flame grows. "He gives them all equal opportunity to engage with him," Brand says. "See?"

Marcus lets out the breath with a long "ha" sound and the flame grows, sending sparks into the air. Ace echoes him right away, a globe of water swirling in his hand, but he starts at his teammates' burst of laughter. The globe jolts from his hand, splattering the entire group and extinguishing Marcus' flame.

"That was good," Marcus praises Ace, but he laughs along with the rest.

Marcus responds to humour and he acknowledges effort. They love him for it. Am I longing for that love? Am I really so shallow that I just want this team to look at me with googly eyes? That's just scraping the surface. Matta told me to follow my intuition, a very unreliable intuition at that. Something about this space, with these incredibly talented students, and me, a lacklustre, Shadowless halfie teaching them, tugs at me, and it aches.

"I want to do more."

Brand licks her lips, narrowing her eyes. "What makes you think you aren't doing enough?"

"I don't know. I think I might have something to give that's more than just defensive combat."

The air takes on a thickness with everyone converting gulps of oxygen to carbon dioxide and the natural energy in their bodies building and cooling. Without adjusting my own breaths, my essence is settled in an easy back-and-forth motion through my body, as if rocked in a cradle, as if it's sleeping. I rub a hand over my chest as a spike of pain disrupts the slumber.

Taking off her glasses, Brand sets them on top of her curls. "Tomorrow, I have to go out of the city during my regular training time with Rin. Hans will be there, but it's been good to have two of us working with her. Would you be willing to step in for me?"

"Yes, of course. What have you been working on?"

"Rin relies on her essence strength in a physical capacity. What she needs to do is focus on its spiritual capacity to master her spirit affinities. The thing is, she doesn't have much awareness around her physical form. She's sort of disconnected from her body, or at least that's my observation."

While the others are taking full belly breaths and trying out new breath cadences, Rin stands off to the side, hand on her stomach and eyes trained on the floor. With a subtle lift of her chest, she drops her hand and shakes it out. Tapping her thumb and pointer finger together, her brow furrows.

"Hans and I have been taking her through a progression

of awareness in the physical body, working to connect it with her essence energy specifically with the life affinity," Brand says. "What I need you to do is get her one step closer to her spiritual energy. How would you do that, Adrianne?"

I'm getting there. I know I am. The tug stretches through my spine. It tingles in my chest; it is heavy like the weight inside me. Last night, I questioned my efforts. Valencie, unexpectedly, helped me see where I can direct a bit of it.

"I guess if you're starting in the body, then you have to move on from the action to what spurs that action. The awareness of what's going on inside you. The emotion, your mind."

A light sparks in Brand's eyes. "Very good. The life and death affinities are closely linked with strong emotions. I know there are a lot of big emotions inside her. She's never had the chance to express them though."

"Rin, keep your hand on your stomach and try holding the other in front of your mouth to feel the change in breath," Marcus says.

Johana scoffs. Every time I hear that laugh, it makes my fists itch.

"Ghosts don't breathe, Marcus," she says.

The cool, glassy eyes, her pale complexion, her quiet, unbashful presence . . . Rin ticks all the boxes for an apparition. Though I wonder if Johanna has missed the mark with that barb. I think Rin is haunted in the same way I'm haunted—by the past.

"Did you know Rin before she came here?" I ask Brand.

"No. I knew her parents." The casualty in Brand's communication hits a wall as she pulls the glasses off her head again and places them on her nose to write a note. "The school archives might have some information about spirit affinities and their emotional connections. I suggest you take a look before tomorrow afternoon."

With that, she leaves me to watch alone.

I keep the idea of ghosts in my mind as Professor Hans and I wait for Rin in the weapons training room the next day. It's Freeday, so most students are studying for the next week of exams, Something I should be doing, but I'm captivated by this harsh duality of ghosts and their haunted counterparts. I want to be here for Rin.

"Is she usually this late?" I ask Professor Hans as I pull out a piece of gum.

"Late, yes." He holds out his wrist and shakes his sleeve away from his watch. He tsks. "This late, no."

Ten minutes past four, the doors swing open. Rin marches over to us with her arms crossed over her chest. Wavy blond hairs stray from their usual pattern as they sprawl over her shoulders and there is an unsteadiness to her steps. Her eyes scrape over me, landing on Hans as he sighs.

"Come, we mustn't waste time. We haven't made nearly as much progress with the life affinity as we should have by now," he says.

Not even a hello or a chance to breathe. I shake my head and stick the spicy gum in my mouth.

"Where's Brand?" Rin asks.

I steel myself with my hands behind my back. This posture really is effective. No wonder Marcus gets such good results. He always stands so tall. But Rin shuts out my presence with tight eyes. She doesn't want to see me. I'm not the one who is supposed to be here. A squeeze in my chest asks if I believe that. Cutting myself out of the equation, I focus on the girl standing like ice before me. Brand was supposed to be here, but today I am.

She's still alive, isn't she? That's significant today.

"Miss Highcaller had an errand to run, so she asked Miss McCarthy to join us today," Hans explains.

Rin moves to a punching bag with a star crystal. Her walk isn't one you see much around here. It's fast and directed. The sway in her hips is minimal. To me is says she's spent a lot of time having to manoeuvre and even hide her presence. Her eyes are locked on the ground until she takes a Telando stance by the bag. Fists by her jaw, feet hip distance apart, and an easy bend in her knees.

"All right." Hans follows after her. "Let's start with a three-strike combination, jab, cross, front kick. Three times through. First, just against the air to feel the movement of your body. Second, slowly, paying attention to every muscle engagement. With the third strike, use your awareness of your body to draw out energy to form wings, like you would a projection."

Rin shifts her weight to her toes and bounces a few times.

"Breathe in," Hans says.

Taking a breath, that same furrow from yesterday pinches her brow.

"And exhale with each strike."

Rin runs through the combination. Her body makes the movements perfectly, there's no doubt that Rin knows what she's doing. But her air is tangled around her as she breathes in laboured bursts. Her eyes flash with a pale-blue light. If I had blinked, I would have missed it.

I glance at the professor. "Hans?"

As if I didn't even make a sound, Hans continues to urge Rin into a slower pattern, drawing control from her core. My heart pounds in my chest as Rin's breath shakes her. The pink colouring drains from her pale skin. She presses her hands to her face and collapses into a crouch.

"For Carnity's sake," Hans says. He plants his hands on his hips, but I grab his arm and turn him to face me and save the hyperventilating girl from further torture.

"Professor," I say. I swallow hard as his sharp, dark eyes dart to me. "Hans, may I have a word with Rin alone, please?"

Hans dips his head to me. "Well, I can't seem to get through to her," he says under his breath. Casting another glance at Rin, he worries his bottom lip with his teeth. He puts up such an air of superiority and poise most of the time that this simple motion of fallibility sticks a pin in my heart. "Yes, of course."

Whether it steals your breath, or makes you break out in a cold sweat, paralyzes you, or knocks you off your feet, panic never hits the same, but it's always terrifying. I ran, slept, ate, and fought just to take it down. There's only one thing that really makes a difference in the end.

I step to Rin and crouch before her. Her shoulders are trembling and bony under my hands.

"You're safe, Rin," I say through a tight throat. "You're safe. You're okay. It's just a panic attack."

I fill my lungs with air and send essence in a steady stream to my hands so they're warm as I run them up and down Rin's shaking arms.

"I need you to just listen to my voice and take slow breaths," I say. "Nice and easy, don't force them in or hold them. Panic attacks are nasty little motherfuckers, but they only seem scary.

Show them a little kindness and they melt like butter."

Following my instruction, with a shuddering breath, the air to follow is a little less turbulent.

"Did something happen today?" I ask to try to ease her attention away from the act of breathing so it's not so much of a chore.

I don't want to force it, but this is what Brand wants me to get at. The energy behind the panic. Something like this isn't always triggered by a specific incident, making it far worse to handle because there's nothing to pin it on. I have a feeling Rin has a pin, but she's just not ready to stick it into the culprit.

"Rin, what happened?"

"Nothing. It's fine," she whispers.

Matta would ask what's in her head. Taking my hands off her shoulders, I lay them on my own knees. I don't want pressure on Rin.

Quiet settles in on us, but Rin breaks it fast and stands to take up a stronger pose with her arms crossed again.

"I . . . engaged the life affinity earlier," she says.

"Did you mean to?"

"No."

This seems to be a trend with her. She never means to engage it. Her connection to the life affinity bears a resemblance to my ability to transform my eyes. It came back to me so suddenly. I had to learn to control it before it got out of hand without even time to think of why it came back. We both owe it to ourselves to face what our essence is trying to tell us.

"All right," I say, standing to face her again. "Let's walk through it."

"Walk through it?"

"Yes. Why do you think you engaged the affinity?"

I rest my hands on my hips. With the pause, voices from the school halls echo, creating a contrast between me and Rin in this room alone together and whatever is going on out there.

"I don't know," Rin says, and snaps her head to the side.

"What were you feeling before it happened?"

"I was duelling with some guys. I don't know. I felt ready to fight."

I rock back on my heels and forward to my toes. Stiffness creeps around my jaw. What did I feel before I transformed? I was alone in a shrine. Serenity saturated my bones, prodding something close to home, close to my spirit. Close, not head-on.

"That's not what I mean. Just listen, okay?"

"Fine." Rin looks everywhere but my face. The lights, the walls, the clock. So, I close my eyes.

"Brand told me that the spirit affinities are linked to strong emotions. So, I want you to think back to the first time you engaged the life affinity. What were you feeling?"

"Wha—I . . . "

We are in a vulnerable state with this conversation. No wonder I can't hold her eyes. The wooden floor creaks as Rin shifts, her eyes trailing the rows of practice swords on the wall behind her. With every move she makes, my skin prickles, getting closer to what she's feeling. My hand wanders behind me to an itch.

"You don't have to tell me," I say. I haven't told anyone. "Just think about what emotions come up before you engage the affinity. For some, the life affinity is triggered by feelings of peace or even sadness. Others describe loneliness, fear." Rin recoils, shrinking into herself so fast my chest aches. "The death affinity can be triggered by love or hate, anger. Think about how these emotions feel for you. Do you get a headache, feel sick, chills up your spine, an overwhelming heaviness? You can use the emotional energy to direct the affinities."

There are two feet of space between us. Her eyes are worlds away. Turning to the side, I motion to the door.

"You're free to go. Or we can work on a few things together," I say setting my hand back on her shoulder to bridge some of the space.

"I'm doing just fine on my own." Rin jerks out of my grasp.

The door creaks as she leaves. I clasp my hands behind my neck, holding myself so I don't crumple on the floor too. I think I missed something here. I was so excited to have an opportunity to work with one of the advanced team members that I moved too fast, embarrassed her, frustrated her.

Being here to help her through a panic attack was surreal. Matta sees my anxiety but never the sheer panic, and even then, she tells me not to worry. I shouldn't worry because it will all still work out and to ask the ancestors for help because I need it more than most without a Shadow. But I don't think anxiety has anything to do with strength. It has everything to do with what is wrong, in the world and in our hearts. I know there is something wrong inside me, Shadowless, or something else. Having someone here with me, breaking and confused by essence, made me feel less alone. But it's selfish to force that kind of bonding too soon. Twisted.

Textbooks trail from my desk to the bed. Each one is marked with neon sticky tabs and open to the most crucial concepts—or at least the ones that make no sense to me. I crouch next to the text on hédin physiology. If I go through the coagulation cascade one more time, no two more times, then I'll switch to ethics. I'll hit the main concepts and then review tactical field care.

I brace one hand next to the text and rub the ache in my stomach as I run through the intricate tandem of molecules that facilitate coagulation. Eyes closed, I recite the cascade. My hair trickles over my shoulders to hang in front of my face. A strand brushes my nose. I recoil with a shiver and rub at it. I can't remember the next factor anyway. I throw my hair back and tie it in a knot. Exhaling, I close my eyes again, searching for the missing factor in my mind.

The bristles of the carpet dig into my knees, the only place in my legs that has feeling.

What if I just stop now? Wing the test. If I fail . . . maybe I'll just quit.

The thought makes its rounds through my head, repulsed by my rationality and shaken by the erratic energy of my anxiety. I let it find my younger self in the back of my mind. She reaches for it and thinks it's a pretty thought, a ray of sunlight breaking through the rain clouds. What if that's what she should have done? Quit. Maybe we would have been better off.

I jolt myself upright. It's not a pretty thought. I have to go through with this for myself because I made this choice, and for Matta. Somehow, I need to find a way to stay awake and remember this stuff so I can pass.

Holding on to my bed, I stand. My back cracks and my legs are fuzzy cotton between my knees and my feet. I spit out my gum, and it twangs the side of the metal trash bin. Downing the dregs of my tea, I cringe at the contrast of clairmint and cinnospice. I have a few hours of viable study time before I collapse, but I'll need some air if I'm going to get through all this material.

I pull on a sweater and leave my room. A few other girls are still chatting in the halls, reviewing material for their own exams and running through combat forms in their pyjamas. I move past them in my bare feet with my head down. If Rin, Eliote, or Johanna come into the hall, my nerves might experience spontaneous, unexplainable necrosis, and that will be the end of me.

The main floor is quieter. I skirt through the lobby, my feet slapping on the cold marble. A draft skates through the wide room, shifting the chandelier so the crystal tinkles above me as I push open the front door.

I ease myself down to the front steps, the tightness in my chest loosening with a clean breath. The campus grounds have walkways of grey slate, and the patches of grass between training grounds are cut short, no weeds in sight. There are a few flower planters along the steps with some roses, but other than that, the grounds are caged in with the city wall on one side and shrubs along the cliff facing the sea. The rush of the waves creates a pleasant loop of unintrusive noise for my brain as I stare at the arena on the other side of the path. Lights on the ground shine against the metallic panelling so they reflect it, giving the arena an appearance of a glowing orb.

Marcus comes out of the side door from the training room. He carries a gym bag and makes the journey across the campus slowly, his limp pronounced more than usual. He raises his eyes from the ground. I give him a quick wave. Changing course, he limps over to me.

"What are you doing here so late?" I ask.

Taking a seat beside me, he says, "I was just clearing a few things out of the arena for the Medic exams. Sounds like they're going to be tough."

"Don't remind me." I wrap my arms around my stomach as it gives a dizzying lurch. Pulling out the pack of cinnospice gum from the pouch of my sweater for a fresh stick, I say, "But it's your day off."

"Yeah, I don't mind helping out." Marcus eyes my fingers as they unravel the gum.

"You don't want to hate all this anymore?" I ask, leaning my head on my hand.

A soft smile crosses his lips as he tilts his head up, taking in the stars. "Well, I've been hating it for a while now, so I might as well make a positive impact while I can, balance out my *Ha'ken*."

"What's *Ha'ken*?"

"It's an Earthkin teaching. The energy we put into the world affects the Karess long after we die, so everything we do counts. A little positivity goes a long way."

That's sort of like a Vow. With both concepts, you have a prerequisite of willingness to follow in a certain moral code, ruling your life by it, letting it guide your decisions. My Vow to protect all life should produce a positive *Ha'ken*, shouldn't it?

Marcus drops his eyes to his hands and stretches out his legs. "But I have a long way to go before I make up for all my complaining."

"Complaining? I think you're allowed to be upset, Marcus, for as long as you need to be. Isn't that what you told me? Aren't we all allowed to be a little pissy?"

"I guess so," he says. Even with the cool wind, his chuckle

calms my heart. "Hey, shouldn't you be studying or sleeping or something?"

"I have a lot more studying to do. I just can't concentrate."

"Something on your mind?"

The question of whether it's worth it—if I am worth all this trouble and stress—hasn't left me. I've come this far with my Guardian training; it would be a waste to throw it away. Does that mean the stress is worth something? And if I'm stressed, then I'm worth something? It's a meaningless loop because I don't know where worth comes from.

"Sort of," I mumble.

"Want to talk about it?"

I shake my head. "No, I'm trying not to think about it."

"Well, do you need a study buddy? I could sit with you while you study. Sometimes it helps to stay focused if you have someone keeping an eye on you."

What a wonderful thought. Someone to sit with me while I struggle. My eyes are glued to Marcus, taking him in while I methodically work the spicy gum with my teeth. He can't really be suggesting this just because he wants to. It's positive *Ha'ken* to babysit someone in distress, right?

He scratches his jaw and shrugs. "I have a book with me, and my echo buds. I'd just go home and read for a while alone anyway. What, you don't want me to?"

A moon beetle on a rosebush beside him flicks its wings, sending a wash of iridescent light through the dark.

"Uh . . . yeah I would like that." The words come out before I can make an excuse.

"Are you working in the library or your room?" he asks, offering me a hand up.

"All my stuff is in my room."

My feet are chilled, and I can't seem to move them. Marcus motions for me to lead the way. I sniff, turn to the door, and lead us up to my room. My floor has cleared all but for one girl sitting in the hall with a text propped on her knees. I open my door and step back into the half moon of school notes I left throughout the room.

"You can sit at the desk or the bed, wherever you want," I say.

"Where are you going to sit?"

"Probably on the floor."

He nods, but both the bed and desk are blocked by texts and notes. He steps over my hédin physiology text to the space between my bed and desk. Settling himself on the floor, he situates his back against the wall and pulls out a book, his echo, and echo buds from his bag.

For a few moments my brain reminds me of all the scenarios I've played through revolving around having someone I liked witness my living space for the first time. I wonder if Marcus sees an invitation into someone's personal space as intimate as I do. Here, there's not much personality on display, and my room at home is still pretty bare, but it's more about what the room is used for. Sleeping, dreaming, crying, dark thoughts. Putting all that aside, I join him on the floor and focus on my text. His smell is light and fresh with a hint of body odour, probably from clearing out the arena. Legs stretched out and ankles crossed, he's settles into my space so easily. It brings an order to the chaos in my room and in my head. I focus in on my studies, and for the first time tonight, I get the coagulation cascade down without mistakes.

As I close the text and swap it for another, I catch Marcus lean his head back with his eyes closed. He taps his fingers in time to his music, and a few things tap together in my head. We hit traffic a lot when he comes to pick me up. He never complains about it taking too long. He goes to parties in the middle of the week, and he volunteers his time on Freedays. Now, he's here late at night instead of going home to relax, sleep. I get the feeling he's not doing all this for the socialization or even the *Ha'ken.*

I nudge his foot. His eyes flutter open and he takes out his echo buds.

"You don't want to go home," I say.

"Not exactly. I like to be at home. I like my space." A line deepens across his forehead.

Home is an enjoyable space, and he's drained by people, but ultimately spending more time with them than he needs to. He's trying to tire himself out.

"Are you not sleeping well?"

"How can I?" he says, his voice tightening as he draws in his knees.

It comes to me as a light in my mind. Nightmares. He must dream about the essence syphoner attack. Having your essence ripped from you can't be left in the past.

Marcus clasps his head in his hand, throat bobbing with a slow swallow. "Do you believe in the All Creator?" he asks.

I push aside my text and crawl closer to him. "I wasn't raised that way."

"I was taught that the All Creator has a divine will for our lives. He has a plan for each of us, and we should seek that will. I believed that. I wanted that. I was prepared to face hardships as a Guardian because I thought that was the All Creator's will for me. I have now. But am I really suffering because maybe I didn't follow the right path?"

My dad grew up this way, but he rejected it. I doubt he communes with the All Creator at all anymore. But it's very clear that Marcus has a solid relation with this form of divinity, and it's important to him. I don't think following the will of the divine is so far removed from the ritual of making a Vow. A Vow was forced on me for not making my own. The will of the Beastblood is for no one to lose their way—the lineage's way, not the individual's.

"Am I even free to choose something on my own?" Marcus says, staring at the ceiling. "Is that like spitting in divinities face?"

I search for answers up there too sometimes. Should belief in something you love be so hard?

"Marcus," I say slowly. "Do you have to believe that? Do you have to believe in his will to love the All Creator? I mean, I don't believe in him, but you do. Do you have to believe in the same teachings to know the same divinity as the next person?"

Our eyes trail down to our shared space in unison.

"Take me and Eila. We both call on Carnity, but Eila's devotion is far greater than mine." I shift to cross-legged and hold out both hands to weigh out imaginary bundles of devotion.

The shame I felt in Carnity's shrine jumps up my throat. We like to put the judgements we hold on our revered ancestors, as if they had the same biases and hurts as us. In Carnity's day, she was the only reference to essence. I thought she might be repulsed by me, but I think it might be the opposite. My halfie essence is only a problem because other people with different affinities said it should be.

"Does devotion change who Carnity is?" I ask.

Marcus' chews the inside of his cheek, his eyes focused on my hands like they might actually hold our faith. Maybe they're glowing balls of light to him. To me, they're stones, like anchor points.

"If I believe that our great ancestors are integrated beings, what's the point if they still react in petty ways to their followers?" I take a strand of hair and twirl it through my fingers. "If I pray once a month for Carnity to help me, I hope she's honoured I called at all. Same for the All Creator. If he is divine, I doubt he takes such a harsh eye to his followers. If you can't accept that he has a divine will for your life, does that cancel any love that you share?"

Marcus nods along. "I hear what you're saying. I like what you're saying. But devout followers of the All Creator would say I have to sacrifice my will to really know him." Taking a breath, he lets it out in a long, controlled stream. He closes his eyes for a moment. "If you don't feel like you have a purpose, do you feel like you still have the freedom to make your own?"

I scan my room with all the medical texts and medical supplies on display—a testimony to the path I've chosen. It's a path. Is it a purpose though? If anything, I don't feel freedom in it. There's just always been a necessity to find it.

"I don't have an answer for you," I say.

"That's okay. I shouldn't keep you from studying anyway."

Our dinner the other night ended in a similar way. We got to a deep discussion, and when we parted, I let it crash down on me. It dug up a lot of hurt. This is doing the same. I'm not as shaky though, because he's still here. He can stay as long as he needs. I need him to stay as long as he needs.

"You're doing amazing, Adrianne," Marcus says softly as he takes out a book.

The continuous tightness in my stomach relents. Tomorrow, that won't be the case. A moment of ache-free studying is what I need.

CHAPTER 14

Oɴᴇ ᴘɪᴇᴄᴇ ᴏꜰ ᴛᴏᴀsᴛ and a few pieces of fruit. The exam is in one hour. I need to eat. I need the energy. My tongue is too dry, though, my throat thick. Layers of memory hide inside my head, weighing my eyelids to the point of blurring my sight. Four years ago, on this day, I woke up in the hospital. A nurse made sure I ate, at least something.

I pick up the fruit and put it in my mouth. The tangy juice spreads over my tongue, and I let it sit there. Eyes closed, I suck on the fruit, breathing through my nose, the voices in the dining hall shifting around me.

There's a bridge in front of me—this exam leads me to different paths. If I want to be any kind of Medic, I need to pass. It'll show my grandparents that all this wasn't a waste of time, and maybe it will show my old self too. I hope she'll see it.

I focus on the sweetness smothering my tastebuds to show her it's worth it, worth it to swallow, to step forward. She's so strong though, grabbing my hand and sitting down on the floor, unable to move. All she wants to do is cry, to lie on her back and watch the clouds pass, let them wash away all the bad and the questions in the world. She seems peaceful there, breathing, sinking both into her pain and a void of nothing. But I have to push through, so I swallow. I'll cross this bridge, then I'll complete fieldwork, finish my clinical hours, and my public-aid. That's where the path is going now.

Each piece of fruit goes down faster as I focus on the logical steps of my journey out of the academy. A good grade on this exam will offer me the best opportunities to come. I bite into my toast, and the raw ache in my stomach turns into a pounding heart. My body seems to be on the path already, exerting energy too fast. I need to keep up.

Lifting my laser gaze from my plate, I blink my eyes a few times. I tilt my head from side to side, stretch my arms above my head, and take a long breath. Let's get this exam done.

Papers rustle. Pens click. I flip my page back-and-forth to review each question, making sure I used the right gauge needle to insert a catheter and the right fluids in each scenario. In the anatomy section, I find the questions I've skipped. It won't do me any good to leave something blank.

Come on, Adrianne, what's the largest axillary essence node? I can never remember if it's posterior or anterior. How did I remember it again? Total bullies poop acrid nuggets. Triceps brachii posterior accelerator node.

I scribble the answer and fold up my paper. Marching up to hand in my test, my knees knock together. My pits are nice and sweaty, even though I've only been sitting here a little over an hour doing nothing but scribble and wrack my brain for answers. I know I answered some of them wrong, but I can't think of anything better. The proctor takes the test and the pocket of air that has been accumulating in my chest explodes in a sigh, drawing a few heads.

The second I'm out the door, I pull a cookie from my bag. Not only do I deserve a reward for finishing that test, but I'll need the energy for the practical exam. A cookie may not be the best option, it's what I'm eating though, and my stomach seems happy with it. The practical exam is scheduled by clinical study groups, and mine has the first slot. I sit down on the bench outside the classroom to eat. Leaning my head back to savour a moment of peace, I draw in a long breath to replace that bubble I sequestered in my lungs before. Slowly, I release it, so it doesn't get stuck again. Brushing the crumbs from my breasts, I stand and head to the arena.

Eila and DiHan wait outside the arena door. A crash sounds from inside and the ground trembles. My stomach lurches. I plant my hands on my hips, coax my breaths to follow an even cadence, and stare at the ground.

The flowery scent that clings to Eila wraps around me as she steps over.

"May I help?" she asks, eyes trained on the ground.

"With what?"

"Your anxiety. I can help."

"Oh, I guess. At this point, it's mostly permanent, but you

can give it a shot."

As she places her hand on my back, I shiver with the scratch of her nails. She tilts her head to me, eyes finally making contact in a silent inquiry. With a quick nod, she closes her eyes and holds out her free hand. She is still for a moment, just her pinky finger twitches, then the tips of her fingers glow neon green. She presses all five fingers to my chest. My eyes grow wide as my breath lurches inside me with a subtle and lively heat that expands over my skin.

"W-what did you just do?" I ask.

"The plants around us are often ready to lend their energy."

"Wow." I swing my arms a little. "I was feeling like this day was going to knock me on my ass, but I feel so much better. Like a fuckton."

Her lips twist into a grimace. Her eyes, dark and sharp, stab through me right where her fingers were.

"Why do you speak that way?" she asks in a hushed tone. "I thought you were different than that."

My lips twitch, and my tongue is lost and lax in my mouth. Eila's eyes drop back to the ground. Of course she's surprised. For all the years she's known me, I was the quiet one, never talked out of turn or hurt people with the fire of my tongue, and I didn't show off like other Beastbloods. My teeth dig into the inside of my cheek. I tap my toe against the cobblestone with one foot and then the other, creating a rocking motion that is soothing.

"I thought I was different too."

I huff a hot breath, and she crosses her arms, turning her dagger eyes away from me, so they don't do anymore damage.

The minutes tick past, allowing me to acquire that lovely,

sweaty second skin, even though the air has cooled off for the fall. The door opens and headmaster Evelyn calls me into the arena. She gives me a swipe of her eyes, and a smile that I will not let throw me off course. This exam is not going to land me on my ass. That pious energy Eila stuck in me is still doing its job.

Inside, the arena is completely terraformed. Rocky formations rise out of the usually open area, obscuring the stands from sight except for small slivers to my right and left. Medic gear is strewn on the floor in front of me. Two professors are in the stands, and a final Medic professor accompanies Evelyn. Each one of them holds a PAT ready to take notes on my performance.

"Our next Medic is Adrianne McCarthy," Evelyn says, raising her voice so all the professors can hear her.

"Adrianne, ahead, we have stations for you to demonstrate practical treatment skills. Suit up, perform each skill, then report for your field scenario. You will be timed for each portion." Evelyn nods and looks at her PAT.

My feet are glued to the floor. The air is thick. My heart beats in a heavy, even rhythm inside me.

Evelyn lifts her eyebrows. "Are you going?" She taps something in her notes.

Fuck.

"Yes!"

Dropping to my knees, I scan the medical supplies and an empty medkit. There's everything I need and more. I start with protection equipment, masks and gloves. Next, I make sure I have everything I need to treat hemorrhages, obstructed airways, respiration traumas, circulation, and hypothermia. With my essentials packed, I scan the rest of the items for versatile options. Scolya root tonic for essence pressure, I'll need that. Curestones, obviously, can't compete with the natural healers without them. I grab the star crystal vest for active combat zones, slip it on, and strap my scissors to the front.

I pack the kit as fast as I can, making sure everything is in a pocket or fitted tight together so nothing jiggles. Slinging it on my back, I buckle it around my waist and chest. Finally, I secure a Medic badge around my biceps.

"Three minutes, thirty seconds," Evelyn announces my time to the rest of the professors.

Damn. Those are thirty seconds wasted.

I scramble over to the skills station. There's one medical dummy of a chest with a firestone rifle wound, another with a major bleed, a head with an airway device next to it, and another with a line and fluids. Evelyn didn't say I had to do them in a certain order, but I'll do them in the order we're trained to, starting with the bleed. My heart pounds, but I've lost the shake in my hands since doing everything in repetition in clinical and Medic classes. The procedures are easy, my hands are swift.

Evelyn calls out my time as I stand at attention. "There's a wounded Protector in the canyon. Find them, treat them, return them here. Be creative with essence manipulations to get your comrade back safely. You may begin."

I dip my head and sprint into the constructed canyon.

As I come upon the first walls of rock, I catch a glimpse of a Luminee professor who teaches advanced combat. She waves her hand in the air and shadows spill into the arena, making it darker than night. Fog sifts through the pillars. Slowing my pace, I focus the flow of my essence to my head and centre my attention at my ocular transform point. I close my eyes. The fine muscles twitch with the pulse of essence headed straight for my glowing transform point. Opening them again, my night vision takes hold.

"Ocular transformation with singular transform point," the Luminee professor calls out.

That's ought to earn me some points. But I can't hold the transformation long, so I'll need to find the Protector soon or else I'll have to resort to flame to light my way. That's too abrupt, and it would alert a beast in a real field situation. I sprint a little faster, weaving through the stone walls, dashing through long, narrow passages, with sweat and mist dripping off my face. My turns are etched into my mind, creating a map that I hope will stick. Zenta, please let it stick.

My lungs pull air in quick bursts. Essence pulses in my forehead. I whip around another corner. Laying on the ground, slumped over a pool of fake blood, is my wounded Protector.

Step one: Check the area for danger. Note number of wounded. Evacuation plan.

Slowing to a walk, I trail my eyes from the top of the canyon to the bottom. The terrain slopes down and there is a cluster of sharp rocks in my path. On the left, there are dark crevasses in the walls leading further through the arena. I keep to the right, shoving stray stones out of the way to create of better path to get the Protector out of here.

Step two: reassure your comrade that you're there to help.

Gravel grinds under my feet, and my breaths are just as rough. I crouch in front of the Protector.

"My . . . my name is Adrianne, and I'm here to help you." My voice is raspy, weak. The energy coursing through my body doesn't make it to my lips. "Can you hear me?"

A sigh slips into the darkness. "Yep."

The pulsing on my forehead intensifies with a pinch. The Protector on the ground has rusty red hair, dark skin, and a muscled body.

"Marcus?" I stare at him as my transformation releases, diminishing his form into a shadowy lump. A laugh trickles through me. "This gettin' you *Ha'ken* points?"

"That's not how it works. It's not points . . . never mind. Just do what you have to do," Marcus says, his voice muffled as he talks into the ground. "I don't know what it is with Brand and Evelyn making me participate in stupid drills." He lets out a fake cry of pain.

Stifling another laugh, I wipe my face on my sleeve and take off my medkit. If he's screaming, then that ticks one element off my list. Airways are clear.

Step three: put up defences.

Steadying myself, I set my stance and remove all distractions from my mind. With one full-body movement, I thrust my hands forward and a sheet of glimmering orange angles itself over me and Marcus so that we are protected from one side as well as above, with the cavern wall as the final protection. I don't think I can make it any bigger without using up too much essence.

Step four: Treatment.

"Any shortness of breath?"

"Yes."

I pat him down, checking for the source of the blood and any other bleeds. My hands come away red from a fake wound patch on his left side. I make sure his spine is straight and it's safe to move him and then heave him onto his back. I move the excess fabric away from the patch that is still seeping blood.

"How did you obtain the wound?" I ask, stuffing it with

gauze. If this is an active danger zone, I'll have to skip curestones for now.

"Beast attack. It was"—Marcus pauses and pretends to be out of breath—"A four-legged beast, green eyes . . . I feel dizzy." His performance is stale. The poor guy.

Green eyes, poison for sure. Once the bleeding's controlled, I change gloves and rip open a poultice patch that is great in a pinch. It's embedded with curestone powder and lightwood serum, which is an antivenom, and will keep the wound covered until I can properly heal it. I dress the wound and give him a scolya root tonic to reduce essence pressure, which in turn prevents excessive blood loss. Marcus just holds it in his fist.

I continue my assessment by checking his chest and making sure his lungs are rising evenly. Finally, I check both radial arteries. Quick, warm pulses tap through my fingers.

A low rumble shakes the ground. Stone grinds against stone. A flash of light in front of me. My heart lurches to my throat. Five paces away is a stone animation in the form of a four-legged beast.

"Here we go again," Marcus says.

"Fuck."

My barrier doesn't protect us from that side, and Marcus' head is right in the beast's line of sight. My defence is broken. Shit. I didn't think this through. Should I have taken the chance and done a bigger projection?

I'm not supposed to engage in combat unless it's absolutely necessary, and for me that combat needs to be nonlethal, no sharp points, nothing to burn or maim. Stomach churning, a slimy slug inches its way up my throat, and the beast takes another grinding step forward. My limbs are like rusted metal. So far, none of my patients at the clinic have been close to death. It doesn't matter that the beast is made of stone or that this wound is fake, the reality is setting in. My vision clouds. *Shit.*

Marcus stirs, palpable tension in the air.

The beast charges toward us, its stoney paws clobbering the ground.

I blink away the haze. Planting my hands by Marcus, I release my hold on my barrier. The orange plates fuse to my legs as I fling them to the side. Both my feet, armoured in flame, smash into the beast with an explosion of sparks and rubble. The beast slumps against the wall. But the awful grinding sound continues with more flashes of light down every corridor.

"We're going," I say.

I haul Marcus over my shoulders and reinforce my strength with fire armour around my torso, following the line of my vest to make the process smoother. This will have to do for armour. I don't have enough essence strength to make a whole suit, let alone maintain it in a fight.

The mist and shadows have a mind of their own, assaulting me with cold tentacles. I get Marcus moving, but we are surrounded by stone beasts. My armoured kick wouldn't kill the beast, they're too tough for that, so it would only knock out a real beast. Practicing a killing blow won't help me uphold my Vow on the field. My mind storms trying to figure out what I should have done to avoid them getting this close. Damn it, I did everything wrong.

Skin slick and Marcus' fake blood seeping into my clothes, ice infests my heat. It prickles along my neck and black spots fill my eyes. *I can do this.* A sob threatens to undo me. I harness it with a grunt and lurch forward, locking the beast in front of me with a glare and bare my teeth.

The beast inches forward with guttural snarls and stone claws scratch the earth.

I may not have much fire manipulation left in me, but I still have the strength in my transform points. Maybe if I use a beast projection. I don't know what other option I have. I draw in a deep breath and lock the pressure in my bones. Tracing my body with my mind, I illuminate my transform points. My forehead pulses. My gut churns. I clench my fists to force my essence into my triceps brachii posterior accelerator nodes. A force slices through my arms. I let my fists unclench. A burst of light showers the beasts. Orange tendrils of energy swarm around me, weaving into the face of a tiger, a ferocious glimmer in its eyes.

Marcus gasps as the ethereal projection encompasses us on all sides.

The projection bursts forth, slamming the beast into the cavern walls. Strings of light sparkle all around us. They stay in place, pushing back any beast that tries to attack as I haul Marcus to the arena entrance.

The shadows fade and the mist lifts. I pant like a fucking dog, and I'm an absolute mess with fake blood stuck in my hair and under my nails, and dirt covering my knees.

Evelyn steps forward, high heels crunching over the rubbly floor. She keeps her eyes on her PAT, face stern, but a slight curve at her lips makes my heart flutter. I set Marcus down as my armour fizzles out, and wrap my arms around him, waiting for Evelyn to calculate my grade.

"Well, Adrianne," Evelyn says. Her head tilts to the side as the smile spreads her lips. "Written and practical exam included, your overall grade is 83% and you—"

"Fuck yes!" I holler, letting my head tilt back and my body slump into Marcus. He wraps his arms around me, and I yelp as he squeezes and spins me around. Tears spill down my face. Laughter and sobs gush out of me and get caught by Marcus' strong embrace. I bury my face in his shoulder once he sets me back down. He keeps his arms around me and strokes his hand carefully down the back of my head.

"You did it," he says into my ear. "You did it. You were amazing."

Evelyn clears her throat. "You are cleared for a field mission. Be ready for a placement when your supervisor can afford to lose the extra hands in clinical. Most likely in mid-Otsven, just a month away. Once you receive your placement, you'll report to the Guardian station on the start date and follow any orders your Commander gives you. You may or may not be the only Medic on your squad, so make sure you prepare yourself for either situation." She folds her hand around her PAT and nods me to the door with a sliver of a smile.

Marcus squeezes me, and I'm grateful. My head pounds and my legs are like jelly.

Was it the energy that Eila put into me, or was it just the adrenaline that propelled the beautiful projection? Either way, holy Fōsten, maybe I can actually do this. Having a nonlethal essence ability at my disposal might make fieldwork a little more attainable.

CHAPTER 15

"YOU KNOW YOU DIDN'T HAVE TO DRIVE ME."

A smile spreads over Marcus' lips. The side of his face might be more preferable to me than the front, maybe because I've gotten used to sitting next to him rather than facing him, or maybe because he smiles more when he doesn't see people looking at him.

"You wouldn't want to ride transit to the Guardian station with all your gear," he says.

Guardian station. My first time departing from the station, not just working there. Everything inside me squirms like my body is rearranging—my heart to my throat, my insides to the outside. My bones don't want to be bones anymore. I lean forward and open my pack.

"It would have been fine," I say, sorting through my provisions, medical supplies, and bedroll.

"If you had taken transit, you wouldn't be able to check your pack for the third time."

Supplies, carefully curated for the nasty climate of Toreth alongside the essentials, overflow around me. My hands stop and I shoot a glare at him. "Don't make fun of me. I'm nervous."

The smile lingers on his lips. He turns his face to me, his golden-brown eyes glinting. "I know you're nervous, and I like driving you. Now"—he takes one hand off the wheel and picks something out of the cupholder—"chew this." He hands me a pack of gum. "I know you like the cinnospice, but mint is better for your stomach."

I take the pack. It's clairmint, known for its calming properties, with no artificial sweeteners. I melt back into the seat, relaxing my neck to let my head rest, and I put a piece in my mouth. My heart steadies a little. The clairmint gum is sweet and soothing, the music just loud enough for me to make out the words, giving my mind a distraction. Still, my fingers are restless, and I run them over the smooth edges of my triangle pendant.

"Hey, how do you think Rin is coming along with her spirit affinities?" Marcus asks. His face has retained its natural rigidity, tightening his brows.

"Well, I haven't seen much progress since I worked with her a month ago when Brand was away."

"Did something happen?"

"She started panicking while working on it. Something happened or has been happening with her, I think. I'm worried."

The connection I feel with Rin is strong, but the way I communicated with her was too much. Brand wanted me to get to her spirit connection. Rin isn't ready for that. I started to prod too soon. I was able to help her through the panic attack because I've had them before. The fear they produce knocks you on your ass. I tried to guide her through it, and I tried to help her connect with her emotions, but she didn't know that I've been perpetually on my ass. As her instructor, I was there to teach, help her. Would expressing that part of me even be appropriate?

"Yeah, I'm a little worried too." Marcus swallows and nods. "The rest of the team is doing well, I think. They're not fighting as much. They still need work, but they're taking on new skills really well."

I press my lips together. Marcus glances at me.

"What?"

"You care about them," I say with a hand to my heart.

He shakes his head, but a glow livens his cheeks as they raise in a smile. "I just don't want the next generation of Guardians to be totally incompetent. Well, I guess it's still my generation."

With this fieldwork assignment, no one knows me or has preconceived perceptions of me to compare to what they get in the moment—the two won't clash. Maybe, for once, I can be myself, do my job, and avoid being the incompetent one.

We pull up to the Guardian station, and my insides have settled back into their rightful places, all but my pounding heart. I step out of the cruiser to assemble my layers; I was too hot and nervous to do it before I got in. I pull on a black zip-up jacket and my vest. The vest is orange. It has a fire-breathing tiger on the back. Matta made it for me to give me confidence in all of myself. I need that today.

"Do you think I should put on another pair of socks?" I ask Marcus as I fiddle with the straps of my gloves.

"You're going north to the Toreth ice-wastes, right?" He leans against the cruiser with his arms crossed. A cool wind blows a few leaves around his feet.

"Yeah."

"You've got leggings on under your pants?"

"Yes."

"And your socks are long enough so your boots don't chafe, and they cover the space between your boots and leggings?"

"Yes."

"Then you're fine." Marcus pushes himself away from the cruiser and comes over to me. "You'll want dry socks to change into. Your essence will keep you warm."

Even though I've become accustomed to the weight of my medkit ever since I was forced to wear the kit on my back for weeks in my first semester as a Medic, Marcus carries it for me to the entrance. Once we're there, he helps it onto my back. I pull my headband out of my pocket, but Marcus cups his hands around mine before I can put it over my ears.

"You'll need to put on a communication device. Better keep this off until then so you don't mess up your hair."

I bite my lip. I love how he knows that would be upsetting to me. It's not important for me to have perfect hair, but it does take a long time to do. Staring at our hands, pressure builds behind my eyes.

"Thank you for driving me," I say through the choke in my throat.

"My pleasure." His voice is low and smooth.

The doors are two paces away, but just like before my first clinical, my feet are sealed in place. A push-back, a barrier that I have to hurdle over to get to my next step, is always present.

"Are you going to be okay?" Marcus asks.

The step to him is easy, and he steps to me. In the time of one heartbeat, I am in his arms, my head against his shoulder, his hand smoothing my hair.

"Stay safe," he says. "Please."

In my heart, the words have been a truth that I've known for a while—they're not just for this departure. If I have to stay safe, that means I already am. There is already safety between us. I hope the meaning is shared.

I release him from my grasp. His arms are tight around me while mine dangle at my sides. The crisp air evaporates, the solid ground crumbles, and all that's real in this moment is the pressure of his embrace like a reset for my nervous system.

Gently pressing away from me, his face trails close to mine, and he kisses my temple. My eyelids flutter closed. He lingers, his hands gripping my shoulders.

His lips leave me. I glance at his face, but his eyes are on the ground. Thankful, I let my eyes fall, too, as I head into the station, taking a left turn to the precinct instead of a right to the clinic. There are no words to be attributed to the peace we just found in that hug. There's assurance that he might feel something for me, the way I feel it for him.

Inside the station, I'm met with a murmur of voices from every corner of the wide room. My lungs fill with stale air, tainted by cigarette smoke, boot polish, and old canvas. At the front desk, I show my registration card and my Medic training ID.

In return, the Protector at the desk hands me a Medic arm band. "Squad B105 is waiting for you. Commander Karf will be your squad lead."

"Thank you." I strap on my armband with fumbling fingers.

I heave a breath, let it go, and march over to my squad. As I approach, a tall woman with an avian Vishal on her forehead, jet-black hair, and tan skin turns to me. She wears all black, with high-heeled boots, a fur-lined hood, and a compound bow strapped to her back. Her eyes narrow as she nudges the man next to her.

"Commander Karf?" I ask, still looking at the woman. She chuckles and elbows the man again.

"Trainee McCarthy?" the man asks as he turns. His voice grates on my nerves with an apathetic growl. "About time."

Glancing at the clock on the wall, I resist the temptation to growl back that I'm five minutes early—he must be Emberstead, no doubt. I nod to him, hands at my sides.

"You've had your physical check?" he asks. Red eyes meet mine with impatience. He has three raised scars across his leathery face. His communication device is already in place around his head.

"Yes, just yesterday."

Stepping to the side, Commander Karf reveals two more team members. He runs a hand over his face. "You wouldn't believe how many trainees show up for duty without their physical done."

"Right, uh, could I get the team's physical records for vitals reference?"

"Nathal"—Karf nods to one of the squad members on the bench—"our tech specialist. They'll transfer you the records." Karf steps further away from the group and lights up a cigarette.

Nathal stands. Their hair is a bright, Nytrue blue, cut short to frame their face. Every available space of their ears is pierced with studs and rings. They have a lanky but muscular build. Setting their shoulders back, they smile wide and pull out their echo. "What's your lightstone registration number?"

"2-5-48-7031," I say.

Nathal's fingers tap swiftly over their echo, and within seconds, I have the team's most recent physical records.

As I save the files and Nathal's number, Karf blows smoke into the centre of the group. "Like I said, Nathal is our tech support. Vera"—he motions to the woman—"is our scout." Vera raises her chin in greeting, sharp eyes narrowed, and a confident smirk on her lips. "Lotic is our frontline man."

Lotic sits bent over his knees. He has swirling Lifeblood tattoos over a shaved head. But as he turns his face to me, there are no healing rings in his ears. I'll be the sole Medic for this mission.

"If all goes well, getting the physical records will be the extent of your medical duties. You're just along for the ride. If there's a beast attack, we'll deal with it. I haven't had an injury on my squad in three years, don't need a newbie getting in the way of a flawless mission. You got it?" Karf hands me a communication device. "You put that on and keep it on at all times."

"Make sure you turn off the ampliphone when you take a piss though," Nathal says.

I chuckle and exchange a smile with Nathal. Vera's dark eyes scan me from head to toe. Raising one eyebrow, she plops down in the seat by Lotic. Crossing her legs, she whispers something in his ear. His only response is a quick swipe of his eyes over to me and back to the ground.

"Our mission is to escort scientists doing research at a facility in the ice-wastes back to Emberstead. It's standard practice for remote powerstone dig sites. There are no trains or motorways in the area, so we will be taking an airbus to the nearest station and then making the rest of the way on foot." Karf drops his cigarette on the ground and stamps it out. He straps on his pack and slings the strap of his firestone rifle over his shoulder. "Piss, say your prayers, and meet in the airbus hanger in five."

Thank Zenta and her blessed flames. I do not want to set out on this mission with the urge to pee and have to do it in the freezing winds of Toreth. I locate the bathroom across the room.

As I hurry over, thankful not to have barf lurching up my throat, Vera's voice prickles the back of my neck. "At least if she lags behind, we'll be able to spot her in that vest."

It's not necessarily malicious, and I don't think the eye swipe was critical either—keen maybe, like a bird. Still, it sends a twitch to my shoulders.

I grab a stall and pull down my layers. As I pee, I thumb through the team's physicals. Looks like Karf's essence pressure is way too high, so is his blood pressure. Lotic has type one insulin dysfunction, Nathal has more allergies than seems possible, and judging by her essence analytics, Vera is at the beginning of her monthly cycle. You don't have resting energy output like that unless your stored essence from the month is making its way back into the system. With Carnity's eyes on Vera, at least one squad member will be at full strength.

My face twists into a snarl as I mumble Karf's words, *"Just along for the ride."*

I stick prostaglandin blockers in my chest pocket in case Vera has pain. Shuffling the contents of my pack a bit, I stick a Muncho bar for Lotic in the front pocket, along with antihistamines and an epinephrine syringe for Nathal, and a scolya root tonic for

Karf.

At the mirror, I get my communication device on and situate my headband over my ears. I'm about to switch the ampliphone on, but leave it off as Vera comes in. She strides to the mirror, hips swaying.

I pick the pack of blockers from my pocket. Handing it to her, I say, "Carnity's blessings."

Vera eyes the little silver packet with four white tablets. She snatches it from me and pops one in her mouth. "You'll soon figure out that none of the damn ancestors have their eyes on us. Especially Carnity." The tablet crunches between her teeth. A smile quirks her lips as she raises the little packet like she would an ale to cheers. "She leaves the Great Gate to the Lesser Worlds wide open."

Vera slaps the packet to my shoulder. I fumble to catch it as she disappears into one of the stalls.

I step to the door with a shiver and the imaginary taste of the blocker powder on my tongue.

"Never assume anyone's got your back, Adrianne," Vera calls after me.

The warning sinks in as I make my way to the airbus hanger. It directly contrasts what Karf told me, that they'll take care of everything, yet both attest an element of self reliance.

Since Vera is still in the bathroom, Nathal is fiddling with their tech devices, Karf is nowhere in sight, and Lotic has an otherworldly glaze to his eyes, I head to the hanger and get on the airbus. There are enough seats for a ten-man squad—five seats on each side of the cabin. Taking the seat nearest the pilot on the left side, I strap myself in where I'll be out of the way until we touch down in Toreth. I hope someone gets a bloody nose from the cold. Or Karf has a heart attack. Frostbite is a definite possibility.

Vera and Lotic take seats on the opposite side of the cabin, closest to the door. Karf sits across from them. With the pattern that's setting in, I expect Nathal to sit across from me or even on the other side of Karf, but they settle in right beside me.

I take a deep breath of metal and hot firestones as the airbus hums to life. Something whirs, something hisses, and still another something makes a big clunk. My hands clutch the seat. The bus jerks and rises off the ground, and my stomach protests with a violent clench. I'm beginning to think that Muncho bar I intended for Lotic might make it into my mouth first.

CHAPTER 16

Marcus' lips pressed against me. It's a nice image, one that I've always liked to play with in my mind, and now I have something to connect it with. A touch. It's almost a relief that the first time his lips touched me wasn't on my mouth. There was such an intense energy between us, I think we both are reeling. The energy lingers inside me without a hot, heavy pull of lust or the heart-twisting effect of romance.

I hold the image tight behind my eyelids as Afa's icy winds threaten to bring the airbus to the ground before we make it to our designated landing zone. It howls outside the tin can and will be the first beast to battle out there in the ice-wastes. The airbus trembles, jiggling every inch of my body. My stomach is in knots and my chest is tight.

I ate the Muncho bar in my pocket, since I don't want to become known as the hungry, pissy Medic right from the start, so I had to fish out another one from my pack to have on hand. I just need to get to the facility without barfing, without having to nervous pee, and without falling behind. Karf's demeaning task of sitting back and shutting up has become my focus.

Filling my empty mouth with the precious clairmint gum, my stomach lurches as the airbus touches down with a heavy clunk of landing gear. I pull the cowl sewed into my vest over my nose and zip the vest as high as possible. Flipping up the hood, I secure it with buttons that connect to the collar. Matta thought of everything.

"Move on out." Karf's gravelly voice comes through the coms loud and clear, grating against my pressure headache.

The door to the airbus screeches open, letting in a torrent of angry wind, and racks up a few too many heartbeats. *Come on, Toreth. Bite one of us. Give this Medic something to do.*

The door hits the packed snow, and Karf's boots are on the ground. I trail my team out of the airbus. To the left is the air traffic tower. In front of me, flat fields of ice stretch on for miles. To the right, jagged spikes of ice split the endless, frozen void like the skin of the Karess has been broken with protruding bones. The spikes tower over the wastes. They glisten as the sun peeks through a patch of clouds, but as shadows descend, they are painted a range of blue hues from sky blue to the dark blue of bruising flesh.

"Vera, scout ahead, but stay close," Karf says.

Vera's dark hair whips across her face in sleek strands. With a nod, she sprints away from the group. A flash of light bursts from her and a shockwave washes over us as she transforms into her beast form. Ebony wings beat the air. She soars high above us, a majestic raven, and the icy gale is no match for her.

"Nathal," Karf growls over the wind. "I want you scanning for core-energy pulses at all times."

Without delay, Nathal has two tech devices in hand. One of them looks like it is used to gather energy waves, the other displays the energy reading for the area. The devices flash and make blipping noises as we move forward.

"Trainee."

I spin around to face Karf.

"You stay behind Lotic, and between me and Nathal. Got it?"

"Got it," I say. Nathal winces and adjusts their comm in their ear. I lower my voice to a less enthusiastic decibel. "Like I'm not even here."

Karf grumbles and his eyes roll. He starts to trudge, his feet following the lead of his eyes. Lotic starts into a steady march, taking his time to move to the front of the party. Nathal matches Karf's position on my other side, creating a triangle around me.

Every month of third year, when I started as a Medic, our instructors had us climb Moon Hill. Every single month, so we could endure all the seasons as we hulled dummies on stretchers and carried Medic supplies on our backs. Today, I'm grateful for that training, but an Akinnera winter is not nearly as bitter as Toreth.

We've walked for ten minutes, and the skin around my eyes is numb. My feet sink through snow that is less packed and skid over patches of ice I don't anticipate. I keep my hands in motion, scrunching my fingers, pumping my arms, anything I can do to keep movement in my essence to build heat.

After two hours of walking, Karf hasn't called for a break. I pick up my pace and pull up next to Lotic, slipping a Muncho bar into his hand, and rip open another for myself. He gives me a quick side-eye, but nods and peels open the packaging. Another half hour of trudging and silence, Nathal bridges the gap between us.

"Adrianne," they say.

My stomach gives a pinch, and I swallow hard, my jaw sore from working at my gum that is tough and flavourless. They nod to the right. "Check this out."

We've long since left the ice-bones to rot behind us. All that lies on the horizon is a cluster of ominous clouds in all shades of grey, ready to shit a pile of snow on us.

"Yeah, ice-wastes," I say. My breath fogs around me and the wind whisks it away. "Seen it once. Never want to see it again."

"Just watch." The very edge of the screen in their left hand flashes bright green.

The Karess groans, and a tremor reverberates through the ice. In the distance, the wastes split. A stream of core energy jets out of the earth. My blood churns like my veins are being wrung out. The energy glitters and twists through the air, bending over and freezing in a perfect half moon arc. An eery pool of core-energy mist billows at the base of the moon, glittering like crystals.

My heart flutters as a smile springs to my face. "Okay, maybe I would like to see that again."

Nathal throws their head back and laughs.

"Why does it do that?" I ask.

"It's utanic energy."

The wind howls around us, whipping stray hairs around my

eyes.

"It's what?" I ask.

Nathal picks up their pace, and I follow them back to the group. "Chaotic energy."

"Oh right. What was the word you used?" As we leave behind the twisted crescent, my insides loosen.

"*Utanic* is the ancient Slyvic word for chaos. Utanic energy comes from the mixing of jint, unama, and fann essential energies. There are pockets of it only in a few places on the Karess. In the ice-wastes, we've got huge deposits of pressurized ice, organic matter from fossils, and core energy. Perfect recipe for utanic energy. That spiral motion is a defining characteristic."

"Why does it come out so forcefully? It's so different from the core energy that seeps out of boulders. And we only have core energy bursts in spring and summer in Emberstead."

"It's the goddamn cold." Nathal spreads their arms wide to the blank white space around us. "It irritates the energy. It's the opposite of a geyser where heat boils the water. Cold makes the utanic energy testy. You know, Sii is a utanic energy reservoir."

"That's why it floats?"

"Exactly. The circular motion is enough to push it away from the Karess, but gravity keeps it in place. The two forces are balanced. Did you feel it?" They point their thumb at the arch as we continue to trudge.

"Feel what?"

"A sort of circular motion inside you."

I rub my chest. "Yeah, actually I did."

"It's because you're a halfie. Halfies have essence variations that guard against chaotic energy. In a way, you're more sensitive to it, so you feel it, but in other ways you're less affected by it."

I smile as Nathal falls quiet again, checking their sensors and taking in the wastes with their own small grin. A few minutes in silence again, and my skin starts to tingle. There's a tinge of sulphur in the air, and energy that makes my heartbeat fast. I rub my nose.

"Uh, Commander Karf?"

He grunts.

"I think there's a beast nearby. Thought it would be good to—"

"For fuck's sake, they step out of the academy and think they know everything, don't they?" Karf grumbles and shrugs his pack up higher on his shoulders.

"You don't have to worry about that kind of stuff, Adrianne. Vera will tell us when there's trouble." Nathal gives me a slap on the arm.

But the wind sets an itch in my bones. I know it's there. It's big, threat-level four probably. Hungry.

As if she were an omen of death, Vera soars overhead, casting a shadow over us. She screeches a long, high-pitched note, and Nathal's smile fades. Vera swoops down to us as Lotic and Karf draw in close. The instant she touches the ground, Vera transforms back into her hédin form and draws her bow. My essence rushes through my hands and the hair at the back of my neck stands on end.

"Beast up ahead," Vera says.

Karf draws his firestone rifle. "How many?"

"Just one," Vera says and throws her fuzzy hood over her head. "An unstable Ice-Behemoth, threat-level four. It's near the bridge over the ravine, the only passage for miles. It would take us into the bloody night to go around."

"We stay our course. Only engage if it approaches. Nathal and Lotic create some cover."

With a deep breath, Nathal turns their palms to face the ground. Small bits of ice and snow rise as they bring their hands up and flip them to the sky. Lotic raises one arm and with a sharp swoop toward his chest, he stirs the wind. A small snowstorm envelopes us, and Vera takes to the sky to be our eyes.

Though I still have no apparent part in this mission, I keep my eyes vigilant, searching through the snow for anything at all. My heart pounds, and I've sweat through my first layer of clothes.

We trek for about ten minutes before we come to the passage over the ravine. The ice dips straight down into the Karess on both sides of the passage. Lotic leads us onto the ice bridge without slowing his pace. He keeps his gaze forward, and so does everyone else. But my head spins as a block of ice from the ravine wall slides off and plummets down into the dark, shattering as it crashes into the side. Wind and snow whistle around my legs. Halfway across, and I wish Lotic would walk faster. I'm so hot in my layers that my feet might burn through my boots and melt the ice keeping me from dropping into the belly of the Karess.

The scientific research facility appears in the distance beyond Lotic and Nathal's storm just as my feet step off the ice bridge and onto more solid ground. My stomach roils inside of me. Heavy breath spews from my lungs.

"Come on team, almost there," Karf says, letting his rifle hang at his side.

A growl shunts an icy wave through my blood. I turn my gaze across the ravine. On the other side, a silhouette fades in and out of visibility as snow falls in heavy gusts over the ice-wastes.

A flicker of muscle, a massive grey tusk, a glint of an amber eye. A groaning shriek bellows from the beast and steam spills from its nostrils.

"Get a move on, trainee. We're not about to fight it today."

I stretch my fingers, warming my blood enough to get my feet to move again.

A chain-link, electrowire fence opens into the research facility. The facility is built with bland stone walls surrounding a cavern similar to the one we just crossed. Another Protector meets us at a hulking metal door to let us in.

Earth and metal and the unmistakable musk of water damage greet us as the door hisses shut. A focused murmur swells over the clatter of our boots. Scientists work in pairs at cluttered workstations or individually inspecting powerstones. Workstations are set up one after another along a railing that looks over the cavern. Down the cavern, the stations circle the edge at least five floors below the surface. Red glows from firestones, flashing lightstones, and shimmering core-energy particles litter the drab facility with colour.

"We have barracks ready for you since it's so late in the day," the Protector leading us says.

"Well, we had a trainee with us so we couldn't have helped that," Karf says.

My eyes dart to him. "Maybe Lotic should have walked a little faster."

"Mind your mouth." Karf glares at me with dead eyes. He lets out a breath through his nose, wafting his disdain over me.

"He does walk kind of slow," Vera says, inspecting her nails. A smirk plays on her lips. She sweeps that smirk over to me as Karf and Lotic grumble.

Forget Karf with his condescending looks and passive-aggressive shit. Vera just smiled at me. A female Guardian just backed me up. If that doesn't say "buck up, girl, you've made it," I don't know what does.

Our guide gives a stifled chuckle. "It's fine. The scientists you'll be escorting only just got back from a final dig. They're right over there."

At the elevators, two scientists wait for us. They wear heavy coats, protective eye covers, and helmets. One steps forward, removing his helmet and tucking it under his arm. He holds out a gloved hand, smudged from searching the ice-wastes for powerstones. A boyish smile spreads over his pale skin. "I'm Stephen."

My head ticks to the side. Something about his smile, and the way he holds himself closed but relaxed reminds me of someone.

Not even looking at the guy, Karf takes out his echo. "Stephen and Adia?" he mutters.

Stephen nods, and a soft smile touches Adia's lips.

"Holy ancestors, the two of you ever see the light? About time you got back to Emberstead," Karf says.

The smile drops from Stephen's face. It prompts dark bags to grow under his eyes as his head tilts down, dark hair obscuring his gaze. Adia shifts beside him—a silent stir of energy. Lifting his head again, Stephen's throat bobs, and his smile returns to his face with just the motion and no good will. "About time."

Cold grips my heart with the steel in his silver eyes.

"We should change. I'm sure we'll see you down in the dining hall," Adia says, her voice light and sleepy, her eyes shadowed. She tilts her head to Stephen so her long, black hair shifts over a rippling pink scar on her cheek.

"Of course," I say before Karf can get in another gruff piece of nonsense. Both sets of scientists' eyes land on me. "We'll talk later. I'd love to hear about your research."

The murmurs of researchers and clack of stones spikes in our silence. Stephen nods, his neck stiff, as the facility Protector steps between us to press the elevator button. We pile inside the cramped space, away from the breezy workstation platform, but the chill follows us, weaseling its way through all my layers, and my head spins as the elevator moves down a level.

Making a quick stop at the barracks, I deposit my pack and shed some of my layers. The section of the facility that houses the barracks and dining hall are enclosed underground, and poorly lit. The air is stale. I take a deep breath of it and it sloughs through my windpipe, taking its time to get to my brain.

The Muncho bars I've been devouring through the day have worn off again. I scoop some sort of potato slop onto my plate, with adrenaline still shaking my hands and a pain shooting through my stomach—a mix of anxiety and hunger that is way too familiar and takes my breath hostage. I take two heaping scoops of the vegetable mix, unable to spot another vegetarian option.

My squad has dispersed around the facility and only Karf sits in the corner downing a plateful of mystery meat. Adia sits at the opposite end of a long table from a small group of scientists deep in discussion. Keeping her head low, her long hair falls around her boxy shoulders.

I sit across from her. Swallowing hard, I press my eyes shut for a moment and bring my attention to my shoulders, forcing them to drop. With my hands pressed on the table, I inhale, eyes still closed. The stuffy air expands my stomach, tugging the cramps. Sending my awareness to my legs, the tension follows, so I anchor my feet flat on the floor. For a moment, nothing squirms and all that's left is hollow. Seizing the moment, I shovel in a mouthful of mush.

"This place is awful," I say through my food.

Adia jerks her head to the side. Her hair swishes around her porcelain face, but not quite far enough to cover the reddened skin along her nose. The scar tissue stops right at the midline of her face, as if it couldn't go any further, like whatever torment afflicted her right side wasn't allowed to cross her nose.

"I guess there's not much in the budget for a paint job," Adia says.

As she lowers her face to her food, the rippled skin of her face sucks in shadows. Only one thing could make a scar like that. Not a beast, not a sword. Fire. My fingers itch, heart pounding in my chest.

I smile at her even if she can't see it from inside her cover. "What powerstones have you and your partner been researching?"

"Waterstones," she says to a piece of fish on her plate without missing a beat.

With a wad of potato split between my cheek pouches, I say, "They just added a whole unit on waterstones for Medic studies. I didn't know they were so good for anxiety. I need to invest in some." I chuckle to hide a cringe and run my hand over my sore stomach. "What exactly are you studying about them?"

"Things in the same vein as that, you know, health effects and, uh"—she dips her fish into a pool of sauce a few times and clears her throat—"long term use." With a quick swipe of her hand, she tucks her hair behind her ear, and just as fast, untucks it. "Early stages of research right now. Just gathering enough stones for the project."

I nod along. "What made you want to research waterstones?"

Adia draws a breath of the reluctant air around us. I take one as well, heavy with grease and stone dust. A moment passes, and years of life on this planet pass behind Adia's eyes. They meet me with a gripping energy as her shoulders straighten and her hair lays flat against the vulnerable plane of her face. "People like me need this."

"People like you?"

She drags her fork through her sauce, creating a channel that appears and floods in quick succession. "It's an underestimated stone. I think it could make a change in this world. It will be unexpected. But when I'm through with this research, people will finally give me the recognition I deserve."

What kind of people though? Maybe she's talking about her scar. Burn victims. If a wound like a burn isn't treated by a curestone or a healer before it scars, there's no way to reduce the scarring since it's already healed by the body's natural process. Or maybe she doesn't have enhancements, like Eliote. Unlocking the full effect of a powerstone would give power back to hédin with low or non-existent essence power.

There's no draft, no air movement at all, but my hands go cold. "Well, I can definitely relate to wanting a little recognition. Being a halfie, there're a lot of expectations of how I should act and how my essence enhancements should progress."

"You're a halfie?"

"Yeah, Emberstead and Beastblood."

Adia's eyes narrow. She sets down her fork, and it makes a

defined click against the ceramic plate. She stands, jostling the table and picking up her plate. "I think I will turn in for the night. Goodnight—"

"Adrianne."

"Goodnight, Adrianne. We'll meet you tomorrow at eight by the entrance."

My foot slips from its planted position, and my leg starts to jiggle.

"Goodnight, Adia," I say with a quick nod. "I hope you find everything you're looking for in your research."

Giving me one last look, Adia exudes a strength as bitter and scathing as ice. Only one other person has given me such an unsettling yet undeniable gut feeling before. Rin. And I don't think Adia has such pure intentions of studying waterstones. One conversation can't confirm that though, can it?

CHAPTER 17

THE ICE-WASTES AND THIS FACILITY DON'T SLEEP. The walls vibrated through the night from machinery, generators, and the energy from powerstones. Over all those waves, vibrations, and thrumming noises, something else kept me up all night. Not even the constant pain in my stomach distracted me from the clawing awakening that set in my spine. Something has upset the beasts scattered through this frozen death zone. It's not normal for Beastbloods to sense beasts, but I'm long past hoping I'll ever be a typical Beastblood. First the Rover at home in the forest, then the behemoth at the bridge to the facility. I can't deny that I can sense them, and they were all awake with me.

This morning, I skip breakfast because I know I'll just throw it up. I pack up my things as fast as I can and corner Nathal.

Something about my conversation with Adia still keeps my attention.

"Nathal, can you look something up for me?" I say, rubbing at a knot in my neck.

"Sure, what is it?" they say, turning a bright smile to me as they fold up a sweater and stuff it in their bag.

I scan the room. Lotic is still dozing on his cot and Vera pulls on a shirt while simultaneously brushing her teeth. "Can you look up what advanced ed academy Stephen and Adia attended?" I ask, lowering my voice.

Nathal squints their blue eyes at me. "Well, yeah, but why?"

"Adia was telling me a bit about her research last night. It was interesting, so I was just wondering what programs they have at the schools."

"You want to leave Guardian work already?" Nathal shifts on their cot so I can sit next to them. "I swear Karf is the worst of the bunch. We're not all that bad."

"No." Shaking my head, I bring a smile to my lips, but it twitches. "Can you just look it up?"

Nathal shrugs and whips out a Personal Automated Technology device. After tapping and scrolling for a minute, their face crinkles. Cocking their head to the side, they say, "I can't find a record of Stephen attending any advanced ed, but Adia went to the Braya Advanced Education Academy and majored in hédin physiology with a focus on lifeline code."

I chew the inside of my cheek. Why would someone who studies lifeline code be focused on waterstones? Could waterstones really make that much of an impact on a molecular level?

"And Stephen has all the credentials to be working at this

research facility, even though he has no record of advanced ed?"
I ask.

Nodding, Nathal holds up the PAT with the documents. Why would someone who never went through scientific study end up here? And how could they get the credentials to be here?

"I think we should tell Karf, or whoever runs the facility," I say.

"No use really. Karf's not going to delay this mission for anything. How this facility runs isn't really our business unless we're assigned to investigate." Nathal shrugs and continues to pack up.

Pressure taps at my temples like the fist of a prophetic wraith begging me to pay attention to this. I push up and pace through the narrow space between the rows of cots.

Nathal peeks over their shoulder at me. "Nothing to worry about, newbie." They flash a toothy smile.

My stomach turns in quick, pinching twists. I take a long breath of the damp air and leave the barracks with my pack.

Heading to the front entrance, my boots hit the metal flooring in heavy beats. As I zip up my layers, the twists and turns of my gut cinch the muscles throughout my body. In one of the dark corridors off the main hall, Stephen and Adia are turned toward each other, huddled over their packs. I slow my steps and backtrack behind the wall with a sudden ache pressing into my temples.

"I think I should carry it," Adia whispers. "It affects me less."

"It's fine. I can handle it for a day," Stephens says, his whisper harsh and weighted.

"But if you can't, there's no way to swap it with eyes on us." Adia holds out her hand.

Stephen crosses his arms tight over his chest. Untucking one hand, he runs it through his hair. "We should have just left when we found it."

"I keep telling you, we have to do everything by the book here. It's the only way to get this done quietly."

I press myself as close to the wall as possible to hear their conversation. A sigh washes out of Stephen. As I take a peek around the corner, Adia whips her hair out of her face and ties it while Stephen crouches down to open his pack. In the dark corridor with only the green exit sign for light, their forms are lost in shadow, their voices lowering to an incomprehensible hush against the constant click-clack of stones. Stephen hands a single stone wrapped in a white cloth to Adia. A jet-black stone pokes through the folds of the cloth.

I pull myself away from the corner. My hand grasps my pounding chest. An uncanny energy wafts down the corridor. It curls around me, rooting me in place. Crawling up my body, it digs under my skin. Shadow spreads like slime inside my heart. My head becomes heavy. My neck weakens and my face nods to the ground.

Why am I even here? I've hated every second of this fieldwork. If I can't do this, then what? There is no use in a life without purpose. I am nothing. I am no one. I won't make it. I should kill myself. Now. Don't wait. Don't suffer.

Just as my eyes shut, the energy leaves from the top of my head and air rushes into my lungs. I yank my slack body back to attention. My mind prickles with the lingering thoughts that the dark force latched onto. Those thoughts are always with me, but usually they're subtle, lingering like wraiths hiding in the dark, not demons, so loud and taunting. They bolstered out of nowhere.

Stephen and Adia have a Death stone.

My professor said we don't know how the stone affects beasts. That clawing in my spine, it's not just anxiety. The beasts and I were awake because those two brought a Death stone to the surface. I don't think Stephen and Adia know that.

The elevator doors open and Karf leads Nathal, Lotic, and Vera to the exit. I swallow hard, my mouth dry, and peel myself away from the wall.

"Karf, may I speak with you?" My voice shudders from my throat.

Karf just brushes past me with a sour frown and lights up a cigarette. "Everyone, move out. Keep our researchers and our trainee in the centre of our band at all times, no slowing down. I want this mission over with as soon as possible."

"I really need to talk to you before we go," I say, sprinting up to him.

"We're on a schedule, trainee." Karf punches the button to open the door. It screeches open. The bitter air wraps around my legs and scrapes like needles over my face.

"It's about the mission," I say, grabbing Karf by the arm. I tug him back before he can step into the snow. Smoke catches at the back of my throat, triggering my gag reflex. I grit my teeth.

The sickly grey of his skin darkens under his eyes. "What could you possibly need to tell me about this mission, huh? You have zero experience. Now get to your position."

The electrowire gate opens to the ice-wastes. My blood is on fire, coursing through me in gushing waves. I scan the horizon, fingers twitching at my sides. "We can't go out there."

"Aw, she's just a little nervous after seeing that beast

yesterday, hey?" Nathal says, nudging me with their elbow.

Lotic chuckles as he pushes past me.

"It's not *one* beast we're going to have to worry about."

Who knows how many beasts that stone will attract? I glance at Stephen and Adia. Stephen's grey eyes are glued in front of him, his long face like stone. A flick of Adia's eyes catches my attention before she lets her hair fall, and she adjusts her pack.

I grab Vera's arm. "Vera, we can't go out there. Please believe me."

Vera squints her eyes at me. She shrugs me off but stays put. "You sense something?"

"Yes. We should call for backup."

A roar of laughter erupts around us as the rest trudge through the gate, leaving me and Vera frozen at the entrance to the research facility.

"I'll take a look. I told you, no one's got your back, but I never disregard the warning of an intuitive woman. Stay alert," she says.

With a nod, Vera takes to the sky in a flash of light, but she'll be back on the ground with word of beasts in no time.

I sprint to catch up with Karf. Just a few paces behind Adia, my heart pinches, the darkness claws into my skull. I shake my head and grit my teeth.

"They haven't been truthful with us," I say in a biting hiss, trying to get through Karf's thick head while not being overheard by Stephen and Adia.

"Who the hell are you talking about?"

I fight for breath and my body crawls with sweat. "They weren't looking for fucking waterstones, they have a Death stone."

"Girl, if you don't stick to your post and stop talking nonsense, then I'm leaving you in the snow. Got it? Now walk."

"I'm telling you, it's not safe."

"You have no right to tell your Commander what is and is not safe. You have a duty to patch up injuries. You see any beasts out there?" He bares his yellow teeth. "I'll tell you when to stop moving."

The nausea evaporates from my gut, replaced by a strong grip on my whole body like hands supporting me from every angle, pushing against the pull of the Death stone and the ache of anxiety.

"Hells of Dien," I say. "Put down your damn pride and get your team to safety, now!" I grab Karf by the collar, his grey skin flushing with fire just like my own. My essence spikes inside me, sending sparks around my fist.

The wind howls and everyone turns to stare at me. A shadow passes over us as Vera swoops overhead. A screech like bone grinding against bone rips through the ice-wastes, searing my eardrums. A Noltwyn Alzuke dives for Vera.

Light flashes through the sky. Vera drops in her hédin form. She draws her bow and fires at the Alzuke. The arrow sticks it through the chest with a plume of red and gold. Vera shrinks and her wings propel her to greater height.

Another black form streaks across the sky. The Noltwyn Alzuke opens its jaw and clamps down around Vera's raven form. The sound of teeth sinking into flesh jolts me away from Karf. The sky rains crimson. Blood splatters my face as light bleaches my sight. Vera's hédin body plummets to the ground, silver essence snaking out of her wounds.

Vera stares at the heavy clouds above, her mouth agape, her

eyes wide and glassy.

"No, no, no." I drop beside her, my knees soaking up blood and snow. My hands tremble as I check for her pulse. Nothing. I bend over her, hoping for a puff of air from her nose, a heave of breath. "Shit."

No pulse, no respiration. That's polytrauma. Do not resuscitate. A deep ragged gash sinks straight through her heart and blood seeps from her smashed skull.

My priority is to prevent additional casualties now.

Iron tingles my nose and acid crawls up my throat as my eyes cloud.

The crack of Karf's firestone rifle splits the air, and the Alzuke crashes into a frozen arch of utanic core energy. The ground trembles.

"I've got energy readings on land coming from the northeast," Nathal shouts, holding out their beeping tech devices.

Body shaking, I lock eyes with Adia.

"You," I say, rising with blood and snow dripping off me. "Hand over the stone. You're under arrest for possession of an illegal powerstone."

She doesn't move a muscle.

Her dark hair swishes around her pale face, eyes like steel, her fists clench at her sides.

"Having that stone is endangering everyone," I say, stepping closer to her. My knees buckle, but I right myself and plant my feet in the snow.

"Adrianne, behind!" Nathal shoots a stream of ice into the air.

An Alzuke smashes through it and dives for us, wind from its wings rupturing the icy patches of snow. I lunge forward, throw my arms around Adia, and hurl us both to the side. A shadow crashes over us. The Alzuke rams into me, its talons ripping through my side. I scream as blood spills and pain lances through my body. Lotic roars, sending a torrent of wind against the Alzuke, throwing it off me.

Bracing my hands on both sides of Adia, I push away, my blood pouring over her and my essence obscuring her face in a silver mist. Her clothes are torn, and her pale flesh is exposed without the slightest scratch. Ironskin. Her chest rises with a breath, her eyes capture mine with ice, and her teeth appear in a snarl.

"*Hon nahack slyv, mas des hon lotnaha zethalash en des slyv lotnasold.*" Her Slyvic words slide off her tongue, venomous.

A siren swells from the research facility, and the Protectors on guard shout orders to each other.

Blood gurgles in my throat, and I clutch my side. Adia throws me off. I land in the snow three paces away, crumpling in on my wound, hands slick with hot blood and essence. Snow crunches beneath Adia's feet as she approaches with no regard for the repetitive blasts of firestone rifles, shouts, and the ground trembling with approaching beasts. A trickle of salty blood sneaks out of the corner of my mouth as Adia crouches in front of me. A spike of adrenaline urges me to scramble away from her. The gash in my side screams like the talons are ripping through it again. I slide across the snow, leaving a dark smear of red.

"One by one, the fires will go out," Adia says. Her bulky form looms over me. The bright peach scar is all I can focus on. "People like you killed my family. Someone like you left me with nothing but this scar." She points a finger to her face and pulls me close to look at it.

Beastbloods sided with the Emberstead in the Fourth Great War. All my people sided against hers. Tears spill from my eyes, a groan grows deep in my lungs, and pain radiates through my torso as she lifts me clean off the snow with one hand. The metallic scent of blood smothers me, and I choke back a sob. My vision blurs as Adia shoves me back to the ground.

"Stephen, let's go!" she shouts.

Electro-blue light flares around her, blinding me with her projection of energetic wings. Adia dashes forward, her wings sparkling behind her. She grabs Stephen and lifts them both into the air.

A beast roars and Karf hollers in pain. Nathal battles a beast with ice and water, Lotic fends off another with a gale force wind, and Vera's lifeless body lies in the middle blossoming a pool of blood.

I heave rapid breaths through my teeth. Bracing myself in the snow on one hand, I coax my essence to follow my breath away from my gaping side. Without the essence near the open wound, my skin won't resist my flame. I surround my hand in fire armour and press it to my side. I scream as it sears my flesh. The acrid stench fills my nose and I bite my lip, whimpering. The flow of blood stops, my skin pulls and smarts against the cauterized wound. I push away from the snow.

Karf slams to the ground under an Ice-Behemoth twice his size, his rifle braced between the beast's jaws. Saliva sprays around them. I let go of my breath and heave another. It rips through me. My vision goes spotty; it sharpens and wavers. Blood pounds through every limb. My bones grind, my muscles tear, and an unfathomable itch fills my joints. Hédin flesh vanishes, replaced by thick fur. I blink, it flashes in my eyes, orange and black.

My breath stops as pain engulfs my face. My incisors grow pointed and long, pricking my lower lip. The pulse of blood vanishes. My heart vibrates like a gong and then is stilled with a clamp of darkness.

I watch. Watching has never been such an active, harsh reality before. My body runs away with my heart. I am above the wastes, above myself, shrouded in a thin veil of shadow. Lights glimmer around me while my team battles the beasts. As I am hovering, I am still conscious of the skin and bones of this foreign being, the muscles writhing with strength.

I burst forth at full speed, legs exuding power as energizing as acid. My fur glistens and bristles as my palms hit the snow. My transformation takes full effect, and I leap at the beast. I am drifting further away, further above, gauzy black wrapping me up in a breathless heap. As I drift, my fangs clamp around the behemoth's neck. The crunch of bone and the squelch of flesh sends a tremor through my body, and my mouth fills with blood. The veil, where there is no blood in my throat, is heavy and vast. My body, with the guttural cries of the beast vibrating through my fangs, through my bones, is hot. I can't grasp the air to scream. My mind, it's hanging by a thread in the space.

The beast roars.

The veil heats. Sparks engulf the darkness, burning at the dense tendrils binding me away from my body. A pair of eyes stares me down. Flickering and shifting, a face looms, just a breath away. Fangs and fur and an inferno of fire lunge for me. It smacks my face, and I am shunted back into my body.

My neck jerks, and I slam the beast to the ground. Vision clouding and breaths wracking my body, light wraps around me as I regain my hédin form. Fire burns in my veins. I spit blood over the snow, but it's still hot and slick over my tongue. I slam my fists together, creating a loop of energy. Every inch of my skin burns as a projection of essence and flame bursts forth, blasting the beasts backward. Throaty screeches echo through the ice-wastes. One by one, the Alzukes take to the air, and the behemoths' paws beat the earth in escape.

I turn to Karf with bloody arms held away from my shuddering body. His eyes are wide, and his teeth are bared. He trembles as I approach. I rip off my sodden gloves and slap them down in the snow beside him. As I get new gloves and treat his wound, Karf's eyes never leave my face. I unwrap a curestone and press it to the gash on his shoulder. Karf's upper lip curls, the muscles in his neck crane away from me.

Mist twists in the icy air as skin knits itself back together under the glow of the curestone. Curls of our breath mask the blood on my vest. I turn, still grasping Karf, and stare at the behemoth lying on its side, no breath in its lungs, golden essence running dry, and blood streaking its neck. My heart rips, a weight plummets in my gut, and tears slip down my cheeks, falling red on the snow. I tried so hard, I did everything right, and this is what I get? The moment I act on a pure gut instinct, everything completely crumbles?

Snow crunches and I turn to Nathal. They stand above me, trembling. The winds press on them, and they sway. "Adrianne, you're—"

"I'm fine." I zip up my medkit in a swift motion. My heart is back with a passion. My blood is hot and my essence is hotter. Energy radiates through my clothes and cuts through the frigid Toreth air. It clears my mind and body of pain.

"You're hurt. You need to get inside."

I stand. My body jerks with energy and rights itself at the same time.

"I can walk." I shove my hand at Karf and heave him off the snow. "Let's get Vera's body and get to the airbus station. Got to stay on schedule, right?"

Karf nods, a snarl as grotesque as a beast's on his mouth.

Grabbing my litter, tears shiver from my eyes. I swipe them away and focus my blurry vision on Vera, rolling her stiff body away from me. Nathal takes one end and I take the other, and we lift our comrade off her frozen death bed.

C H A P T E R 18

After hours of walking and the agonizingly bumpy flight back to Akinnera, I step off the airbus and my knees buckle. Nathal grabs me by the shoulders to steady me.

"We've got to get you to the clinic," they say.

I just need a fucking moment of quiet.

Shrugging them off, eyes fixed on the door out of the hangar, I say, "Leave me alone."

"You, of all people, should know you can't let an injury like that go untended."

Everything inside me vibrates. I can't bite my tongue any longer. Nathal just pricked the bubble that reins in my thoughts.

I whirl around. "Don't worry about it, right, Nathal? It's not your concern. 'Don't worry, newbie.' 'We'll take care of it, newbie.'"

Nathal's blue eyes are locked on me, their shoulders low under the weight of their pack. Karf brushes past them, eyes averted, and Lotic is still in the ship with his head in his hands and tears wetting the floor by the body bag.

"Adrianne, I didn't mean anything by it." Their voice cracks.

My throat is thick, but I force out the words. "*Of all people.*" I squeeze my eyes shut, my body aching as the last of my energy dissipates. "I knew something was wrong. I told you something was wrong, and none of you listened. Now Vera is dead."

The heat of the airbus tangles around my legs. The stench of the burnt-out firestone core sinks into my skin and my stomach churns.

With slow deliberation, Nathal nods, and says, "I'm so sorry."

Their quiet voice digs into my ears. I shield my face as the tears break free again and I burst through the door into the main station.

I cross to the bathroom where this whole mission started. At the mirror, I freeze.

Dried blood stains my skin around my mouth. It streaks from my chin, up my cheek and into my hair from my attempts to swipe it away. My lips are cracked, and my skin is blanched. The green of my eyes is sick. Strands of hair stick out of my braid in every direction. I swallow. The effort to wash down the metallic taste on my dry tongue shakes my whole body.

Outside the bathroom, the Guardian station buzzes with activity. Lotic's cries over Vera are prominent but muddied by shouted orders and a beeping noise. Inside my head, there is nothing. The image before me in the mirror is all-consuming.

This is all I have, a shredded orange vest binding me together.

I slide the straps of my pack off, but the pressure remains on my shoulders. As the pack slams to the ground, an echo rings somewhere deep in the station. I dip my shaking hands into the sink and run the water. Every one of my muscles is a rubber band ready to snap. As the water washes away a layer of blood, the jerking motion of my hands splashes bloody droplets all over the sink.

I swipe my face. Water and blood rain off me. A sickening twist in my gut pushes up a slimy lump in my throat, increasing pressure against my lungs. I gasp, and a cry escapes my mouth. Hot tears burn my eyes.

I couldn't do it.

My numb shell cracks. A lancing pain strikes through my forgotten cauterized wound. It smarts as my shoulders shake.

I tear off my jacket and my shirt, so I stand in the middle of the public bathroom in my bra with a beast's blood and my own blood covering me head to toe. The wound on my side is its own demon with gaudy red colouring, yellow pus, and fangs digging into my flesh. Knees trembling and my eyes clouding, I fumble with the buckles of my pack to find a curestone and a dressing.

"She's in here."

A Medic bursts through the door, Nathal behind him. Nathal's eyes are wide and red and wet as they search me.

The Medic rushes over to me just as my knees give way. He wraps his arms around me, easing me down to the ground slick with bloody drippings.

Reaching for my med kit, I say, "I–I need the curestone in my . . . "

But the Medic moves my pack behind me before I can get to

it. "Shh, you're okay," he says, pressing me back.

My body is rigid, and the shaking of my muscles pulls open my singed skin. Blood stings the break, my essence curling above it. The Medic's face wavers above me, just smooth brown flesh, no blood. His hands are swift as he pulls curestones, salve, and bandages from his own pack.

"I can do it myself," I say, grunting as the Medic pushes me back to lean on my pack again.

"I've got you covered." The Medic cleans my wound and, unable to remove the pain from my mind, I cry, covering my face with my crimson hands. Behind my fingers is Vera's face, still gawking at the sky, her essence mixing with the wind, her blood becoming one with the snow. Tension washes through my body as another searing pain strikes my side with the pressure of the curestone against my skin. It awakens the beastly essence inside me, releasing a groan. I clasp my hands over my lips to muzzle the beast—the beast that broke my Vow.

The gauzy veil of black sits quietly in my memory. It's not the first time I've been there, surrounded by the brilliant lights. Void Watching wasn't the first time, and neither was the heart-stopping event as I made my Vow. The first time was when I got my scars. I didn't connect it until now because I saw more than the glimmering black expanse that time; it was more of a dream than an experience.

In the dark, pure lights like stars—brighter than any in the Illyson sky—had bored into my sight, inky dark surrounding me. A haze of violet washed over the light with a thrum of energy—a ringing in my ears, and static in my head. It was a whole new world right in front of me, but it cracked into pieces just as fast as it had appeared. I thought I was gone then, but I was faced with a vast expanse of indigo and pale blue. It had trees and beasts of pure light roaming in a great valley. It ached in my skin, and my essence churned in a roundabout motion, slipping over itself as if tumbling down a hill.

A crackle of sparks and a flare of white fire had bleached the colour out of these layering worlds until all I could see was a golden aura. Gold like the eyes I keep seeing. The fiery beacons blinked as I blinked. They flickered as I breathed. And the sparks winked out.

I had been dead, and I had seen three distinct realms. The Lesser Worlds. In my full transformation on the ice-wastes, I was almost dead, only glimpsing the dark of the closest of those worlds.

And those eyes keep watching me, keep bringing me back.

Bandaged and washed, I wait in one of the clinic stalls for Valencie to clear me to leave. I run my fingers along the long, pale ridges of skin on my arms. My fingers are wrinkly, and my skin is tender from scrubbing off the blood; every inch is rosy except for the scars. The Medic left no trace of the talons that shredded me or the fire that seared the wound shut. Pulling the collar of my standard issue Guardian t-shirt over my nose, I inhale the musty, plastic scent that clings to it from the bag it came in. It's better than the other smells of the clinic, but I still have to force the gurgle of acid down my throat.

The curtain shifts. My old Monitor, Officer Pellen, stands before me. Static fires up my spine. He holds my gaze as my mouth drops open. He was only twenty-five when we met, so he'd be almost thirty now. His eyes are still wide and kind.

He caries his weight around his stomach, some in his face, and maintains a clean shave. A sad smile crinkles his golden-brown skin. My hero, the one who got me back on my feet, told me truths, and didn't placate me. I am transported into my old skin, another hospital room, and shorter hair.

Dr. Valencie slips in beside Pellen and closes the curtain around us. "Adrianne," he says with a quick nod. "I've never seen a Guardian walk into this station on their own two feet after a beast wound like that."

My eyes are fastened on Pellen as Valencie sits in front of me to make a note on a clipboard.

"Glad I've found a way to impress you," I say. My monotone voice stops Valencie's pen.

I shift, bunching the sterile paper beneath me. "Why is he here?"

"I brought your Monitor in because in your records it says that you're unable to transform, and yet, your teammates inform me that—"

"You're supposed to contact me any time you experience a disturbance in your essence," Pellen says, the smile gone. He takes the seat next to Valencie.

The air in the small space is hot, and I fan my self with my shirt.

"Have you ever tried summoning?"

My eyes snap to Valencie. "What?"

"I did a few extra tests while doing your essence analysis, tests you wouldn't normally do for routine checks. There is an extraordinary amount of fau energy molecules in your essence."

The muscles in my face have a mind of their own. They twist my eyebrows and my lips part in the beginning of a snarl as I shake my head. "Yeah, I knew there was some fau, but—"

"An extraordinary amount, Adrianne." He turns the report to me, pointing at the measurement with his pen.

The number swirls in the sea of markings. I'll have to take his word for it.

"When we register essence level at seventeen years of age, the metres we use to test essence strength rely on the interaction between the core energy of the Karess and blood. Essence gives blood a specific energy profile based on the combination of jint, fann, or unama energy molecules in a hédin's system."

"Yes, I know. What does this have to do with anything?"

"Fau, primitive fann, doesn't charge the blood with energy, so we used to think that it had no purpose. Recent research has found that Beastbloods with a higher count of fau are able to transform and summon. They still have an affinity for one or the other, but the test only shows specific lineage affinities for Ironskins because their jint essence is in line with the jint core energy." Valencie taps his pen on his notes. "It says here that you've been able to transform your eyes in the past."

The attention of my ears shifts from within the curtained space to the wider clinic. It produces a physical shift in my body, like when I transform. The curtain is that dark veil, and I am aware of both Valencie and Pellen before me and a conversation between a Medic and a Guardian at the other end of the clinic.

Valencie squints and dips his head to catch my eyes. I nod.

"Each of our essential energies, mind, spirit, and essence, is active on its own," he continues. "Our bodies keep them physically contained together, but they are more powerful and stable when integrated. Essence abilities like the spirit affinities of the Ironskins, beast affinities, and energy-imprint sensing abilities of the Earthkin, and even Mind Fire, are more likely to act on their own, especially if there is a shift in mental or spiritual understanding. The essence will respond accordingly."

Understanding. Kind of like discovering a truth inside me—a Vow.

"Our spirits are like a riverbed." Pellen holds his hands out to face each other to make a winding river motion. "They direct where the water—or our essence—will go, how it will act. If you dig a new canal or unblock an old path, the water will flow that direction."

"What about my physical body? It feels like my heart stops when I transform," I say, rubbing my fingertips along my collarbone.

Pellen is a fire before me, burning my eyes. His mouth twitches. He must be able to fill in the gaps, that this isn't the first time I've done a transformation since the last time he saw me.

Taking the stethoscope from around his neck, Valencie motions for me to gather my hair away so he can check my heart sounds. "My understanding is that if your essence acts in a way that isn't aligned with your mind and spirit, there will be a split. To use the river analogy, the river is flooding over into the town, causing damage. Your heart doesn't stop, in fact, it's probably overworked. You just can't feel it because your spirit has jumped out of your body. You're evacuating your flooded town. You are more conscious of your spirit than your mind because the spirit realm, the Higher Plane, is layered over our physical reality. And if you stay too long in your beast transformation, your heart will eventually stop." Valencie checks over my charts again. "Slight murmur. That's new for you," he says and jots it down.

It's a fine balance, it seems. The transformation of my arms saved my life years ago, and I'm sure this transformation took some damage from the wound I obtained from the Alzuke. It's probably why I could stand on my own two feet coming in here. Partial transformation, protective. Full transformation, lethal.

"You're saying that my essence affinity is for summoning, not transformation?" I ask.

I could laugh if my lungs weren't so stiff, and my side wasn't so itchy. Some people believe in a continuous connection of mind and body, two inseparable parts of a whole. Some take to the body and spirit model, or no distinction of parts at all, just matter. But my dad was so invested in the research of the three vital energies model. Maybe it's exhaustion, or the way my parents raised me, whatever it is, I believe it. Every word makes sense.

But how could I not know what my affinity was? Transformation seemed obvious; my eyes make a clear transformation. Does this mean I'm not really Shadowless?

Sitting down and crossing his legs, Valencie twists one of the gold rings in his ear. "You're the only one who can really answer that question, but, yes, it is a possibility. If you were taught to use transformation techniques, then when your emotion is heightened, your essence reacts with that training. I'm sure there's someone at the academy that can teach you a few summoning techniques."

Or Dano. How would I even ask him? How would he react?

I shiver. Gathering my hair over my shoulder, I slide off the bed.

As I bend and wrap my wrinkly fingers around the plastic bag with my bloody clothes, holding my breath against the stench, Pellen says, "But before that, I think it's best if you take a few days at home."

I stop with my hair obscuring my face from his view. "I can't do that. I have to finish my clinical study."

"I agree with Officer Pellen," Valencie says. "I know Medics are always trying to scrounge up recommendations at this point, but I'm going to be straight with you." He stands beside me, bringing the pinching scent of medical grade hand soap into the aura of nervous energy around me. "I'm not giving you a recommendation. You'll pass clinical whether you finish your last week or not."

Pellen stands. "It's my professional opinion that you should take time to rest."

"No." I push aside the curtain, and as I walk out, my heart jumps into an erratic beat.

I haven't put my shoes on, so there's no satisfying stomp to accompany my storm. But the tread of Pellen's runners follows me.

"Adrianne, wait," Pellen says, grabbing my arm.

I yank myself free, pressing to the far end of the clinic with the scent of blood clogging my nose. The tap of Pellen's runners stays on my trail. "I think we need to reinstate Monitor checkups. But now that you're over twenty, you have to be the one to consent."

I whirl around and Pellen doesn't even flinch. "You're the one who said I was Shadowless." My hands shake at my sides. "A broken spirit."

A frown mars his face, drawing it long, and his shoulders drop, lowering to my level. "Oh, Adrianne," he says through a breath. "I never told you your spirit was broken."

"You didn't have to say it. Everyone else did." My voice

screeches out of me.

"I told you your *essence* might never be the same. There's a lot of misunderstanding of what Shadowlessness actually is. Essence is a physical part of us. Of course a near-death experience is going to affect it. But your spirit can't be broken, Adrianne."

I don't believe that.

I shake my head. Turning on the stone-cold ball of my foot, I march to the station lobby.

Tapping out a simple message for Marcus to pick me up, I sit in the lobby where I first came in. Blood pulses in my fingers as I grip my medkit in one hand and the plastic bag in the other. My eyes sting. I can't close them though. There's too much blood and too much darkness behind them. I can't let them rest until I can lie down and sleep.

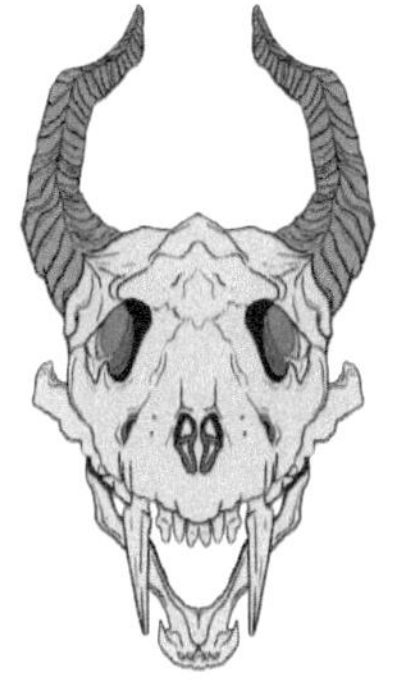

CHAPTER 19

I *CAN CLOSE MY EYES WHEN I GET TO MY ROOM.*

Lotic sits across from me by the window. His muffled sobs lick my ears like a heavy fog.

I want to cry. Maybe the tears would wash away the blood, and it wouldn't be dangerous to close my eyes. But tears are for sadness. How do I rid this body of its guttural hate? In my first year of Guardian training, I stepped to the line of death. Look at me now. Unable to live my life in accordance to my Vow— I'm a killer, a shit Medic. I've been using my essence all wrong without even knowing it. What else have I been doing that's been keeping me from living the way I'm supposed to? I thought I was doing it all right. Vera did it right. A noble Beastblood who took on the duties of a Guardian. Now she's gone. Is that it?

Sacrifice your life and you've lived well?

My fingers tremble, and I drop my bags to stick them in my ears. I hold my breath. Pressure builds against the echoing cries and crunch of bone between my teeth and the thud of Vera's body slamming to the ground. Cold seeps into the skin of my knees as if plummeting into snow. My stomach flips with a gripping spasm, and I heave a breath.

Hands are on my shoulders. I jolt, taking another, sharper breath and drop my hands as my head spins from the rush of air. Marcus kneels in front of me. A clammy heat breaks out over my neck.

"Adrianne, what happened?"

I stare into his deep-brown eyes. All I can do is shake my head.

Marcus runs his warm hands down my shaking arms. The friction soothes a bit of the tremor stemming from my heart. Leaning forward, his grip tightens, his eyes close, and his lips graze my cheek. The touch of blood still lingers there with the slick, metallic sludge on my tongue. I recoil, drawing in another breath to hold against the stir in my essence.

"Sorry," Marcus says. Letting go of me, he flexes his fingers as his eyes trail away. "Let's get you home." He helps me out of the chair with strong arms.

I let him steady me but not hold me. We walk close together to his cruiser. He opens the passenger door. I stare at the clean interior as my skin aches with grit and blood. Heat pulses on my back as Marcus nudges me to sit. I jerk away from his gentleness and cage myself in his cruiser, slamming the door shut.

Marcus ducks into the cruiser. Starlight washes over him as he sits still for a moment with his hands resting on his legs. The bright, orange scent he carries stings my lungs.

"Do you want to talk about what happened?" His eyes take in my hands going white at the knuckles and the bloody clothes in the plastic bag.

"No, just drive." My voice is husky.

Marcus opens a bottle of water sitting between us and hands it to me. "Well, I'm glad you're back."

"Yeah." I take a sip and stare straight ahead. The moisture on my tongue tugs at my eyes. *Not yet.*

Putting the firestone key in the ignition, Marcus says, "So, you know I've been talking to Brand."

I glance at him from the corner of my eye. He catches me and licks his lips. Leaning back in his chair, he takes the key back into his lap. Why won't he just drive?

"She says she might have a job for me." The space in the cruiser shrinks as he runs his hands along his knees, creating nervous energy that jolts through the air. A twist hits my gut. "It wouldn't be Guardian fieldwork, but she wants me to work with her in a private organization. Hasn't told me much about it. We have another meeting lined up though."

"That's fucking great, Marcus." The words bolt off my tongue. Their venom must be masked somehow because his face stays still in its neutral, angelic way.

Stay safe.

Marcus is safe, he's steady, and confident. But I'm not safe. The path I'm on, the way I've lived my life, it's wrecking me. Like my first year. The longer I stayed at the academy, not knowing where I fit in, not knowing what I wanted to do, let the depression sink deeper and the anxiety shred my nerves to bits. If I go home like Pellen suggested, then I've come full circle.

"Well, no, not really." Marcus runs his hand over his face. The bristles of his beard scrape his skin, and the sound is as loud as metal on stone. "I mean, the opportunity is great, but it would mean moving to a base in Sarr."

"I think you should do it." I try to dig for a sweet note in my voice, but it's all flat.

"What do you mean?"

The cruiser is still cold, the Guardian station still looming ahead of us. Out the side window, I spot Lotic stumbling out into the green glare of the night.

"It's no use sticking around here when there's a clear opportunity that would suit you somewhere else," I say.

Marcus shifts so his torso is facing me. His hands keep moving from his face to his knees. "I just . . . It's not that simple. I—"

"It is that simple. We do what we have to do to find our way."

"So, you're not at all . . . upset that I would be leaving?" The starlight reveals the quick rise and fall of his chest.

"No, and it's not like you need me."

No one really needs me. I wish I was Vera. I wish I could meet a quick death and stare at the sky in a peaceful daze in a pool of red. Then I wouldn't have to face the stress of finishing training. I wouldn't make people worry. I wouldn't be a disappointment to my family. But I can't tell Marcus that. He'd worry.

Marcus squeezes his eyes shut. With a heavy breath, he says, "Adrianne, I thought about you the whole two days you were gone. I checked the Guardian casualty report and saw a death on your team. My heart stopped."

"It's not fair, Marcus. It's not fair that I can't get out of this academy barely scraping past death's door. So, take this job that showed up on a silver platter for you and go. You might never get another chance like this."

"It wasn't handed to me. I worked with Brand, and we came to an agreement."

"A few little conversations and just like that, wow, a new job!" My voice pitches high and a vile chuckle slips off my lips, using up all the clean air in the cruiser that would order my thoughts. "Every choice I make, if it's even a little out of line from the norm, comes back to bite me in the ass. My teaching methods, defying Karf's orders to try and keep us safe, my own Vow."

"Why are you being like this?" Marcus slaps his hands on the steering wheel. He could have slammed them, and I wouldn't have flinched, but he just holds the wheel, to keep his control.

"Why the fuck did you think it was a good time to bring this up?"

His keys jingle as he shoves them in the ignition again. "I–I don't know, I was just making conversation. I wanted to talk to you."

My side stings, and I squirm in the small space as heat fills me from head to toe. I shove my bag off my lap and roll down the window.

"You're the only one I want to talk to," Marcus continues. "Zenta, this doesn't come easy for me. I don't have the regular romantic feelings for people just like that. I feel something for the first time. For you, Adrianne. I want you to let me in, tell me what's going on, but you didn't. I thought if I went first, it would help."

One of his hands stretches into the space between us.

Everything about him is strong, from his gaze to the hard planes of muscle along his arms to his words. Today it is stronger. The openness. His outstretched hand. I could reach for it, any time, any place, and he wouldn't let me fall.

His openness is beautiful. It's been gradual and sweet as we've been able to be together this year. But there is no prettiness in the thoughts that break into the static of my mind. Damn it. He should back off. I'm terrified of him seeing me fall back into a dark place. I'm scared it will hit so hard I won't get up again. What I've been longing for with him has finally come to be, and it stings like salt in the festering wound in my soul.

"Just take me back to the academy."

If I were standing, his sigh would blow me over. His shoulders are slumped as he manoeuvres out of the station parking lot and onto the motorway.

"Are you sure? Maybe it would be good to take some time away. I have an extra room. My apartment's just a few blocks away on Weckler Drive."

I throw my arms in the air. "I just want to fucking sleep!" I yell, and the sound shatters the tension in me.

"You do this all the time," Marcus says. He shakes his head and clenches his fists. Lines carve in his forehead and right into my heart. "You let things build up inside you. Then you take it out on other people. It's not fair for you to take it out on me." A pause stabs into the cab. "And you can't take it out on yourself either."

"Just take your job and leave me the fuck alone. I don't want to think about my own shit or process anyone else's."

Marcus' whole body is tense like a statue. I face forward as the cruiser rumbles to a stop outside the academy. My pack is ten times heavier, and my bloody clothes are putrid as I gather them and slam the cruiser door behind me. It's always back-and-forth with me. Hot, cold. Numb, angry. Understanding, jackass. No middle ground. No rest. No direction.

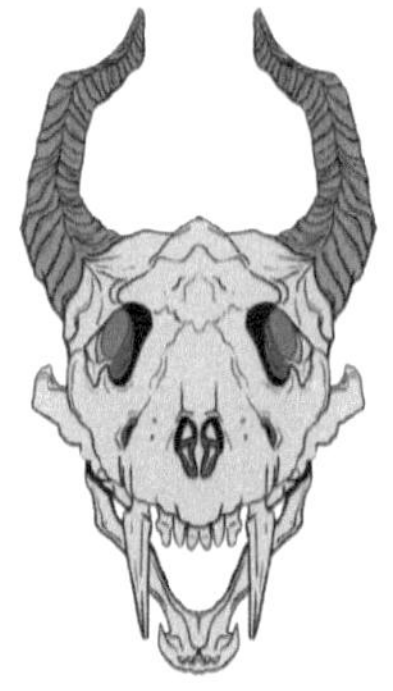

CHAPTER 20

I ALMOST DIDN'T GET OUT OF BED THIS MORNING. It was quiet there. But I'm here at my clinical, going to finish strong, like my dano. He experienced a death on his squad when he did his fieldwork. He kept going. And even though my heart is revolted by my awful words to Marcus, and my head is reeling from the possibility that I might be able to summon, I'm here.

The skin on my stomach is still pink. I turn side to side, and it stretches with a pinch, pulling at the other cells that aren't so new. The raw flesh takes in the touch of my hand with a curious prickle, like it's wondering why there are scars, salty sweat, and dirt on my skin. It's baby skin. It doesn't know how hard this world is.

I put a dressing over it to keep it clean; it doesn't hurt, but it's just a little too sensitive to have my Medic uniform rubbing against it. Pulling on my shirt, I take a full breath to expand my lungs to capacity—five counts won't do it today. The skin of my body that is hard with callouses and tense muscle shivers with lingering sensations of beast breath and blood.

Swallowing hard, I slap my hands on my thighs to get my blood flowing. Stamping my feet, the other Medics whisper around me. I wonder if Eila had fieldwork as fucked as mine. If she did, I can't tell. She doesn't seem to have ghosts in her head or a garbage bag full of clothes sodden with blood. She's serene, chatting with a senior Medic across the room.

Shaking my head, I slap my legs again.

I have a few minutes to spare, but I leave the locker room before I get stuck. Every beep of a monitor and call over the ampliphone system has extra volume today. They jostle my skull, giving me a headache. My steps are slow but determined. The hall to the clinic is longer than I remember. The shadows between patches of fluorescent lights pull at me. A janitor mops the floor, flooding my nose with disinfectant as he sloshes his mop back-and-forth. Back-and-forth. Wiping all the dirt away.

The air around me has an odd shift to it, like there's more space between molecules. My blood goes heavy with ice. Something twists inside me, cranking my muscles to move faster to the clinic.

The second I step through the door, Dr. Levis shouts, "I need help over here!"

I sprint to the furthest stall in returns.

A Medic straddles the bed, giving chest compressions to a Protector in cardiac arrest. Another stands at the Protector's head with a ventilator, and Dr. Levis' hands glow in bright white light over the man's exposed chest. I swallow, but my throat is numb. Dr. Levis turns to me, hands still outstretched and pulsing.

"McCarthy, trade off chest compressions."

My brain pings with a jolt of adrenaline. I come up next to the Medic on the bed. He makes eye contact with me, and I nod. The Protector's pale skin is bright red. The ventilator hisses and Levis' manipulation makes everything waver in its energy. All that fades as I climb onto the bed for better leverage and set my fist over the man's chest. I press down hard, engaging my whole body. The skin is hot and sweaty.

I press again and again. I match my breaths to the beat, so I don't forget to breathe. All I know is my hands and the crunch of bone inside the man's body. Dr. Levis shouts commands. My ears only listen to the ones that concern me.

"McCarthy, switch off."

I drop off the bed, panting. My arms hang away from my sides, shaking, and I swipe away sweat. Heart clambering in my chest, I count a five-second breath, but that breath splits into two, and by five seconds, I've taken well over ten breaths. They swim in my head, turning to hot gas in my chest.

Two-hundred compressions go by in an instant.

"McCarthy." The voice sloshes through my brain.

I'm back on the bed, pumping the Protector's heart.

More Medics arrive, and we cycle through compressions. The moments between contact with the patient are cut from my mind. I am mechanical.

"Time of death, 9:24 a.m.," Dr. Levis calls out. "McCarthy, it's done. There's nothing more we can do."

A hand is on my shoulder, pulling me away from the dead man.

I slap the hand away.

They resuscitated me. I'm still here. I didn't even try with Vera. And this guy? We just stop trying? I'm not an idiot. I know we're not miracle workers, and essence manipulations can only get us so far, but I don't know if I can be this close.

I press again, but the man's chest doesn't move. My arms bend at the elbows, and I collapse on one arm, the dead man breaking my fall. Sliding off the bed with a few other Medics bracing me, a murmur shuffles through my brain. None of the Medics' mouths move.

"Thank you."

The murmur rings through me. Weight plummets in my stomach as a heat drifts past my face.

I'm delirious, exhausted.

"Get the fuck off me." I shove away the hands supporting me.

Valencie stands outside the stall. He slips his glasses off his nose with a crinkle infesting his brow. "McCarthy, a word."

Hand clamped over my eyes, pressing at the ache in my temples, I set my other hand on my hip as tears churn in my eyes.

Everything that usually soothes me is useless. No breathing, no focus, no running can fight my heart pounding to be free with a slight extra pulse in each beat. Tears stream down my cheeks, and I brush past Valencie. My lips part, and a stream of hot air slips out with the pinch of a silent scream.

"Adrianne."

My feet keep moving, through the doors into the hall, walking right over the janitor's clean floor. The moment I turn the corner, I stop my feet. One hand on the wall, my body trembles. As I shake, the tears sprinkle the ground. My knees go weak. I shudder all the way down to the ground, head spinning.

"Would you leave us for a moment?" Valencie says softly to the janitor.

The janitor's footsteps fade down the hall, and Valencie crouches down in front of me, his white coat falling over his knees to touch the floor. As he braces his elbows on his knees, hands clasped between them, Valencie is quiet. It's the quiet that draws my face away from my hands. Quiet I've been craving.

Minutes pass and he doesn't budge. Not even the sound of his breaths meet my ears. The quiet attunes my attention to the weight inside me. It's like the girl I was in first year who just wanted to quit, to sleep, to just be and simultaneously not be for one second. The girl I've always been has crawled out of the cell I locked her in. I take her hand.

"I'm still going to pass if I skip out on clinical this week?" I ask without hiding the thick sob that accompanies my voice.

"Yes. Would you like me to arrange a pay cruiser to take you home?"

"Can you call Officer Pellen instead?" I whisper, wiping the tears from my face with the heel of my hand.

"I'll arrange for him to pick you up from the academy," Valencie says. "Grab your things and head on out."

I stay on my knees for a moment until he's out of sight.

The beast, Vera, this Protector whose name I don't even know. All this death is part of the job I signed up for. And I've even gotten better, more confident in my work. I know everything I need to know, everything I need to do, and I do it well enough. But once a living, breathing hédin is facing Carnity's Gate, I don't know if I can be the hand they let go of.

Nana Atherie would tell me not to cry. Dano would tell me

to keep my head up high, to continue working for the greater good. Matta would get me to help her with beading or work in the garden because she grew up with them, and that's how she learned to deal with her pain. She got more clients when Dad went to prison, she made bread for the neighbours every week. She got up early in the morning and went to bed late. None of those things work for me, and I can't make them.

CHAPTER 21

PELLEN AND I SIT IN HIS CRUISER outside my house late in the evening.

"Are you ready to go in?" he asks.

Hugging my backpack on my lap, I sink my chin to lean on it. Beyond the hood of the cruiser, my childhood home waits for me, crawling with ivy. My garden rings around the left side, and the hill into the forest cradles the right. There is a cast of frost forming on the scattered leaves at the base of the front steps. I rarely take the time to look at it from this angle. Inside was always where the magic happened. It held my family. It's where we ate and laughed and communed with each other, wrapped in all the beautiful colours my matta chose.

I clear my throat. "Sorry you had to go out of your way to

do this." Pellen is quiet, and his lack of words prickles inside me. "Sorry for yelling at you at the clinic."

"This is my way, Adrianne," Pellen says. His voice is soft, like cotton on my ears. "I work with one person at a time so there's room to make runs back-and-forth to people I haven't worked with in years. I work with people who scream at me and swear at me all the time. It's the hardest thing I've ever done, but I do it because it means that they've still got air in their lungs. And they're fighting to keep it there."

He turns to me, face glowing in the light of his smile, and pats my knee. My face is like putty. I'd have to force my fingers into it to get it to match his smile. I can't use up strength, though, not until I'm safely inside.

I open the door and struggle out of the cruiser with my bulky backpack. I stand for a moment in the crisp chill of my hometown, letting the pack fall to the ground. Pellen follows, hands in his pockets, gravel crunching beneath his feet. I take a few steps to the garden, dragging my bag behind me. The energy suckles are as brilliant as the sun.

Matta is always the energy in our house. Dad and I found little pockets to share with each other, but for the most part we followed Matta's lead. When I came back home first year, I planted all these flowers. They were my contribution to our eclectic home. I only had the idea and the willpower to plant them because I'd rested.

"I really am fighting." The words crack out of me.

"I know."

Drawing a breath, my body sinks heavier on my heels. I'll rest again, here in the quiet of Neejaan. In the quiet Valencie gave me, I found respect when I was looking for approval. In all aspects of my life, that's what has driven me—other people's opinions. Now I don't know what I really want and who I really am. If I keep pushing, my heart and my essence will become too dysregulated, and who knows which will kill me first. If I rest, maybe I can get up the strength to ask Dano to help me.

"It's still empty," Pellen says.

"What?" I lift my gaze from the golden flowers.

"This plot in the corner. When we dug this garden together, you said you wanted to keep this space for something specific."

Bits of frost melt through my canvas shoes as I cross the yard to where Pellen stares at the hard, empty earth.

"I wanted to put a rillia bush there."

Pellen acknowledges the sentiment with a low hum. "Why is the bush important to you?"

Letting my head hang back, I take in the stars above. "The colour of the blossoms reminds me of something I saw." The vast, misty blue of the Lesser Worlds. I think it was the Lower Void. As the shape of a pale-blue rillia blossom blooms in my mind's eye, the disembodied 'thank you' I heard in the clinic passes with it. "Do you think we can hear spirits in the Beginning? Like ones that have passed on from here?"

"We? No not we. You maybe. If you're asking, then you probably do hear them."

"You're not gonna put this in your psych report?"

Pellen chuckles. "Nope. But I am going to order you to get inside. It's freezing. I'll check in at ten tomorrow." He swings his keys around his fingers.

My gut twists. "Actually, can we make it in the evening?"

"Sounds good," he says, giving me a quick hug. "I'm glad you called."

As Pellen leaves, the door to the house creaks open, letting out a ray of light and a gust of sweetly perfumed air to greet me as I fall into my matta's arms. She presses a long kiss to my forehead, her fingers trailing through my hair. Gathering me inside, she sits me down with a massive cup of rose tea.

I squeeze a drop of honey into it. Tears prickle my eyes as I stir it in.

"Do you want to talk about it, sweets?"

"No," I say without missing a beat. "Not yet."

Why does this refusal to give her information make my bones as strong as steel even as she frowns at me? I dip my nose to my tea. The steam layers over my cheeks in a sweet spiderweb. The tea warms my tongue and washes through me like a wave. Matta's hand settles on my knee under the table.

The fight with Marcus surges back into my mind. Every time it replays, it sinks a lump further into my stomach. With Marcus, I kept it all to myself because I didn't want him to see the failures I despise so much.

I take in Matta's face and the brown hairs going grey at the edges. She wears a silk night-robe with roses on it; I think Dad bought it for her. Sewing supplies are scattered all along the kitchen counters behind her, and there's a mannequin with half her bust covered standing in front of the icer.

In first year, I never told Matta I was struggling because she was dealing with Dad's trial. I found it easy to listen to Matta as she expressed her concerns. It was easy to empathize with Marcus' experience in the Guardian system, and easy to care for his struggles with his god. I don't express my feelings because they always feel less important than someone else's pain. I keep it inside until it hurts enough, and then it's too late. Or the opposite. I express too much in a way that hides the truth. I get mad instead of telling people why there was even an emotion to begin with. I guess it's only easy to take someone's burdens until you've pushed your own down too far that they spill onto them at the wrong time.

Expressing myself and my needs will come with time—I'm out of practice and too tired. I know Matta will try to make the situation better. I have so much love for her, but right now, Matta doesn't get to make things shine. Because I don't think I've fully grasped everything I need to from this string of events that has the pillars of my world crashing down. I thought my problems were less important than others, but they're only less important when looking through a lens outside of myself. So I get to look at them and feel them first. This moment is for me.

I drain my cup, and Matta takes it from me to wash. I follow her to the sink and wrap my arms around her from behind. The one pillar left standing.

The floor creaks as I cross the kitchen. Eeny weaves through my legs, and I stop to pet her. She's longer and thicker, but her fur is still fluffy with kitten fuzz. I hold my hand still for her so she can lick my fingers. Scooping her up, I stand, shut myself in my room, and kick off my shoes.

We crawl under my covers and sink into the familiar groove of the mattress. My spine clicks as it relaxes. Surrounded by stiffening joints and blurry vision, my heart's not a heart but a rock. A hot rock. Boiling lava. An angry monster writhing within me. No, a child throwing a tantrum. My heart's not a heart; it's a malfunctioning piece of machinery not working in the way it's meant to.

It sickens me how conscious I am of this depression because

it's been building for a while, and now that I see it, I can do something about it. It's so thick I could roll it in my hands like a lump of clay. These deaths I've experienced are a suffocating weight locking me in with this muck covering my heart.

I need to be here right now—slowly drowning, compacted under mistakes. Maybe sinking right to the bottom is where I'll collect all the pieces of myself. I'll make sense of all the horrors that have strung together on a wire of my life. One by one, they've slipped off and fallen into the dark because I couldn't hold them and mould them into something wearable. I have nothing to show for it. My younger self has been tugging me to rest all along so we could plant something new inside me this time.

It's been quiet for the last few days. Mostly I slept and studied the chapters I will miss for my Medic classes. But I only study at night after checkups with Pellen. My brain feels better with the dark; my eyes don't get so tired. Matta didn't push me to tell her what's in my head even though I know it's killing her. She's bound to have seen the Guardian reports and pieced together my return home.

Muffled chatter drifts to me from down the hall. As I blink the sleep from my eyes, soft, orange light sifts through the opening between my drapes, and the conversation in the kitchen is just as heated. I roll out of bed, hair trailing me in a knotted sheet. The clock says 4:30 p.m. I take the brush from the drawer in my nightstand. If I'm going to make an appearance to someone other than my matta, I might as well take a moment to clean up.

I run the bristles of my brush through the ends of my hair.

It's not that I don't want someone else to see the knots—I just know I need a moment before I go out there.

The sunlight warms my hair as I continue to work upward. I brush from shoulder height to the ends in one long stroke, one long thoughtful stroke to take care of my hair. My fingers start to shake. Almost every strand has a break in it or a split. The ends are dry, and my roots are oily. You have to take care of long hair for it to be healthy. You get two different problems if you don't pay attention. Aside from washing and keeping it out of my way, I didn't care for it.

I split it into three sections and weave them together, slowing my fingers from their usual frantic manipulation to a peaceful rhythm. To my Beastblood Lineage, this long braid is a visual representation of an unspoken Vow. But to give such a Vow to me, my elders had to know how difficult and time consuming it would be. This braid is me.

My elders were urging me to take care of myself and find what I truly desired, not force me into a Vow I couldn't keep. Using pretty words and pushing myself through Medic training to get to an end. A badge to my name and more stressful jobs won't get me anywhere. Pellen said he works with one person at a time. I didn't realize how much ease that concept gives my soul.

I set my brush on top of my nightstand so it's the first thing I see when I wake up and the last thing I see when I go to sleep. As I make my bed, a pressure builds in my chest, tugging me out of my room. I press my hand over it, like it's something precious—pressure forming a diamond.

In the hall, I stop right in the middle. My nana's voice stings my ears from the kitchen, and behind me, images of my younger self line the gaudy yellow walls like a hug. As I stand in the liminal space between her and who I'm trying to be, a beam of orange light from my window grounds me. Air fills my chest. We're all the same person. With my exhaled breath, the tug grows stronger.

"Finally awake, I see." Nana stands right in the doorway with Matta behind her shaking her head and pinning her one breast clad mannequin. "When are you going back to the academy? You can't just sleep your life away."

I skirt past her, eyes low, and round the mannequin to the icer.

"Young lady, I think you need a refresher on the values of our people." Nana mounts her hands on her hips, shaking the gold hoops in her ears.

I take a long chug of orange nectar straight from the carton.

"We are not called Beastblood to indulge in savagery and sloth." Nana snatches the nectar. I grip the carton, but the condensation lets it slip out of my hands and a splash of bright orange hits the floor. "A beast is any being not hédin that has essence, so when we transform, we are beasts and when we are hédin we are not. The two work together to create fervour for life! Anipa, did you not pass down these values your father and I gave you?"

"Hey," I say.

My stomach turns itself over. I point a shaking finger at Nana. She recoils, her lips pursed. Every time I act on a gut instinct, someone gets angry and the earth beneath my feet seems to be turned over. The earth is disrupted, but you can't plant anything in untilled soil.

"Don't take this out on her. I'm the one you have a problem

with, so let's hear it."

"What has happened to you? It's like everything we've taught you to make a good life has gone into that head of yours and fallen right out."

Matta stands and brushes stray threads off her skirt. "Look, Adrianne is on her own path and just needs—"

"No, Matta, I've got this. I love you, but I've let you direct me longer than I needed you to."

Her eyebrows shoot up, and her lips curl into a smile as she takes a step back with her hands folded.

"Direction is what you lack, that's for sure. When will you make a Vow for your life?"

"I did!" I throw my hands in the air. My voice is full, and it sinks into the space around us, stretching to the far corners of the room. "I did Vow, and it made things worse. Besides, a Vow is for me, not for you, so I don't think you should get to know it."

It was right in the moment. It encompassed one part of me. I didn't want to hurt the Rover, I don't want to hurt anyone. But I've been hurting myself for so long by thinking that I could be as productive as my family hoped I would be, clinging to one idea of productivity.

Nana's lips work around the air I burned with my words. It must taste bitter, but she's given me so many bitter words to count without regard for how they could affect me. I don't mean harm by this, I don't mean to be disrespectful, but I just can't give her what is mine and let her try to regulate it.

There's a spark in her brown eyes, a nod from her head as she looks up at me. She turns in a slow half circle to the kitchen table and picks up the orange nectar. Handing it to me, she says, "Anipa, my bag, please."

Matta takes the leather purse from the back of a chair and hands it over, her chest held up tight like she's holding back a laugh. Nana's silks shuffle as she crosses the creaky kitchen floor, and the door clicks behind her.

Letting out her breath, Matta looks at me. My heart pounds in my ears. I take a swig of nectar, let the tang wash through my mouth, and I raise the carton to Matta. "I think that went well."

I head back to my room, with a chuckled, "okay," from Matta trailing in my wake. Tears trickle down my face. We've been in this situation before, a blowout resulting in someone walking out the door, and me crying. It's not me walking out first, though, and I think I've cleared up at least some of the blocks in my heart. Tomorrow, I'll talk to Dano—without breaking out comfort foods or spilling on the floor.

CHAPTER 22

THERE ARE WHITE ANTLERS painted on my grandparents' door in reverence for Fōsten and Annat'an. Above it is the silhouette of a panther in black for Dano's familiar, below, two lynxes in yellow for Matta and Nana's transformations. My eyes lock on the antlers. I don't want to yell; I want to share something with Dano. What to share? About Vera? My ability to project my beast form but not transform without splitting my being? I press my hands to my cheeks to warm them as the night cools.

It all swims in a sludge in my stomach, dissolved and mingling, not easy to separate.

Dano taught me the Fōsttimdato forms I still use today, and Nana taught me to transform. Maybe we can start there. I mark the sign of Fōsten with a finger over my head, then the sign of

Zenta, and Carnity's sign for good measure. Sucking in a five-second breath, I knock on the door.

It opens immediately, and Dano's large form steps into the starlight. I step back a little, adjusting my sweater.

"Hello, Adrianne." His voice wraps around me in a low, even tone.

"Hello, Dano."

His pause starts my armpits sweating.

"Your Nana told me what you had to say yesterday." This information lies in the air between us without an inflection of judgement. He turns to the side. Nana is behind him, gliding ancestral beads between her fingers. She holds her head up high and nods to me.

Dano clears his throat. "Would you like to come—"

"Practice Fōsttimdato with me."

A piece of gravel grinds under his foot, and a prickle trails down my spine. "Yes, of course," he says, and leads me inside.

I follow him down the long hall through the centre of the house. All along the walls are memories of Matta and me as we grew up. Matta's are in black and white and mine are in colour but still blurred by a finger in the way of the shutter of the memory tech or a glare of sunlight. I rub at the tug in my chest. Dano opens the door to the back patio, where I learned my first punch.

We've spent hours together in this court under the blistering sun and the cool, minty glow of the stars. Soon we'll celebrate the Festival of Two Moons. Every year, when our second moon comes into the sky, I used to ask him to train because I felt so powerful. My feet are familiar with every chipped tile, so Dano and I fall wordlessly into our warmup drill, with my back to the house so I don't have the light in my eyes. The hairs on my skin stand on end. Nana must be watching from the window.

I hold up my open hands and take a wide stance. Dano holds up the pads, and we get to work. We exchange combinations for ten minutes until I build up a sweat. Swallowing hard, I remove my sweater. My scars glow white in the dark. The thick ink lines of my tattoo are more aggressive than in daylight. Dano's heavy tread is like rocks in my ears as he turns his back to me and takes a few steps toward the house.

"It's hard for me to look at myself too," I say.

His is always the loudest voice in the room, but right now, he is silent.

"These scars are not lessons or curses. They just are."

Dano slowly turns to me, eyes still on the ground.

"I guess they're reminders. They remind me to be what I am. Even though I can shapeshift, I am not a shapeshifter."

Lifting his face to mine, his eyebrows furrow and a frown pulls on his wrinkles. "I don't understand."

"Neither did I. When I was little, transforming my eyes was easy, but trying to follow Nana and Matta's instruction to go any further was exhausting when it should've been exhilarating. With essence maturity, it's dangerous. I think I lost the ability to transform my eyes because . . . after trying to take my own life, my spirit put blocks on anything that might hurt me."

I pick at my nails. "My eye transformation came back before I left this year. I took a Vow. I think I was ready to see my true potential. It's just, I don't know, I was trying to achieve this potential in all the wrong ways."

Dano takes both my hands and holds out my arms in the space between us.

"When I transform more than one part of my body, I lose myself. Everything goes black, and I can't control it. I fully transformed during my fieldwork, but that was only because everything was going to shit. Sorry." I put my hand to my lips as Dano grunts. "It was all . . . No. It was shit. I was frantic. A doctor at the Guardian clinic told me it might be because I have a summoning affinity. The amount of fau in my essence makes it possible for me to transform and summon, or well, that's what he thinks might be going on. I think he might be right. Would you—"

Dano raises his hand. I jolt, ice flooding my veins, but Dano's hand stays put hovering at his side, silvery tears glinting in his eyes. A gust of wind wraps around us and a pure white light flashes under his palm. I throw my arm up to shield my eyes. As the wind dies down, every inch of my skin crawls, and I drop my arm. Before me, at my dano's side, stands Rahkanu, his panther familiar.

Settling his hand on Rahkanu's head, Dano says, "Summoning relies on your connection to yourself."

Rahkanu nuzzles Dano's large hand with his nose, and the tiles vibrate from his rhythmic purring. Dano kneels and motions for me to follow. I sit with my back straight, hands on my knees, and my essence running in cleansing bursts through my body. The body may have to regenerate essence molecules to fill our channels, but the base molecules, the ones inherited from mother to child, are everlasting. The essence that persists knows the shift isn't right for the rest of me, my spirit, my mind, but I didn't realize that until now. Even the potential to transform, to be great, to do marvellous things, will be corrosive if it's not what I need. Just the beginning of this lesson eases the tension in my stomach. All my energies know it is right to hear these words.

"When your connection to yourself grows or is threatened," Dano says, "you have greater capacity to summon because your familiar is a guide for you and is there because they chose your company."

Holding up my hand, I dart my eyes to Dano. He nods and I stroke my hand down the silky fur of Rahkanu's neck.

Dano rubs his hands together. "Before you left this year, I heard what you said. It challenges me. You challenge me to be better, to be kinder. Ever since the first time you flipped me on my back in this very courtyard, you've challenged me." The brightest smile reveals itself to me on his face, gapped teeth and all.

A chuckle releases from me. I scratch under Rahkanu's chin, and his white teeth glint as he raises it for me. I say, "That was the first time I met this beautiful boy."

"There won't be much I can teach you until you find a way to naturally connect with your own familiar. If a familiar has chosen you, they'll have shown themselves somehow. But you have to be willing to show yourself to summon them."

I stare at Dano and this magnificent animal before me. There is acceptance between us where there used to be dysregulation. Nana's bristling presence at the window reminds me that I am a challenge for both of them, just as Dano said. I can't expect her to bridge this gap so soon after I yelled at her yesterday.

Marcus told me he wanted me to let him in. I pushed him away because of fear. Fears about my failures, about my true self. But of all people, I feel like I can be open with him without scrounging up courage for words. Never once has he faulted me for swearing like Eila or Dano. Even if we don't share the same beliefs, we still encourage each other to build faith and persevere.

I brush away the tear that's made it halfway down my cheek. "Thank you, Dano. I think there's something I have to do."

Dano sets his hand over my tattooed shoulder. "Strength of the ancestors, my child."

My face scrunches, and I whisper another quick thank-you and throw on my sweater. My hair tangles through the arm and neck holes—but I can't move my fingers to undo it, not when they shake like I'm hopped up on caffeine. I bolt through the side gate to my cruiser.

C H A P T E R   2 3

Tʜᴇ ᴡɪɴᴅsʜɪᴇʟᴅ ɪs ɪᴄɪɴɢ from the cold outside and the heat expelled from my body. A cool sweat takes the heat's place, and tears and snot slime down my face. The person in the cruiser behind me honks as I swerve for the fifth time to wipe it away.

My heart bangs against my chest so hard it aches. Every deep shadow and bright light along the motorway is an affront to my sensitive body. I clutch one hand over my chest. It stings that a person I felt caged by all these years for their ideals on Vows and duty and direction is the one who has helped me clear the path to my self. We've released each other from our cages, I guess. The bars angered me, then I lashed out so many times that I wounded someone precious to me.

I was so shit to him.

"Shit!" I slam the steering wheel.

I may be a shit, but at least I can recognize it. At least I can admit there is something wrong. I have to admit it to Marcus, to tell him I'm sorry.

After an hour of reckless driving, I'm three blocks away from Marcus' street. My cruiser gives a low fizzling sound.

"Of fuck." It groans and slows. "No, no, no." I veer to the side of the road. The second the cruiser dies, I fling open the door and slam it shut with my foot.

I sprint, engaging every muscle, letting my feet pound the cobblestone, not worrying about how loud my ragged breaths are. I need all the air I can get. White clouds of breath burst from me and trail in my wake. At the corner of his street, a cramp hits my side like beast claws tearing through it. I yelp and clutch my side. I stumble to someone's fenced-in yard and crouch down, gasping for breath.

He won't want to see me. I was horrible to him and left without saying anything.

This is the way you are, and it doesn't have to drag you down.

Throwing up before heading off to school. So anxious I can't see straight. Being an ass to someone so kind. That's me? I slam my fist against the fence. It's like my body resists the choices I've made. Something's not right about me or the choices.

The resistance, it tells me something. It shows me when the two halves of myself are breaking apart. In situations where I know there's something not right, the choice isn't the problem, it's why I make the choice. Be a Medic to make my grandparents proud, to show other people I can do it? Or be a Medic because it was the first thing that sparked a fire inside me? I get sick when I try to do things I don't really want to do, when I have somehow spun other people's expectations too deeply into the choice. It's the same resistance my essence has against my beast form. It's not right for me.

A flash of a cruiser's headlights refracts through my tears, and they wash down my face.

No shame, sweets.

All this time, Matta was just trying to get me to forgive myself for being me. For being imperfect. Forgive myself for not letting her love really get to me. Forgive myself for my darkest times. And forgive myself for not listening to myself.

No shame, sweets.

No shame, Adrianne. I'm sorry for hurting you. I know I do it every damn day. Please forgive me.

The torrent of breaths still inside me. I count them. One breath bites the cracks on my chapped lips. The second burns through my nose. Breath three deflates in my lungs and rushes out too fast. Four spills out all my poison. And five brings in air. Just air. The next breaths don't need counting.

I brace myself on the fence and take a shaky step. With a few more uneasy steps, I settle into a jog, searching for Marcus' cruiser. The tension that pushed my legs to sprint has dripped away. I think I'm ready for Matta's positivity. All those choices I've made run through my mind in her voice.

Punching Johanna means you're not afraid to try new methods, sweets. Using Dawnranfet means you're adaptable. Defying Karf means you look out for the best for your team even though it means going against a superior's orders. Trying to Void Watch means you're not willing to give up on yourself.

I find Marcus' clunky, green cruiser parked outside a plain two-story apartment building. Someone is just leaving, and I snatch the door behind them before it closes. With a shaking finger, I search for Marcus' name on the panel with apartment numbers. My heart pulses a heady rush of blood through my body as I find it, and I lunge up the stairs.

My mess fills the small hallway to Marcus' apartment. My breaths bounce off the walls, the smell of sweat oozes off me, and my hair is a messy halo around my head. But I knock.

I squirm with each passing second. Maybe he's not home, or if he is home, I should leave. Maybe I'm too raw to do this. I've just jumped to another drastic measure to dispel the ache inside me. Swiping my face with the ends of my sleeves, I stop wondering. Raising my hand to knock again, a crash sounds from inside.

"Marcus," I call, moving my ear closer to the door.

The answer I get is a grunt. I try the handle and the door opens. At my feet is Marcus' echo with the case broken off, and his keys are a few steps away. I push the door open all the way. The small table that I assume held his keys and echo lies on its side, and Marcus leans on it trying to get up, his bad leg stretched out stiff.

"Marcus, what happened?"

Marcus looks up, his eyes wide, taking in the girl who took a big, sloppy bite out of his heart. His eyes shudder as he winces in pain and collapses back down to the floor. I rush over to him, dropping to my knees.

Taking a laboured breath through his teeth, he says, "I was coming to the door, and my leg just gave out. I've been having pain all day."

"Here, let me help you." My voice is scratchy and quiet.

I move to him, but he holds up a hand.

"I've got this." He presses off the ground, but as he goes to put pressure on the leg, the muscle seizes, visible even through his sweats.

"Ah, sh . . . "

"Shit, Marcus. You can say it."

His face pinches with pain and a curt laugh. I wrap my arm around his waist and put his arm around my shoulder, supporting him on his bad side. His torso is firm and sweaty in my arms. I stand and he leans his weight on me. Slowly, we stagger to his room, and I help him onto his bed.

Just as I prop his leg up with a pillow, it seizes and Marcus groans. I cringe at the sound.

A tear slips from his pinched eyes. "It's so bad. It's like the essence is being sucked out all over again." He pants and clutches his leg.

"The essence channels are deteriorating. I can only imagine the pain you're going through. Your doctor should have given you something for the pain."

"He did," he says between breaths. "I just didn't pick it up." Marcus flops back, both hands hiding his face.

He probably didn't have the time or energy to pick it up. With me taking the week off, I'm sure he's done more with the team than normal.

You're a fucking asshole, Adrianne.

I shake my head. Yes, it's true I didn't think how this would affect him, how any of my actions would affect him, but I needed the rest. It brought me back here, and I'll make it right.

Ice helps overactivity in essence channels, but the opposite is true for deterioration. I take a breath, attempting to calm my heart enough to connect with the flow of my essence and trap enough in my palm to plate it with a small projection. Armour would be too hot. The plate radiates a subtle warmth, and I press it to Marcus' thigh. He sucks in a quick breath with a jolt through his whole body.

"Shh," I say, resting one hand on his shoulder and squeezing gently.

His chest heaves and he lets one hand drop.

"I didn't mean it," I say.

"What?" he says with a release of breath.

"Any of it. I'd hate it if you left. At least if I made you hate me before you left, it would be easier for one of us."

"Nothing you do could make me hate you." His voice isn't the usual smooth rumble that stirs my heart, but thick with emotion and pitched higher, almost panicked. "I've always cared about you. Always have, always will."

I want him to move his hand so I can see his eyes while he says it. But I haven't apologized yet. He may care, but he's still wounded. His body sinks deeper into the pillows, the tension in his leg releasing with the heat of my projection.

"I'm sorry I pushed you away." I drop my eyes as they prickle. Shaking out one hand as the projection wanes, a cloud of smoke twists between us, and I keep talking even as the tears fall free. "I'm sorry I didn't share what was bothering me and then lashed out. You knew what I was doing. What I always do."

Marcus' rough hand wraps around my wrist. Outside, a siren wails, and inside, deep inside, my heart screams.

"My comrade died during my fieldwork. There wasn't anything I could do with bandages or curestones." Prying my left hand away from Marcus, I make another projection and press it to his leg. "I tried to stop us from making the journey across the ice-wastes because the scientists had a Death stone that would attract the beasts in the area. I should have tried harder to convince my Commander to delay the mission. Or maybe if I hadn't argued with Karf, we would have been on our way, and Vera would have had time to warn us of the beasts."

Glancing up, Marcus' eyes finally find mine. They're bloodshot and puffy, but they're still the same kind eyes I love.

"When I got back and went to clinical, a patient died right under my hands."

My face is slack, and there's a pull inside me to cry, but it's just another expectation that I should emote in a certain way. Marcus tugs at my hands. I release the projection. It's all out now—my confessions, my tears—and my back can't support the weight of my body. Marcus tugs me again, and I crawl into him, leaning my head on his chest.

"I'm sorry," he whispers into my hair before pressing his lips to my forehead.

He wraps his arms around me, stroking my hair like I'm still something precious to him, someone to be forgiven. I cling to him, and he clings to me, two halves of a very dark place.

CHAPTER 24

THE TIME WE SPEND WRAPPED IN EACH OTHER, my hand on his chest and his fingers tangled in my hair, pulling me close like I might drift away, is uncountable. I'm thankful for his strong arms, because I really might drift away.

I told myself at the beginning of the year that I didn't want to hide anymore. Those events that I used my matta's voice to transform, like punching a student in the face, are where I stood on my own two feet. I've let other people's reactions push me into confinement and push myself to do what's expected of me. But that cancels out my efforts to reveal myself. I have to challenge myself to not give in. Being open with Marcus and receiving who he is might help me learn to do that with my familiar. No, first it will help me do that with myself.

With the moment drawing longer, my stomach growls. Marcus' chest vibrates with a chuckle.

"I'll make us something to eat," he says, sitting up and bringing me with him. Giving me a quick squeeze before he slides off the bed, a smile creeps to my lips as I lean into him for one more second, humming a note of pleasure from his closeness.

Standing slowly, he tests the strength of his leg. With most of his weight on his right leg, he pads across the room in his socks and sweats, shirt crinkled. I blush behind him. I almost lost the chance to see him like this—soft and dishevelled. I lean over to finally take off my shoes and make my way back to the door to set them out of the way, all the while taking my first real look at Marcus' apartment.

The walls are a light grey. The bed has a simple metal frame with white sheets. Only one lamp by the bed to read the neatly stacked books, one dresser for clothes, shoes lined by the door. There may be only one lamp, but he has two nightstands, one on each side of the bed. My cheeks heat again. What would it be like to have my own lamp on that side to read beside him? I shake the thought and turn the table in the entry way back on its feet and set his keys and echo on top.

In the kitchen, Marcus has bread toasting, and he is chopping vegetables. The kettle sings with two mugs waiting beside it. I sit at the round, wooden table.

The night sky casts a green glow over his living room—just a brown leather couch, a coffee table, and a white rug. A plant takes the place of a vision tech in the corner. The only thing out of place is his tote bag thrown on the floor. There's no excessive energy in this home—he is the energy, and there is still room for me.

As I pull my knees to my chest, Marcus sets a piece of toast on my plate with the nut spread I told him to buy once.

"You got the spread," I say.

"Yeah, I think I'm addicted." He smiles to himself as he pours our tea. But it slowly fades. "I was nervous to tell you about Brand's job offer."

I scoff. "No wonder," I say, scrunching my sleeves in my hands, my stomach dropping.

Marcus brings his cup to his lips and the tea quivers inside. His throat bobs as he swallows. Setting down my piece of toast, I clasp my hands between my legs to listen. His eyes flick to me and back down to his tea.

"I didn't think you would get mad. I wasn't really thinking at all. I was just excited. Excited to be with you, excited to tell you."

My chair creaks under me as I shift with heat crawling up my neck.

"If I had thought about it, I would have been able to see that it wasn't a good time. I would have been able to see that you needed space." He's quiet for a moment, a light smile taking over his lips.

"Are you going to take Brand's job offer?"

"I don't know. I'd still like to work with her, I believe in the work she's doing, but I kind of like what I'm doing now. Teaching the advanced team grew on me so fast."

"Do you think that the All Creator is calling you to one or the other? Both maybe?"

As he stretches his legs under the table, his calf touches my shin. It rests there. "I thought I was best suited to serve my community through Guardian work because that's the way the

All Creator made me. Now I just think he'll be happy to see me happy. I find happiness supporting those idiots on the advanced team, and I think I could enjoy teaching the students that come after them too."

I snort. "They're such precious idiots, aren't they?"

Marcus laughs. The sound gives me permission to move again.

"Are you going to come help teach tomorrow?" he asks. "Brand's got them doing these intense drills, and we could really use an extra person."

"Yes, I will be there."

I take a bite of toast and he munches on a carrot.

"I don't know how Johanna still has her head. I thought Rin would have torn it off by now. Or you would've," he says.

"You've seen all my finest moments, haven't you?" I say, holding my mug to my cheek to hide my flush.

"I have," he says, slowly slipping his fingers around my free hand.

He strokes me with his thumb. My eyes are magnetized by the motion, and the sensation of his skin on mine sends a tingle up my arm. The beat of my heart picks up, like it's a fist rapping on a door.

"What you said in the cruiser," I say slowly, "that you don't have the normal romantic feelings. What did you mean by that?"

Marcus leans his head on his hand, eyes gazing off to the side. "It's hard to explain. Remember when you thought I was asking you out on a date?"

I nod, sending more pressure into my fingers around his.

"For a lot of people, it makes sense, you know, to ask someone on a date. But for me, even if I find someone attractive in some way, the idea of being romantically involved is separated from it. I dated a bit in basic ed because that's what people do, and I was encouraged to date by my family. It always felt like there was something missing though."

So maybe it was a practiced speech. He knew he had to say something when I got embarrassed, and he had it prepared. This is something he's had to learn and let grow into his life.

"I had a girlfriend once. She was smart, beautiful, funny, and we got along well. But the relationship didn't feel right to me for a long time. It was like I was playing a role in a play. I only started to feel a real connection after months of dating. I started to really want to take her out on dates, and pick up foods she would like, or make sure I said goodnight to her over a message. I think we both wanted to be in a relationship the whole time, but I was meeting her in a friendship mindset for most of it, and she was meeting me in a romantic mindset. The two are on the same level of importance to me, but for her, it didn't feel that way."

"My dad says that Emberstead people are very passionate about love," I say.

"Yeah." Marcus' eyes drop to the table. "And I am too. People don't see that in me though."

"I do." I shake his hand so he looks at me. "You telling me not to be embarrassed was one of the most passionate things I've ever heard. You gave me a chance to put expectations down and just see you and myself."

Marcus' eyes trail my face, lips parting, muscles in his jaw relaxing.

"I . . . " It's on the tip of my tongue. After being buried so long, it's become too heavy for my lips to speak. I squeeze

Marcus' hand hard and shut my eyes. Behind my eyelids, with only Marcus to grasp, I see myself with Pellen, the one person I would call a hero. "Marcus, I want to be a Monitor."

"I know." His hand matches my grip.

"I don't know if I can do it though."

"You're exactly the kind of person who makes a good Monitor. Someone who cares for the physical, mental, and spiritual state of a person, who can meet them where they are so they can grow and take control of their lives."

My breath catches in my throat. He paints a different picture of me, walking a path that has always been an option, but I was too afraid to take it. Even though we sit beside each other, it feels like he's given me a hand up, up from the bottom of a dark pit where I've let myself collect, and I'm finally ready to stand.

"Thank you," I whisper.

We finish our nut toast and veggies in silence, sipping tea and stealing glances. After we're done, he washes the plates and I dry them.

"Is there still something missing between us?" I ask, my eyes hooked on the motion of his hands.

They are precise with all his movements, and I can't seem to look away. If I look away from them, I'll look at his mouth. My beastly mouth will want to caress his face, my clawed hands will want to touch his. I stack the dishes in the cupboard as fast as I can and turn away.

My feet take me to the living room as I chew on my thumbnail. Marcus' energy follows me, full and warm. I turn back around, and he's right there looking down at me, his dark skin glowing in the dim light and his eyes sparkling.

My heart pounds, shaking my breaths. He steps closer,

sliding his hand up my neck to my jaw. Eyes fluttering closed, I lose the sound of my heart. All I know is the strength of his hand cupping my face. Whiskers graze my skin, then the soft velvety touch of his lips releases my breath. Up my jaw and down my neck, he trails sweetness over me. I drink in the smell of his skin.

"There's nothing missing," he whispers.

His lips find mine. I lean in, pressing my body to his, wrapping my arms around his neck. His mouth opens and closes as he breathes into me. Delightful sounds send shivers down my spine as I circle kisses around his lips. An ache sinks inside me, following his hand from my waist to my hip.

My back arches, trying to keep my lips on his. Cradling me with one arm, he braces the other on the couch as he lowers us down. His muscles tense as he tries to keep some of his weight from me. But I pull him, and he relaxes into me.

The kisses come faster, easy now that we've rehearsed enough. A smile lifts my face as Marcus leaves a trail of wet kisses along my collarbone. He sighs with my hands under his shirt, sliding along hard muscle and smooth skin.

"Do you want to go further?" I ask into his ear.

His kisses slow, coming back up my neck, and he rests his lips on my chin. "I'm not there yet, I'm sorry. I'm not sure if I will get there."

My heart swells around this patient man and my arms follow, hugging him tightly. I don't mind if he never gets there. "We don't need to go anywhere but here."

Placing one last kiss on my lips, he lays his head on my chest. My heart pounds right under his ear. Arms tucked around me, breaths slow and steady, his eyes fall closed.

From this angle, the contents of his tote bag on the floor next to the table are revealed. Two balls of new yarn and a crochet hook bring a smile to my face. That shirt he wore the night we went to dinner comes to mind. I drag my nail in a circle over Marcus' shoulder and he shivers. "You make your own clothes."

His heavy breath heats my chest. "I make one piece of clothing for myself and everyone thinks I'm Mr. Fashion Man."

"Well, you do look very fashionable when you wear it," I say with a laugh. "What are you making now?"

"My cousin's having a baby, so I'm making a blanket for them."

"Can you teach me to crochet?"

"Sure, in a minute though." His voice fades into me.

I stroke his cheek and let my own eyes shut. In the stillness, the beat of Marcus' heart matches mine.

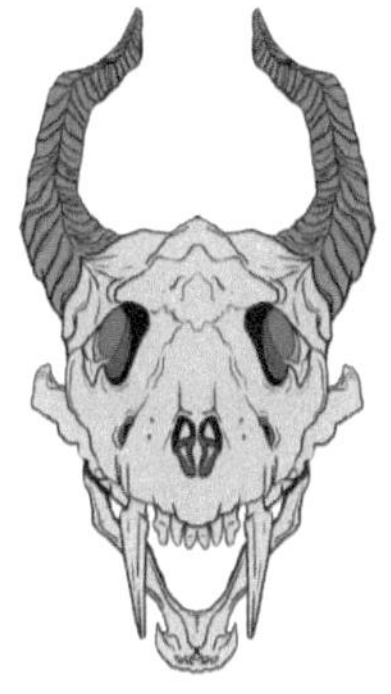

CHAPTER 25

THIS DAMN TRAINING ROOM DOESN'T BREATHE. Frost covered the campus this morning, but this room traps any morsel of heat. Maybe the heat is just coming from me. Everyone's focus is cutting as I try to resituate myself back into this world after being at home.

Brand's been pushing the team hard with the drill where they carry Marcus to the library. She's added a few more aspects to it though, a rope climb, carrying a dummy, dagger throwing, and ending with a one-on-one duel with an instructor. Each of us, Brand, Hans, Marcus, and I will take on one of them, and we've brought two other instructors in as well. I did it with them once before my fieldwork, but as they shuffle into the training room with Marcus holding his arms over his chest like a corpse,

I can't hold back a chuckle. They set him down and then burst into a sprint to their individual lanes to six climbing ropes. They are silent except for their clattering feet and huffing breaths.

Pain runs through my head. I rub my temples as I wait for my part in the drill. Five days away, sleeping through the day and studying at night, has my body moving slowly. It is good to be back, despite the heaviness of my heart, and I want to pay closer attention to training with this team, without the obsession of getting a recommendation or worrying about who's watching.

I stroll by the team as they climb the ropes. Jeff-Ray pulls himself up, hand over hand, in a methodical, smooth motion. Niko and Ace alternate shuffling their hands up and then their feet, the ropes shaking below them. Somehow, Rin makes her way up without shaking the rope more than an inch. Eliote throws herself, hand over hand, her face pinched, arm muscles bulging, making it to the top before all of them.

"That's right, Eliote, use those arms," I say, forcing the words through my constricted throat. "Better wear a sleeveless dress to formal tomorrow to show 'em off."

"I thought we were busting our butts to kick ass in battle, not a dress." Johanna grunts.

I laugh, and it shakes some of the drowsiness from my body. "Doesn't hurt to do both."

One by one, the team hits the ground and sprints to the other end. Niko slides down the last few feet of rope, landing hard on the edge of his foot. The impact jolts him to the ground. A chain with a Warrior tag on it slips from the collar of his black t-shirt.

"Niko, you okay, buddy?" I ask.

"I'm fine." He grunts and takes a few staggering steps, then bolts after the others.

I rub my eyes. Just the thought of sprinting makes my lungs hurt. There is a cloud over me, heavy and dark, quieting the intensity of my thoughts and feelings. It's a lonely shield, but the slowness helps pick out information outside of me. Niko isn't fine. That tag isn't his. Someone left it behind.

Marcus' arms slice through the haze and scoop around my waist. The pressure of him close around me in such a sweet gesture lightens the ache in my head. I shift my weight to lean on him a little, despite the heat radiating off me.

"So, tomorrow is the winter formal," I say. "Are we going?"

"Absolutely not." His low voice tumbles through me.

"You would deny me the pleasure of taking Marcus Ericson to the winter formal in my final year?" I say with a gasp.

"You've already been to three of those things."

"I haven't been to one with you though."

"And you never will."

"Fine. Will you let me take you to the Festival of Two Moons in Sii?"

Sighing, he leans in to kiss my cheek. "That we can do."

Part of me wants to throw myself at him, to be kissed and held until the cloud is gone and all I know is his touch. The rest of me wants to crawl away where I can be alone in the dark and not let anyone be touched by it. Both are so extreme and so me. What feels even more me is to stay right here, leaning into him. It's him too. Touch is how Marcus shows affection, and it's how he likes to receive it too. Even back when we went out for dinner, he touched my hand at the end.

"Adrianne, when Rin comes back in, I'd like you to duel with her." A less perfect voice than Marcus' bites through my fog with a hard edge.

Marcus breaks away from me, rubbing a protective hand over his smiling face. Brand stands behind him.

Pulling my gaze away from Marcus, I say, "Sure, Brand."

"And, Marcus, call Eliote over when she comes back in."

"Right." He dips his chin in a respectful nod.

Marcus and I wait for the team to come back in after the weapons drill with an inconspicuous amount of space between us. Although Rin's become better at controlling her Ironskin strength, she's the toughest one on the team. In every sense. She radiates a strength that is inexpressible and undeniable. The toughness that comes through trials no one sees. Am I tougher now? Or softer?

Eliote storms back in and Marcus calls her over. She strikes with a wide roundhouse punch. Marcus blocks, and in seconds, they're locked in a quick back-and-forth. Rin sprints inside on light feet. She slows her pace, looking around at all the instructors. Her eyes lock on to me, cool grey, and intense as the hells.

"Rin," I say, and she bolts toward me.

All she has to do is land one shot on me.

I swallow hard and spread my feet into a solid stance, holding up my open hands to block my face. Rin leaps at me like she has springs in her legs, the essence in each of her cells giving her otherwise impossible physical strength. Her leg whips through the air, speeding toward me like a hammer. All the heat in my muscles sparks, and I duck right under her. She lands behind me with just a tap of her feet on the ground.

I spin around, and she bridges the gap between us with a smirk on her face. That first kick was just to wake me up. Thank Fōsten, I needed that.

Circling around each other now, she keeps me close. I test my own strength, thrusting a jab at her face. Her head slips under my arm, and her left fist comes at my stomach. I crunch, blocking her fist with a lowered elbow, and follow with an uppercut. She blocks it with a quick snap of her hand. Her fist flies past my face faster and with more weight, getting closer to my skin with each strike. I evade the last blow, throwing my body weight to the side and letting her momentum throw her past me.

She back-kicks and twists around, engaging her entire body to swing both fists at my face. A grunt bursts from me. I swing one arm under hers, bashing them to the side, and hammer my fist to her throat, pulling back just before impact. She keels backward.

The girl is smart, pulling out Dawnranfet moves because she knows her Telando can't beat my defensive Fōsttimdato techniques. Dawnranfet is frowned upon in Guardian circles, but the amount of times I've seen her pull out a Dawnranfet move tells me she's not only watched but fought in the ring. If you fight those brutal fights, you fight to win. And she wants to win this fight. Even with all the distractions around, her eyes are linked to my every move. But they are dull with focus, like it's the only thing keeping her going right now.

Darting to my right, her arm circles my neck. She drops to the ground, taking me with her. My body slams to the gritty training room floor, and the air leaves my lungs, Rin's elbow looming above me. Right before the boney elbow hits my stomach, I thrust the current of my essence to one side, rolling and standing upright in a fluid motion.

Our eyes catch. A tinge of electric blue blinks from Rin's eyes, not enough to shake her focus or draw attention, and I might be the only one who notices. The fight fades for a split second. Blood rushes in my ears, and my essence churns back to my core in searing jolts. My energy pulses and latches on to the blink of light that has left Rin's eyes but is locked in my mind. A tremor passes through my body. My mind sinks in my skull, resigning to sit out for a minute, and my flesh turns to corded muscle, my skin to fur, my nails to claws.

The eyes that keep haunting me in the space outside my body loom before me, but for the first time, they have a form beyond a face. Swirling light and shadow with four legs and a long tail. It comes closer. A roar bursts from the being, and a scream rips through the training room.

Rin is below me, pinned beneath my paws.

Fucking hells. What am I doing?

I back away, transforming back to the Adrianne I see in the mirror. Rin's face is blanched, her eyes wide like silver shields. I slap my hands over my face, tears brimming so hot they sting. The contortion of my body leaves my bones aching, and shivers crawl down my spine. My energy is thick and tired.

"Everyone, stop." Brand's cutting voice stabs my ears.

Rin stares at me from the floor. She is ice, not sweating at all, just pulling in breath after breath, the calm shaken right out of her.

From a few paces away, Johanna crosses her arms and looks down her nose at us. "The idiot's afraid of cats, Adrianne," she says.

"Shit. Sorry, Rin." I catch Rin's eyes. I shifted her focus from the fight to something else that lives in her, something only her eyes know. There is no judgement, only shock in her curious gaze. But her light made me snap out of my body. For a moment, we were both protecting ourselves from something neither of us could see. "I didn't mean to."

Gasping at the spike of pain in my chest, I turn on my heel and march outside to the training grounds. The moment I'm out of sight, the tang of blood covers my tongue, and I gag. I clap my hand over my mouth. Behind me, a presence of fire and strength sparks my senses. Marcus takes me into his arms, rocking me, as an Alzuke swipes past my face. I flinch. Vera's skull cracks on the snow.

"Marcus, why did I do that? Why did I transform? There wasn't any threat." I sob into his shoulder. "Valencie said the fau in my essence should let me summon, that transforming into my full form is going to hurt me, and it does, it hurts. What is making me transform?"

"I . . . I don't know. It's almost like you know things before they happen sometimes. I remember in first year, you were panicked about beasts being outside the school. Everyone laughed at you. But the next day, a beast got through the wall and was found digging up the rose bushes. A professor killed it right on the grounds."

I had the same itch in my spine as I did in the ice-wastes that day the beast came on to the campus. The tug in my chest was there too. The blue in Rin's eyes was a feather-light touch, and yet it triggered my senses like she had activated her life affinity with maximum control. The light touched something in me like it was creating a path to those haunting eyes that keep me from drifting too far away from myself. Each time I see them, they urge me back into my body to fight in my hédin form. But what if they could come to me before my transformation? Maybe my familiar has been staring me down from beyond the Voids.

Tremors race through my body at different spots and different speeds. The pain in my head has intensified between my eyes and my heart pinches with every pulse accompanied by a ragged extra beat. I don't think my body can take another transformation like that. But my familiar doesn't have a body I can summon in this world. It's a mystic beast. Being Shadowless, I was told I was tied to the Lesser Worlds and, oh Dien, I really am, but in such a different way.

After an essence control drill outside with Marcus, the team files away from the training field. My heart storms as they leave, each one stretching their muscles and limping from aches in their bodies. I head back into the training room to help Hans clean up the dummies. Marcus is wrapped up in conversation with Eliote. As she asks him questions, Marcus faces her directly, nodding along. His eyes are bright, intent, and as he gives her input on her performance today, his gestures are animated. The confidence looks good on him.

I squat low by one of the dummies and heave it over my shoulder.

"Fuck, I forgot how heavy these things are," I say, a new admiration for Eliote sparking inside me. Even after that nasty drill with no extra oomph from essence, she stands with her back straight and her purple hair is sleek.

"Yes," Hans agrees as we shuffle our way to the storage room. "They are exceptionally unwieldy."

We stack the dummies in a pile in the far corner. There're four more to go, yet Hans takes a moment to adjust his shirt and swipes at the dust that will only reaccumulate with the next burlap sand person. Unfamiliar voices sound from outside along with headmaster Evelyn. Hans nods with a glance at his watch.

"Perfect timing," he mutters. I barely catch the words through his sigh as he walks out. I follow after him.

"Why are you looking for Brand?" Marcus asks two uniformed Local Protectors. He takes up a shield of confidence, crossing his arms and holding his chin high.

"I told you we will discuss this in my office," Evelyn says.

"I'm sorry, we have a warrant for the arrest of Brand Highcaller, there won't be any discussion needed," one Protector says. He holds out his shield badge. "Now where can we find her?"

Hans steps forward. "I believe she was talking to a student in the side training field." He holds out his hand to the open door letting a nasty chill in to eat away the stale heat. "Please follow me."

"What's going on?" I ask, grabbing one of the Protectors by the arm. He turns on his heel and looks down at me with a dark glare.

"Brand Highcaller was the last person seen with an Ironskin Local Protector who went missing. Many Ironskins are disappearing. We believe it has to do with a rebellion of sorts."

Marcus scoffs. "That's ridiculous. I know the Commander, she's not doing anything—"

My heart leaps as the other Protector, just as tall and twice as wide, steps forward with his hand on his pistol.

"We have our orders. Do not get in the way," he says.

Their boots clatter on the floor, leaving black scuffs all the way to the door. Hans ushers them through, but his eyes are on me. His face is blank except for a slight pucker between his brows. He did this. He turned her in, but why on the Karess would he do that?

"Evelyn, what the fuck is going on?" I ask.

"This is none of your concern," she says, her face in tempered neutrality. Marcus gives her a quick side-eye, and Evelyn shakes her head. "Now, the day after Freeday, we'll need you both to step up and teach as Brand was scheduled for an instruction."

My stomach turns over. I know Marcus isn't doing well with his leg. He needs to rest just like I did, and I can't get what he said out of my head, that I know things before they happen. I think I can sense beasts because of their fau essence, but that doesn't explain how I knew a day early that a beast would be crawling around campus. That flash of blue in Rin's eyes, her limping teammates; I think this team is about to break.

"I'll instruct. Give Marcus the day off," I say.

Evelyn draws a long breath through her nose, giving me a cynical side-eye. "Thank you, Adrianne, but I think I would prefer to have the two of you."

"I can do it. Please trust me." My voice wavers, but that doesn't break my eye contact. The tension in my chest is pulling me to this team right now. I'm needed here, and I don't need anyone to watch me. "I won't let you down."

Evelyn's mouth quirks. Releasing my eyes, she says, "Very well. Thank you. Please finish cleaning up."

The headmaster leaves us behind in her signature sweet, smoky scent.

I grab Marcus by the arm. "You know something," I say through gritted teeth, eyeing Evelyn as she takes Hans aside.

Marcus rubs his temples. "Yeah, I do. Brand works for an underground organization that advocates for Ironskin safety and equality as well as fighting for opportunities for other minorities. They have people in government, lawyers, doctors. They're making a change in the background. But Brand wants to bring them out into the open. Her goal is to establish this organization as a branch of the Guardian system."

"But what does that have to do with Brand being arrested?" I ask.

"The Ironskins in her organization haven't always been on the same page. Years ago, a group of them broke away to pursue more drastic measures. They want to revive the Ironskin nation from the dead. Brand makes personal visits to Ironskins who might not know about the organization who need the connection. My guess is that someone pinned Revival activity on Brand's efforts of simple connection."

He presses his lips together, and I step to him, putting my hand around his waist.

Secret Ironskin organizations. Like two Ironskins disguising themselves as scientists to obtain a Death stone. But what would Death stones do for them if not used as a weapon?

"My fieldwork mission," I say. "The two scientists who found the Death stone were Ironskins."

"Yeah, that's significant, but it doesn't track. Wouldn't they need a Revival stone?" Marcus says.

We stare at each other. My heart beats hard for him. Brand asked him to help her, to work for her organization in Sarr. I rest my eyes for a moment and the memory of Adia's defiance drills a dull ache through my side. Brand is one side of the Ironskins dilemma, searching for connection, and Adia is the other, longing to revive what's lost, to grasp their power once again. Two extremes, and I know what it's like to get caught on one side.

"Brand wants her people safe. And the way she puts it, her people are Ironskins and you and me. Everyone. She doesn't want division."

I take a deep breath. "It's going to be hard, dangerous. But you need to take that job."

"Yes," Marcus says. His jaw works. "But I'm not going to Sarr. Their council doesn't have an Emberstead member though. If I can get on that council, then maybe I can keep my connections with the Guardian academy as a teacher and be the Guardian link Brand's been looking for."

I was a fool to think this job was a handout. He was picked specifically for it. Brand sees the Marcus I see, passionate about the right things, gentle but firm when necessary, stable.

Walking over to the dummies, his limp is heavy, and he winces.

I put a hand on his chest. "I'll take care of this, but first I just want to make sure you know I'm really sorry for the way I acted," I say.

His eyes are warm, and they dance all around me.

"I know," he says. "You're easy to forgive."

My breath catches in my throat. It wasn't easy for me to forgive myself. It's taken me years to even think about it. And yet Marcus looks at me, all a mess, and forgives the piece of shit that I am. How big is his heart?

I lean into him, hands on his shoulders, bringing him down to me for a kiss. His lips are soft on mine, and his hands are gentle on my waist.

I think I might love him.

But is it too soon to know? Is it too soon to have these words running through my head?

I shoo him away to go eat and rest without an answer, the words dancing through my mind as I start to prepare a lesson for next week and lug the rest of the dummies to the storeroom. Throwing the last one down, it flops on its side, staring at an identical model. If the dummies had real eyes, one could see what's behind the other. If they communicated, they would see the whole room.

Eila told me it was a responsibility to Void Watch. If I have a familiar in the Lesser Worlds, then don't I have a responsibility to share my knowledge with them? Are they already trying to share by sending me knowledge of what's to come?

I click out the lights, rubbing the ache in my chest. I think it's time to try it again without a transformation.

CHAPTER 26

A LIMINAL SPACE. That's the first step Eila taught me.

It's one in the morning, and I gather a blanket, my tea, and a book I found on Void Watching from the library. I brewed my tea strong—lavendorin for calm. I take a sip and slip out of my room.

There are many liminal spaces in the academy at this hour. I could pick any deserted hallway, a stairwell, the parking lot, or even the empty dining hall. The central courtyard calls to me though. Under the crisp, utanic starlight, in-between classrooms and dormitories, learning and rest, it's the perfect place to cross the Voids. I cross to the fountain in the centre that's been turned off but has icicles glimmering from its spouts. Blanket folded over my shoulders, book open on my lap, I sip the cup of tea while skimming the chapters I read between classes this afternoon.

Essence seems to be an important part of the equation for the lineages that have pure essence. Focusing on essence helps them move their consciousness quickly to the level of the Lesser Worlds that corresponds to their energy. A regular Beastblood would probably find themselves on the Void Bridge between the Lower Void and the Silent Realm because of the unama and fann energies within them. If I use essence to focus with a transformation, I'm not really going anywhere specific; I just see the Higher Plane because it's the closest to the physical world and my vital energies are all out of sync.

Essence really only makes it faster, providing something to focus on in meditation, making meditation the true key here. I've had enough snapshots of the Lesser Worlds and the glowing eyes to visualize what I'm trying to connect with. If I focus on these aspects, maybe I can connect with my familiar and learn about them before the real Void Watching begins.

I snap the book shut, sucking in a deep breath, and take in my surroundings, like Eila taught me. The sorrow-blossom trees are dark and spindly, the gardens surrounding me display muted tones of green, and the walls of the academy are dotted with dark panes of glass except for one. My room. I mark the distance between me and that light, the soft threads of my blanket, its weight over my sweater, then close my eyes.

Bringing colour out of the dark, I start with the Lower Void with its indigo and other blues, the violet of the Silent Realm, then the shimmering black expanse. The Higher Plane is the most familiar, so I rest there, constructing the mountains.

I hold a breath until the air is warm inside me. Painting the golden eyes in the dark, I wait, focusing on the flicker and their similarity to my own eyes, with a sharp gaze and an elegant curve.

A metallic screech spikes through the quiet in the physical world around me. This must be why it's important to take in my surroundings before, so I'm alert. I blink a few times and my eyes land on Niko shuffling down the path to the bench. His eyes are on the ground, a bottle of ale swinging from his hand. Staggering, he flops onto the bench across from me.

"Uh, hey, buddy."

Niko starts. "Adrianne, didn't see you there. You were so still." There's a flush to his cheeks, but his speech is clear. Probably not too many drinks in yet.

"You doin' okay?" I ask, eyeing the ale in his limp fingers.

"Aw, yeah, I'm great. What's more Beastblood than pretending you don't have feelings with a bottle of ale?" He breathes a mirthless chuckle and takes a swig. "That's what I am, Beastblood. Nothing more to me."

What a lie.

Slumping a little more, his bright-orange puffer coat hangs open with the black t-shirt from this morning and the Warrior tag on full display.

"Who died, Niko?" I ask.

"Shit, Adrianne, talk so bluntly about the dead, and you'll give us both bad luck." He tips the bottle to his lips again, but I snatch it out of his hands. "Hey," he yelps.

"Who died?" Raising my eyebrows, I take a long drink. It's good. I draw my knees up and settle into my blanket a little more to enjoy it.

Niko's eyes track me, dark and beady. "You know what I hate about you?"

"That I don't just let you be a dick?"

"You walk around here like that braid means nothing."

He's wrong. It was a heavy shame for a while and now it means everything to me. But in-between all that, I get his interpretation, because it meant so much for my lineage, and I didn't create something for myself. In that respect, it was meaningless to me.

"It's like you spit in my face every time you walked into the training room." Niko's eyes shift away from me. Head tilted back, they target the light on in the girls' dormitory. "You spit in my great dano's face. My great dano fought in the Fourth Great War. He told me it's what we fight for that counts. He fought for the peace. And I want to make sure that the generation after me gets to live in a relatively peaceful world the way I did. I had a safe life because of my great dano. That's why I Vowed to follow in his footsteps and fight for that safety."

His words sit in the frosty air with us. The skin of his cheeks twists as his lips press together. Gasping, he bends over his knees. "I made that Vow two months ago, and now he's dead. He didn't even get to see me finish my first year. It's almost like the universe is laughing at me." The pinch in Niko's voice steals my breath away. He presses at his eyes while I clench his ale. "There's nothing special about me. I'm not smart or super talented. I worked my ass off in junior training. Being a Warrior like my great dano, protecting my family, our culture—all that gave me some sort of framework. Without it, I don't know who I am."

His disdain for halfies, however distasteful, makes a little more sense now. Halfies create branches in those clear-cut cultural paths. Like a tree, it's beautiful to me now, but for someone who stays so true to the Beastblood way, I suppose there's pain from the break. A growing pain. A good pain. He can't see that it's good though.

"Niko," I say, tentatively putting my words out into this fragile place. "Your desire to maintain the safety you've been able to experience is so amazing. That's the collective Beastblood spirit. But you don't have to follow someone else's footsteps to do that. Make your own steps. Huge ones."

Niko pushes off the bench and punches his fist at the wind with a grunt. "I don't know how to do that, Adrianne!"

"Yeah, you do." The words come so easily. A smile tugs at my lips as he pulls at his hair. "Somewhere along the way, someone told us that our ancestors knew best. They took their own steps. The moment we start to follow, we start to fall, I think. I fell. Really fucking hard."

Turning to me, hands in his pockets, his eyes are softer now. "Is that why you weren't working with us last week?"

I nod and he sits back down. Taking the blanket off my shoulders, I spread it out over both our knees. Niko traces the whiskers of the embroidered cat with a finger.

"If this is the path you want, then it's yours," I say.

Niko's throat bobs. With a sniff, he brushes his eye.

"It's not fulfilling your duty or expectations. It's yours. No one gets to put any claim on it just because someone else has done the same thing."

Unmoving, Niko is quiet, like he is inside himself for the first time—awake but stunned by the sense of self.

"Tomorrow's winter formal. Keep grieving your great dano, but wear your Vishal, honour yourself."

Standing, Niko says, "Any chance there's some ale left in

there?"

"Saved you a sip." I hand over the bottle.

Dangling it between his fingers again, he starts to walk away.

"You think Rin's just looking for a little safety too?" I ask, stopping him. "Think you could offer her a little of yours? Your great dano might not, but you could."

"I'll think about it," he says quietly, a curl of air rising above his head. He downs the last of the ale and heads back into the building.

I run my cold hands over my cheeks. Finding a few tears, I wipe them away with my blanket, and settle my hands on my lap. One last try at this meditation, and I'll go inside too. My shoulders are heavy with cold; my heart is achy and full. But I paint the eyes in the Higher Plane expanse and settle my mind on it.

The image is steady, unchanging. An energy is added to it though. It exudes a playfulness with a poke at my heart. It is caramelized sugar, melting and swishing back-and-forth on my tongue. Warmth taps on my forehead. My own knowledge sings inside this energy but is fuller and layered with intricacies. Undoubtedly, this energy has a feminine strength. She laughs at me like I finally found her hiding in the most obvious spot. She gazes at me with love, deep into my past. I stare back at her, over her shoulder into the future. One moment is clear, filled with bright blue.

CHAPTER 27

ALL MEMBERS OF THE ADVANCED TEAM are in the training room waiting for me the morning after the formal. Without the other instructors, the room is more open, more daunting, and it's filled with a strained, pointed energy, like broken glass, that sets me on my toes. The guys talk in a circle, rubbing sleep from their eyes and stretching out muscles after a night of food and dancing. Rin and Eliote are stretching out close to each other but are silent, and Johanna keeps her distance. I'd like to close the distance between these little clusters. They've all worked as a team this year, but that doesn't mean anything's changed inside them—they've just followed orders.

The soreness that usually hangs out in my stomach while I teach is missing today. I built that cloud over my head and now I've pulled it down. "Everyone, please gather around," I say. My voice swells through the room, touching the ceiling and the floor as it draws the team around me.

Propping my hands on my hips, I swallow. Instead of pushing everything that's happened in the last few weeks behind me, I let it sit with me in this lesson. The events put weight on my heart, so I have to attend to my words with more precision. I don't want to be harsh, but I also don't want to pretend everything is okay.

"I know you're supposed to be working with Brand today," I say. "Brand has been arrested, and that's all the information I have."

The silence lands like a hammer. Niko's eyes catch mine for a second and drop to the ground. Jeff and Ace exchange a look with slack jaws, and the girls just wait for more info with wide, bloodshot eyes. Rin lets out a sigh, resting her hands on her head. Her jaw is set, ready to break, the ice in her eyes about to melt.

I take this as my cue to ease into a simple lesson.

"So, today we're gonna go over the same things as last week, blocking and avoiding attacks to warm up, then go on to counterattacks later on. I'm going to pair you off, and I want you to switch up who's attacking and who's defending every few minutes. I want Jeff-Ray and Eliote together, Ace and Niko"—it might be a huge mistake; what's one more to add to the pile?—"and Johanna and Rin."

Johanna's eyes flash, and I swear there is steam coming off her. The minimal colour in Rin's face runs dry.

"Choose who's going to start attacking. We'll switch after five minutes." I clap my hands to move them along.

The team pairs up to spar. Without the eyes of other

instructors on me, my mind is sharp like crystal, focusing in on detail. I take a deep breath, circling around Johanna and Rin. Johanna's form is sloppy as she punches, a ragged look in her eye. Her hair flops in kinky curls around her shoulders. The pinch between her eyebrows deepens as her fist makes contact. Rin blocks Johanna's punch with her arms, absorbing the full impact of the hit with a snap. Each attack is taken like she wants it. She expects the blow, not anticipating it, but accepts it like she deserves it.

I shake my head and cross my arms as my stomach cinches. "Johanna, tone it back a bit, keep it controlled," I say, moving on to circle around Jeff and Eliote, keeping one eye on Rin and Johanna.

Jeff attacks and Eliote alternates between blocking his strikes with her arms and bobbing and weaving. Every time she uses a physical block, she winces, and every time she ducks his fists, he's ready with another hit, making her move in hurried jerks that aren't normal for her.

"Hold up you two," I say as Jeff throws a jab and Eliote lets out a heavy breath. "Okay, so Jeff's got a lot of power and a lot of reach in his arms. Focusing on your footwork is going to give you more of an edge in a spar like this, Eliote. When your opponent is so much bigger than you, you want to avoid blocking with your arms, and bobbing is just going to tire you out. Instead, I want you to get used to moving back. Just a simple step back. Move in and out to slip past attacks and avoid any quick jabs to your core as you duck." I get into my stance and show her a quick step back. "Now you."

Eliote holds up her guard and steps back as Jeff slows his punches to let her get used to the new movement.

"I know it's tempting to lean back but keep your core solid, move your whole body, and incorporate side movement too. Good." I nod to them.

They continue to spar as I back away. I bite my lip with a wave of heat spreading through me. I still get the quiet obedience from these kids, nothing else. It's a dull exchange. That's okay, right? A lump forms in my throat, and it's a harsher squeeze than normal, extra force for extra release. I sigh it out.

A few paces away, Niko and Ace stop. They mutter between each other for a moment and then Ace pats Niko on the shoulder. Niko turns to me and raises his hand.

No one sees it except for Ace waiting with an approving smile.

"Uh, Niko? You have a question?" I say, pressing a hand over my heart.

Niko jogs over to me. He rolls his shoulders back. His eyes shift from side to side, but as a flush spreads through his cheeks, he says, "I want to thank you for training us this year." The words come out with too much breath. He dips his head, his shaggy blond hair shielding his eyes. "I can't speak for the others, but having you come in here and teach this boring shit to us day in and day out has taught me more than anything. Every bone-splitting, repetitive drill taught me perseverance."

My throat aches as if my heart is inching up my esophagus and I might vomit it up at their feet. I scratch the sensitive skin on my side where it meets my bra, fighting my heart back into place so I can speak.

"Thank you, I—"

"You had to protect yourself from me." It's whispered but the sentiment rings through me. "Of any Beastblood in our lineage, I admire you the most." Pounding his fist to his heart, he offers me his hand.

I mirror him, except for the tear streaking down my face, and clasp his hand. My face is burning as I say, "Thank you, Niko, but you've got to get back to work."

"Got it, boss." He gives me a wide grin and trots back to Ace.

I turn to the corner of the room and paw away my tears, heaving breaths to still my heart. I've barely made any connection with half the team. Even if I wanted to give them something more than defence training, Ace, Jeff, and Eliote didn't need much from me. Niko, on the other hand, we needed to rub edges.

A flash of orange light blazes behind me. I turn on my heel, snot still trickling from my nose, and Johanna has formed herself a full suit of fire armour and the two girls whale on each other, holding nothing back. The room heats and the air is sucked dry as Johanna starts screaming at Rin.

The purpose of the exercise is completely lost as Rin leaps at Johanna, and Johanna adds blazing flames to her hits. Ducking, Rin sweeps Johanna's legs, taking her clean off her feet.

Jeff cringes as she hits the ground, and Eliote's eyes grow wide as she tracks her movement, but Johanna rights herself easily and screams, "Damn it, Rin. Why'd you turn your back on me?"

I just worked my heart back down to my chest, and now it plummets to the bottom of my stomach. Shaking my head, I march over to them.

"Rin. Johanna," I yell. "What the hells are you doing?"

"Tell her, Rin. What are we doing?" Johanna says. Her chest

rises and falls with heavy breaths. Her eyes never leave Rin, they are locked like chains, the connection unbreakable.

"Nothing. I'm not getting into this right now, not in front of everyone." Rin's steely eyes glance at me, and her face flushes.

"Of course," Johanna says with a scoff. "Of course you don't want to talk. So, fight me." Spit flies from her mouth, and her hair shakes around her head as she challenges Rin.

I roll my eyes. Huffing, I push the two of them away with fire projections.

"No," I say.

But Johanna's malicious smile slinks across her face, and she dashes away. Rin spins behind me, running after her.

"You little shits," I mutter.

That's all the reprimand I can muster as the air in my lungs goes still, and my feet stay planted. I wanted them to work together. But they beat each other, and I take in every hit and every word like I watched Dawnranfet, letting the meaning of each offence sink in.

Why'd you turn your back on me? The clarity of the question is a sheer force ringing through my ears. It infuses ice in my veins and weight in my heart. This fight has been brewing beyond my control for a long time now. Under my nose, these two girls were hating each other, and I did nothing. I've been so caught up in my own shit I just let this happen. What else have I missed?

I should stop them, make them talk it out. But Johanna knows this battle better than I do. Maybe she's right. Maybe fighting it out is the only way.

The other students murmur around me, but I can't make out words until Ace grabs my arm.

"Shouldn't we do something?" he asks. His sapphire eyes

shake as he waits for me to respond.

I open my mouth to speak; the air in my lungs won't move. I shake my head instead.

Ace huffs and starts marching over to the girls just as Rin's fist plows through the wall, leaving behind a gaping hole. The entire arena trembles, and Ace stumbles back.

Tears spring from Johanna's eyes as she darts away from the blow. Rin throws her fist at Johanna's face again. It collides with fire armour with a sizzle. Johanna laughs, a bubbling, maniacal sound that churns my blood.

"Pathetic," she says. "Show me how you really feel. Outside. Now."

The two jump through the hole in the wall like two bad little bunnies.

Ace dashes after them, pulling up short as the hole closes with fire. He slams his hands against the wall. "For Carnity's sake, how many times does she need to be beat down before she can get up?" He grabs his hair.

I go over to him while Eliote, Niko, and Jeff scurry to get the door open to the outside. "What if she doesn't get back up? Damn it, I-I know she's been doing bad again. I just didn't know what to do. I didn't know the first time either." His eyes roam the ceiling, a glimmer of tears cresting his bottom lids.

I'm not sure if he's talking to himself or me, but Ace's shoulders are shaking, and he hides his face. A series of thundering crashes shakes the arena.

"It's okay, Ace, I know you're worried about Rin, but—" The ground shakes again.

"Yes, yes, I'm worried about Rin because Johanna won't stop until Rin's broken."

I put a tentative hand on his shoulder. "Take a breath. She's going to be okay. They both are. Let them work it out." Ace wipes his face on his sleeve. "So, let's go make sure they don't kill each other." I steer him to the doors.

As we step outside into last night's snow, the icy air sings with a moment of silence, weighed down by the stench of ash. A screech breaks through, and Johanna flies through the air and slams into the arena wall. The building shakes, Johanna's armour fizzles out, and she hits the ground.

"Fuck, are you sure Rin's the one to worry about?" I ask.

Johanna's body lies limp on the ground, bits of cement raining down on her. The courtyard is littered with fire-sword manipulations lodged in the cobblestone. Rin stands in the middle of the flames, breath enveloping her in a white cloud as the blue life affinity light pours from her eyes. Stringy hairs quiver around her face as the blue light goes out, and her body slumps over and she braces herself on her knees.

I clutch my pounding chest. My essence struggles inside me. It's her life affinity that drew my beast to me the other day. The spirit affinities connect to the Lesser Worlds, and maybe that glimpse of Rin's light sparked a connection in my mind to this event unfolding before us. None of us on the sidelines breathe. All our eyes are glued on the two girls.

Johanna pulls herself to her feet. "I needed you," she says through a gasping breath.

The words are a resounding gong through my being. I just can't figure out why this little bitch's words are hitting me so hard.

Johanna thrusts out her hand and Rin flies through the air toward her. The faintest flicker of amber energy connects the two of them. I've only seen Johanna use Mind Fire once—a powerful manipulation of the energy in the nervous system far beyond my own fire-manipulation capabilities. Her veins stand out from her skin, and her eyes cloud like she's in another world.

I wince as Johanna's fist collides with Rin's face, and Rin shrieks, "I-I couldn't."

Johanna pounds the ground with her foot. "Why?"

"It was too much," Rin says, stumbling away from Johanna. She grabs on to one of Johanna's flaming swords still glowing like a torch, the essence in her skin repelling the heat so all the sword can do is turn her sweat to steam. She lets a sob escape her. "Everything was crashing down on me. My dad died—"

"My dad died too, Rin. You should have known how I felt. We should have got through it together like we always did."

"Shut up. You wanted me to talk, so I'm talking. My dad died. My mother killed herself. She killed herself and I didn't know what to do."

My gaze is narrow, centring on Rin and the sobs gushing out of her heaving chest.

"You punished me," she continues. "You said you hated me and yelled at me for not being able to deal with your pain right away. And you've punished me every day since."

A deep ache grows inside me. It's like I'm watching myself fight myself.

"So the blame's on me then," Johanna says. Her shoulders hunch, and she clutches a bloody scrape on her arm. "Fine. I'll take it. But that's only half of it. Come on, Rin, why'd you leave me?"

She throws a punch, and another and another, and Rin is forced back, blocking each blow as they inch closer to landing a hit.

Rin ducks her head and crosses her arms like a shield over her face and screams, "I was scared!" She trembles under her confession. "I didn't want to be left again, so I left first."

"Look what happened. Look where *we* are. And you made new friends. Ace. Eliote."

"I know, I know, and I hate myself for it. I hate myself for everything."

The wind shifts around us. Jeff hangs his head, hands braced on his hips and his face only holding together with a grimace, like he's humbled to have witnessed such a vulnerable moment. Eliote clutches her chest, eyes wide. Niko's a stone pillar beside her.

The howl of the wind, the bite of the cold, the crumbling plaster and cement, fades as Rin says, "I didn't want to make it through."

Johanna steals a sharp breath, pressing her eyes shut. In a flash of fists, Johanna engages Rin again. Their movements blur through the shell of tears in my eyes. A flash of fire, the smack of a foot hitting flesh, and Rin hits the ground.

There's no wonder why I feel so connected to Rin. It doesn't make sense though. I couldn't have known she struggled with the same things I did. It's not like suicidal tendencies have a certain smell. It's not like you can see them, you get used to masking it.

Johanna drops in front of Rin. She cries over her as if lamenting the punishment she's inflicted on Rin.

I'm sorry, Adrianne. I'm sorry I punished you when I thought you were broken.

A breath expands inside me, shaking me. It's going to take a lot longer than I thought to forgive everything.

"We need to get Rin to the infirmary," I say before tears can take hold.

"She won't want to wake up there. Not again," Ace says under his breath.

Damn it. It's the only thing I can think to do.

"The kid got knocked out cold. She needs medical attention." My voice shakes. I don't know how to soothe the ache that cuts through this courtyard in relentless sweeping waves, knocking away smiles and energy. It's too heavy. I stand, empty-handed, in front of my students. Snow leaks through the fabric of my shoes, the sweat in my pits taking on a brutal chill.

Ace runs a hand over his face and says, "If you heard any bit of what those two just said, you have to know that Rin won't want to wake up anywhere but her own bed. What are the nurses going to do for a weak spot that you couldn't do?"

"You're right." I swallow and force my body not to shake. I move to Rin and Johanna, wiping tears from my eyes. "I'll monitor her until she wakes up and get high-grade curestones."

I press two fingers to Rin's neck. Her pulse lashes out at me, her skin cold and sweaty. I roll her into my arms, but just as I'm about to lift her, Ace stops me.

"I'll take her," he says.

The ache clutches me with phantom hands, wringing out another tear. I unfold Rin from my arms.

"Thank you, Ace. I'm cancelling training for the rest of the morning. Eliote, Niko, Jeff, and Ace, please attend classes this afternoon. I will go talk to headmaster Evelyn about the incident."

In the lobby, I stand at Evelyn's door, fanning myself with my shirt even though I'm chilled, and I swipe my eyes. Behind me, Eliote helps Johanna to her room. Johanna's sniffles prickle the back of my neck. Her attitude irritated me this year. Not anymore. I'm learning to read my gut reactions better. I think she is my aspiration. I want to *be* angry, not just let anger explode out of me to mask something else. I want to be angry and anxious and empathetic and rested all at the same time and not let any of those things hide. Johanna's angry words to Rin stunned me today. They woke me. I am honoured by the messiness of their relationship. It is a beauty.

Evelyn trusted me with her students' safety today, and I let them beat each other up. Oh Zenta, help me. The cold from outside has worn off and a wave of heat fills my body as I rock back-and-forth on my toes, creating murky puddles over the marble floor. Niko and Jeff shuffle through the lobby in heated but hushed conversation.

I take a breath, banish the need to knock, and barge in.

Evelyn sits at her desk, gold pen in hand poised over a notepad as she talks on her echo. Her brown curls bounce as she looks over the rims of her spectacles at me.

With a slight roll of her eyes, she runs her tongue over her teeth and says, "Something just came up. I will echo you back in a few minutes."

I plop myself into a chair opposite her desk, rattling a single tear from my eye.

The roll of Evelyn's eyes softens to a gentle glimmer of brown. She pulls out a box of tissues from one of the desk drawers and pushes it over to me. Checking her watch, she frowns. "It's only halfway through the first time-block."

"Yeah, something happened," I say.

"Mm, and what is this something?"

"We were working on a defence drill to warm up, and Johanna and Rin started beating each other. I tried to stop them but then they . . . ran around me . . . and I let them fight it out. Rin's unconscious."

Evelyn stares at me, her eyes pinched and lips pressed as she listens. "We take fighting outside of instructed combat seriously. I should write them up," she says.

I run a hand over my face. "No, no, please don't."

Evelyn is still as my hand drops to my lap.

"I didn't say I was going to. I said I should." Her head tilts to the side. "I need to treat my students with fairness, you know that."

"They've had punishment enough from each other. And I know, everything's gotta follow protocol. If you don't take action with this case then what does it say about the establishment, right? But I'm telling you they're going to be safer now that they've fought it out. If they hadn't, Johanna wouldn't have been able to say what she needed to say, I wouldn't know that Rin's suicidal, but now I do, and I can help them." I deflate back into the chair; my knuckles are white from clutching the arms. A breath shakes out of me.

Thumbing through a stack of files on her desk, Evelyn says, "You raised a lot of doubt in me this year. I told you at the beginning I chose you for a reason."

My heart beats in my throat, and I wish I could melt into the chair.

"I told you inflicting harm on my students was not it.

Yelling at them wasn't it either. Letting them beat each other up doesn't hit the mark."

Tears gush down my face. I slouch deeper. She's going to cut me from the team.

Evelyn opens a file and adjusts her spectacles. "Your evaluation from Commander Karf came in today. He wrote: *Trainee McCarthy has no unique skills to offer, just another Medic who thinks they're better than everyone, forcing me to check my essence pressure, acting without orders, and meddling in duties not her own causing casualties on the mission.*" She clicks her tongue and flips the page. "Your companion Nathal also submitted a report. *Adrianne was a fantastic support. She took careful medical notes, offering pain medication, monitoring essence pressure, and making sure we were informed of any harm that might come our way. Because of her, I was able to inform the Local Protector units of two individuals with an illegal Death stone. McCarthy knows that being a Medic isn't just bandaging wounds and stepping behind her companions. She knew when to fight. She's a Guardian first and foremost because she values life.*"

They said all that just by watching me for two days?

"Karf is a typical Guardian jackass, if you ask me, but between the two of them, they paint a pretty accurate picture." Evelyn puts down the file, setting her glasses on top.

Pulling myself up by the arms of the chair, my body follows slowly like a child gone boneless in defiance of bedtime. I loosen my grip on the wooden arms, shift on the lopsided cushion beneath me, and focus my attention on Evelyn as best I can. Her gaze is iron, her fingertips poised together.

"You make choices, and then you accept the consequences," she says. "You look deeper than the surface. I don't trust you'll do the conventional thing, but I trust you'll do the right thing. The doubt I held wasn't in my choice to have you teach. I doubted my understanding of what it means to teach. Which is why I won't punish them or you. You let the scene play out because you knew it needed to."

Lower lip quivering, I wipe my eyes. My spine straightens one vertebra at a time. "Thank you," I whisper. "But these qualities aren't suited for a Medic. Not a field Medic at least."

A smile quirks Evelyn's full lips.

I lean forward, running my hands along my knees. My eyes fall closed as I wait for the words to form on my tongue. "I want to apply for the Monitor program."

Evelyn takes a sheet of paper sitting by itself on the side of her desk. Her long fingers select a stamp and an ink pad, and after signing a swirling signature at the bottom of the paper, she stamps a bright-red Akinnera seal on it. "Fill out this form and return it to me by the end of the week. I'll send it directly to the Guardian Medic Commander's office. I will send Nathal's report with it as well, and my personal recommendation."

I shake with her words, heart swelling, blood rushing in my ears. After fighting myself all these years, all it took was a little trust in myself. I hide my face from her again, knowing it's tomato red.

"Monitors work one-on-one with people who suffer," Evelyn says. "People who suffer losses, anger at themselves, guilt, anguish. There are few people in this world who have a heart soft enough and strong enough to help them out of that."

Tears gush down my face. Soft and strong. Two extremes, and I'm finding a bridge between them.

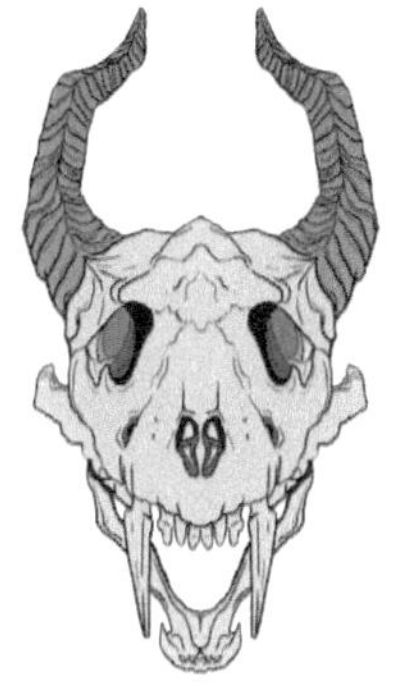

CHAPTER 28

RIN IS LIKE A MAGNET TO ME. I slip into her room for the fifth time today. Every time I check her pulse, her breathing, they are as strong as ever, but her eyes won't open. For a moment, I'm glad she doesn't open her eyes. I crouch beside her bed in the dark and slip my hand into hers. Taking a long breath, I let my essence speed up to heat my hand. My skin pulses and in a few moments, Rin's clammy hand is only cool at the tips of her fingers. Her cheeks grow pink even in the dark of her room.

A thought warms with our skin. Rin's mother killed herself.

That knowledge pulls at me like the Death stone pulled at my deepest, darkest desire. My eyelids grow heavy. The quiet rushes in waves through my mind. These last months have been so emotionally draining. The Voids between life and death call a little louder in times like this.

As I run my thumb over a small patch of skin on Rin's hand, her chest rises and falls. With a sharper inhale, air rushes into her. Energy travels like grains of sand trickling up her arm. I pat my fingers carefully up her arm as it moves—a chain reaction of her cells bolstering and decreasing essence production. The touch of her skin is calm in her hand now, but around her trunk, where Johanna hit her in the back, the pulse is palpable even without touching her. Her essence has adapted to heal her weak spot.

My hands slip away from Rin into my lap. I stare at my fingers—the tips, where the claws come out. I am worlds away when my beast form shows. It is wrong to transform out of my skin. When Rin used her life affinity today, it was as if her spirit wanted out of her body, to be free, or to be at peace within herself. That's all I want. For me and for her.

Energy radiates through me from my temples to my toes, stopping ever so often to swell with warmth at my transform points. If I knew her name, I could call her, my familiar.

I take one last look at Rin and leave the room, trying not to wake her.

The hall is quiet since the rest of the school is still in classes. I rub my arms, goosebumps spilling over my skin with the bite of winter infesting the air. My hands slide over the long, raised scars on my forearms. Smooth pink skin, regrown, pronounced to the world. I keep even pressure with my fingers up and down the scars. The motion is soothing.

Tears fall without a choke in my throat, without tension in my shoulders, without a sting. They fall and a presence stirs behind me—a gentle earthquake beneath my feet and a soft breath on my back. A wild urge sparks fire in my blood. I turn.

Basking in the cool afternoon light stands the form of a tiger made of pure flickering gold energy. Breath gushes out of me as she blinks, and the essence in my body shudders. My knees go weak as the tiger chuffs, bowing her head to me. Her fur is rippling flame, and my essence pulses in time with each flicker. The light darkens and waves across her back to create her stripes. Her eyes are vast and inky, her fangs, daggers of light. She is like Ōna, our sun, a fann energy star. And since she is a beast, this energy that flows in her is fau, akin to the energy in me.

Trembling, my lungs expand with a slow breath, taking in the electric scent of essence and her warmth. The tiger paws the carpet in front of me. I stare at the divots left behind by her claws, trying with every ounce of strength not to let my body collapse under the strain of coursing energy inside me. But she paws again, coming closer.

I swallow, even though my throat is dry, and raise my hand. It wavers in the space between us, delicate and frail in her presence. Hot air from her nostrils bathes my hand, and she presses the side of her face to my palm. She's the mystic beast Matta told me about. She's the one who heard my Vow. No one's known her name before, but it twists inside my mind with her heat—Kai'trish.

The floor dips away from my feet. Darkness swarms me. It churns and presses on my chest, pushes me from behind, swerves my balance. I throw my arms around Kai'trish. Somehow, I tumble, but she is still, her essence solid in my arms. The temperature drops, sending a crashing pain through my skull. I shriek and clench every muscle in my body to keep myself from shattering.

My feet slam down on solid ground. A sensation I've never experienced before wraps up my legs. Radiating through my body, it is a knife shattering bone with no pain; it slices through like butter with an odd discomfort all the same. A pale, periwinkle mist billows at my feet. My heart pounds in my chest and my vision tilts, but as I clench my fists in Kai'trish's fur, the world and my body stills.

Kai'trish chuffs, her essence vibrating around me. Releasing one arm from her neck, I keep hold with the other and lift my eyes to my surroundings. My breath curls around me with the mist.

The walls of my dormitory hallway have morphed into two towering trees. Their trunks are thin, their bark flaky and crystalline. A bit tears off, and as it floats away, it morphs into a small fish, wispy and glowing.

My jaw drops and my legs go stiff. "Holy Zenta's tits," I mutter.

The fish moves away in undulating swishes through the mist.

There is nothing for miles, only periwinkle haze. And beyond that haze, indigo. Shit. I'm not Void Watching this time. I am here physically. This can't be happening. I can't be here.

The cold is hot, the air is thick and twists inside my lungs. My head throbs as I suck in breath after breath. "You"—a tear escapes my eye—"you brought me to the Lesser Worlds." A shiver washes over my knees and echoes over my shoulders.

Kai'trish stares me down with her brilliant eyes.

"Why'd you bring me here?" I double over, my stomach in knots, still holding on to her pulsing fur. "I don't want to be here," I scream. "I–I never did. I'm not ready."

With a shake of her head, a spark jumps from her fur onto my skin. I start, but as the heat washes over me I know I'm not here to stay, I'm not here for me—she wants to show me something.

Kai'trish takes a step. I follow on wobbly legs.

Setting a foot on the pale, cracking ground, the haze liquefies to a slime-like texture. I raise my foot, and the slime stretches. It clings to itself like spiderwebs, beading with condensation that catches glints of unearthly light. A stringy bit snaps, springs into the air, and returns to the swirling mist. It's as if this haze is an alternate form of core-energy mist.

I let my hand fall from its death grip on Kai'trish's fur. Heat drips off my fingers, replaced by a crackle of cold. It doesn't sting or hurt, and I know it won't harm me, but it's intense, a stranger clutching my skin.

A shift in the cool air moves the haze, revealing a jagged cliff face reaching higher than even the trees I entered through. On the other side of us is a giant with glowing silver eyes. It stares at me and my bones shudder, but it only stands from its kneeling position to sway in the strange air and the strange curling substance all around us. The ground trembles as another stands beside it, and then another. They sentinel the path that stretches on forever with weary eyes, their bones creaking, and quiet storms rumbling in their chests.

An ache fills me alongside my quivering breaths. I stare back at the gargantuan forms. Matta told me that the hells are not a place, they are not synonymous with the Lesser Worlds. The hells are the fracturing of the vital energies. This, here, is the third hell of the Lower Void—an essence root. I may be in the land of the dead, but I am wrapped in flesh that contains my vital energies. These giants are manifestations of essence, grown out of control and grounded here, separated from their minds and spirits.

Kai'trish brushes my side with her face. Her warmth soothes the ache. With her close to me, I know what she knows, and she knows what I know. We're here to help an essence root.

Grabbing my hair, I braid my first Vow and throw it over my shoulder. Nodding to Kai'trish, I say, "All right, let's go."

I take a few steps on my own along the path, but Kai'trish comes behind me, her great paws shaking the ground, and steers me off the path with her head pressed to my back. The instant she makes contact, I know that through is down, and down is back. Around is our way.

"Okay, I get it." Kai'trish increases her vigour, and I lurch forward, forced into a jog and nearly catching my foot on a stone that was not there a moment ago. Through is down. Down is back. It's unnecessarily confusing, kind of like life itself.

"Some have to go back, don't they?" I ask Kai'trish. "To make things right with themselves."

She prances next to me, her luminous coat glowing brighter.

We press on in silence. As I sink into the rhythm of our steps, letting my thoughts fade, I ease myself into the peculiar ways of this world, and the speech of the Lower Void hits my ears. It hisses with whispers; it crackles and strikes; it is smooth and dark. The pattern of speech is lonely. I've always known that pattern—the heaviness of it and the comfort too. It's odd and the only thing that I've felt shake it is Marcus. And now Kai'trish. It's not as if I was looking for them. I didn't need to look. Kai'trish only came to me once I had made amends with myself, and Marcus and I wouldn't have worked if we had become a couple in any year before this.

But the lonely vibration of this land is broken into pieces with a new energy. It carves through the mist, drawing in streaks of light in erratic paths. I pick up my pace, the cold around me digging deeper into my bones. With a pulse of heat, the haze clears. In the wasteland ahead of me, a mass of essence tangles in a sphere anchored to the ground. This is the root she wants me to see, but this one doesn't take any hédin, beast, or animal shape. It has corrupted so far that it is now a writhing mass, reaching for more with tentacles clawing into the ground, its core radiating a deep pink, almost purple glow through a necrotic black crust.

Kai'trish prowls back-and-forth in front of me, sniffing the putrid stench tangling around us. As I raise my hand over my nose, the lights that move toward the essence root come into focus. They are glimmering forms, hédin, animal, and beast. The delicate fish is here, taking a curving path through crevasses in the root. These essences are mobile, searching, retaining their forms from their Beginnings on the Karess. They're only lesser essences, the first hell of the Lower Void. Some of them with more erratic patterns, that streak from one plot of dehydrated ground to the next in starts and stutters, are essence terrors—the second hell.

Every essence I've come across until now retains their legs, their fins, their wings—their ability to move. All except this massive orb. It's as if it has chosen to stop in this very location. The other essence fractures are still willing to search for their other vital energies, to integrate and move on to the beyond. This root is blocking them. No, it's attracting them. It's fann essence. Fann always takes from its environment. This is what Eila warned me about. The Poison.

Eila told me to avoid it, but I follow Kai'trish into the throng of glimmering essence fractures. The ground crunches with each step. A substance oozes from the cracks in some places, and in others, a gas seeps into the air. Are we moving in because we are drawn by the root or something else?

Under an arch of flaking root, a lesser beast-essence paces. It snarls at the root, leaping toward it and jumping back, shaking its head, its tusks glimmering gold. The little fish wiggles to the base of the root and the beast pounces in front of it. The fish staggers, but instead of trying to go around the beast, it heads out, away from the root. As the beast continues to snuffle back-and-forth, head up in the air, and back down to the ground, my jaw aches. Hot blood drips down my neck, coating my tongue and seeping through my teeth.

"Fuck." I drop to my knees. Tapping a shaking hand to my face, my fingers come away clean.

Kai'trish nudges my hand away from my face to stretch out before me. I hold it there, a prickle setting into my fingertips. The distressed beast slows, its grunts quiet, and it lifts its head to me. A tear slips from my eye as it blinks, a puff of steam billowing from its nostrils.

"It-it's okay. I want to help you." My voice cracks out of my throat, spilling like the sludge beneath my knees. "I want to help this root, so it doesn't claim any more energy for itself. I want to help it move on."

The beast steps forward. Its growl is low and thick, but I stay put, my hand out strong. There is a break in its essence on its neck. Curls of gold energy break away from its body there. My fangs did that. And yet the beast comes closer, its head low, tilted to the side, its eyes wide as it takes its killer in. My heartbeat merges with the thundering pulse inside the beast as it presses its head to my palm.

"I know this root is hurting everything around it, but it's okay for you to move on. You've been so strong."

The beast, Kai'trish, and I rise from the mire. Kai'trish leads us through the tangle of roots and dripping, wine-coloured sludge. We pass other essence fractures, their energy pulling at my skin, but none of them follow. The pull of the root is too great. I reach my hand to these glimmering fractures. They aren't fazed by my presence. Kai'trish nudges her head to my shoulder. This is what she's been calling me for. She wants me to find a way to heal this root and take away this Poison.

"I don't know how to do that."

And she knows it too. She knows it will take time—she's waited for me, and she'll wait again for me to find a way to help this root, whoever it is.

Our path moves around the right side of the root. As we clear the tangled mess, a stirring sensation pulls me forward. The swirl and churn I felt as I dropped into this world grips my insides as we near a bridge spanning a break in the earth that dips into total darkness. The twist is the same as when I was in Toreth and the utanic core energy burst from the ice. This must be a Void Bridge to the next level of the Lesser Worlds.

Kai'trish and the beast bound ahead, taking the bridge across with their tails swishing behind them. The bridge is simple, just an extension of this plane to the next. Its periwinkle shine glimmers. Energy reverberates through my feet and a ripple expands over the plank with each step I take. I fill my lungs with breath and step into the Silent Realm.

CHAPTER 29

MY BREATH EVAPORATES without leaving my lungs. Darkness tinged with violet stretches on before me, under me, above me. All that keeps me company are my beasts. They trot to the right, keeping close to the churning pull of the Void barrier. I continue to follow. The beast I slaughtered plays with Kai'trish, its mouth parts as if in a grin, and its essence ripples. It has peace here. Is that why there is nothing? At least nothing that I can see? Matta says the Silent Realm is shaped by the mind. If I sense nothing familiar to me, and nothing from the beast, then maybe we are both at peace with our minds. I never would have expected such a clear space because I still have so many questions.

Kai'trish, I say. My mouth is still. My mind heats as she turns around and waits for me to catch up. We fall into step with her tail tapping my legs.

I was wondering if all this happened, all this connection with the Lesser Worlds happened because of my suicide attempt?

Kai'trish growls.

So, it's not like that then. But you did help my spirit block off my essence abilities for a while.

She hated to see me in so much pain with such a powerful essence that might hurt me if I couldn't gain control. Our connection didn't start there though. Kai'trish could see me from the moment I was born. Living a lonely life, shepherding energy to union for millennia, how could she not notice when a soul came to the Beginning that looked just like hers?

What happens when I Void Watch with my transformation?

Kai'trish bounds out into the glassy violet light. With a large gap between us, she and the beast sit and stare at me. I smile at her. With a simple eye transformation and meditation, I can see where Kai'trish is. Kai'trish takes her place next, so we both look at the golden beast. This is what I will see when I Void Watch without transformation. I'll see what she sees.

What about the lights in the Higher Plane?

Kai'trish takes a step forward.

I'll see soon enough.

The three of us continue, never faltering through this dark along the churning, curving wall, until we come to another bridge.

Again, the world of dark drops, but instead of darkness beyond the edge, there is light. It twinkles in winks of blue, green, and purple. The colours swish, waving in greeting to me, and my heart lifts. The ground meets my feet once again. It is soft, like grains of sugar. A sweet aroma washes over me as green foliage sprouts out of the fine earth. Golden energy suckles, delicate whisper weed, tall grasses build around my feet.

The bridge is a white lattice spreading out from its sugary base. The beast vanishes across the bridge without a glance behind it. Kai'trish waits for me at the base of the bridge. She sits on her hind legs, her fur flickering in delicate wisps all about her. On both sides of the Void Bridge are rillia bushes bathed in a murky, neon glow.

A moment passes as I stare at this creature who has found me. It draws out long, longer than any breath. I crouch and set my hands on the ground. The grains of earth build up around my flesh of their own accord. Energy suckles bend low to kiss my arms. A thrum of power rolls over my skin, merging with heart and essence and spirit as Kai'trish circles me in long, smooth steps. There's something about this bridge. There is clarity in my mind.

We'll be back here, won't we?

Kai'trish circles me one more time, stopping behind me so her warmth presses me forward. We'll be back here, it's why we have to go. Dragging my fingers over a pale rillia blossom, I cross the bridge.

My breath comes back to me in full in the Higher Plane. It rushes me, filling and emptying, swaying me one way and then another. I wrap my arms around myself. Never having enough breath has left me desperate for this and now it shakes me to my core—I'll still never have enough of the sweet air. My vision goes spotty, and my skin becomes lively with energy. I am light on my toes once I drop my arms. Blinking away the spots, layers of twinkling lights wrap around me backed by the deepest inky black.

One stands out to me, pure white light shining out, demanding attention. The beast I sent here with my unhinged transformation into a form not my own, stands before it. The beast faces a shimmering form. Energy radiates over me as they merge together—body and consciousness. Its form expands with one last breath, and it paws the ground. Taking a step, it vanishes, and the light implodes around it, and with it, fulfillment of my Vow. I may have killed this beast, but I've protected it too. Now it is whole and at peace.

The lights, they're not stars, they are gates to the Beyond. I spin slowly, taking in the vast expanse of rolling blackness, with high peaks and low valleys, all dotted with sparks of light. Some stay shining, others seem to fade and reappear every so often. Still others shimmer and implode like the beast's.

This journey has sewn me together. I stand strong and still under the weight of it, under the weight of my life—the pain I've faced, and the pain I will face. I have to move forward from here, take steps, be something. But there's a pull to the past, a *hiraeth* for who I've been, because I was home in myself even if I didn't realize it. I long to be gentler to that skin. I wish I could go back to the first time my mother assured me I was stronger than I could imagine and believe her. Maybe I wouldn't have touched death so many times before calling out to myself.

Kai'trish stands at my back. I nod. "I'm ready."

She presses her forehead to my back. Her glow surrounds me, and shivers bleed around my shoulders. The churning fills my stomach as we cross the Void back to the Karess.

With a flash of gold light, I am back between the walls of the academy dormitory. The mystic beast is nowhere in sight. My body is coated in sweat, and the tender skin on my side pinches. Beyond the window at the end of the hall, the moon hangs lazily in the emerald sky. The cold sweeps around me. But I'm too tired and mesmerized from my unexpected journey for it to take hold. I'm not sure if Kai'trish needed me to guide the beast to peace, but maybe she knew I needed to be there. There's forgiveness for a broken Vow. And now I can let it go.

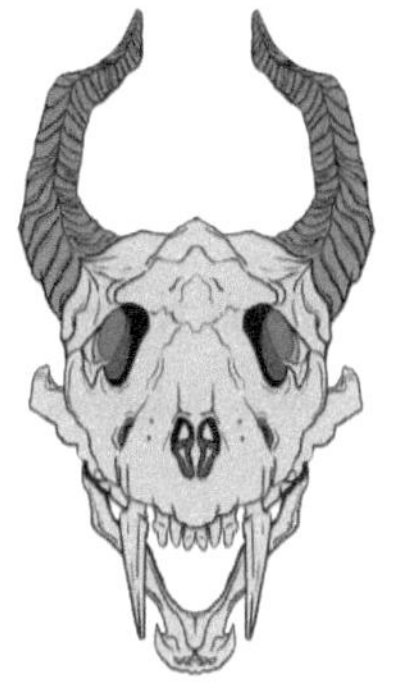

C H A P T E R   3 0

The academy is silent, and I am too stunned to move. Lifting my wrist to check my watch, my arm is heavy; the bend in my elbow is an effort. Just past midnight. Time wasn't my concern in the Lesser Worlds, but I think the length of time feels consistent with our notion of time on the Karess. I've been gone all afternoon.

From Rin and Eliote's room, I took all of five steps before I summoned Kai'trish. I turn and backtrack to check on her once more. Easing the door open as smoothly as I can, I peek my head into the room. A thundering crash shakes the floor. A scream rings through the hall, and my blood rushes to my head with a jolt. Eliote bolts upright from her bed, her eyes wide, and she throws off her covers. I move to her as she stumbles through the dark, and I catch her around the waist.

"It's Rin," she says, her voice shaky. She strains her neck to see past me out into the hall as sleepy faces peer out from every doorway.

"I should help her," Eliote says. "I–I don't know what to do though." She presses her fingers to her quivering lips.

I pull her back to her bed. "I know. It's okay, I'll help her."

"I should—"

"Sleep. What everyone needs to do is sleep. Rest. She'll need you in the morning."

Eliote slumps onto her bed. Her eyes follow me, squinting as she pieces together my words and what she sees in my aura. She nods, and I leave her bent over her knees in the dark.

Closing the door behind me, whispers drift between rooms. I rub my hand over my chest as my heart beats fast, and say, "Go back to bed. I'll check it out."

Cold and heat crawl down my spine as the girls vanish. I grab my med kit from my room, and as I near the bathroom door, two murmuring voices catch my ears. It's Rin, and I have a feeling Johanna is with her.

Placing my hand on the door to push it open, the murmurs come through in fits wrapped around heavy sobs. My hand falls, and I slide down the wall into a crouch. The conversation isn't angry anymore. There isn't a threat, nothing to be broken up.

I touch my palm to my heart again as I wait, the tips of my fingers of my other hand bracing my crouch. My heart beats a heavy rhythm. It is strong. The strength is unnerving as it fills me. It's like I've stepped into a suit of armour and could face an army. But stepping into strength is no easy feat. Confidence takes practice. Forgiveness takes time.

I catch my breath in my lungs and hold it. Churning inside me, the air is a comfort. I exhale and move into the bathroom as their voices fade.

Rin and Johanna sit side by side along the back wall. One of the mirrors is shattered, its remains covering the white tiles with glinting shards of glass, and the wall is caved in. There's a puddle of vomit on the floor, adding bitterness to the air.

Rin looks up at me and I catch a glimpse of her red-rimmed, storm cloud eyes before she hides her face behind her knees.

I sit in front of the girls. I am stiff and reverent with my hands placed on my legs.

"Hey," I say.

The whole team took on this stillness as we watched their fight. I think we all know we were witnessing something far too intimate for spectators. The fight was public, but I wait for an invitation into their space now.

Rin is stone still. Johanna's frame shifts with even breaths. She has a cut on her upper lip. The skin is pink around it.

I take a deep breath of my own. "I should disinfect that cut, Johanna."

"It's fine," she says.

"I should really do something for it, or it will scar." I turn to my med kit, my eyes still glued to Johanna as she licks the cut on her lip with a wince. My hands stop moving to my kit.

Despite her discomfort, her eyes are soft.

"Let it," she says and pushes away from the wall. "I'm going to bed."

I smile to myself at her ability to take pain—physical and emotional. Maybe she understands healing more than I do.

With Johanna gone, I give my undivided attention to Rin as

I cross my legs and get back to collecting a curestone. Rin runs her pale hands up and down her legs.

"Johanna hit your weak spot, didn't she?" I ask.

Ace and I assumed this earlier, but I know Ironskin weak spots aren't something to chat about, and they don't give out the knowledge willingly. I want to make sure I'm not jumping to conclusions.

Eyes glazed over, fixed on her knees, she nods.

"Seemed like she knew where it was."

She nods again.

"Bitch." I dip my head to see her face. She smiles, but she taps her fingers to her lips as a frown takes hold. "Do you mind if I take a look?"

Her breaths come short and quick as she turns for me. She gasps with a twist and slows even more.

My hands are cold but I'm not sure if I should warm them, given the nature of her injury. I lift her shirt. Her entire lower back is inflamed around a raised bump. The skin is deeply bruised. The bruising and redness farther away from her weak spot take on an interesting pattern. It follows tiny, jagged paths, not along nerves or blood vessels, but between skin cells. Some patches of her skin are unaffected. Her essence must move from certain cells, allowing bruising in those areas, as the essence is directed to the areas in her weak spot with the most damage.

Amid all this damage is a scar, from one side of her back to the other. It's raised, crude. It wasn't treated with stitches or curestones.

I let my hands be cold to soothe some of the swelling, and tap from the top of the bruising to the bottom, noting where the swelling begins and ends. My eyes stay on the scar. I think she did it to herself. And it's not easy to let someone help you clean up wounds like that.

"She really did some damage on ya, girly. You're in a lot of pain, hey?"

Rin shrinks into herself with sharp breaths.

"I'm going to use a high-grade curestone on it, if that's okay? It should take away the bruising and make sure there's no nerve damage."

"'Kay," she whispers.

The curestone is big enough to span the length of the swelling. The stone is smooth and cool. It catches the fluorescent lights and shimmers.

"All right, I need you to take a deep breath for me. I'm going to put the curestone to your weak spot. Okay?"

I may move the curestone toward the injury, but the attraction between it and Rin's wounded flesh is instant. A pale glow builds around the stone as a shadow sweeps between Rin and the smooth white surface. The shadow ripples in one direction—skin to stone. The glow brightens even as the pale surface gets dimmer with inky-black swirls infesting it.

Rin gasps and sniffles

"Shh. Breathe," I say.

As she inhales, I inhale. With my free hand, I run my fingers through her hair. It's something Matta would do. My chest swells with heat at the soothing image of my mother, but my heart aches. Rin hasn't had a mom to run her fingers through her hair in a long time. And I'm guessing she wasn't around to try and heal that wound on her back before it scarred.

"I'm going to hold it here for thirty seconds."

I keep raking my fingers through her knotted hair, taking

care not to pull too hard. Her head leans into the touch.

"Ten more seconds," I say.

But as swelling lowers and the trails of bruise fade and Rin's skin becomes pale, the stone cracks in half.

Rin turns all the way around to look at me without flinching in pain, and her cheeks are rosy. "What happened?"

"Well . . . " I purse my lips at the tiny bits of stone crumbling over my knees at the touch of my thumb. "It died."

I've never seen a curestone do this before. Usually, they just stop being effective.

Rin's eyes fall closed. The muscles in her jaw go slack, her lips part, and her back relaxes into an arch. As the seconds pass, she tries to form words.

Clearing her throat, she says, "Adrianne?"

"Mm?"

"I don't know if I can do it."

I set aside the broken curestone and shift to sit right in front of her.

"Johanna wants to start over," she says, moving hairs out of her face. "But how do I start over when . . . I don't feel like I can go on?" Her whole body moves with her breath—a form of control that suppresses everything trying to come out. The control and focus to keep breathing, keep moving, after breaking.

"I know what you mean," I say. The words slip out of me. Soft but clear.

That's not enough. Tingles crawl over my arms. They spread over my shoulders, merging into a soft buzz in my chest. I clear my throat. It's choked—not from an urge to cry, not yet at least, but the part of me that still hurts doesn't want to say it. It's raw, even after four years, and it wants to stay covered, not carved open again.

I'll risk it for her though. Sharing this part of me is what I needed to do when she panicked in front of me. She didn't need a lesson that day, she needed to be validated.

"I want to tell you why I'm here," I say.

The storm in Rin's eyes meets mine. It tugs and pulls the words out of me.

"I don't talk about this a lot. I mean ever. The only people at the academy who know about this are Evelyn and Marcus." I twiddle my thumbs to try and ward off the numbness crawling my skin. "Fuck, this is hard to say," I say with a laugh.

I keep fidgeting—with my hands, my hair—until it all centres with a buzz in my chest and I can push it all out in one big rush.

"When I came to the academy," I say and clear my throat once more. "I was really self-conscious. I constantly worried what others thought of me. I struggled with identity and tried to find it in all the wrong places. I saw myself through the eyes of the people around me, or the way I thought they saw me. Too fat, too skinny, my weight and my emotions were all over the place. I tried to find myself in my lineage, but was I more Beastblood or Emberstead? I was really lost, you know? I didn't think I could go on either. I attempted sui—"

I said it in past tense.

I wish I could take it back, say it all over again, in present tense because all that is still true. All those confusing thoughts slice through a mangled heart. They bleed and create running rivers. I've created bridges over those rivers, though, new ways to think for myself and to see myself.

My stomach flips with a sinking nausea. It jolts up my throat, so I set my focus on my hands, stirring my essence to warm myself.

"I attempted suicide," I say with my eyes fixed on my flushing fingers. "Sometimes I look back on it and it seems . . . silly, or my reason was too small. But when you don't feel alive in your own skin, when you can't hear your own thoughts or find your own way, it doesn't feel small. Nothing feels small. It's all totally overwhelming."

Lifting my eyes to Rin, I set my hand on her knee. The warmth of my skin responds to the cold seeping through her sweatpants.

"Since then, I've learned to look for myself in myself and accept what I find. I had to redo first year, but I didn't have all that pressure on myself to do it right. It's not like everything got better after that. Every day is still a battle against depression, self doubt, and anxiety is a motherfucking asshole, but I started making choices for myself.

"Choosing to be a Medic was the first choice I made without thinking about what other people wanted from me. I still don't know what I really want in life, but I know that choices define us more than our desires. The choice to keep going after already going through so much is the hardest."

Glistening tears stream down Rin's face. I have to fight to keep my own tears in. My pain has snuck into the present, but hers is here too. I told her this for her to know she isn't alone. She needs to know because it doesn't get easier, and the pain never goes away. We need people who understand that, who aren't going to break when we tell them our biggest pains.

I run my hand over her back. Her shirt warms as I make small circles, and the motion soothes my restless hands.

"But how did you move on . . . from your attempt?" Rin

asks.

The question is welcome in my heart; I'm still asking it myself. It's a good question, even if there is no good answer and the answer changes from time to time. Asking the question means you're not thinking about the other side—not wishing to cross the Voids.

"You never really get over something like that. It stays with you forever," I say.

Rin swipes her eyes with her shirt, as if to punish her eyes, her heart, and everything that hurts. I take her hand, the hem of her sleeve soaked in tears, and rub my thumb over her cool skin.

"I still struggle with the same thoughts and feelings I had back then. I still take my days five seconds at a time. But at one point, I just had to forgive myself for it."

Her face flushes and her eyebrows cinch together. "Just forgive?"

The fire in her words matches the raging regret in my heart. I would have cussed her out if she had said the same thing to me a few years ago, or even at the beginning of this year.

"How do I forgive her for leaving us?"

I try to keep hold of her hand, but she pulls it away, clenching and unclenching her fists.

"How do I forgive her? How do I forgive myself? How do I forgive myself?"

I know, hun. I know.

"Didn't she want to be with us anymore? D-didn't she care what would happen to us? And I almost did the same thing to my brothers—I was this close!"

Rin gasps and sobs and doubles over, her body shaking. My eyes fill and I cannot blink. I pull her into me, ready for her to pull away, but she lets herself collapse onto my lap where I hold her and keep rubbing her back.

"My mom didn't want to be with me," she mutters. "Stephen doesn't want to be with me . . . I don't want to be with me. I can't imagine why Johanna would want to be my friend."

Heaviness sinks into my arms, not tension. It takes a moment before it's apparent that the heaviness is relaxation. I think Rin feels it too. She's released the lies and expectations into this room just as I have, expressing how awful it is to hate yourself and wonder why anyone would love you.

I lift Rin off my lap as tears cascade down my face.

"Forgiveness isn't saying it was okay that something shitty happened," I say through the choke in my throat. "It wasn't okay that your mom left you. But I can tell you this, she didn't want to leave you. She was in pain. You'll always feel that pain when you think of her. You've been carrying her pain and your own for years, girly. Don't be hard on yourself for wanting out. Forgiveness is giving yourself permission to step away from the bad and into something new."

She can't escape the pain. I know I never will. But I've found some new parts of myself that are just for me and no one else, and I hope she finds those too. I hope she finds new, beautiful things about herself, beautiful to the extreme to outweigh her pains.

I've lost her eyes again, so I tilt her face toward me. "You are not your mother," I say with a clean wave of tears.

I wrap Rin in my arms. She fidgets, but I can't let go until all the hope and all the love that I've locked away from myself and only grasped now pours onto her. Rin leans into me, my neck catching her tears, but her breaths have nowhere to go. So I let her go. Let her breathe.

"All right," I say, getting both of us off the cold tile.

I sling my arm around her and walk her back to her room.

"Get some sleep, and in the morning, no coffee, just scolya root tea. And have a cup before bed too. It will help you regenerate your essence throughout your body," I say.

Rin meets my eyes. Her cheeks are full of colour, and her eyes are bloodshot. A beautiful picture of life.

One more time down the hall and maybe I'll make it to my bed. But Johanna leans against the doorframe of her room, her arms crossed. She eyes me, a laziness to her gaze. No defeat, no regret, not anymore. I stop a few feet away from her, rubbing my temples.

"Are you going to be able to sleep tonight?" I ask, also crossing my arms.

Johanna flicks her gaze to the ceiling. "Yes," she mutters.

"Okay, well—"

"Thank you for taking care of us, for teaching us this year." She drops her arms and straightens up, still not looking at me, but her feet face me.

I chuckle. "Oh, I'm sure you could've gone without a few of my lessons."

"No, actually I couldn't have. I've learned more than I hoped to learn this year. And it all started when you punched me in the face. I had to pay attention."

Pressing my lips together, I try to hide a smile.

"Brand taught us to fight for our team while in the field, and you taught me to listen up. You let me do both those things today."

The smile breaks over my face, and I can't stop myself from hugging her. Groaning, she says, "I am so done with all the hugging and crying."

Still, she leans in a little as I give her a quick kiss on the cheek.

"Okay, okay, that's it." She pushes away, her face crimson, and holds out her pinky fingers to me. "Fuck off. This time I'm really going to bed."

The little Rover in the cage. I had to free it and guide it to its escape. The truth inside me wasn't about never killing or never spilling blood. That's too specific. It was about reducing harm by any means necessary. Even if it's hard to admit, I don't think any of us would have made it back from my field assignment if I hadn't killed that beast. I wouldn't have gotten through to Johanna if I hadn't punched her. Today, I saw Johanna in all her glory. The day I punched her, she saw the real me, and that's what made the impact. I immediately tried to cover it up, and she was horrified. I hurt both of us when I began to tailor my lessons to expectations.

Sometimes people need to get punched in the face. Sometimes someone has to die. Sometimes you need to fight it out. Sometimes you have to turn into a beast. But only sometimes. My intuition, listening to myself, builds the bridges I need to learn to cross. My full transformation into my beast form was the wake-up call I needed to see the two lives I live more clearly. A heavy hitting, foul-mouthed beast on one side and a peaceful guide like Kai'trish on the other. I was never broken, only caged. I've freed myself now and I won't get caught again.

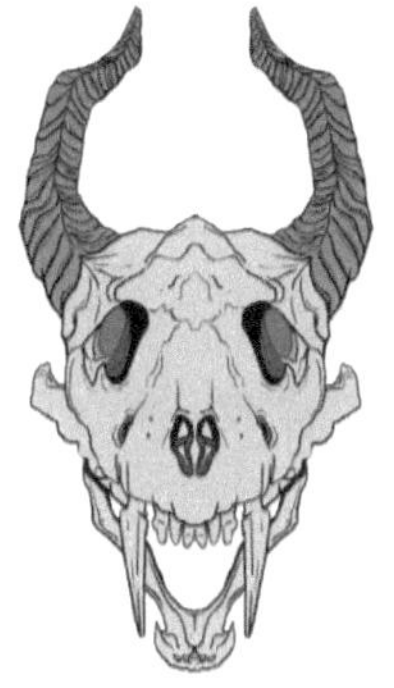

C H A P T E R   31

A week passes, and I haven't been able to summon Kai'trish back to the Karess. I was starting to worry that it was just a one-time thing, but as the two moons have risen tonight, I know that's not the case.

The Festival of Two Moons is a time of anticipation, renewed energy, transformation, and shift. For most, it's just a festival, but for me I've always felt it more. A deep, excited understanding of our universe. It's the only time I've ever felt free of worry.

The shift at this time is more of a stir, a roundabout motion. It's common knowledge that the bright green stars in our sky are chaotic energy, but the effect of that energy is minimized by the atmosphere of the Karess. Since Nathal told me about the halfies sensing the energy more than other lineages, it makes sense that I would feel this time of year deep in my bones because the second moon balances the energies within our atmosphere to produce utanic energy.

And the Voids between realms are utanic. I think that makes it easier for Kai'trish to cross. I also think she's not constantly at my disposal, especially if she has to go through the worlds instead of around to help souls integrate. She's close tonight though. Her breath reaches me and strengthens my heart.

Marcus holds my hand in his lap. His fingers are locked with mine, and he cups his free hand over them to keep them warm. The airbus shudders as it lifts from the platform, taking to the air up to Sii. The city on the floating boulder glistens in the fading daylight, core energy streaming from its base to meet the stars. Now, with Marcus' presence, the energy of this time of year is amplified, more chaotically delicious than ever. I squeeze his hand, and he leans into me, resting his scruffy cheek on my head.

Today is about remembering to break. Not emotionally, but I need to remember to give myself breaks so I don't have to shut down so severely. I like to think that I honour Vera this way— watching my own back. Spending time away from the school, the stress, the pain, and letting myself be in the moment. This is what I need before the last few weeks of school and graduation. And deep-fried keeta greens. I need that too.

The heat from the airbus's firestone core radiates through the metal floor. The windows of the bus are wide open, never shut, even in the dead of winter. The forest around the city comes into view, blanketed by a thin layer of snow. Touching down in the outskirts of the sky-city, the whir of the engine quiets. As we exit the airbus, the two moons loom overhead. The silver moon that is always present is called Aniso. The smaller, honey-yellow moon, Ryo, adds a new dynamic light to the green sky. From somewhere deep in the fairgrounds, a singer changes to a minor key, filling the cold air with a weighty, satin touch.

"So, food first, right? Unless you want to do the two-slide?" I jab my thumb in the direction of a crowd stomping and shuffling to the mysterious melody washing through the festival grounds.

Marcus cringes. "Not in a million years will you see me dance."

"Mm, I can wait a million years."

"We're going to live that long, hey?"

I study him, his handsome face, unpolished soul, earnest eyes. "Maybe we'll dance in the Lesser Worlds together."

He takes a breath, chuckling. "I guess once I've discarded my bones, then maybe, maybe you'll see me do the two-slide."

"I'm gonna hold you to that. Or if I die first, I'll become a Wander Wraith and haunt you until I get my two-slide with you."

Marcus smiles. Lifting his face to the jade sky, he says, "Actually, before we eat, can we stop at a shrine?"

"Yes, of course."

The stomping and shuffling dancers fade behind us as we make our way through a row of booths. Each one is draped in silk and sparkling designs to indicate their wares. We pass one selling jewellery with powerstones set in them. The air is heavy with the different energy frequencies of the stones. On the other side of the cobblestone path is a booth for homemade incense, adding a smokey perfume to the energetic air. Behind the bedazzled booths are whitewashed buildings like the ones down in mainland Akinnera. There are long streamers crisscrossing overhead from building to building and all different ancestral symbols in the windows for protection.

At the end of the row is an Emberstead shrine. The building is made from a simple wooden frame with burgundy leather panels embossed with flare-wing moths. In the centre of each panel is a ring of suns. At the apex is one large golden sphere. The subsequent spheres completing the ring decrease in size on both sides. It depicts Ōna and the changing hours of daylight she provides the Karess. Like for Ōna, we are thankful for Zenta and the various ways she is present for us.

Marcus pushes aside a thick, black velvet curtain in the doorway. Inside, firestones line four different paths to representations of the revered ancestors: Carnity, Dien, and Zenta, as well as one for the All Creator. Most Emberstead shrines are like this, some even have extra stations for the dual pure spirits Ashnaho and Neuoa.

Marcus takes the path to a tall, masculine-looking visage of the All Creator on the far right. With a flick of his wrist, he lights a candle and sets it with a dozen other flickering flames. I take the path next to him to an oil painting of Zenta. She is painted with flaming red hair cut in a sharp bob above her shoulders. Her skin is pale and smooth, her eyebrows angular and dark.

As I kneel in front of her, lighting my own candle, Marcus whispers a prayer.

"Nialle, dantes enhir dan tascaternacht ō ketz nanehall eront."

The last time someone prayed so fervently near me, she made me question everything. It stung. She drew me into her own prayer, acquitting me of sins I didn't even understand. Marcus softens his prayer as he appeals for himself. I wait with my hands together and eyes closed. The warmth of the stones seeps through my coat, and their orange glow flickers through my eyelids.

Once Marcus stirs, I open my eyes. "Say 'hi' to Vera and my beasty for me," I say and wink at Zenta.

"That's it?" Marcus says, holding the heavy curtain for me. "That's the prayer you give to the first hédin to manipulate the element of fire? Who led the way for everything we teach today?"

I step out into the cold, snowflakes kissing my cheeks, and stretch my back. "Yep. I said what was on my heart."

Marcus sighs. "I guess that's all prayer is."

"Plus, I'm hungry."

With a playful roll of his eyes, he shakes his head. "Right, right, sorry for making you wait so long. Guess my heart is just heavier than yours."

"No, just bigger."

"Oh, is that what it is?" He darts his eyes to me, a shy smile on his lips.

"Huge." I grab his hand.

Glued together, we search for as much food as we can possibly handle. We start with deep-fried keeta. The thick, green medallions doused in vegetarian batter and fried to crispy perfection, crunch and ooze as I bite into them. Steam seeps from my mouth. Marcus laughs at me as my feet stamp in the snow in delight. He plants a kiss on my forehead and pops a piece of keeta into his own mouth.

We move on to the next booth and purchase a steaming pile of barbequed meat. There's a vegetarian Beastblood special, too, but that's not right for me now. The meat spills warmth and even more grease through my mouth. Finally, we sit under the stars with syrup-glazed fruit and honeycombs, giggling and shivering together in sugary delusion. I am so at peace with Marcus near,

I can eat without a stomachache, I can speak without having to tailor my words.

To the left, familiar voices prick my ears.

Jeff-Ray's voice sails over the din. "I can't believe you missed every single one, Johanna."

"I swear, you have no tact when it comes to anything that doesn't involve fire or a fistfight," Niko says with a cackle.

"You're going to have a fistfight right here if you don't shut up and give me some of that candy fluff."

I grab Marcus' hand.

"I know, I know. Just be very still and maybe they won't see us," Marcus says through a mouthful of fruit.

I freeze, cupping my plate close to my chest.

Jeff swipes the candy fluff from Niko just as they pass us. Jeff holds it high in the air as he stuffs a piece in his mouth while the other two reach for it unsuccessfully. They disappear into the mass of bodies.

"We get one day away from them, and I still have a headache from their bickering." Marcus rubs his temples and gets back to eating.

As he licks syrup from his fingers, his face hardens, a furrow touching his brow.

I nudge him. "What's up?"

"I feel like the gate is just being thrown open and the rules I thought I knew for life have been erased. Working with Brand, I"—he brushes his mouth—"I have no idea what that will look like. There's no guidebook for working with an organization like that." He swipes the last bit of glaze from his plate with his finger and mumbles, "And maybe none of it will happen since her arrest."

I note the far-off look in his eye as I take a bite of too-sweet, too-sour fruit. He's not done his thought yet. So, I munch and listen.

"I'm not saying there should be rules, I think the rules I've followed all my life were just put in place by other anxious idiots who crave control just like me." He plops his empty plate down on the bench beside him and leans forward on his knees. "I think we've missed a lot by following their plan."

"So, what you're saying is that you're scared."

Marcus looks me dead in the eye. His mouth pulls tight, eyes searching and gentle. He swallows, the ball of his throat bobbing. "Yeah."

"Scared of the things you've missed and the things to come?" I say, gripping my plate.

He nods.

Taking his hand, I say, "Me too. But I think we've punished ourselves enough for being scared. As if it was a fucking sin against the ancestors to not have it all together, to mess up. You still okay with the big guy?" I point a thumb at the sky.

"I haven't given up on my faith in the All Creator, I've just let go of some things people insist I believe in, a strict divine purpose being one of them." He rubs a hand over his chest. "My prayers feel stronger, like wherever I find purpose, he'll be with me, even in my fear."

"Mm, I like that. I think creating our own purpose is hard though, so it's something only some of us can do. For me, having my feet on the Karess is purpose enough."

Marcus cups my face with his hand. It's warm and gentle despite the frigid cold and snowflakes dusting the air. My heart calms with his breath skimming my cheek. His lips press to mine, and just as my head starts to rush with dizzy euphoria, he pulls away enough to say, "I don't want to mess this up."

Eyes closed and head resting on mine, he breathes me in slowly, as if savouring something sweet.

I clasp his face in my hands, tears stealing his beautiful face from my eyes. "You won't. Because I already love you."

My heart ricochets inside me. Marcus leans forward and whispers in my ear, "I love you too." He kisses me again to seal the truth.

For a moment, I am safe in my skin, skin with scars. My mind is quiet, my heart is content. Each heartbeat is full of fresh flow, each breath life giving and not a fleeting entity to grasp on to. The crowd flows around us. From each booth and cluster there seems to be a contest to out-do each other with the loudest laughter.

A scream breaks past the barrier of sweet kisses keeping us safe. It rips through the night. The music stops and screams cascade into each other. And the crowd moves. Marcus braces me as people stumble past us.

"What the hells?" I say, trying to stand, but I get pushed back into Marcus.

Everyone scrambles in one direction. Still planted on our bench, I try to get a glimpse of what everyone is running from. Screeches and screams meld together, crashing, searing sickness in my gut. Through the tangle of sound, my heart pounds, and my essence is hot inside me. A palpable but invisible stream of energy passes over me in the opposite direction of the crowd. It pulls and claws at me for a moment, but never takes hold. My essence churns into a thickened sludge that is protective and solidified. It thrums inside of me. It is a rhythmic chant, casting away the energy swarming the environment.

"Marcus, do you feel that?" I yell over the crowd with shivers prickling my skin.

I turn to him. His hands have let go of me and he stares at them with wide eyes, mouth parted.

"Yes," he says.

Local Protectors shove through the terrified crowd, hollering commands to each other that my brain can't comprehend. My vision clouds with spots, and my ears start to ring as my eyes catch sight of what's caused the frenzy. I grit my teeth.

A monster of lifeless bones and skin streaked in moonlight lashes out at a man struggling behind the rest. Its gnarled hand is a vise around the man's arm. It yanks with a hellish scream, and the man's arm rips from his body. Blood arcs through the air. The monster drops the arm, and the man crashes to the ground, crying, face pinched, his only hand grasping at his mangled shoulder and ungrasping in shock of the blood and essence streaming from his body.

Metal tinges the air and my stomach flips. The monster slashes at the man's throat, drawing blood and muscle through his skin and keeps running, stomping over the corpse and barreling forward with jerking movement, blood trailing behind him.

Despite the tension in my jaw, my teeth chatter and my body jolts. Tracking the monster, my trembling body takes its stance. I thrust my hands forward, propelling my essence from my feet to my hands. A projection bursts in front of me in brilliant orange light and solidifies. The monster slams into the barrier.

One of the Protectors unsheathes a long blade and rams it into the monster, pinning it to the barrier. The tip of the blade is buried in slack folds of grey skin. No blood, no essence. The monster's eyes glint, slobbering teeth appear from its mouth. A sound escapes—chittering, gurgling. Desiccated laughter.

Shivers cascade down my body.

I turn in a circle, hands up, breaths rapid, mind calculating where I'm most needed. The crowd has thinned, but down the cobblestone road, more of the terrible monsters slink out of alleys. I step forward, around my barrier. Focusing on the heat of the pentagon, I expand the wall from one side of the street to the other, blocking off the citizens on one side and the Protectors and these monsters on the other.

Marcus spreads his feet wide, taking a stance that is strong and supportive, balancing his weight so his bad leg doesn't have to overcompensate. He pulls in a full breath, drawing his fists in close to his sides. He expels his air, and orbs of fire burst into being above his head. He punches one fist and then the other, alternating in quick succession. With each punch, the orbs speed away from him. They dial in on the monsters scrambling toward us. With his measured breaths controlling his manipulations, the orbs burst open and slam into their faces. With the hissing of flame solidifying into armoured plates, Marcus spreads his fingers wide, outstretched in front of him. He clasps his hands together. In unison, the plates cinch over the monster's faces, stopping them in their tracks. Like he's swinging a bat, Marcus whips his clasped hands from one side of his body to the other. All the monsters' heads tick to the side with a violent crack. Marcus pulls his fists back to his sides as the monsters clatter to the ground in heaps of angular limbs.

More of these vile creatures leap forward attacking other Guardians, and the one that took the man's arm is still locked in battle with the Protector and his blade. It slashes its fist with such strength that it breaks the blade. Without hesitation, the Protector shifts his stance and wields an ice sword, covering himself in ice armour. But as the ice shoots up his body, the monster jabs both fists at the man, slamming the Protector's heart and shoulder. The ice cracks and sheds off his body in shards, a scream ripping from his lungs.

The cry is a call to my heart to move blood faster. Marcus' ability was effective, but how could this Protector do nothing to defend himself from the monster? I don't have enough control to do Marcus' ability, and I can't get distracted by figuring out how these monsters work. I need to help this injured Protector.

Saliva splatters me in the face as the monster lunges at me. I plate my arms with flame, heat billowing around me. The monster's fist slams into my armour. Sparks explode as I skid backward, arms still braced and trembling. I step back from its boney, flailing limbs, duck under a high kick, and step to the side until I'm between my injured comrade and the monster. The demon slashes an open hand at me, sneering, the chittering sound gushing from its mouth.

I suck in a gritty breath. It strikes my lungs, expanding a flame inside me that presses on my soul. With a pulse of light, golden tendrils burst from my core. They bash into the monster, sending it flying as an image of my beast form flashes through the dark. She chuffs and growls inside me, itching to be released fully through my flesh. I can't transform or I'll lose control. I channel the ferocity, sinking her into my hédin bones. The golden energy expands wider, blocking the snarling monster from getting any closer.

I drop to my knees by the writhing Protector with my projection still shimmering around me.

"My arm," he says. "I can't use my essence." He strains his fingers, his arm solid with tension, jerking and spasming with no manipulation.

The monster hit his shoulder and chest, so this man's brachial essence path is blocked between those areas. I know how to unblock pathways, but I've only practiced on a dummy.

The Protector stares at me, eyes quivering. Wafts of heat permeate the air with the stench of char and mingled blood.

"Your essence flow is blocked." I push up my sleeves. My breaths are heavy and my mind is spinning under the commotion around me, but my essence is still strong and oddly solid inside me.

I can unblock it. I know I can. But my hands shake, hovering over the man.

I try to centre myself and bring to mind all I've learned this year, in training and outside of training.

The man screams as his arm spasms with essence surging with nowhere to go.

"My name is Adrianne, and I'm here to help you," I say over his screaming.

The man gasps for breath, grunting and moaning. I grab him by the shoulders, my hands shaking.

"Look at me," I yell in his face. "Look into my fucking eyes." Not your textbook definition of calming your comrade, but his eyes are locked on me. Tears snake down his tan cheeks.

Shutting my eyes for a moment, I just say what I need to hear right now. "We're gettin' through this shit. You are strong. You are brave. We are going to get your essence flowing, okay?"

He stops screaming and nods his head, taking long breaths through his teeth.

I flinch as a monster throws itself at me. My beast projection pulses and bashes the monster away. The golden wisps settle back into a gleaming lattice around us.

Here we go. There is a pressure point and an essence node right beside each other in the wrist. I need to stimulate them at the same time. I place one thumb on the pressure point and my other thumb over the essence node.

"This is going to hurt," I warn the Protector.

He nods. Using the force of my whole body, I press down on the two points. The man screams. There's a pulse of energy from his hand. I find the next two points along the elbow.

The fight against every distraction burns away worry; I have no nausea. Eyes trained on my work, breaths full and fast, my focus creates its own buzz of energy that drowns the roar of commotion around me. My body responds to the command of my mind without hesitation.

I press again. The man groans—a flash of light.

"One more. This one's gonna hurt like hells."

The core channel. I press my knuckles down below his collarbone and plate my other arm with fire armour to get more force. With a deep breath, I simultaneously press my knuckles into his chest and slam my elbow down on the core node just above his heart. He howls as a surge of essence flows from his chest through his arm, meeting the essence that was caught in his hand.

I slip my arm around his shoulders and prop him up.

"Try it out," I say.

Wincing, he wiggles his fingers. With gritted teeth, he creates a swirling globe of water. A smile spreads his lips, and I cheer for myself and for him. A rush of excitement washes over me, and I yank him right off the ground.

His smile—no, not just his smile, the transformation of the man's whole demeanour, from anguish to delight—that's why I want to be a Monitor, because I want to see transformation in the world, in people. Because I allowed myself to transform from a girl who lost herself to whatever I am today—still lost, but searching, moving.

With no monsters in sight, I bring down the barrier. The rolling streams of invisible energy gush like a river over me. Screams swell through the city, amplifying the horror in my heart and a thundering crash shakes the ground. I stumble into Marcus and turn to the origin of the crash.

Above the city, far in the distance, under the light of the dual moons, a giant bellows to the night. It's just like the monsters that swarm the city, but this one doesn't have the mischievous grin and gut-churning giggle. Its body writhes with power, and its outraged cry sinks into my bones. Marcus grabs me as my knees go weak. He pulls my face into his chest, his arms trembling. I shriek as Marcus draws us down to the ground, and we cling to each other until the ground stills.

The Protectors in our area rush past us. But another torrent brushes my face. One Protector stops in his tracks, spinning around to his comrades. His chest heaves, his arms tremble, outstretched, riding the wave of this phantom in our midst. His eyes lock with mine—deep brown and shaking. Lavarian wings sprout from his back, but his skin is dark—he's Earthkin.

I stare at him, then at Marcus. We're all halfies. We all feel it.

The Protector grits his teeth. At a loss, he shakes his head and sprints down the street in the direction of the giant at the other end of the city.

Marcus lifts me up and takes my hand, tugging me along after the Protectors. I set my heels on the cobblestone and don't budge.

"Adrianne, what are you doing? We have to go help." His dark brows furrow, his frame a silhouette in the moonlight.

"We do," I say in a quivering voice, the tinge of iron in the air itching my nose. "But not that way."

Marcus sputters and runs both hands over his hair.

Up and down, the churning lingers in the air. Invisible to my eyes, the energy snakes around my legs. I turn, following its path.

"You said you felt it," I say, whipping my arms around me at the sensations pulling at my skin.

"Yes, but what about that?" He shoves one hand at the sky. The giant swings its arm through the air at something. The ground quakes.

I take a step toward Marcus, toward the giant. A growl in my soul makes me step back.

"Adrianne, come on!" His brown eyes plead with me. "I don't know what this is, but I know we have to help the people that are still out there screaming for our help." He takes in a long breath, his face twisting in a grimace, longing to get out there and fight. "This is my chance." His words barely reach my ears as his arm drops to his side. "This might be my only chance."

I shut my eyes, grunting with the rushing energy around me and the tug in my heart to follow it. Opening them again, flashes of red and blue burst around the giant.

"Marcus, trust me—"

"It's our duty as Guardians not to run away from something like this." Grabbing my hand, he yanks me forward.

"No, Marcus. We're going to miss something if we follow the rules." The force behind my words is like a bark, no, a roar. They burst from me as I keep my feet planted, resisting Marcus' pull. "You might not know what is doing this but . . . but I think I do."

His chest heaves and the muscles in his face are taut, but he stops tugging me.

"This, I feel it every year, it's utanic energy building in our atmosphere from the interaction between the moons, the Karess, and the sun. But I never feel it like this. It never has direction like this. Something is drawing it in."

"How? Why? What could do that?"

I ground myself with a breath of bitter air. "An Ironskin with a Death stone."

"Death stones aren't utanic." Marcus' grip tightens around my hand, and his voice strains.

No, but they draw in beasts, they draw in mental energy that is chaotic and desperate, like fear, like vengeance, like the desire for death.

"That stone is here, I know it, and we have to find it. Because then maybe we can find Stephen and Adia. If we bring them in, they can be questioned about the Revival. Just trust me."

Marcus shakes his head. Still gripping my hand, he grunts and turns away from the giant.

We sprint at full speed, following the winding trail of energy.

CHAPTER 32

W E SPRINT FARTHER AWAY from the visible threat thrashing through the city, chasing after the invisible snakes of energy churning over the cobblestone. They stream from every alley, from every corner, slithering out of the city.

I bolt through the gate, but Marcus' footsteps slow behind me. Skidding, I turn back to him, lungs burning. Marcus is bent over with both hands braced around his bad leg.

"This isn't right, Adrianne," he says, his breaths ragged.

"I know, I know, hun," I whisper, crouching before him. I send essence to my hand and place it on his leg. He grimaces. "I just know we have to go this way. There are people fighting that giant now. I can see the essence pulses—"

"No, I know. It's my essence. It's"—he shakes his head—"I

don't know, it's fortifying or something, getting more and more tightly wound inside me. I know we're going the right way. I just can't keep up."

"It's our halfie essence. It has some sort of fortifying effect against chaotic energy."

The pinch in his cheeks and the huff that escapes Marcus are not out of place for all the crazy words I've been saying tonight.

"We'll go slow. I'm right here with you, and I need you." I look him straight in the eyes. His jaw tenses in my hands clasped around his face. The wind whistles through the gate, the stars paint us in green. "I need your control, okay?"

Pressing his eyes closed with a deep breath, Marcus nods and straightens. We breathe together, fogging the air, and follow the energy as it twists down a path in a patch of forest that cups the west side of the city.

I keep my arm around him as we walk through the clumps of trees, their branches tangling over the path. Tucked in the darkness of the forest are core-energy boulders. Glimmering streaks of white energy carve through the stone. At the top, bits of core energy escape their crevasses and float away from the stones in twisting motions, adding to a thick mist that pulls at my clothes as we wade through it. A spark of utanic core energy comes close to my cheek. My essence pulses, and the spark jets away in a corkscrew pattern.

The path leads up an incline to a stone staircase. At the top of the stairs is an archway. Under it, a red glow pierces the night. The utanic energy thickens, forcing itself on me and dispersing a moment later.

I glance at Marcus, whose eyes are already on me. He gives me a squeeze around the waist. "I trust you," he says and nudges me forward.

Ascending the stairs, my heart beats in the same forceful rhythm as my essence. My breath is heavy and fast. My head is clear to the point of dizziness. As I push myself the last few steps, the clarity compounds with a heavy force as my mind latches onto the dark thoughts I've harboured inside me. I breathe through the unrelenting pull and lean instead into Marcus. His arms tighten in response.

At the top, shivers attack my skin before my eyes even comprehend what's going on. Beyond the towering arch made of wood and iron is a stone. On that stone, three prongs of iron protrude from the top, and between those prongs is the black Death stone. Stephen holds his hand above it, causing it to glow blood red, just like his energetic eyes—the activated death spirit affinity. The veins under his eyes pulse through his fair skin. Rin mentioned someone named Stephen. Could this man in front of me be the sibling of the cold-eyed girl I know?

And this is what he wanted the stone for? To syphon utanic energy?

"Stephen," I yell.

Marcus' hand keeps me back.

"He can't hear you." A voice comes from the shadows of the trees surrounding the platform of stone.

Heavy tread. The mist parts and a shape emerges from the shadow. Black boots, sturdy legs, a woman's figure, full and curving. Adia's pale face appears with the bloom of wrinkled skin, her black hair cascading over her shoulders in a silky sheet.

"Adia," I say between breaths. "What are you doing?"

"Oh, just a little project. I told you about it, remember?" Adia paces between me, Marcus, and Stephen. Ruby-red light of his death affinity rims her silhouette, the green stars glimmer above her. She glares at me from the corner of her eye. "I told you, 'One by one the fires will go out.' We just need a little power boost." She looks back at Stephen.

Under his palm, the inky-black Death stone splinters with an ear-piercing screech. The blood-red light engulfs all of us as the shards hover and twist and rearrange themselves, so the pointed ends face outward and they solidify back into a unit.

A low hum comes from Adia's throat as her silver eyes glint in the deathly glow. "Looks like it's starting to fill. And our other project is just wrapping up too." She points back to the city.

A fire-bright glow of red energy, just like Stephen's eyes, swarms the giant. A roar thunders through the night.

"She did it faster than I expected." Adia's voice is thick with admiration and a deep dark satisfaction.

"Who?"

"Rin, Stephen's sister. She finally activated her death affinity."

Beside me, Marcus bristles. "You put a young girl and thousands of people in harm's way, and for what?"

"Her abilities needed a push. And we need her abilities to bring our people back." Adia sweeps her hair behind her.

"You're sick," Marcus says.

Adia's smile drops, and her face snaps to look at him. "I'm a genius."

All those monsters just to get Rin to activate her Death affinity? My stomach gives a dizzying lurch. "How did you know she would do it?"

"I made the giant, and as its creator, I knew exactly who could destroy it."

The jagged utanic Death stone spins beneath Stephen's

hand. For a moment, Stephen's body wavers, his fingers tensing around the stone, and his lips part. But as the world writhes with power around him, the stone drinking it in, he stays upright, entranced by the stone and his death affinity.

"I was just hoping to fill the stone before anyone found us." She cracks her knuckles. "But I get to stamp out your flame today. You must be more sensitive to the stone than I thought to have found us so fast."

My jaw is like iron, my muscles tense and ready, essence hot inside me. "I followed the utanic energy."

"Ah yes, you're a halfie, and the worst kind, too, Beastblood and Emberstead." Adia's eyes squint, her eyebrows pulling together.

The greedy claws of the Death stone play inside my head. The utanic energy nips at me, but my essence repels it. My eyes are heavy for sleep, a deep one, a forever one. Marcus is beside me though, and he won't let go. Kai'trish, her energy supports me day and night, especially now. "Why do you have to do all this anyway?" I ask Adia. "What does utanic energy do for your ritual?"

"Adrianne." Adia sways to one side, letting out a sigh with an eye roll. "You can't tell me you don't know what I need the energy for when you've walked through the Lesser Worlds."

Marcus glances at me, a waver in his eyes. Not of judgement, but of worry, concern, and love.

"You saw me? You're a Void Watcher?"

"Mm, yes, but you see, when I Void Watch, my energy is caught in the Hold, the great invention of the Fourth Great War that traps my people so they can never integrate." Her eyes get lost in the mist surrounding us, but she steps in front of Stephen so he's protected at her back. "I saw you through this prison."

A Hold full of unintegrated souls from the Fourth Great War? How could I have missed that? "I didn't see anything like that. It all felt so free there."

"You wouldn't have seen it unless you went through. Through is up, and up is—"

"Forward," I say, nodding along.

There's a pattern to madness in the land of the dead. Through is down, down is back. And if in the Higher Plane, through is up, up is forward, then that means in the Silent Realm, through is back, and back is up. Kai'trish and I go around though. We can guide energies to unity because we know the way. But some energies need to journey on their own, to take twice as long as others with these cryptic riddles. The long way still leads home.

"Good, so you did learn something. And to cross between the Lesser Worlds, you . . . " She swirls her hand between us.

"You have to cross the Void Bridges. You're going to make a bridge from the Hold to the Karess."

Marcus throws his arms up, resting them on his head, muttering, "unbelievable," with a heavy exhale.

"Why can't you fill the stone with utanic energy from the ice-wastes, or even Sii itself?"

"The energy has to be free flowing, not encased in ice or stone," Adia says with a shrug. "It would take years to extract enough energy like that. We've waited long enough."

"All this will do is start a war and then no one will be free," Marcus says. His voice booming through the haunted night. A stone grinds under his foot as his stance widens.

With a twist in my gut and a pull in my chest, I lock Adia with my eyes. Her jaw twitches, a blue light cresting the rims of each eye but not flooding them. Her readiness to kill us is only hindered by Stephen's vulnerability behind her.

"I get it, Adia, I really do," I say. "Once you get your people back, you'll have all the power. All the natural power of your lineage home again."

A whistle of wind cuts through the platform. Adia is exercising divinity. Divinity with her own plan, to fight her war. But it's not her war, it was passed down to her. And true benevolent divinity sets people free of prescribed destinies.

"Do you know how hard it is to come back from the dead, Adia? Do you know what happens when power comes back once everything has changed? Dysregulation."

"I'm not going to let you stop me. I put my life into this!" Spit flies between us. Her chest heaves, hair quivering forward—hiding her again.

"And who are you now, Adia?" I shift my stance, my heart pounding with boiling blood. "We're taking that fucking stone."

A smile pulls at Adia's lips, dark and knowing. Her head tilts back and she chuckles. "You think your little mixed energy is a match for pure jint?"

I plate my fists in armour, and Marcus' orbs surround his head again.

But the glow of our embers is like a shadow compared to the light that spills from Adia's eyes. With a shockwave of power, the mist lingering on the platform is swept away. Adia lunges for Marcus. Her hand clamps around his neck. I jolt toward him, but an explosion of light bursts in front of me, and an icy grip squelches a scream from my throat. My feet leave the ground. The skin of my neck is stretched, my airway crushed. The joints of my neck and shoulders strain with the weight of my body.

The light fades, and my vision comes back blurry and darkening as my air is restricted, but I have enough light to see what's in front of me. Two Adias. One flesh and bone holding Marcus by the neck as he struggles against her strength. One Adia of light and energy, blue like the sky, powerful like lightning.

I thrash against her. Her energetic fingers dig into my skin. Hot blood trickles down my neck. I grab at her arms with my plated fists, but they grind against her like stone. The strength in my arms gives way, and my hands slip right off her.

In Rin, her life affinity is contained inside her. I could feel that it wanted out though. The life affinity is Adia, just like Rin's life affinity is her. Adia has separated herself. She is whole in flesh and whole in spirit, made solid with essence.

I'm not like them. I have two halves, but I am whole. Emberstead and Beastblood, hédin and beast, fire and fang. I am burning passionate life and teeth that dig deep into death. I have not lost my beast soul. I have found her. She is me, and my Shadow is Kai'trish. I am no longer Shadowless.

Only a small dot of light makes it to my eyes. But I hold on, calling to the power within me and across the Void. I focus on the splendour of the moment I first saw Kai'trish in her full form. The relief that washed through me is the energy I need. Essence spasms through me, but I urge it to calm as Adia's hand crushes my throat.

From the dark behind me, flaming energy leaps at Adia— Kai'trish, my Shadow. Adia hits the ground in a crashing thud under the mystic beast. Marcus tumbles to the ground beside her. The ghost of Adia vanishes, and my feet hit the ground. The beast roars in Adia's flesh face. She pinches her eyes shut, her hair spraying to the side under the tiger's breath.

I have to get that stone.

I sprint at Stephen.

Energy bashes me in the gut, and I'm flung into a tree. A snap in my side reverberates through my body. The pain strikes through my side a second after, stealing my breath.

Adia is on her feet. She has merged with her spirit again, and her blue wings spread around her. My familiar prowls to my side. Marcus pushes himself up from the ground, grunting, sweat streaking his face, but his stance is strong. The orbs flare to life and they stream toward Adia. They slam to her wrists and grow long. Sparks burst around her as the orbs turn into chains shackling her to the ground.

Adia screams at the top of her lungs. Her life affinity ghost rips from her body and dashes to the stone pedestal. She snatches the utanic Death stone and sprints away into the forest. Stephen jolts as his connection to the stone shatters. The red of his eyes flickers. All the colour drains from his face, and he hits the ground. Adia flexes her arms, breaking the shackles into tongues of flame. But there is no light in her eyes as her ghost gets farther and farther away. With her grey irises striking through me, she throws her fist at me.

I fling my arm up to counter, a rabid rush revitalizing my strength. I kick her back. Marcus grabs her from behind before she can strike again. She whirls around striking high and low. Marcus evades her, giving me time to reposition. I swing my leg, taking her clean off her feet. Kai'trish leaps on top of her, pinning her down again.

"Adia!" Stephen's voice shakes me. His eyes flare. He stumbles forward, gasping and weakened from the Death stone transformation. "The stone . . . it wasn't full."

"We'll find another way. Let's go!" Adia grunts, throwing Kai'trish off her. She rolls away from me and dashes to Stephen just as he stumbles. She catches him and projects her wings. They flicker and she screams in pain, but they solidify, and she lifts them into the air with a powerful burst of energy that splits the earth.

She flies them to Sii's edge, and they plummet off the side into the night.

As the dust settles, I fall to my knees. Marcus rushes over to me and wraps me in his arms. Sweat and the tinge of essence fills my nose as I lean into him.

Adia's scream lingers, taking up space in my head. She's pushing so hard to the point of breaking. That last projection of her wings would have been all the essence she had left with the rest running ahead of her in her double. Pushing down a path of power and recognition. We are kin in that respect, or at least we used to be, both swallowed by pain because of it.

"We didn't get the stone," I say into Marcus' shoulder. "I–I'm sorry we—"

"We stopped them from filling it though." He turns me to face him. "We have names, and we know what they need it for. That gives us time, and we can do something with this information. It was a small win, it wasn't for nothing."

A small win. A win no one would see if we hadn't gone this way.

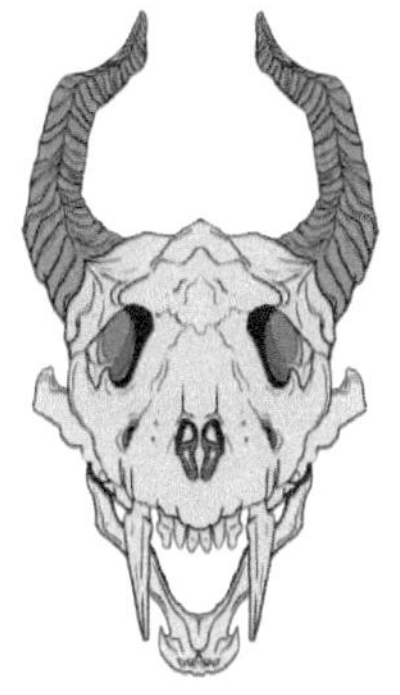

CHAPTER 33

MARCUS AND I MAKE OUR WAY BACK TO THE AIRBUS STATION on the south side of the city. All life has abandoned the streets. Monsters lie limp on the cobblestone, souring the air with their necrotic stench. Tables are turned over, stoves left to smoulder under charred food. Trinkets and bloodied bodies litter the city. Outside the station, the glow of firestone cores and the flash of headlights fill the airspace as medical units and extra airbuses hurry people back to the mainland. The station is abuzz with Medics, families huddled together on blue, plastic benches, and people wailing over lost loved ones.

We wander with stiff limbs through the crowd until we find a free bench. A man sits hunched over beside me. His elbows are on his knees, and his hands are poised as if to cradle his head, but they don't make contact with his skull. Blood is crusted over his fingers, and they shake with nervous energy while the rest of him is unmoving.

Marcus watches him with careful eyes. Pressing his lips together as he scans the crowd, he takes in a long breath. I follow his gaze from one Medic to another. They're all busy with more than one patient in their care at a time. I squeeze Marcus' leg, my heart swelling with his caring eyes making the connection that we need to help this man even before I do.

I scoot over to the man. As if he can hear me but can't find a word to acknowledge my presence, his hands quiver faster. Slipping my fingers around his wrist, I check his pulse. It's even but rapid. I press his hands down away from his face to his knees. I hover one of my hands over his bloody fingers and place my other hand over his back. Now that my essence is fluid again, I coax it to my hands to warm his core and hope to Zenta he will stop shaking.

Minutes pass, and I shiver, shoulders slumped. Even though my eyelids are heavy, I keep my eyes on the man. His hands warm as my body cools with the strain of using so much essence tonight. But I keep my hands poised around him as the crowd thins and the voices quiet to murmurs. Tears trickle down the man's face as he finally closes his eyes. I take a shuddering breath. My body sways without command. I grit my teeth and force my essence to keep circulating.

Marcus' arms wrap around my middle. Pain lances through my side like a hot knife. I wince, and Marcus pulls away.

"Don't let go," I whisper.

His arms return to support me as I work. He kisses my cheek, then leans his head on my back.

The man squeezes my hand with a weak jolt. I squeeze back, fortifying myself against his weakness. He's lost someone, someone he probably tried to save but couldn't. Behind those eyelids, I know he sees demons and blood and a singular dying face, and through it all wonders why it wasn't him. Wondering if he can ever trust himself again. I just want him to know that he can, he will, but it's okay if he doesn't for a while. No point in adding shame for slow healing on top of it.

It's nearly midnight as a Lifeblood Medic arrives at the scene to relieve another unit. Her eyes are bright, alert as she scans the station. Striding over to our bench, she takes the man to her med-ship and comes back when her eyes catch me clutching my side.

"You're hurt," she says.

"I'm fine—"

"She has a broken rib," Marcus says.

"No, really, it can wait. There are so many other people who need help."

The Medic sets her kit beside me and tucks her long dark hair behind her ears. Its clean scent floats past the aroma of blood and body odour clinging to my clothes.

"Can you open your jacket for me?" the Medic asks. She rubs her hands together, taking a minute to engage her essence with a few hand gestures. Nodding to Marcus, she says, "You might want to hold her steady. This will take a while."

I lean on Marcus as the Lifeblood woman hovers her hands over my ribcage. Her eyes close, and she takes in a long steady breath through her nose. As she releases it in an audible rush through her mouth and a prayer to Afa, a pain like icy wind chafing my insides takes hold of my ribcage. The Medic works on restructuring my bones, and I rest my eyes. An investigative Protector questions Marcus as he keeps me steady. He tells the Protector about Stephen, Adia, my experience with them, the Death stone, the utanic energy, the monsters, all with a sad reverence.

His voice fades, and the sting in my side subsides. I blink away the daze in my mind and straighten my spine. The Medic has left. I don't know when, but for the second time this year, the pain has been taken out of my body by someone else. I didn't have to fight with it. Marcus squeezes my shoulder and helps me onto an airbus with the last of the festival goers who have had their night of renewal tainted by death.

"What are we going to tell Rin?" I ask.

"I don't know." Marcus runs his hand over his face, dark bags weighing down his eyes. "We'll see what Evelyn has to say in the morning."

I nod in and out of sleep throughout the airbus ride—pulled back to consciousness by the icy air whipping through the open windows and drawn back to sleep by the weakness in my body. Every time I stir, Marcus pulls me in closer, urging me to rest. My body is weightless with him supporting me as he leads me to my room.

At one point tonight, he was leaning on me, and now, I'm leaning on him. I trust his support. I trust I need it, and I'm not too much for him.

He lies beside me, and I reach my hand to his face. My hands are cold now, the pads of my fingers wrinkled from dehydration. But his skin is smooth under my thumb, his beard divinely prickly. The dark room is lit by his smile as he watches my eyelids drop. Gentleness and strength radiate through me as he presses his lips to my palm.

The morning light comes with strange ferocity. It's like the light that burst from the Death stone as it transformed. It's bright but not brilliant, strong but not warm—the sun holding its breath. So, I hold mine too.

I swing my legs over the edge of the bed. My movements are sluggish but not painful, thanks to the Lifeblood Medic. Images waft through my mind on repeat like a vision reel of yesterday's highlights. I'm tempted to think that it's fate, how Stephen and Adia have come into my life. Maybe I'm supposed to stop them, or maybe help them even. There's a tight bond of hate between the Ironskins and the Emberstead. It creates tension throughout Illyson. The Emberstead took their power, and continue to take power, use it and build it, no matter what is in their way. Some lineages follow their lead, some resist, both build the tension. Do I wield a blade against it? Move my feet toward a bigger picture? Would that take me away from who I am becoming, who I feel stirring in my soul, waking from the dead? I know my truths have been found in the middle of big questions. There's a place for me here.

I tie my hair into a braid and change my clothes. Marcus' breaths are still long and even as he sleeps. He exerted so much energy last night, I shouldn't wake him. The truth I'm still learning to accept is that he would want me to wake him. I can't push myself too fast though. I still need to recharge too. Soon we'll learn each other better, when to bother each other and when to leave each other alone. It will come more naturally. I'm looking forward to that. I leave him to rest.

I also want to find Rin.

The school is just starting to wake. There are a few early risers in the dining hall. Their soft chatter adds to the sense of pause in the air. Such a huge thing happened last night. An attack on Sii, a symbol of peace, a zone safe from beasts. The peace that we've all fought so hard for has been disrupted. We're all making choices in this pause.

I eat in silence, welcoming the food to strengthen my body with slow bites. Leaving the dining hall a little more awake, I follow my feet back to the lobby where Rin is coming out of Evelyn's office. Her face is blank, wet with tears. My gut twists, squeezing out the little breath I have and sending a ringing through my ears. Does she know about Stephen and Adia?

Rin turns on her heel as if she's going to go back into Evelyn's office. But she just stares at the door. I crumple my hands into my sleeves as I approach her.

"Rin?"

Her shoulders squeeze to her ears. Turning, she keeps her eyes low, away from my eyes.

"What's going on?" I ask.

"I have to leave," she says in a quiet rasp.

My throat thickens. "Does it have to do with last night?" I'm sure it has everything to do with last night, but I just don't have the mental clarity to ask anything more insightful. "That giant?"

Rin nods, wiping her cheek with the back of her hand. "An Ironskin group, the Revival they're calling themselves, directed the attack at me. They . . . uh . . . they need my abilities for something. They're going to hurt more people if I let them use my abilities." Her body twitches as she speaks, her gaze drifting from one side of me to the other. Holding up a small card, she says, "Evelyn gave me a pass of absence. I leave tomorrow."

I stand with her in silence, stuck in the pause. Tears trickle down her face. "Fuck," she whispers into her sleeve as she brushes them away.

"Are you suicidal?" The words drift out of my mouth, clear and careful.

Rin squirms, folding her arms close, eyes cast away. "No one asks that."

"I know. That's why I'm asking."

Taking a breath, she sets her hand on her stomach. "I don't know." She scrunches her fingers in her shirt. "Not right now, but close."

Both her arms twitch toward me, as if to draw me in, but they fall back to her sides, the movement unfinished. I finish it for her so fast that she topples into me. She shuffles her feet closer and leans her head on my shoulder. A soft sniff breaks the tears from my eyes.

"Thank you," she whispers. "For everything."

Her tears soak into my shoulder and warmth soaks into my heart.

"Five seconds at a time, okay?"

She chuckles into me. "I don't think I could stand much more."

Nodding, she leaves me, re-situating strands of hair that shifted out of place with our hug. I would like her to have something to remember me by. My fingers gravitate to my triangle pendant. The metal is so delicate, but there's nothing to fill the space between the three gold bars that make its shape. I still have the pieces of the curestone I used on Rin, and somehow, it seems right to return them. I'll have a jeweller set them in the pendant for her this afternoon.

I enter Evelyn's office without knocking.

Evelyn's sharp brown eyes dart toward me. Her gold spectacles slide down her nose as she tsks at me with one hand on her hip. Across from her is Brand, hands propping her up on the desk. She looks over her shoulder at me. My mind jumps, taking her in. She was just arrested and now she's here.

"You two better start talking, and you'd better have a good explanation for sending that girl away."

"Adrianne, just calm down, and we'll chat—"

"Chat," I say. Blame it on lack of air, stress, exhaustion, but I don't have the patience to be patronized. "You want to chat, hey?"

I stroll through the room, running my fingers over the supple leather chair backs. Evelyn's eyes track me like a bird of prey. Brand turns to face me with her arms crossed, a slight quirk of the corner of her mouth.

"You want to chat about monsters of death terrorizing innocent citizens to get to one eighteen-year-old girl? Sure, we could chat about that, 'cause, you know, chatting involves a back-and-forth. We both know the attack happened so we can exchange stories. But no one knows about what happened outside the city."

Both women's eyes fix on me with varying levels of contempt and intrigue. Brand straightens, squaring her shoulders toward mine. "What happened outside the city?"

"Rin's brother and a woman named Adia created a utanic Death stone by syphoning the utanic energy buildup in the atmosphere from the two moons."

Brand and Evelyn turn to each other. Evelyn steels herself

with the exchange of information from Brand's eyes that I can't see.

"Did you report it to the LPs?" Evelyn asks.

"Of course I reported it to the fucking LPs."

Evelyn rolls her eyes and waves her hand in the air. "I am so glad to be rid of you after graduation."

With a flare of satisfaction pulling a smile to my mouth, I take the liberty to sit.

"This is a huge breakthrough, Adrianne," Brand says in a flat, unwavering tone. "I'm sure Marcus has told you about my job offer. But I could use someone like you to get to the bottom of this."

The steel in Brand's eyes, the bluntness in her statements, catches me off guard. My hands sweat and my breath catches in my throat as I wait for her to continue.

"Would you be interested in a position on the counc—"

"No." I match the strength of her gaze. "You have the best man for the job."

"The Revival is planning to bring the Ironskin Lineage back from the dead, to reverse the effects of the Death Ritual in the Fourth Great War. Your experience with Stephen and Adia could be a real asset."

"No. I care about Adia." I drop my eyes to my lap. The statement doesn't make much sense, but I feel it in my gut. Seeing their eyes, questioning me, would take the words out of my mouth before I could speak them. I focus on the sound of Adia's screams from last night. I clear my throat. "I would rather her kill me out of rage. I respect her way too much to get in her way."

"You support her illegal activity?" Evelyn asks.

"Not in the slightest."

Evelyn shifts in her seat, fingers poised at her lips. Brand takes the arm of my chair and leans down to me. "This affects us all."

"I didn't stand down when trouble stared me in the face," I say, looking up at her. "But I did it by following my path. Being true to myself won't deny me a place in this fight. I think people need me, as a Monitor, as me." My sweat cools on my skin. My heart slows to heavy, steady beats. "I think we'll both know when you need me, Brand."

My responsibility to the world lies in my actions, my choices. I choose to do what I do best. Help people. One-on-one.

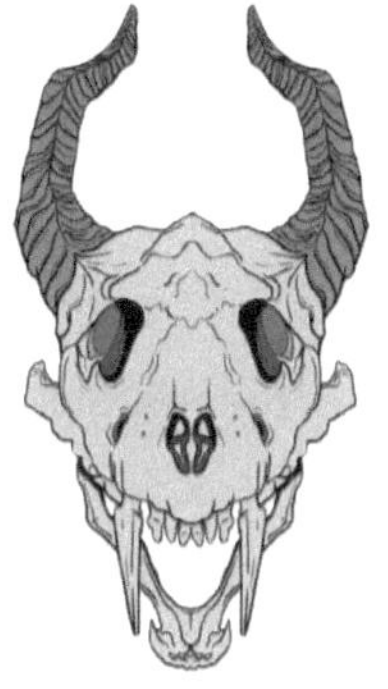

C H A P T E R   3 4

On graduation day, Matta arrives early, bearing everything I could possibly need to get ready for the ceremony. She shuffles over to me, still fumbling my dress in its carry bag and a makeup kit, and bends over me, setting a kiss on my forehead. As I push myself out of bed, Matta hangs the dress on my curtain rod and sets out makeup and pins for my hair. I grab the paper bag she dropped by the door. Opening it, the sweet smell of homemade pinichu berry buns envelopes me.

I sit in front of my mirror with Matta's hands already in my hair. I nibble on one of the buns and hold one up to her to take a bite. She braids half my hair into a low crown around my head and lets the rest fall naturally down my back.

She starts work on my makeup and Vishal without

consultation. I don't have space in my head to pick out a lip colour.

This Guardian academy was a box I stepped into because I thought it would make my family and my lineages proud. It was dark, cramped. I took a Vow to help me define a path out of it. Breaking that Vow showed me that my path is twisting. It bridges the world of the living and the dead. In both, sometimes I'll go around, sometimes I'll go through. I didn't make anyone proud at this academy, except for me.

"Talk to me?" Matta says quietly as our eyes meet in the mirror.

My gaze tilts down at the half-eaten bun in my hands, but Matta tilts my chin up. Staring at my face, made up with a beautiful black Vishal, gold eyeliner, and a bright-red lip, a buzz starts in my chest. It's heavy, swelling through me, touching the frayed edges of my nerves, sparking a little fire in my heart. My eyes prickle. Thank goodness she didn't line my bottom lids.

"I'm a summoner."

Matta lets the chunk of hair she's brushing out fall. She sets her hands on my shoulders and looks at me in the mirror, skin crinkling around her eyes. "Your dano told me. Who did you summon?"

I turn to face Matta as she sits down on my bed, her cheeks growing rosy. "The mystic beast you told me about," I say. "Her name came to me without sound. Kai'trish."

Matta claps her hands together and draws them to her mouth. Her eyes mist with tears and glitter with delight. "Kai'trish," she whispers.

The unfamiliar name is hushed between us, our secret. It is sweet and mysterious. I press my hand to my heart as her amber eyes appear in my mind.

"She's shy," Matta says. "Intuitive and immensely powerful. She's never been summoned before. Perfect for you."

I drop my head to my hands. My heart floods with pride and humility all at once. Kai'trish has been waiting for me to summon her for so long. The root she showed me is one of the reasons I can't get involved the way Brand wants me to. That root is part of a hédin soul. Helping it integrate, that's Monitor work. My body shakes with sobs flowing out of me, but Kai'trish's undeniable presence urges me to look up, to accept her.

"Has she given you any gifts?" Matta asks.

Cocking my head to the side, I say, "She saved my fucking life."

Over and over again.

But Matta's fuzzy lynx ears twitch. I don't have any physical representation like that, nothing that has developed over time, only what I've had all along—the ability to transform my eyes, to see through the dark.

I nod.

"And your Vow?"

Smoothing my fingers over the braided crown, I say, "I just need this one."

Matta wraps her arms around me, and I sink into her.

"Now for your dress." Her voice is choked as she lets me go.

The black dress is heavy with the intricate beadwork stitched by Matta's hands, and mine, with such care and purpose in mind. The beads are bright yellow and orange at the bottom and flare up the skirt to deep red and swirl into wispy smoke patterns at the heart-shaped neckline. Thick velvet caps my shoulders, but the sleeves are sheer, draping elegantly over my scars and my tattoo. I sway a little and the beads clack together, the sheer fabric of my sleeves shimmers in the morning light that is now un-paused, energetic.

The arena skylight has been cleared of snow, but Seena will do as she likes, and heavy snowflakes blot the glass. My pits are already sweating as if the stale sweat stench that lingers through the arena draws perspiration from my glands. I keep my arms close to my sides as I wait on the stage for my name to be called.

Evelyn is at the front of the stage, her royal-blue uniform dripping in gold and silver badges. She shakes each graduating student's hand, and each time my heart skips a beat as she presents their Protector or Warrior badge.

I find Matta in the sea of parents and academy students in their multicoloured uniforms. Matta taps her fingers to her Vishal. I tap my fingers to my matching pattern. To her left are Nima and Nipan McCarthy. They watch the procession with their heads held high, faces impassive. On the other side of Matta, Dano wraps his thick arm around Nana as she dabs her eyes with a handkerchief. Dano's gaze finds me and he gives me a wide grin and a nod.

Fixing my eyes back on the audience, I find Marcus. His Protector uniform hugs his muscled arms. He stands at the back with the rest of the Professors, his hands folded in front of him. After a few seconds of his stoic frame resting in my line of sight, his eyes raise, his mouth turns up in the tender smile reserved for me. Heat crawls up my neck. I smile so widely, my cheeks twitch and the sweat that's collected on my upper lip spreads thin.

Eila is next to me. She waits with her head bowed and her